Victoria Hislop

Inspired by a visit to Spinalonga, the abandoned Greek leprosy colony, Victoria Hislop wrote *The Island* in 2005. It became an international bestseller and a 26-part Greek TV series. She was named Newcomer of the Year at the British Book Awards and is now an ambassador for Lepra. Her affection for the Mediterranean then took her to Spain, and in *The Return* (also a number one bestseller) she wrote about the painful secrets of its civil war.

In her third novel, *The Thread*, Victoria returned to Greece to tell the turbulent tale of Thessaloniki and its people across the 20th century. It was shortlisted for a British Book Award, and confirmed her reputation as an inspirational storyteller. It was followed by her much-admired Greece-set short story collection, *The Last Dance and Other Stories*. Her new novel, *The Sunrise*, was published to widespread acclaim, and was a *Sunday Times* hardback bestseller.

Victoria divides her time between England and Greece.

Visit www.victoriahislop.com to learn more.

Praise for
The Thread

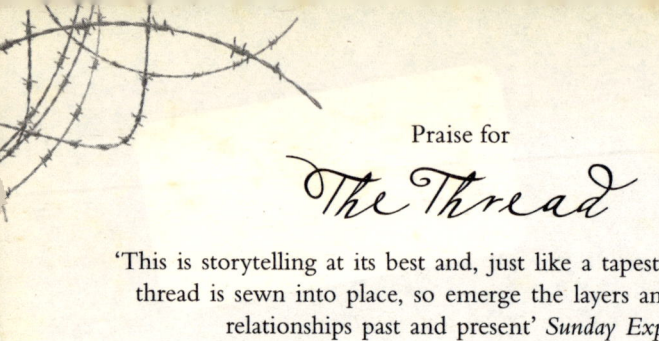

'This is storytelling at its best and, just like a tapestry, when each thread is sewn into place, so emerge the layers and history of relationships past and present' *Sunday Express*

'A sweeping, magnificently detailed and ambitious saga' *The Sunday Times*

'Hislop's fast-paced narrative and utterly convincing sense of place make her novel a rare treat' *Guardian*

'She has brought something fresh, unusual and rather intrepid to an often vapid genre, with a tenacious attention to the tangled and controversial history that fuels her plots . . . *The Thread* will entertain and enlighten legions of readers' Boyd Tonkin, *Independent*

'Pleasingly complex . . . Hislop has done well to tell a story as diverse and tempestuous as Thessaloniki's with such lightness of touch' *Spectator*

'Very good at interweaving the lives of individuals into the backcloth of great events, giving the reader a history lesson that doesn't feel like one . . . Recommended' *Daily Mail*

'Hislop's view of history in her novels is, just like the writer herself, a compassionate and generous one . . . Her many, many fans will be delighted with what is her best novel yet' *Scotsman*

'Reflects [Hislop's] obvious love of Thessaloniki and its inhabitants. The characterisation is sure and the historical insights fascinating' *Mail on Sunday*

'Meticulously researched and compellingly told' *Woman & Home*

Praise for

the Return

'Aims to open the eyes and tug the heartstrings . . . Hislop deserves a medal for opening a breach into the holiday beach bag' *Independent*

'Like a literary Nigella, she whips up a cracking historical romance mixed with a dash of family secrets and a splash of female self-discovery . . . What sets Hislop apart is her ability to put a human face on the shocking civil conflict that ripped Spain apart for three bloody years between 1936 and 1939' *Time Out*

'[The Return] should be required holiday reading for anyone going to Spain' *Daily Mail*

'Fear not, Hislop fans, there was more where [The Island] came from . . . The story of the Spanish Civil War is . . . executed with verve and sensitivity' *Sunday Telegraph*

'Excellent' *Sunday Telegraph*

'Hislop marries an epic family saga with meticulous historical research, and it's a captivating partnership' *Easy Living*

'Brilliantly recreates the passion that flows through the Andalusian dancers and the dark creative force of *duende*' *Scotland on Sunday*

'This atmospheric novel beautifully evokes the minutiae of traditional Spanish life' *Psychologies*

'Captivating and deeply moving' *Look*

Praise for

the Island

'Passionately engaged with its subject . . . the author has meticulously researched her fascinating background and medical facts'
The Sunday Times

'A beautiful tale of enduring love and unthinking prejudice'
Express

'The story of life on Spinalonga, the lepers' island, is gripping and carries real emotional impact. Victoria Hislop . . . brings dignity and tenderness to her novel about lives blighted by leprosy' *Telegraph*

'A vivid, moving and absorbing tale, with its sensitive, realistic engagement with all the consequences of, and stigma attached to leprosy, elevating it beyond holiday literature' *Observer*

'Hislop's deep research, imagination and patent love of Crete creates a convincing portrait of times on the island. She writes evocatively of the minutiae of traditional life . . . A moving and absorbing holiday read that pulls at the heart strings' *Evening Standard*

'Hislop carefully evokes the lives of Cretans between the wars and during German occupation, but most commendable is her compassionate portrayal of the outcasts' *Guardian*

'War, tragedy and passion unfurl against a Mediterranean backdrop in this engrossing debut novel' *You* magazine

'A page-turning tale that reminds us that love and life continue in even the most extraordinary of circumstances'
Sunday Express

'Wonderful descriptions, strong characters and an intimate portrait of island existence' *Woman & Home*

Praise for
The Last Dance
AND OTHER STORIES

'A master at evoking a sense of place . . . At turns romantic and melancholic, these stories offer memorable portraits of ordinary Greek life' *Mail on Sunday*

'Beguiling . . . Her characters are utterly convincing and she has perfected her knack for describing everyday Greek life' *Daily Mail*

'Stunning . . . Intricate, beautifully observed and with a painter's eye for imagery, in these stories Hislop evokes Greece, its people, its customs and traditions with a sensitivity that reveals her deep knowledge of not just the place but also the human condition' *Express*

'Lyrical, twisty short stories' *Evening Standard*

By Victoria Hislop

The Island
The Return
The Thread
The Sunrise

The Last Dance and Other Stories

Victoria
Hislop
The Sunrise

headline
review

Copyright © 2014 Victoria Hislop

The right of Victoria Hislop to be identified as the Author of
the Work has been asserted by her in accordance with the
Copyright, Designs and Patents Act 1988.

Map and timeline design by David Smith

Cover photographs © Hans Georg Roth/Corbis (Famagusta, front) and
Andreas Manolis/Reuters/Corbis (Famagusta, back); sea-shore © plain picture/
Cultura; cactus © Irina Fischer/Alamy. Other images © Shutterstock.com

First published in Great Britain in 2014
by HEADLINE REVIEW
An imprint of HEADLINE PUBLISHING GROUP

First published in paperback in Great Britain in 2015 by
HEADLINE REVIEW

1

Apart from any use permitted under UK copyright law, this publication may
only be reproduced, stored, or transmitted, in any form, or by any means,
with prior permission in writing of the publishers or, in the case of
reprographic production, in accordance with the terms of licences
issued by the Copyright Licensing Agency

All characters – other than the obvious historical figures –
in this publication are fictitious, and any resemblance to real
persons, living or dead, is purely coincidental

Cataloguing in Publication Data is available from the British Library

ISBN 978 07553 7780 0 (B-format)
ISBN 978 07553 7781 7 (A-format)

Typeset in Bembo by Palimpsest Book Production Limited, Falkirk, Stirlingshire
Printed and bound in Great Britain by Clays Ltd, St Ives plc

Headline's policy is to use papers that are natural, renewable
and recyclable products and made from wood grown in sustainable
forests. The logging and manufacturing processes are expected to
conform to the environmental regulations of the country of origin.

MIX
Paper from
responsible sources
FSC® C104740

HEADLINE PUBLISHING GROUP
Carmelite House
50 Victoria Embankment
London EC4Y 0DZ

www.headline.co.uk
www.hachette.co.uk

For Emily
λαμπερή όσο κι ένα διαμάντι

With huge thanks to the following people
for insight, inspiration, love, friendship and hospitality:

Efthymia Alphas
Antonis Antoniou
Michael Colocassides
Theodoros Frangos
Alexis Galanos
Maria Hadjivasili
Mary Hamson
Ian Hislop
William Hislop
Costas Kleanthous
Yiangos Kleopas
Stavros Lambrakis
David Miller
Chrysta Ntziani
Costas Papadopoulos
Nicolas Papageorgiou
Alexandros Papalambos
Flora Rees
Hüseyin Silman
Vasso Sotiriou
Thomas Vogiatzis
Çiğdem Worthington

Cyprus, 1972

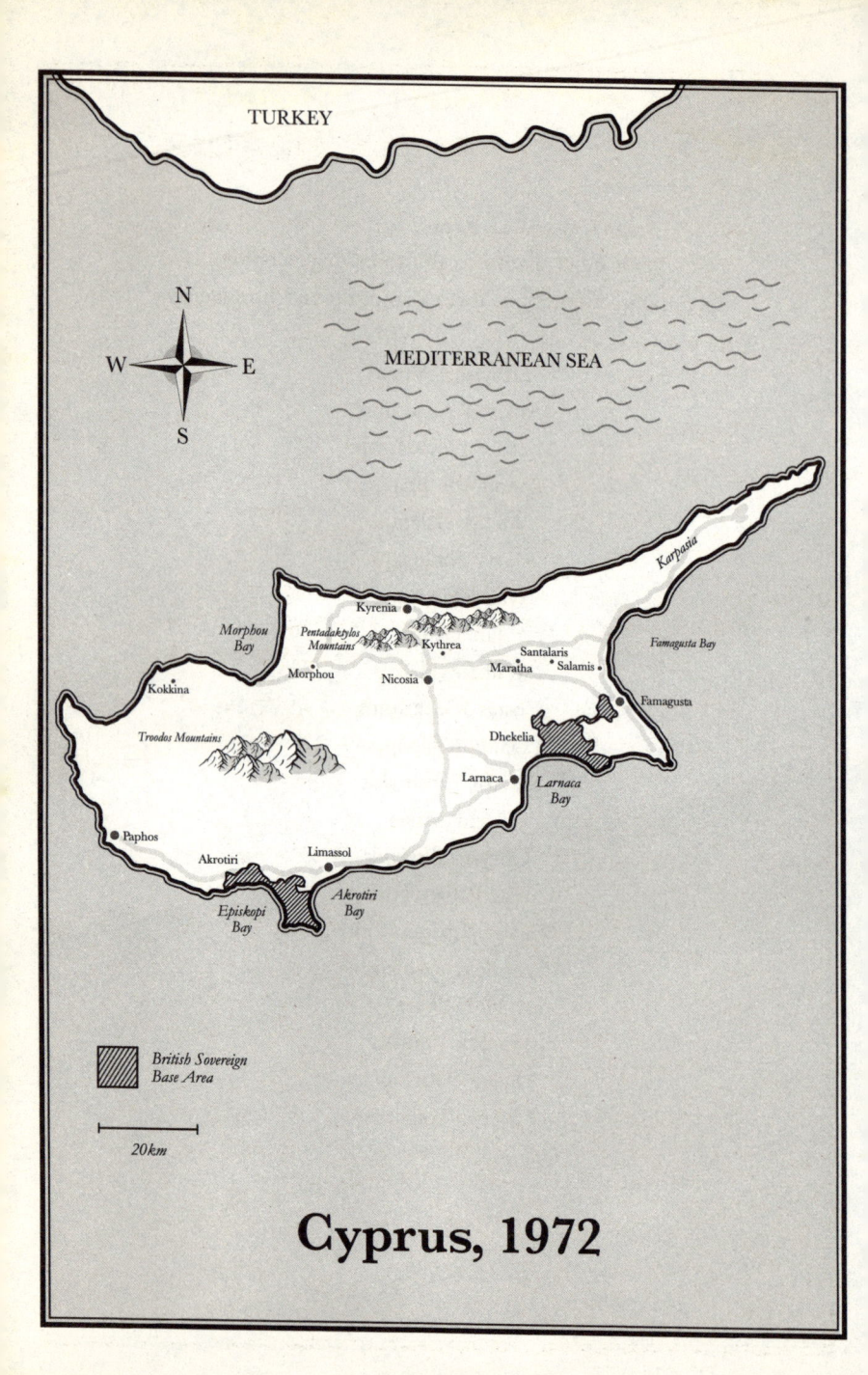

Before this story begins...

1878 The British Government negotiates an alliance with Turkey and assumes administration of Cyprus, while the island remains part of the Ottoman Empire.

1914 Britain annexes Cyprus when the Ottoman Empire sides with Germany in the First World War.

1925 Cyprus becomes a British colony.

1955 EOKA (the National Organisation of Cypriot Fighters), under George Grivas, begins its campaign of violence against the British. Its aim is *enosis* (union with Greece).

1959 Britain, Greece, Turkey and the Greek and Turkish Cypriot communities agree on a settlement for the Cyprus problem – the London Agreement. Archbishop Makarios is elected President.

1960 Cyprus becomes an independent republic but the Treaty of Guarantee gives Britain, Greece and Turkey the right to intervene. Britain retains two military bases.

1963 President Makarios makes 13 proposals for amendments to the Cypriot Constitution and outbreaks of fighting take place between Greek and Turkish Cypriot communities. Nicosia is divided and the border is patrolled by British troops. Turkish Cypriots withdraw from power-sharing.

1964 There are further incidents of serious inter-communal violence. United Nations sends a peacekeeping force. Turkish Cypriots withdraw into enclaves.

1967 Further incidents of violence between the two communities occur. There is a military coup in Athens and tension builds between President Makarios and the Greek regime.

1971 George Grivas returns secretly from Greece and forms EOKA B, once again aiming to achieve *enosis*.

Famagusta was once a thriving city of forty thousand people. In 1974, its entire population fled when Cyprus was invaded by Turkey. Forty years on Varosha, as the modern city is known, remains empty, sealed off behind the barbed wire put up by the Turkish army. It is a ghost town.

Chapter One

Famagusta, 15 August 1972

FAMAGUSTA WAS GOLDEN. The beach, the bodies of sunbathers and the lives of those who lived there were gilded by warmth and good fortune.

Fine, pale sand and a turquoise sea had together created the most perfect bay in the Mediterranean, and pleasure-seekers came from all around the world to soak up its warmth and to enjoy the sensual pleasure of the calm waters that gently lapped around them. Here was a glimpse of paradise.

The old fortified city with its strong medieval walls stood to the north of the beach resort, and trippers went on guided tours to learn about its origins, and to admire the vaulted ceilings, detailed carvings and buttresses of the magnificent building that had once been the cathedral of St Nicholas but was now a mosque. They saw the remnants of its fourteenth-century history, heard tales of the Crusades, the wealthy Lusignan kings and the arrival of the Ottomans. All of this information, given by a well-meaning guide in the heat of the midday sun, was soon forgotten when they returned to their hotels, dived into the pool and felt the sweat and dust of history wash away.

It was the twentieth-century development that people truly appreciated, and after their excursion into history they happily came back to its straight-walled modern comforts and its characteristically huge windows that looked outwards on the glorious view.

The arrow slits in the old walled city had been enough to give a sighting of the enemy, but let in almost no light, and while the design of the medieval stronghold was aimed at keeping invaders out, the new city aimed to bring people in. Its architecture opened outwards and upwards to the brilliant blues of sky and sea, not inwards; 1970s Famagusta was inviting, light and designed to welcome the visitor. The image of an invader needing to be repelled seemed something from another age.

It was one of the world's finest resorts, purpose-built for pleasure, with little in its conception that did not have the comfort of the holidaymaker in mind. The tall buildings that hugged the coastline mostly comprised hotels with smart cafés and expensive shops beneath them. They were modern, sophisticated and reminiscent of Monaco and Cannes, and existed for leisure and pleasure, for a new international jet set ready to be seduced by the island's charm. In daylight hours, tourists were more than content with sea and sand. When the sun went down, there were hundreds of places to eat, drink and be entertained.

As well as its allure for the tourist, Famagusta also possessed the deepest and most important port in Cyprus. People in faraway destinations could enjoy a taste of the island thanks to the crates of citrus fruit that left in ships each year.

Most days from May to September were broadly the same, with a few dramatic leaps in temperature when the sun seemed almost savage. The sky was consistently cloudless, the days long, the heat dry and the sea cooling but always kind. On the long stretch of fine sand, tanned holidaymakers lay stretched out on sunbeds sipping iced drinks beneath colourful umbrellas, while the more active frolicked in the shallows or showed off on waterskis, slaloming expertly across their own wake.

Famagusta thrived. Residents, workers and visitors alike enjoyed almost immeasurable contentment.

The row of ultra-modern hotels stretched all along the seafront, mostly a dozen or so storeys high. Towards the southern end of the beach was a new one. At fifteen storeys it was taller than the rest, twice as wide and so recently constructed it did not yet have a sign with its name.

From the beachfront it looked as minimalist as the others, blending into the necklace of hotels that lined the curve of the bay. The approach from the road, though, was grand, with imposing gates and high railings.

That hot summer's day, the hotel was full of people. They were not in casual holiday wear but in overalls and worker's dungarees. These were labourers, technicians and artisans, putting the finishing touches to a carefully conceived plan. Although the outside of the hotel seemed to conform to a standard scheme, the interior was very different from its rivals.

An impression of 'grandeur' was what the owners were aspiring to, and they considered the reception area one of the most important spaces in the hotel. It should be love at first sight for guests; unless it made an immediate impact, it had failed. There was no second chance.

The first thing that should impress was its size. A man would be reminded of a football pitch. A woman would think of a beautiful lake. Both would notice the impossible gleam of the marble floor and experience what it might be like to walk on water.

The person with this vision was Savvas Papacosta. He was thirty-three, though he looked older, with a few wisps of grey in his otherwise dark crinkly hair. He was clean-shaven and thickset, and today, as every day, he was wearing a grey suit (the best available air-conditioning system kept everyone cool) and an off-white shirt.

With one exception, everyone working in the reception area was male. The lone woman, dark-haired, immaculately dressed in a cream shift, was Papacosta's wife. Today she was there to supervise the hanging of the drapes in the foyer and ballroom, but in previous months she had been overseeing the selection of fabrics and soft furnishings for the five hundred bedrooms. Aphroditi loved this role and had a great gift for it. The process of creating a scheme for each room, using a slightly different style for each floor, was similar to choosing clothes and finding accessories to match.

Aphroditi Papacosta's taste would make the finished hotel beautiful, but without her it would never have been built. The investment had come from her father. Trifonas Markides owned numerous apartment blocks in Famagusta as well as a shipping business that dealt with the vast quantities of fruit and other exports shipped out of its port.

The first time he met Savvas Papacosta was at a meeting of a local trade and commerce association. Markides had recognised his hunger and been reminded of his own younger self. It took him some time to convince his wife that a man who was running a small hotel at the less fashionable end of the beach had a promising future.

'Aphroditi is twenty-one now,' he said. 'We need to start thinking about her marriage.'

Artemis considered Savvas to be socially beneath her beautiful and well-educated daughter, a little 'rough', even. It was not merely the fact that his parents worked on the land, but that their acreage was so small. Trifonas, however, saw this potential son-in-law as a financial investment. They had discussed his plans to build a second hotel several times.

'*Agapi mou*, his ambitions are immense,' Trifonas reassured Artemis. 'That's what matters. I can tell he is going to go far. There is fire in his eyes. I can talk business with him. Man to man.'

When Trifonas Markides invited Savvas Papacosta to dinner in Nicosia for the first time, Aphroditi knew what her father was hoping for. There was no *coup de foudre*, but she had not been out with many young men and did not really know what she was meant to feel. What was unsaid by any of them, though Savvas himself might have noticed it if he had studied the photograph given pride of place on the wall, was his resemblance to the Markides' late son, Aphroditi's only sibling. He was muscular, just as Dimitris had been, with wavy hair and a broad mouth. They would even have been the same age.

Dimitris Markides had been twenty-five when he was killed during the troubles that erupted between Greek and Turkish Cypriots in Nicosia in early 1964. He had died less than a mile from home, and his mother believed that he was just a bystander accidentally caught in crossfire.

Dimitris' 'innocence' made his death all the more tragic for Artemis Markides, but both his father and sister knew that it had not been a simple matter of bad luck. Aphroditi and Dimitris had shared everything. She had covered up for him when he sneaked out of the house, told lies to protect him, once even hidden a gun in her room, knowing that no one would come looking there.

The Markides children had enjoyed a privileged upbringing in Nicosia, with idyllic summers in Famagusta. Their father had a magic touch with investments and had already poured much of his wealth into the property boom that was taking place in the seaside resort.

When Dimitris died, everything changed. Artemis Markides could not and would not emerge from her grief. An emotional and physical darkness descended on all of their lives and did not lift. Trifonas Markides buried himself in his work, but Aphroditi spent much of her time trapped in the stifling atmosphere of a silent house where shutters were often kept closed throughout the day. She yearned to get away, but the only escape would be marriage, and when she met Savvas, she realised this could be her opportunity.

In spite of the lack of spark she felt with him, she was aware that life would be easier if she married someone of whom her father approved. She could also see that there might be a role for her in his hotel plans, and this appealed to her.

Within eighteen months of her first meeting with Savvas, her parents laid on the grandest wedding that had taken place in Cyprus in a decade. The service was conducted by the President, His Beatitude Archbishop Makarios, and there were over one thousand guests (who drank as many bottles of French champagne). The value of the bride's dowry in jewellery alone was estimated at more than fifteen thousand pounds. On the day of her wedding, her father gave her a necklace of rare blue diamonds.

Within weeks, Artemis Markides began to make it clear that she wanted to move to England. Her husband was still benefiting from the burgeoning growth of Famagusta, and his business was thriving, but she could no longer bear to live in Cyprus. Five years had passed since Dimitris' death, but memories of that awful day remained vivid.

'We need a fresh start somewhere,' she nagged. 'Whatever we

do here, wherever we live, this place can't be the same for us now.'

With huge reservations, Trifonas Markides agreed. Now that his daughter was married, he felt her future was secure and he would still have a part of his life on home soil.

Savvas had not been a disappointment. He had proved to his father-in-law that he could convert bare soil into profit. He had spent his childhood watching his mother and father alike toil on the land, producing just about enough to live on. When he was fourteen, he had helped his father build an extra room on to their house. He enjoyed the task itself, but more importantly, he realised that things could be done with the land other than scratching the top layer, and planting a few seeds. He despised the endless cycle of this process. It seemed utterly futile to him.

When he had seen the very first high-rise hotel going up in Famagusta, he had, in a quick mental calculation, worked out how much more profit could be made per acre of land by building upwards than by digging down to plant seeds or trees that needed tireless and repeated tending. His only problem had been how to buy the land so he could put his plan into action. Eventually, getting a few jobs, working round the clock and finding a bank loan (the manager recognised naked ambition when he saw it), he scraped together enough to purchase a small, undeveloped plot and built his first hotel, The Paradise Beach. Since then, he had watched the resort of Famagusta expand, and his own aspirations grew with it.

Trifonas Markides was a major investor in his new hotel project and they had drawn up a business plan together. Savvas aimed to build up a chain that would one day be an international brand name, as recognisable as 'Hilton'.

Now the first stage was about to be realised. Construction of the largest and most luxurious hotel in Famagusta was complete. The Sunrise was almost ready to open.

Savvas Papacosta was kept busy by a constant flow of people asking him to inspect and approve their work. He knew that the final picture was made up of a thousand details and he took a close interest in them all.

Chandeliers were being hoisted into position, and their crystals created a kaleidoscope of colours and patterns that danced on the ceiling and were reflected in the floor. Not quite satisfied with the result, Savvas had each one lowered by just two links of the chain. It seemed to double the radius of the pattern.

At the centre of the vast space was a trio of gilded dolphins in a pool. Life-sized, they appeared to spring out of the water, their glassy eyes meeting those of the observer. Two men adjusted the flow that gushed from their snouts.

'A little more pressure, I think,' instructed Savvas.

Half a dozen artists were meticulously applying gold leaf to the neoclassical details on the ceiling. They were working as if they had all the time in the world. As if to remind them that they did not, five clocks were being lined up and fixed to the wall behind a mahogany reception desk that stretched for thirty yards down the side of the foyer. Within the next hour, plaques with the names of the world's major financial centres would identify them, and their hands would be accurately adjusted.

Decorative pillars, spaced to echo the layout of the ancient agora at nearby Salamis, were being delicately painted with veins to simulate marble. Clinging to scaffolding, a team of three worked on a *trompe l'oeil* mural that depicted various classical scenes. Aphroditi, the goddess of the island, was a central figure. In this image, she was rising from the sea.

The Sunrise

In the floors and corridors above, working ceaselessly like bees in a hive, pairs of chambermaids stretched cool new linen across king-sized beds and coaxed fat feather pillows into their cases.

'I could fit my whole family into this room,' observed one.

'Even the bathroom is bigger than my house,' responded her partner, with a note of disapproval.

They laughed together, bemused rather than jealous. The people who came to stay in such a hotel must be from another planet. In their view, anyone who demanded a marble bath and a bed wide enough for five must be rather peculiar. It did not occur to them that they were to be envied.

The plumbers putting the finishing touches to the bathrooms and the electricians scurrying to fit the final light bulbs had the same thoughts. Many of them lived cheek by jowl in homes with three or more generations. They could almost feel each other's breath when they slept; they waited patiently to use an outdoor toilet, and when the evening light faded and the low-wattage lighting began to flicker, they went to bed. Instinct told them that extravagance did not equate with happiness.

One floor below, close to where an indoor swimming pool was still being carefully tiled (there would be no use for it until November), two women, both dressed in white nylon housecoats, bustled about in a dazzlingly lit mirrored room. One of them was humming.

They were preparing the hotel's hairdressing salon for the big opening, and the inventory of everything that had been delivered over the last few days was now completed. The latest design of hooded hairdryer, rollers in every conceivable size, hair tints and processing chemicals for permanent waves: all was in order. Pins and grips, scissors and clippers, brushes and combs were put away in drawers or laid out on trolleys. The equipment needed for hairdressing was relatively uncomplicated. It was all down to the skill of the stylist, as Emine Özkan and Savina Skouros both knew.

Now that they were satisfied that everything was in working order, gleaming and pristine, they gave the counter a final polish, wiped around each of the six sinks and shone the mirrors and taps for the fifth time that day. One of them straightened the shampoos and cans of lacquer so that the brand name, of which they were proud, was repeated in a perfect line: *Wella Wella Wella Wella Wella.*

A great deal of business was expected from the female guests, who would be wanting their hair tamed after a day exposed to sun and sand. Within the next few months they confidently expected that every chair in the salon would be full.

'Can you believe this?'

'Not really . . .'

'We're so lucky . . .'

Emine Özkan had been cutting Aphroditi Papacosta's hair since she was a teenager. Until very recently, she and Savina had both worked in a small salon in the commercial part of Famagusta. Emine had come in on the bus every day from Maratha, a village ten miles away. When the modern resort had begun to expand and thrive, and her husband found work there too, they had uprooted their family and come to live on the edge of the new town, preferring it to the old walled city, which was predominantly inhabited by Turkish Cypriots.

It was the third time that Emine's family had moved in the space of a few years. Nearly a decade before, they had fled their village when it was attacked by Greek Cypriots and their house had been burned down. After that they lived for a time in an enclave where they had the protection of United Nations troops, before settling in Maratha.

Likewise, Famagusta was not Savina's birthplace. She had grown up in Nicosia, but the spate of violence between the two communities nine years before had left her with deep scars too. Such fear and suspicion had developed between Greek and Turkish Cypriots that United Nations troops were brought in to maintain the peace, and a boundary known as the Green Line was drawn across the city to divide the two communities. It had tainted her family's life.

'We hated being cut off like that,' she explained to Emine when they were sharing memories. 'There were good friends we just couldn't see any more. You can't imagine. It was terrible. But Greeks and Turks had been killing each other – so I suppose they had to do it.'

'Maratha wasn't like that. We all got on quite well there, us and the Greeks,' said Emine. 'Even so, we're all much happier here. And I'm *not* moving again!'

'Things are better for us too,' agreed Savina, 'but I miss my family a lot . . .'

The majority of Greek Cypriots were at ease with the Turkish Cypriots these days and no longer worried about paramilitary groups. Ironically, there was now rivalry and violence among the Greek Cypriots themselves. A minority of them wanted *enosis*, unification of Cyprus with Greece, and aimed to achieve it through violent means and intimidation. This was hidden from the tourists, and even most local people in Famagusta tried to forget that the threat was there.

Both women were standing in front of the mirror. They were identical in height, with a similar stocky shape, and wore the same fashionable short hairstyle and salon housecoats. They caught each other's eye and smiled. Emine was more than ten years older than Savina, but the similarity between them was striking.

That day, on the eve of the hotel opening, their conversation was flowing as usual like a river in springtime. They spent six days a week in each other's company, but their chatter was unceasing.

'My youngest sister's oldest is coming next week to stay for a few days,' said Emine. 'She just walks up and down, up and down, gazing into shop windows. I've seen her. Then she just stands and stares and stares and stares.'

Emine did an impression of her niece (one of a total of fifteen produced so far by her four sisters) transfixed by an invisible window display.

'The one who's getting married?'

'Yes. Mualla. She's actually got something to buy now.'

'Well, there's plenty for her to look at here.'

Famagusta had a plethora of bridalwear emporia whose windows were filled with frothy confections of satin and lace. Emine's niece would need several days to visit them all.

'She wants to get everything here. Shoes, dress, stockings. Everything.'

'I can tell her where I got my dress!' said Savina.

The two women continued tidying and polishing while they talked. Neither of them liked to be idle, even for a moment.

'And she wants things for the home, too. The young ones want more than we did in our day.' Emine Özkan did not entirely approve of her niece's ambitions.

'A few lace tablecloths. Embroidered pillowcases . . . It's not really enough now, Emine. Modern conveniences, that's what they want.'

Living in this fast-growing town, where light industry thrived along with tourism, Savina herself had developed a taste for plastic gadgets, which sat side-by-side with more traditional utensils in her kitchen.

'So how will Mrs Papacosta want her hair for the opening tomorrow? Like she had it for her wedding?'

Aphroditi would be the new salon's first customer.

'What time is she due?'

'She's coming at four.'

There were a few seconds of silence.

'She's been so good to us, hasn't she?'

'Yes,' said Savina, 'she's given us a big opportunity.'

'It won't be quite the same here, though . . .' said Emine.

Both women knew that they would miss the atmosphere of Euripides Street. Their old workplace had been a social meeting point as well as a haven for women to come and share intimate secrets, a female equivalent of the *kafenion*. Women in rollers lingered there for hours knowing that their confidences would stay within the confines of the salon. For many it was their only real outing of the week.

'We won't get our old regulars. But I have always longed for my own place.'

'And these ladies will be different. Maybe they'll be more . . .'

'. . . like those?' said Emine, indicating the framed black and white photographs that had been hung earlier that day. They showed a series of glamorous models with bridal hairdos.

'I expect we'll get quite a few weddings, anyway.'

The women had done all they could for now. The next day they would begin to take appointments. Savina squeezed her colleague's arm and smiled.

'Let's go now,' she said. 'Important day for us all tomorrow.'

They hung up their white coats and left the hotel by a back door.

Tourism provided an income for thousands in restaurants, bars and shops as well as in the hotels. Many families had been drawn to the city by the commercial opportunities it gave them, but also by its languid beauty, which they appreciated as much as the foreigners did.

Locals, boys especially, shared the sea and sand with hotel guests. Indeed, the mingling of the two frequently ended with promises of undying love and airport tears.

On this typical summer's afternoon, a small boy, maybe three years old, played on the beach just down from The Sunrise. He was alone, oblivious to anything around him, trickling sand from one hand to the other, digging down deeper and deeper to find the spot where the sand grew cool.

Again and again he passed the sand through his small fingers. He sieved and filtered until only the finest grains remained and ran like water as he lifted his hands and poured them back on to the beach. It was an action of which he never tired.

For an hour that afternoon he had been watching the group of long-limbed older boys playing polo in the water, and he yearned for the day when he would be big enough to join them. For now he had to sit and wait for his brother, who was one of the players.

Hüseyin had a casual summer job putting out loungers and collecting them again, but when he finished, he immediately waded out into the water to join a game. Since a coach had told him he showed great promise as an athlete, he was torn between two dreams: to be a professional volleyball or water polo player. Perhaps he could combine both.

'We need to get your feet back on the ground!' teased his mother.

'Why?' demanded his father. 'Look at him! With those strong legs he has as much chance as anyone.'

Mehmet stood up and waved when he spotted Hüseyin striding

up the beach. Two or three times, with his head in the clouds, Hüseyin had forgotten that he was in charge of the little boy and set off home without him. Mehmet would not have been in any danger, apart from the fact that he had a three year old's inability to orient himself and would probably have wandered the wrong way. In the village where his parents had been born many years before, a small child alone would never get lost, but Famagusta was a world away from such a place.

Mehmet was often told by his mother that he was a little miracle, but Hüseyin's pet name for him, 'little nuisance', seemed to have a truer ring. It was how the boy sometimes felt when his two big brothers were around.

'Come on, Mehmet, time to go home,' said the older boy, cuffing his brother round the ear.

With a ball in one hand and his little brother's hand in the other, Hüseyin made his way to the road. Once they were on the tarmacked surface, he repeatedly bounced the ball. They were both hypnotised by the repetition. Sometimes he could get all the way home, a fifteen-minute walk, without once breaking the rhythm.

They were so absorbed that they did not hear their names being called.

'Hüseyin! Mehmet! Hüseyin!'

Their mother, a hundred yards from the staff entrance to The Sunrise, was hurrying to catch up with them.

'Hello, my darlings,' she said, scooping Mehmet into her arms. He hated being picked up in the street and wriggled furiously. He was not a baby.

She kissed him on the cheek before putting him down.

'Mummy . . . ?'

A few yards away there was an advertising hoarding: an illustration of a smiling boy, his grin wide and cheeky, holding a glass that overflowed with effervescent lemonade. Mehmet gazed at this image every day and never gave up hope.

Emine Özkan knew what he was going to ask.

'Why do you want a drink that's been put in a bottle when you can have a fresh one? There is no sense in it.'

As soon as they reached home, Mehmet would be handed a glass of still, pale liquid, sweetened with plenty of sugar but nevertheless sharp enough to make him draw his cheeks in. It was as flat as milk. One day, after a game of water polo in which he had triumphed, he would go to a kiosk and buy a bottle for himself. It would make a loud *tsok* when the top came off, and bubbles would flow.

One day, thought Mehmet. One day.

Both Mehmet and Hüseyin cherished their dreams.

Chapter Two

At precisely 6.15 p.m., in spite of everything going on around him, Savvas Papacosta instinctively looked at his watch.

It was time to leave for his other hotel. He and Aphroditi were holding a cocktail party for the guests at The Paradise Beach.

Before they left, Aphroditi freshened up in the cloakroom of the now almost-finished hotel. She glanced around at the marbled walls and the sculpted stone shells that held the soap, and noticed with pride that the monogrammed towels were already in place. She applied a fresh coat of coral lipstick that matched the jewellery she had chosen for that day, and put a brush through her long, thick hair. She knew Savvas would be waiting in the car at the entrance.

A few people looked up from their work and nodded as she crossed the floor of the reception. She acknowledged them with a smile. One hundred or more of them would be working until midnight, everyone focused on reaching the almost impossible deadline.

The hotels were mostly positioned directly on the beach so that guests could walk straight on to the sand. As they drove along Kennedy Avenue, Aphroditi and Savvas caught brief glimpses of the sea in the narrow spaces between the buildings.

'What a perfect night,' said Aphroditi.

'It couldn't be more beautiful,' agreed Savvas. 'And tomorrow it will be even more so.'

'Do you think everything will be finished in time?'

'It has to be. Everyone knows what needs to be done. So there's no question of it.'

'The flowers are being delivered at eight.'

'Darling, you've worked so hard.'

'I feel a bit tired,' Aphroditi admitted.

'Well, you look beautiful,' her husband reassured her, patting her on the knee before changing gears. 'And that's what matters.'

They drew up outside The Paradise Beach.

At only five floors, it was modest compared with their new venture, and perhaps a little tired-looking too. Visitors approached through a car park and then up a short cobbled path. Palm trees stood to either side of the main doors; inside there were a few more, but the latter were fake. They had seemed innovative when they were installed five years earlier, but times had moved on.

'*Kalispera*, Gianni,' said Savvas, stopping to greet the man on reception. 'Everything in order today?'

'Busy, Kyrie Papacosta. Very busy indeed.'

It was the answer Savvas liked to hear. Despite his focus on The Sunrise, he wanted reassurance that The Paradise Beach was still full of contented guests. Hosting regular parties was one way he had found to keep their loyalty, but tonight's event had a particular purpose.

That morning, an embossed invitation had been slipped under each door.

The Sunrise

Mr and Mrs Papacosta
request the pleasure of your company
at the Paradise Patio
Cocktails
6.30 p.m.

Now, as Savvas and Aphroditi moved through to the patio to greet their guests, a few dozen people were already gathered there, all of them looking out to sea. It was impossible not to be mesmerised by the sight. In the balmy early evening light, there was a rosy tint to the sky, the sun was still warm on the skin and the lithe bodies of the boys who lingered to play games of volleyball on the beach were sharply defined by the shadows. It seemed entirely credible that Aphroditi, the Goddess of Love, might have been born on this island. It was a place to be in love with life itself.

There was a pattern and rhythm to the way the couple circulated, asking guests how they had spent the day, listening patiently to descriptions of wonderful swimming, clear waters, perhaps an excursion to see the medieval city. They had heard everything before but exclaimed politely as if it was for the first time.

In the corner of the room, a young French pianist moved his pale fingers seamlessly from one jazz favourite to another. The sound of chattering voices and clinking ice drowned out his music here as in every other venue. Every evening he made a journey along the row of hotels, playing for an hour in each one. At five in the morning he would put down the lid of the Steinway at The Savoy, the last of the bars where he had a nightly engagement. He would then sleep until late afternoon and be back at The Paradise Beach for six fifteen.

Savvas was shorter and stouter than most of his northern European clientele, but his suit was better cut than any in the room. Similarly, his wife's clothes were always more chic than those of their guests. However well dressed they were, whether from London, Paris or even the United States, none of the women matched Aphroditi for glamour. Though the American was more than ten years her senior, Aphroditi cultivated a Jackie O style. She had always loved the way Jackie dressed; more than ever since her marriage to Aristotle Onassis, every magazine was full of her image. For years Aphroditi had devoured everything to do with her icon, from the days when she had refurbished the White House and entertained foreign dignitaries with cocktails, to more recent times with images of her on islands not so far away from Cyprus. Jackie's was the style she favoured: immaculately tailored but feminine.

Though the whole impression was flawless, it was her jewellery that made Aphroditi stand out. Most women bought a necklace or bracelet to go with an outfit, but Aphroditi had dresses made to match her jewellery. Usually this reflected a classic Cypriot design but sometimes it had a more modern touch. When people met Aphroditi and were reminded of Jackie Onassis, they sometimes doubted whether Aristotle's gifts to his wife matched up to those given by Savvas Papacosta to his.

Several waiters moved about the room with trays of drinks, but behind the bar, in a dark suit, was the young man who was in charge of the event. Markos Georgiou had begun as a plongeur in the kitchen but had quickly progressed to waiting at tables, then to mixing cocktails. He was ambitious, charming with customers and had spotted Savvas' need for a right-hand man. Within a few years he had made himself indispensable to the hotel's owner.

Markos was the man with whom lone male drinkers drank a late-night whisky (he would memorise their favourite brand and pull it from the shelf without asking). Equally important, he never forgot a woman's name nor how she liked her drink, flattering her by serving a gin and tonic with a twist of lemon rather than a slice.

He had a smile that dazzled both men and women equally. Whoever received a flash of his white teeth and green eyes felt the fleeting touch of his charisma.

Markos, always tuned in to his boss, was ready for the imperceptible nod that was his cue. He came from behind the bar, skirted round the outside of the crowd of milling guests and whispered in the pianist's ear.

The young player smoothly rounded off the melody, and as he did so, the bright tinkling of a cocktail stirrer tapped against a glass silenced the sound of convivial chatter.

'Ladies and gentlemen,' said Savvas, who was standing on a low stool so that he could be seen. 'It is my great pleasure to announce that tomorrow evening we have the grand opening of our new hotel, The Sunrise. This special event marks the beginning of a new era for us and the realisation of a long-held dream: to open a hotel in Famagusta that will rival the best in the world.'

Markos was now back behind the bar. He listened intently to Savvas Papacosta but all the time he was watching Aphroditi, who gazed admiringly at her husband and at exactly the right moment put her hands together. For a few moments there was a warm ripple of applause, then once again a rapt silence that allowed Savvas to continue.

'The position of our new hotel is unmatched by any other in this resort. It faces precisely east, and from the moment the sun rises, guests will enjoy better facilities and entertainment than anywhere on this island. One of the main features of the new hotel will be our nightclub, the Clair de Lune.

'You are all warmly welcome to join us this time tomorrow for cocktails and to see some of the facilities our new hotel will offer. A coach will leave from here at six twenty and bring you back at eight thirty, unless you wish to enjoy a ten-minute stroll along the beach afterwards. Enjoy the rest of your evening and we look forward to seeing you tomorrow.'

Guests gathered round Savvas and Aphroditi to ask questions. Their elegant hosts answered them all with a smile. They hoped of course that some of their regular clients would transfer their loyalty to the new establishment. What they did not mention was that not all of them would be able to afford it. A room at The Sunrise at the height of summer would be beyond the budget of all but the very wealthy.

After ten minutes or so, Aphroditi looked over to Markos and made a summoning gesture. It seemed imperious, unfitting for a woman, but he could not ignore her. She was the boss's wife.

He came over and Aphroditi broke away from the circle to speak to him. They looked straight at each other, eye to eye. The noise in the room meant that Aphroditi had to lean in to make herself heard. He caught the aroma of her perfume and the waft of sweet vermouth on her breath. In spite of the obvious expense of everything she wore, he found the combination of these smells cloying.

'Markos,' she said. 'People will want to look around the nightclub tomorrow. Can you make absolutely sure that everything is ready by six thirty.'

'By all means, Kyria Papacosta, but you know it won't be operational until the following day?'

His response was polite, as was hers:

'I understand perfectly, Markos. But we need to start promoting it and giving people an impression of it. Even if guests continue to stay in this hotel, we will be expecting them to come to The Sunrise for such entertainment.'

She turned her back and walked away.

There was always a measured formality between them which hid a deep-seated mistrust. Aphroditi felt threatened by this man who was always somewhere in the background. She could not help noticing a blemish on his cheek and felt a momentary pang of satisfaction that his otherwise faultless face was mildly flawed.

Though the hierarchy was clear enough, Aphroditi felt that Markos Georgiou's presence challenged her own position. They trod carefully around each other, Aphroditi always expecting some kind of slight that she could mention to Savvas. She had no proof that Markos undermined her but she was always looking for it.

She was furious that Markos had been given freedom to specify everything for the nightclub in The Sunrise. Even its name. It was the only area of the hotel in which Aphroditi had played no part. This rankled with her. She could not understand why her husband gave this man so much liberty when he was so controlling about every other aspect of this enterprise. She particularly disliked what it was called: Clair de Lune.

'It's ridiculous,' she had moaned to Savvas. 'It's the one place in the hotel that will never *see* the light of the moon!'

'But it will only open when the moon is shining, *agapi mou*. That's the point.'

Undaunted, Aphroditi was determined to find something to criticise.

'Most people won't even understand what it means. It's French.'

The argument had taken place one evening when they were in a taverna by the sea.

'Why not "Panselinos"?' suggested Aphroditi, glancing skywards.

'Look, Aphroditi,' said Savvas, trying to keep his patience.

'Because that means "Full Moon", which is not the same. Markos chose "Clair de Lune".'

'*Markos!* But why should . . .'

Aphroditi did not hide her anger whenever her husband put Markos first.

The name of the club itself did not bother Savvas one shilling, but his wife's constant criticism of Markos Georgiou was wearing. He wanted to please Aphroditi, but at the same time he did not want to offend the man on whom he relied for a good proportion of the hotel's projected profit.

The name apart, Aphroditi particularly disliked the decor.

'It just doesn't fit with the rest of the hotel,' she moaned to Savvas. 'Why did you let him do it?'

'It's meant to have its own atmosphere, Aphroditi. It's *meant* to be different.'

Aphroditi did not appreciate that this small piece of the hotel was about the night. It was not intended to connect with the light, airy feel of the ground floor. The Clair de Lune aimed to attract those who preferred night to day, whisky to water, and who relished late-night conversation and cigars.

'I *loathe* that dark purple . . .'

Aphroditi had only been down to inspect the nightclub during daytime hours. It was true that the decor, when strip lights illuminated it, looked gloomy, but with gentle, low-wattage lighting, the space had its allure. There were copious lampshades with gold fringing, thickly piled mauve carpet and low onyx tables arranged around a small stage. Down one side there was a bar with an impressive display of Scotch and Irish whiskies. Even though it could seat one hundred and fifty, the room seemed intimate.

Aphroditi, who had been able to choose the aesthetics of the hotel, was not allowed to influence even the smallest detail of the nightclub's design. Savvas had given Markos carte blanche, and there was not a single aspect that he would allow his wife to change.

In those frantic days before the hotel opened, signs were installed above the door and even the front of the bar was embellished with its name in mother-of-pearl inlay. Aphroditi had lost the battle. She knew it was futile to try to change what was now a fait accompli, but nevertheless bitterly resented Markos' victory.

Markos could not help being pleased that Savvas had been as good as his word. He knew that he was more than Savvas' majordomo, whatever Aphroditi wanted to think. Day by day he had turned himself into Savvas Papacosta's right-hand.

When The Sunrise opened, he rather hoped that the boss's wife would not be around as much. He found her manner with Savvas proprietorial. It was often the way with wives, he felt. They behaved as if they owned their men.

Privately, he wondered why the boss's wife was even working in the hotel. When she was Aphroditi's age, his own mother already had her three children and only left the confines of the house and their orchard in order to go to the village market. Even now, it was just once a year that she left her home in Famagusta to go to Nicosia. The rest of the time she was tending the house or the garden, making *shoushouko* (a grape and almond sweet) or halloumi, or creating lace. Markos accepted that times had changed, and that girls – his sister, even – now dressed differently, thought differently and even talked differently. In spite of all this, the very *existence* of Aphroditi in his workplace bothered him and he treated her with great caution and exaggerated politeness.

One thing he was certain of was that she would play no role

in the nightclub. It would be entirely his own domain. Savvas Papacosta was aiming to attract a set of the super-rich whose taste for cabaret had been whetted in Monaco, Paris and even Las Vegas. He had told Markos that with the right acts and music, they could make more profit for the hotel than the accommodation and catering put together. It would be on a different scale from any similar venue in Cyprus, open six days a week, from eleven at night until four in the morning.

At eight o'clock precisely, Markos watched Savvas and Aphroditi Papacosta say their farewells and slip away. It would be seven or eight hours before he himself left. The pianist continued to play and he knew there would be a core of clients who would linger to enjoy the atmosphere until well after midnight. Some of them would return after dinner and spill out on to the patio to enjoy the balmy warmth of the night. Others, mostly men (though occasionally a lone female guest), would perch on a bar stool to give him their views about business, politics or something more personal. From his position behind the bar, Markos was adept at making the right responses and adjusting to moods that changed with the level in the whisky bottle.

He readily accepted offers of 'a stiff double', clinked glasses with a smile, toasted whatever the customer wanted to toast and stealthily lined up the drinks beneath the bar. Clients happily reeled off to bed after an evening of satisfying conviviality, while Markos poured the unwanted liquor back into the bottle and cashed up.

He drove past the new hotel on his way home. It was two thirty in the morning and lights were still blazing inside The Sunrise's reception area. Numerous contractors' vans were parked outside as people continued to work through the night.

The Sunrise

There to the left of the main doors a huge sign had been erected, ready for illumination: 'Clair de Lune'. He knew that everything inside was in place, as he had already inspected it that morning. Whatever Aphroditi Papacosta imagined, there was little with which she would be able to find fault, and for the group of guests who would be given a privileged preview of facilities that night, he was confident that the nightclub would be the main attraction of the new hotel.

Savvas Papacosta was giving him an exceptional opportunity. It was one that Markos had dreamed of.

Chapter Three

WITHIN TEN MINUTES, Markos drew up outside his home in Elpida Street. Like most buildings in the residential outskirts of modern Famagusta, it had several floors, each with its own balcony, and each occupied by a different generation.

On the ground floor were Markos' parents, Vasilis and Irini. On the first there was an empty apartment that would eventually be occupied by Markos' younger brother Christos; on the second was his sister Maria with her husband Panikos. Markos lived alone on the top floor. If he leaned right out over the balcony, there was a glimpse of the sea and sometimes the possibility of a breeze. Everyone shared the rooftop, a permanent site for drying laundry. Rows of shirts, sheets and towels hung there, dry as paper after an hour. Rusty metal rods sprouted up like saplings, ready for another storey if ever needed for children of children.

At this time of night Markos would not stop at his parents' place, but in the morning he would sit in their small garden for ten minutes before going to work again. His father would usually have left for his smallholding by ten, but his mother would make him the sweet Greek coffee that he loved and take a break from her chores.

When Vasilis and Irini Georgiou had built the apartments in the city, they had replicated in miniature everything they had enjoyed when they lived in the countryside. A vine that grew over a trellis to give them shade, five closely planted orange trees and a dozen pots from which his mother harvested more tomatoes than they could consume. Even the gerania had been propagated from cuttings of their plants in the village. There was also a tiny corner of the *kipos* fenced off with wire where two chickens scratched and fussed at the ground.

For Irini Georgiou, the most important feature of the garden was the cage that hung just to the left of her door. Inside it was her canary, Mimikos. His singing was her joy.

At three in the morning everything was still, apart from the cicadas.

Markos found his key, let himself into the shared hallway and began to climb the stairs. When he reached the first floor, he could hear his brother, Christos, along with some other voices inside the empty apartment. There was nothing in there but the bare concrete of walls and floors and the sounds were magnified.

Markos put his ear to the door and listened. His brother's voice was raised, which was not unusual, but one of the other men inside sounded even angrier. He recognised the voice of another mechanic from the garage where Christos worked. Haralambos Lambrakis had exerted huge influence on his brother.

The two brothers had always been close and fond of each other. There was a ten-year age gap and they had joshed and played around together for Christos' entire life. Since he had been old enough to walk, the younger one had followed the older around, copying what he did and what he believed. He had idolised Markos.

At the age of eighteen, Christos was far more radical than Markos had been at the same age. Just the previous morning they had argued over the burning issue of *enosis* between Cyprus and Greece. As a younger man, Markos had always believed passionately that this union should happen. He had been a member of EOKA, the National Organisation of Cypriot Fighters, and supported its cause when it was fighting for the end of British rule on the island. Since independence had been achieved a decade earlier, though, he had moved away from its extreme ideas.

After the military coup in Athens five years before, most Greek Cypriots valued their independence from the mainland more than ever and no longer wanted unification with Greece. There was now rivalry between the Greek Cypriots such as Christos who still campaigned for *enosis* and those who did not, and between them hung the threat of violence.

'Why have you become such a coward?' Christos had screamed.

'It's not a question of cowardice,' said Markos, carrying on with what he was doing. It was around ten in the morning and he was shaving, methodically passing his razor through thick white foam, watching his face gradually emerge. He looked at his own image in the mirror, apparently ignoring his brother who stood at the bathroom door.

Christos had come up to Markos' apartment to try and win him over to his way of thinking. He never gave up.

'But you used to have conviction! Belief! What's wrong with you?'

'Christos, there is nothing wrong with me.' Markos smiled at his brother. 'Perhaps I just know more now.'

'What do you mean by that? You know more? What is there to know?' Markos' calm manner angered Christos. 'This island is Greek, was Greek, should be Greek, should be part of the *motherland*! For God's sake, Markos, you once believed in the struggle for *enosis*!'

'So did our uncle,' said Markos impassively. 'And our father.'

'So that means we give up? Because people like Uncle Kyriakos died?'

Their mother's brother had been executed by the British authorities during the worst of the violence before independence. His name was rarely mentioned, but a black and white photograph of him on a table in their parents' living room was a daily reminder.

Markos continued shaving. A moment passed. There was nothing more to say about the martyrdom of their uncle that had not already been said during their lifetime. The grief that had engulfed the household would never be forgotten. It had left its own scars. Christos had been seven years old then, and witnessed the wailing and the naked anguish displayed by their aunt and mother.

Markos had hated his uncle Kyriakos and could not now pretend otherwise. When he was little, Kyriakos used to slap him round the head if he was not pulling his weight with the fruit harvest, and if he caught his nephew eating an orange during picking hours, he would then make him eat four more, one after the other, including the rind, to teach him that greed had its own punishment. He was a cruel man, and not just to his nephew. Markos, ever observant of what went on around him, had suspicions that he hit his wife too. The first time he had caught his mother holding a cold compress to Aunt Myrto's cheek, no explanation was given. When he enquired, he was told it was 'no business for a child', but such things had happened so frequently that he had seen a pattern. Markos wondered if this was why God had punished Kyriakos by giving him no children. If so, He was punishing Myrto too.

Seeing his aunt grieve, keening and crying, hour after hour, constantly petted and patted by her family, Markos had wondered how much of it was an act. How could she lament the loss of a husband who had treated her that way? He watched his mother comforting his aunt and was reminded of how many times he had seen her with an arm around the same shoulders after she had been beaten.

During the year that had followed Uncle Kyriakos' death, their father had also been wounded, almost fatally. Even now, Markos vividly recalled the smell of dirt and blood that had seemed to pervade the house when he was carried in. Vasilis Georgiou had recovered, but his chest and back had been lacerated and his upper body was still criss-crossed with scars. The lasting damage was to his leg. Even with a stick, he rocked from side to side when he walked. His left leg could no longer bend and, ever since, he had been in constant pain that could not be alleviated by drugs. Only *zivania* dulled the continuous ache.

'Look at our father, Christos! He's crippled . . . Who gained from that?'

Neither of them knew the full details of their father's activities in the 1950s, only that he too had been an active member of EOKA. Vasilis Georgiou had been decorated by General Grivas, the leader of the uprising against British rule, before he was exiled. Markos knew that Grivas had secretly returned the previous year and was clandestinely leading a new campaign for *enosis*. He had found a new and willing generation of young men such as Christos ready to join his newly formed EOKA B.

'What I can't understand is why you stopped! It's a mission, for God's sake. You don't just abandon it when you feel like it. Not until it's won!'

Christos loved the rhetoric of *enosis*, enjoyed making a speech, even to the single audience of his brother.

Markos sighed. When he himself had flirted with the cause as a teenager, he had even sworn the oath – 'I shall not abandon

the struggle . . . until after our aim has been accomplished.'
Nowadays its aims no longer suited him.

'Perhaps I have other interests now, Christos. Cyprus is becoming something else. A land of opportunity. How exactly is it going to benefit from becoming part of Greece?'

'What do you mean? A land of opportunity?'

'You haven't noticed?'

'Noticed what?

'How this city is growing?'

Christos was annoyed by his brother's bland language.

'What . . . so it's a matter of the money you have in your pocket, is it?'

'Not only that, Christos. Just ask yourself: do you want your precious island to be governed by a dictatorship? From Athens?'

Christos was silent.

'*Gamoto!* Damn!' Markos had nicked himself slightly with his razor and blood oozed out of the cut. 'Pass me that handkerchief, Christos.'

He dabbed at it until the bleeding ceased, mildly irritated by the realisation that a blemish would be left.

'Look at you. Wincing like a baby,' Christos taunted his brother.

Christos continued trying to persuade Markos to see his point of view, but the more desperate and ranting in his entreaties he became, the calmer Markos grew. He looked at his younger brother with sympathy and shook his head from side to side.

Christos stood clenching and unclenching his hands, almost crying tears of frustration.

'How did you change so much?' he pleaded. 'I just don't understand . . .'

Markos did not feel that he had changed. Not inside, at least.

It was the world that had changed, and new opportunities were now presenting themselves and asking to be taken.

'Christos . . .' He appealed to his brother, but was immediately interrupted.

'You've become like our parents . . .'

Markos could not halt his tirade.

'. . . happy with an easy life!'

'And there's something wrong with that at their age?' he asked.

'Father was a fighter once!'

'Once, Christos. But not now. And if you're going to be part of it, just make sure you keep it to yourself. You don't want people finding out.'

Markos was not only referring to their parents, whom he wanted to protect from the anxiety. The police were constantly searching for EOKA B suspects.

He continued his ascent of the concrete stairs and the voices faded. Even with the windows open, the sound of arguing and the noise of the cicadas would not keep Markos from sleeping. A long day and night of work would be followed by a brief but deep slumber.

The next morning he was up at nine as usual, and after the rituals of showering and shaving (he was more careful today), he went down to spend half an hour with his mother before going to work.

Irini Georgiou was chatting to her caged canary when he appeared. She wore a brown chiffon headscarf trimmed with lace which would be kept on all day, and beneath her rose-print apron she wore a floral blouse, the two designs clashing furiously. Everything in Irini's life was similarly busy, from her daily schedule that was full from morning to night with a continuous sequence

The Sunrise

of small tasks, to the decor of the place where they lived. Their house in the village had been larger than the apartment, but they had brought with them every stick of furniture and knick-knack they had ever possessed. The combination of these made the apartment resemble a museum of small objects. Every plate, framed print, vase of plastic flowers, lace mat and postcard sent by a friend had been given a home and, just as before, the icon of Agios Neophytos was in pride of place. Irini felt safer this way, almost cocooned within memorabilia.

Among the photographs displayed in their apartment was a portrait of General Grivas, alongside an image of President Makarios, a wedding portrait of the Georgious and pictures of Markos, Maria and Christos as babies. Irini's adoration of Makarios had increased now that he no longer supported *enosis*. Sometimes the photograph of Grivas, though, was turned to the wall. She said it was an easy mistake to make when dusting. She hoped that her husband had not been involved in any of the assassinations that had taken place, but she had never dared to ask.

She was well aware that General Grivas had returned from exile. What neither she nor her husband knew was that Christos had joined EOKA B.

'Come and have your coffee,' she said, smiling at Markos.

Irini Georgiou adored her firstborn son, and he in turn was always attentive and affectionate towards his mother.

'*Mamma*, you look tired today . . .'

It was true: the dark shadows beneath her eyes were purple-black. Irini Georgiou had not been sleeping well. The past few mornings she had been more exhausted when she got up than when she went to bed. She said it was her dreams. Though they were often illogical and full of tumult, she believed they told her the truth. Whatever anyone claimed, whatever words were used, she believed that peace was contained in the atmosphere. It was an aroma rather than a political situation. Her dreams were telling her that peace was threatened.

When the struggle against the British had ended and the Republic of Cyprus was created, there had been a welcome period of uneventful peace and quiet for the Georgiou family. They were idyllic years of tending their land; of enjoying the quiet rhythm of village life, where birdsong was the only sound that interrupted the silence; of following the pattern of the seasons, the variation in temperature and the welcome arrival of rain. There was space for everyone, land enough to feed them all and warmth between themselves and their Turkish Cypriot neighbours. The only difficulty in their lives had been to manage Vasilis Georgiou's pain, and his inability to work longer than a few hours a day.

The peace was short-lived. Tranquillity was murdered at the same time as their Turkish neighbours, in an act of violence perpetrated by Greek Cypriots. In spite of what their leader, Makarios, said, did and agreed with other politicians, being close to the place where their neighbours had been attacked and killed destroyed Irini Georgiou's peace of mind. Although her sleep had always been dream-filled, it was now haunted by nightmares. It was then that they moved away from the village. Vasilis drove back each day in his small pick-up truck to tend the land, but Irini Georgiou always stayed behind in Famagusta.

Markos followed his mother into the over-cluttered home, where variously patterned armchairs stood on ornately woven rugs. Markos' eyes ached at the sight. He could understand why his father spent so much time away from home, some of it tending to the smallholding they had retained and some of it at the *kafenion*, where he went to see his friends and play *tavli*. Either would be more relaxing.

Markos kept his own apartment entirely without clutter. He had few possessions. Everything had to have a practical use. Bric-a-brac, which gave his mother security, was anathema to him. Even a floral cloth that she wanted to put on his table, 'to pretty the place up a bit', was more than he could bear.

'Such a disturbed night, *leventi mou*,' she said as she put the little cups down in front of them.

She often confided in Markos about her dreams. Her husband, who slept like the dead, was uninterested in such things. He had left an hour before.

'And last night there were such angry voices too,' she added. 'I don't know what took place exactly, *leventi mou*, but nothing good, nothing nice.'

Her son did not like to tell her that she had probably been disturbed by a real argument, between Christos and his friends. It did not seem worth upsetting her in this way. If the subject of *enosis* ever came up, Irini moved the conversation away. She did not want her sons to have anything to do with politics or violence. They had threatened to tear the island apart in those awful years, and she still believed they could. Nothing had been truly resolved.

Markos stroked his mother's hand, which rested on the table. Her skin was paper thin and there was a graze across her knuckles. He ran his fingers across it.

'What did you do, *Mamma*?'

'Just got a bit scratched cutting back the vine,' she answered. 'Nothing serious. It takes a long time to heal when you're my age.'

Markos looked down at his own smooth skin. His father always had rough, lacerated hands too and it was something he wanted to avoid for himself.

Nowadays, when Markos went to the barber for his regular trim (though he was growing his silky hair much longer that summer), he also had his nails manicured. His cuticles were neatened and the nails filed. There was not a speck of dirt beneath them. With their daily massage in olive oil, they looked innocent, almost child-like. For Markos, these perfect hands demonstrated his success, showing that he never held anything heavier than a pen.

'*Tse! Tse! Tse!*'

His mother was feeding Mimikos with his seed.

'*Tse! Tse! Tse!* How are those plants I gave you?' she asked, hardly pausing between talking to her bird and to her son. 'Have you remembered to water them?'

He smiled. '*Mamma*, you know I haven't. I'm sorry. I've been so busy . . .'

'Working so hard, *leventi mou*, working so hard. No time even for a nice girl?'

'Oh *Mamma* . . .'

It was a joke between them. She was always hopeful. Every mother loved her son, but Markos' beautiful looks made him easy to adore. She caressed his cheek as she had done ever since he was a baby, then allowed him to take her hand and kiss it.

'I'm just holding out until I meet someone as beautiful as you,' he said teasingly.

'Yes, my sweetheart, but don't leave it too long.'

Like any mother she was a little impatient. Their daughter was two years married now but she would be very happy if her elder son found himself a wife. Things should happen in some kind of natural order, and besides, he was now twenty-eight.

She was proud that her son had a job in the smartest hotel in town. It had been one of the consolations of moving from the country to Famagusta. She had always recognised that Markos would not be satisfied with a slow, humdrum life caring for orange trees. He might not have achieved good grades at school, but he was bright and she was sure that he had a promising future ahead of him.

Markos rose to leave.

'Look how smart you are!' she said, running her fingers down his lapel. 'You look so wonderful in that suit! Like a real businessman.'

'It's the grand opening tonight,' he said, taking her hand. 'The Papacostas are having a reception and they're expecting lots of VIPs.'

'How exciting.' His mother beamed with pride that her son would be at such a gathering. 'Who's coming? Tell me who will be there.'

His mother lived vicariously through her son's career. She had never been to The Paradise Beach and knew it was even less likely that she would ever visit The Sunrise, but she always wanted to know what went on in these big hotels. Irini Georgiou would buy the next edition of the local newspaper and cut out pictures of the event, which would almost certainly be on the front page.

'The Mayor and his wife,' said Markos nonchalantly. 'Lots of politicians from Nicosia, plenty of businessmen, friends of Mrs Papacosta's father, even some overseas visitors . . .'

'And will the nightclub be opening?' she asked.

'Not tonight,' said Markos. 'Tomorrow.' He looked at his watch.

'I'll go and water your plants later,' Irini said. 'And I'll starch your shirts – they'll be in your wardrobe.'

She was already bustling around clearing the cups, wiping the table, dead-heading a geranium, peering into her canary cage to check if she had put in enough seed. Soon she would start preparing lunch. The whole family appreciated her cooking, especially Panikos, who had put on considerable weight since the marriage.

Maria would come down to help her, and her son-in-law would arrive home from his electrical shop at midday, just in time to eat.

'I must go,' Markos said, kissing her on the top of the head. 'I'll come and tell you all about it, I promise.'

Between now and when the sun set, there was not a moment to waste. By the time it was dusk, the island's biggest social event of the year would be well under way.

Chapter Four

The Sunrise was filled with the scent of hundreds of lilies and the perfumes of as many glamorous women. Gowns were in jewel colours, jewels were in all colours.

The guests were greeted at the entrance and then directed down a crimson carpet that led them towards the frolicking dolphins. Here they were served with ice-cold champagne and then ushered past the murals, which they stopped to admire.

The plaster pillars were entwined with flowers. As night fell, they would also be illuminated.

Dozens of waiters in white jackets circulated with platters of food. The head chef, with a staff of twenty-five in the kitchen, had laboured tirelessly since dawn to create a colourful array of canapés with liberal use of gelatine, piping and puff pastry. They had worked like robots, mechanically cutting and garnishing so that each piece was neat and precise and bore no resemblance to anything home-cooked in traditional Cypriot style. There were tiny vol-au-vents, delicate morsels of foie gras and prawns to be speared with cocktail sticks. The chef was French and his inspiration was Escoffier. He instructed that everything had to be decorated like a dessert. If it could not have a cherry on top, there must be a few grains of caviar, or a tiny speck of tomato to add a finishing touch.

The combined volume of several hundred voices all speaking at once meant that the twelve-piece band was unheard, but the musicians persevered, knowing that later in the evening when the crowd thinned out their carefully rehearsed repertoire would be appreciated. They had been flown in the previous day from Paris, one of the many things specially imported for the occasion. Savvas Papacosta wanted the reception to reflect the international aspirations of the hotel, and the twang of a bouzouki would undo this with a single note. This, indeed, was a sophisticated affair.

Everyone was naturally drawn towards the terrace outside, where there was a suspended centrepiece, an arrangement of white flowers that spelled out the name of the hotel. In front of this stood their hosts, waiting to welcome them.

Aphroditi, in a floor-length ivory gown, seemed to glow from within. Coiled round both of her upper arms were white gold bracelets each with the face of a snake, one with rubies for eyes, the other with sapphires. Some guests thought she looked like a mermaid, others saw Cleopatra's influence. Every woman in the room studied her enviously, analysing the detail closely: the diamonds that dripped from her ears, the dress skilfully cut on the bias that flowed around her body, the way in which the sequins caught the light as she moved, the gold sandals that occasionally peeked through the slit in the hem, the hair wound into a chignon. Emine had created a perfect hairdo for the evening and the women speculated on the number of grips and pins. In spite of their secret admiration, the comments they made to their husbands were reductive and universally scathing.

'And who does she think she is? Everything is just so *exaggerated* . . .'

What the men saw was the whole, the vision, an overall impression. They saw a faultlessly beautiful woman, but knew not to disagree with their wives.

Standing by Aphroditi's side, waiting for exactly the right moment to begin the speeches, Savvas watched the guests surveying what he had created. What he wanted more than anything was to impress them with the quality of what they saw. He had worked every waking hour for several years to complete what they were viewing in a mere hour and could feel their amazement at what he had achieved. Finally, he began to relax.

After the speeches had finished – Savvas, the Mayor and then a member of parliament – congratulations and exclamations flowed as generously as the champagne. When Savvas felt that everyone had had enough time to marvel at the overall impression, politicians, local worthies and potential guests were taken on personal tours. They saw the ballroom, the dining rooms and reaching it via the mirrored lift, the penthouse suite. Every facility was pointed out, the source of the marble tiles, even the thread count of the linen.

Costas Frangos, the hotel manager, and his two assistant managers left guests in no doubt that the quality of everything at The Sunrise was in an entirely new league for the island. It was indisputable. Overburdened with facts and figures, they hastened back to the reception to have their glasses refilled. Beyond question, Famagusta seemed to have grown richer in front of their glinting eyes, and almost all of them saw a personal benefit for themselves.

The wives of the men who owned the neighbouring hotels, however, were eager to find fault. First of all they criticised the food.

'So hard to eat! Everything's so fancy! So fiddly.'

Then they turned their attention to the hotel's decor.

'That floor! And as for those dolphins . . .' whispered one.

'Do you think guests will actually *like* all that fringing . . . and those drapes? And why *have* they tiled the pool like that?' breathed another, almost in earshot of the Papacostas.

These women found their husbands unusually quiet, burdened by the knowledge that they would now be obliged to upgrade their own facilities. Whatever question marks hung over the taste with which The Sunrise had been decorated, the reality was that this new hotel was superior to all the rest. It was not a matter of opinion. It was bigger and grander and, if the canapés were anything to judge by, even the cuisine was going to put the other hotels to shame.

Meanwhile, the government minister was fulsome in his praise. 'Kyrie Papacosta, may I congratulate you on what you have achieved here.' He adopted the tone of a person speaking for others as well as himself. 'I firmly believe that The Sunrise will raise the status of the whole island.'

He offered his hand to Savvas and the flash bulbs went off all around them. Aphroditi Papacosta, standing close to her husband, felt the heat of the lights and for a moment was blinded by their brightness. The photographers could already tell that it would be an image of her alone that would dominate the front of tomorrow's paper. The editor would be more than happy to relegate the picture of the portly politician to an inside page. 'The Sun Rises on Famagusta' would be the headline on the front page.

Like everyone in the room, Markos found his eyes continually drawn to Aphroditi. He was disconcerted to see that she was so much the centre of attention when it was Savvas Papacosta who was the proprietor and the man who had put this hotel together. He saw his boss almost fade away beside his wife.

Markos constantly circulated during the reception, keeping his distance from both of them. The only thing Savvas required of him that night was to promote the nightclub.

Markos could not be certain, but from the years he had spent behind the bar he could guess who was likely to form his clientele. They would be the ones who stayed up till all hours, the heavy smokers, the men who had turned down champagne and asked for something stronger, perhaps those on the edge of a conversation, looking about them, bored or restless even. It was not an infallible test, but it was a place to start. He approached these men, introduced himself and could tell immediately from their response whether his antennae were well tuned. Some of his targets were immediately stirred into life, their facial expressions transformed from neutral to excited. More revealingly, they accepted with alacrity when he suggested seeing the club.

He led his potential clients away from the reception and down an internal flight of stairs that took them to a discreet locked door. He opened it with a flourish, leading them into his domain.

The route into this nocturnal underworld made people feel that they had privileged access to a private space. If he had taken them out of the hotel to the more public entrance, they would not have felt the same connection. Markos was careful to give each one of them the impression that they were the only person to be escorted in this way.

After a few minutes or so, during which he described the cabaret artists who were booked to appear and listed some of the vintage whiskies, his guests accepted complimentary membership of the club. Markos was in little doubt that they would be there again on the opening night.

He delivered them back to the reception, which continued in full swing. Sometimes he watched a man being reunited with his wife and registered her pleasure at seeing her husband's more contented demeanour. It seemed to Markos that women were easily pleased.

Returning from one of his guided tours, Markos glanced out towards the terrace. It was now dark and the sky was dense with stars, all the more visible because of the absence of moonlight. He wandered outside, where the numbers were beginning to dwindle, and looked around him.

He noticed that Aphroditi had moved from her position beneath the floral sculpture and was sitting at a table with an elderly couple. She looked up and seemed to stare directly at him before moving her eyes back to the silver-haired woman. Markos retreated to the air-conditioned reception area. For some reason, he was irritated that he did not even warrant a slight wave or a hint of a smile. Even though the night was cooling, he had felt his temperature rise.

Aphroditi was with her parents. Her mother was dressed in black. Since the day her only son had been killed she had worn no other colour. On this celebratory summer's night, her mourning weeds seemed all the more heavy and sad and made her look much older than her years. Aphroditi's father, Trifonas, wore a dark grey suit and pale blue shirt. He was a handsome man, white-haired like his wife, but still full of vigour. He was enjoying being back on his native island and was particularly happy that this great project had reached fruition. The Sunrise was the first hotel investment that Markides Holdings had made, and Trifonas could already sense that it had been one of the wisest decisions he had ever made.

Nowadays, Trifonas Markides developed property from a distance. He had a company based in Nicosia that looked after the day-to-day running of each investment. From his study in their house in Southgate he spent half an hour on the telephone each day. The money had made them very comfortable indeed. In the cold south of England temperatures, they kept the central heating on for most of the year, matching the Cyprus climate inside their home. They had a Jaguar, thick carpets and what Artemis called a 'char'. Trifonas played golf most days, and on Sundays they drove to the Greek Orthodox church. They were involved with fund-raising for Greek Cypriots who had made their way over to England and needed financial assistance, and occasionally they went to one of the big Cypriot restaurants nearby for the wedding of a child of someone they knew from the church. On the whole, however, although Trifonas socialised at the golf club, Artemis kept herself apart. Life for her had stopped in 1964 and this state of paralysis was her way of being. All the money in Cyprus and Britain could not bring Dimitris Markides back.

Aphroditi knew that she had her father's approval, but she hoped for her mother's too.

'What do you think of it?' she asked.

'It's beautiful, darling. You have done a wonderful job,' replied Artemis, forcing a smile.

'You should come and stay here!' suggested Aphroditi.

Her parents had kept their own apartment in the building that had been given to Aphroditi and Savvas as a wedding gift and they always used it on their rare visits to Cyprus. They almost never went to the Nicosia apartment.

'We couldn't do that, dear.'

Aphroditi had known even before the words left her mouth that her mother would refuse. Such an environment would be far too public for her.

A waiter came up to them with a tray of drinks.

'Hello, Hasan.'

'Good evening, madam.'

'It's gone well tonight, don't you think?'

'The guests have all been very impressed,' the waiter replied with a smile.

Aphroditi took three glasses of champagne and handed one to her mother.

'No thank you, dear. Something soft, if you don't mind.'

'Even tonight, Mother? Just to make a toast?'

Although they only had minimal time together these days, Aphroditi still found herself irritated by her mother. Why could she not lift her mood a little, just for once, on an occasion that meant so much to her daughter?

Even at Aphroditi and Savvas' wedding, Artemis Markides had sat quietly apart from the celebrations. Dimitris' death had been a catastrophe for them all, but Aphroditi yearned for its shadow not to cast a pall over this event too. He was dead, but she was still living.

Aphroditi noticed how her mother avoided looking at the waiter. Her mother's prejudice against Turkish Cypriots upset her, but it was something she avoided mentioning. Aphroditi supported her husband's way of thinking. The hotel must employ whoever was best for any job, regardless of background.

'It's another way to set The Sunrise apart,' Savvas had explained to his mother-in-law, when she had raised the issue that afternoon. 'To make it more truly international, we must have a broad mixture of staff. The chef is French, two of the receptionists are English, our banqueting manager is Swiss. In the hair salon we have a Turkish Cypriot . . . and many of the kitchen staff are too, of course.'

'But . . .' interjected her mother. 'Waiters? Front of house?'

'Well, I don't like to disagree,' answered Savvas, 'but we want the best people. And of course the people who will do the job for the money we're offering. It's business.'

Savvas saw the world through a prism of profit and loss.

Aphroditi got up from the table.

'I must see if Savvas needs me,' she said, making her excuse to walk away.

Something that did not help between Aphroditi and her parents was that the truth had always been kept from her mother. Artemis Markides had been protected from the irrefutable facts about her son, and at times like this, Aphroditi was filled with an urge to tell her everything; to scream out the truth:

'He killed someone, Mother. Your precious son *killed* a Turkish Cypriot!'

She had lived for almost a decade with these words close to her lips, but they could never be spoken.

There had been a careful cover-up, which was easy to arrange for a man with as much money and influence as Trifonas. Paying someone off to change the story was very straightforward. Markides did not want any suggestion that his son had been killed in retaliation for another murder. A fact such as that would taint the family name for ever.

Aphroditi knew that her brother was not innocent. He had been in the thick of the pointless antagonism between Greeks and Turks that had swelled into hatred after the British had left. Neither side had been entirely happy with the constitution of the republic signed in 1960, but when Makarios had put forward a proposal to amend it, violence had erupted. The blood of a Turk meant the spilling of the blood of a Greek, and so it had gone on. It was an animosity that ran deep in some, and at times it had threatened to destroy everything. It had deprived Aphroditi of her only brother, devastated her mother, torn apart her father's life, and if things had carried on as in the previous decade, the livelihoods of everyone on the island would have been ruined, whether they were Greek or Turk. She could see no sense in a conflict where there was no winning side.

She stood for a moment looking out towards the sea. It had been her suggestion when the hotel was being designed that the terrace should reach right out on to the beach so that guests could hear the lapping of the water and step barefoot on to the sand. On a night like this, when the sea was still and the stars were bright, they might also see the most magical thing of all: the reflection of a meteor shower.

In the five minutes she allowed herself to stand beneath the canopy of stars, her anger subsided. Frustration with her mother often got the better of her. Artemis Markides was like an empty shell from which any capacity for emotion had crawled away. It had made Aphroditi even more appreciative of her father's unfailing affection. Since they had moved to England, she had missed him deeply.

When Aphroditi turned round, her parents had gone. Even their glasses had been cleared. She knew that her father would be taking his wife back to their apartment. She hated late nights. The next morning they would be flying back to London.

Markos was standing in the shadows. On this peaceful, star-filled night, in spite of the calm exterior he had on display for the guests, he had been a little anxious. He knew that Christos was in Nicosia meeting up with his fellow revolutionaries.

Suddenly something caught his eye. Against the backdrop of the inky sky, he noticed a pale, translucent statue. It was Aphroditi, motionless and alone. Markos could not decide which weighed more heavily on him that night: concern over Christos, or the vision of Aphroditi like an exquisite marble artefact resurrected from the sands. Both of them gave him a strange sense of unease.

Chapter Five

The last of the revellers left the party at midnight. Less than twelve hours remained before the first guests would arrive with their suitcases.

When Savvas arrived at The Sunrise early the following morning, dozens of people were already clearing, sweeping, dusting and polishing to make everything as perfect as before. Furniture needed to be rearranged. Drinks had been spilled, and debris was littered on the marble floor. The amount of cleaning up reflected the success of the party.

'Good morning, Kyrie Papacosta.'

'Good morning, Kyrie Papacosta . . .'

Savvas heard the words a dozen or more times between the car park and the reception desk.

Members of staff were in no doubt about the standard that was expected in this new hotel. If a surface was shiny, it must be polished so that you could see a reflection of your face. If the napkins were white, they had to be dazzlingly so. Windows must be so clean that they would cease to be seen. The head of housekeeping was tyrannical. Chambermaids had been instructed that unless beds were correctly turned down, they could lose their jobs.

'Who are our first arrivals, Costas?' Savvas asked the hotel manager.

'We have two couples from Geneva, Kyrie Papacosta, and they are coming together. Twenty-six Americans. A group from Germany. Thirty from Sweden. Half a dozen British couples. Some French. A few Italians, and the rest, I believe, are from Athens.'

'That's a healthy start. And exactly the right number for now.'

'Oh – and Frau Bruchmeyer, of course,' Costas Frangos added. 'We're sending a car to collect her from The Paradise Beach later this morning.'

Frau Bruchmeyer had come on holiday to Cyprus the year before and never gone home. That November, her niece had arrived from Berlin with some slightly warmer clothing (a few cashmere cardigans, slacks and a woollen jacket), her jewellery (a piece of which she wore to dinner each night) and some books. The rest of it – her furniture, her family portraits and her furs – was left behind.

'I don't need those things,' she said. 'I need very little here. Just some money to keep me going.'

Day to day, she had little need for cash, just enough to tip the staff, which she did constantly and generously. Her monthly bill was paid by banker's draft.

She began each day with a forty-minute swim from the golden sands beneath her room. Early risers, mostly workers in other hotels, would see her taking her supple body through a routine of stretches and exercises. Then they saw her white-capped head moving towards the horizon and back again. Finally, she sat to contemplate the sea.

'I have swum in every ocean in the world,' she said, 'but in none more beautiful than this. Where else would I want to spend the rest of my days?'

No aspect of her life would have been better back in Germany. Here, her laundry was taken care of and her room kept spick and span. She ate like a queen and, just like royalty, never had to shop or cook. There was a constant supply and variety of company, of which she never tired, and she was only alone when she chose to be.

From her balcony across the bay, she had watched the progress of The Sunrise, and had set her heart on taking the penthouse suite. Until that time, The Paradise Beach had seemed comfortable enough – she occupied the best of its rooms – but she could see that the new hotel was going to be in a different league. With the sale of a few diamond rings, she calculated that she had enough in the bank to last her another fifteen years. She imagined this should suffice, even though she had the energy and vigour of someone half her age.

A few hours later, Frau Bruchmeyer arrived at her new home. The staff at The Paradise Beach had been sorry to see her go. She was like a lucky mascot. A small team carried her luggage down to a waiting taxi. Four expensive suitcases were loaded into the car, two into the boot and the others on to the front seat. She carried a matching vanity case herself, and with promises that she would return to see them all she had discreetly handed each of the staff who came to wave her off 'a little something'.

By lunchtime, she was settled into her luxurious abode, a sitting room with bedroom and bathroom en suite. To her eyes, it was a glorious palace, with huge mirrors on the walls, a large oil painting of a French landscape, a pair of crystal chandeliers, furniture that was upholstered, piped and tasselled, a grand bureau and a four-poster bed. Her clothes all fitted comfortably inside the double wardrobe.

Once she had unpacked, ordered a light lunch in her room and rested for a few hours on the chaise longue, Frau Bruchmeyer then showered and began her slow and elaborate preparations for the evening. The nightclub at The Sunrise would be opening for the first time but, before that, she had an invitation to dinner with the hotel proprietors.

She fastened her charm bracelet, the last gift that her husband had given her, and caught the lift down to the foyer.

At around the same time, Aphroditi was carefully selecting her own jewellery for the evening. She unlocked the top left-hand drawer of the dressing table. Almost without glancing down, she picked up a pair of earrings and fastened them to her ears. They were round, like coat buttons, with a huge stone in the centre. Then she slid on a broad bangle (slightly too large for her slender wrist, but she had not yet had time to get it adjusted) with eight of the same aquamarines set in gold, and after that she slipped over her head a thick chain on which hung a pendant, a single stone that dwarfed the others. Finally there was a ring. The design of the whole set was minimal – the cut of the gems was its feature. They needed no embellishment. The translucent blue and pale gold were the hues of the island, perhaps the reason that the jeweller had named the collection *Hromata tis Kiprou* – 'Colours of Cyprus'. They were the same colours in which every islander was bathed from day to day, but only Aphroditi possessed them in this way.

She had gone with her parents to the airport late morning but had done little else that day. Their farewell was full of unspoken emotion and little outward show of feeling. Anyone observing them might have assumed that the sixty-year-old couple had come home for a family funeral. There was no other reason why a woman would have worn a black dress on such a sunny day as this.

Nicosia airport was very busy at this time of year, with planes coming and going each hour. The arrivals area thronged with expectant package tourists, while the departures lounge was slightly more subdued, with tanned holidaymakers regretful that their time in paradise had ended.

'I am so glad you were there last night,' said Aphroditi, addressing both her parents. 'It meant a lot to us.'

'The hotel is magnificent, *kardia mou*,' responded her father. 'I am sure it will be a big success.'

'It wouldn't have happened without your help, Father.'

'The money was one thing,' he replied. 'The hard work was all your husband's . . . and yours, of course.'

'I hope you'll come again soon, maybe for a bit longer . . .'

Her words sounded empty and automatic. She knew as well as they did that neither of these things was likely to happen.

She squeezed her mother's arm affectionately, and Artemis bowed her head as if to shy away from the kiss that her daughter wanted to give her.

Aphroditi swallowed hard.

A moment later she found herself enveloped in her father's embrace.

'Goodbye, sweetheart. It was lovely to see you,' he said. 'Take care.'

'You take care of yourselves too,' she said firmly.

She watched her parents as they went through passport control and out of sight. Only her father glanced over his shoulder and gave a final wave.

Now that the party had taken place and the hotel was officially open, Aphroditi would have much less to do. She felt a strong sense of anticlimax and emptiness as she drove back from the airport, and wondered how she was going to fill her days. She had worked for months towards the grand opening, designing the flower arrangements, tasting the canapés and compiling the guest list. Her job with the soft furnishings was completed too.

How would she maintain her status from now on, if she was expected to do little more than plan the occasional event and appear each day for cocktails and dinner?

This would be a performance that required careful preparation, though, one stage of which was the daily visit to the hairdresser.

'Kyria Papacosta, what an evening that must have been!' exclaimed Emine when Aphroditi appeared at the salon entrance. The hairdressers had already seen the account of it in the daily newspaper. '*Everyone* who was anyone was there! Everyone important, I mean!'

Emine and Aphroditi shared the easy familiarity of people who had known each other for a long time. To the Turkish Cypriot, Aphroditi played many roles: daughter, client, and now employer. Perhaps the latter should suggest a greater formality, but tacitly they both rejected such an artificial change.

'And you looked so wonderful!'

'Thank you, Emine,' replied Aphroditi. 'My hair certainly had a lot of compliments!'

'We've had quite a few people in today,' said Emine. 'Non-residents wanting the excuse to come in and have a snoop round, I think.'

'But a few bookings from the new guests too?' enquired Aphroditi.

'Plenty!' replied Savina.

Tonight Aphroditi had chosen a bold green dress to offset the translucent aquamarines. The sleeves finished at the elbow to ensure that the bangle was visible. The skirt was full and gathered, accentuating her small waist.

'Those colours really suit you,' murmured Emine, combing through Aphroditi's waist-length hair. 'You look so beautiful!'

'You are very sweet. I feel a bit weary today. It was a long night.'

'Are your parents staying for a while?' Savina was polishing the mirror next to where Aphroditi was sitting.

'No, I'm afraid not . . .' said Aphroditi, their eyes meeting in the glass. 'They've gone already. You know what my mother's like.'

Both the women in the salon understood entirely.

Emine remembered the first time she had seen Artemis Markides after her son's death. She seemed to have shrunk to half her previous size, and Emine swore to friends that the woman's hair had gone from mahogany brown to grey overnight.

'I have always heard it can happen,' she reported, 'and I never believed it. But I swear to you I saw it with my own eyes.'

'Oh, it's a shame they were in such a hurry to leave,' said Savina. 'I've heard the weather is so bad in England. And your mother used to like sitting in the sunshine.'

'I'm not sure she likes anything much these days . . .' said Aphroditi.

There was a pause.

'Can you tidy it? Put it up again, without all those wispy bits?' she asked.

Emine ran her comb once again through Aphroditi's long, thick tresses and divided them into two, then both hairdressers began to plait, eventually winding them round and round, creating a bun that was positioned higher on her head than it had been the previous evening. The hair was heavy and shiny and needed dozens of pins to hold it in place.

The height of the hair somehow emphasised her long, elegant

neck. Swept upwards and away from her face, it also meant that the earrings were more exposed.

Savina held a mirror up behind Aphroditi so that she had a view of the result from behind.

'*Katapliktika!*' she said. 'Fantastic!'

'Almost better than last night,' said Emine.

'Tonight is even more important,' said Aphroditi, suddenly cheered by the familiar company of the women. With Emine and Savina, she found she could relax. She did not have to act the boss's wife.

'It's the first proper evening. The real beginning.'

'You sound excited.'

'I am. I really am. And so is Savvas.'

'Like your saint's day when you're a child. You dream of it but never think it will actually come.'

'We've been planning it all for so long. And now it's here.'

'Who's going to be there?'

'Oh, everyone who is staying in the hotel. And we're having something like a banquet.'

Despite the sophistication of her appearance, Aphroditi displayed the excitement of a child. She was on her feet now and twirled round, pirouetting like a doll on a musical box.

Smiling, both the other women stood back to admire her. All three of them were reflected in the mirror and briefly, with Aphroditi in the middle, they held hands.

Aphroditi released her hold.

'I must go,' she said. 'I'll see you tomorrow. And thank you. Thank you for everything.'

When she reached the foyer, Savvas was already greeting the first guests and guiding them towards the terrace.

Markos was outside, directing his staff to serve drinks. Frau Bruchmeyer was close by, glass in hand, chatting to some German guests. As she waved her hands about to emphasise a point, the heavy rings on her slender fingers rattled, and her charm bracelet tinkled. She was full of enthusiasm for her new home, and the other guests were fascinated to hear how it had come about that she lived day after day under the blue Cyprus skies.

Markos enjoyed Frau Bruchmeyer's company. The elegant septuagenarian had an appetite for life that he admired, and she was often the last person to leave the bar. Sometimes Markos daringly gave her a kiss on both cheeks at the end of an evening.

When Savvas came out on to the terrace, Markos noticed Aphroditi, in green, behind him.

Crème de menthe, he thought. That's what she reminds me of.

It was a dislikeable drink, one that he never encouraged people to have. Serving something that tasted like mouthwash was counter-intuitive to him, even though it was popular among a certain type of guest.

He watched as one of his staff took over a tray of drinks. It seemed to him that Aphroditi did not acknowledge the waiter as she took a glass. At least Savvas had the courtesy to give a little bow before resuming his conversation. If only the boss's wife had the same manners. She was as cool as mint, as cold as crushed ice.

At eight, everyone was ushered away and seated in a small dining room that would be used for private receptions. Tonight there was a buffet, as this was the best way to show off the talents and ambitions of the chef and his team.

The head chef had trained in Paris. He did not produce meals. He created banquets. Colour and shape were important, and if he could make one thing look like another, he would. A fish, for example, might be transformed into a swan, or perhaps a many-petalled flower. Desserts should aspire to some kind of fantasy: a multi-layered castle or an ancient trireme.

Savvas had adopted the manner of a ship's captain, and was professional and courteous at all times with both passengers and crew. As far as he was concerned, the hotel was no different from a cruise liner. It was a contained space in which it was possible for everything to be in precise order. Perfectly precise. Shipshape, in other words.

Aphroditi spoke mostly to the wives, while Savvas discussed politics and finance with the bankers, businessmen and wealthy retirees who were their first guests. It was a relatively intimate gathering.

By the time the desserts were laid out, the guests had almost run out of superlatives.

Frau Bruchmeyer, who was sitting at the top table as guest of honour next to Savvas, clapped her hands together with delight. Though she maintained her slim frame, she had a sweet tooth and sampled a small portion of each of the dozen or so tarts, gateaux, mousses and charlottes. Even then, her bright pink lipstick remained immaculately in place.

The highlight of the evening for her would be the visit to the nightclub. At the end of dinner, some guests drifted away to smoke cigars and drink brandies on the terrace. Women excused themselves to go to the ladies' room to powder their noses. The nightclub was about to open its doors.

The first guests arrived on the dot of eleven o'clock. They were offered a complimentary drink, and with most of the whiskies costing more than one pound for a single measure, few of them turned down the invitation.

Markos moved from table to table, holding out his hand to greet everyone personally and making each client feel that this was his or her own private place. Everybody was charmed. Nobody was in a hurry to leave such an environment or to say good night to the host.

He showed Frau Bruchmeyer to a seat close to the stage. She was a little deaf in one ear and he wanted her to be able to appreciate the act. A couple from Athens whom she had met during dinner were her companions that night, and within a few hours they had already developed an easy familiarity that made them seem like old friends. Frau Bruchmeyer ordered a bottle of champagne for the three of them.

'Hang the expense!' she said as a toast to them all.

'To life!' said the husband, delighted by this unexpected, effervescent company.

Around one in the morning, the piped music faded out and the purple curtains behind the stage parted. A woman emerged. A murmur of surprise rippled around the audience. What they saw was the spitting image of Marilyn Monroe.

She sang the English lyrics impeccably, in a sweet, husky voice that raised the temperature in the room, but when she spoke to the audience between songs, it was with a heavy Greek accent. It made the audience admire the pinpoint accuracy of the impersonation all the more.

Up in the foyer, Savvas stood with Aphroditi.

'Darling, shall we go and have a drink before we leave? Markos told me there is a great singer there tonight.'

Aphroditi felt herself wince even at the mention of Markos' name.

'I really don't want to, Savvas,' she said. 'I am so tired after last night.'

'But darling, it's the Clair de . . . the nightclub's opening night!'

'I know, but I just feel like going home.'

'*Please*, Aphroditi. Just for ten minutes.'

It was an order, not a request. Savvas' voice was unusually firm. Sulkily, she followed her husband towards the unmarked door that led from the foyer to the stairs that took them down to the nightclub.

The muffled sound of applause drifted upwards, and as they walked in via a door opposite the stage, Aphroditi stifled a gasp. The Marilyn Monroe lookalike's platinum-blond hair and peachy skin shone out luminously against the purple velvet backdrop. The singer was taking a bow and revealing plenty of her generous cleavage as a man in black tie continued to play, teasing out the melody of the next song on the Moog synthesiser. The stage was carpeted with carnations thrown by the appreciative audience.

She had already been singing for forty minutes, and the atmosphere was sultry with desire, dense with cigar smoke. Markos had picked up that one of the Americans in the audience was celebrating his birthday, and had asked the singer to serenade him as if he were President Kennedy.

For a subsequent song, she turned her attention to Frau Bruchmeyer, perching next to her on the low padded settee. She lifted one of the bony hands, two of its fingers laden with diamond rings, and gazed into the old lady's eyes like a lover.

'*Diamonds are a girl's best friend*,' she sang.

The audience began to cheer even before the song had ended. The singer was an accomplished actress, too. Now she turned her attention to Markos, who was standing just in front of the bar.

He returned her gaze and smiled, increasingly broadly, as she began her next song:

'*I wanna be loved by you, just you . . .*'

She left the stage for a moment, approached Markos and then

led him back with her, continuing to sing. The combination of pale skin and fair hair against the dark curtains was dramatic. Her breasts were like cushions, her voice sweet and sexy but childlike.

When they had arrived, one of the waiters had immediately approached Savvas to take their drink order. He and Aphroditi stood close to the bar, sipping from their glasses. Aphroditi had refused a suggestion to sit down. She did not intend to stay long.

Savvas noticed how the men gazed at 'Marilyn' and the women at Markos. It was as if his manager had rehearsed the role, reacting to the singer's lines perfectly on cue.

More importantly, he observed that the three waiters were constantly busy, refreshing drinks, opening bottles, crushing ice and shaking cocktails. The air-conditioning kept the room at around twenty-five degrees, warm enough to make people thirsty, but not uncomfortable.

Well done, Savvas thought, silently congratulating his manager.

By the time the song was ending, the artiste was singing close to Markos' ear. *'Boo boo bee doo!'* she whispered seductively. The music faded away, and for a moment, there was silence except for the clink of one ice cube against another.

She took Markos' hand and they bowed together as if theirs was a double act. The audience was on its feet, cheering and whooping.

Markos caught sight of his boss's wife. She stood with her back to the bar, her face as sour as the lemons piled up in a bowl behind her.

Aphroditi touched her husband's sleeve.

'I'd like to go now,' she said, trying to make herself heard above the noise. Her tone of voice was firm, like her husband's earlier.

Savvas looked at his wife. Aphroditi was the only person in

the room not acknowledging the brilliance of the performance. He knew that she still harboured resentment about everything to do with the Clair de Lune.

'Very well, *agapi mou*,' he said patiently. 'I just need to have a word with Markos and then we'll leave.'

'I'll be waiting in the foyer,' said Aphroditi.

Even before the applause had died down, she had left. From the stage, Markos saw a flash of green as she disappeared through the back door. The whole evening was exceeding even his own expectations.

Chapter Six

Hüseyin Özkan began work each morning at six when the sun was still low in the sky but already spreading a warm glow. Laying out sunloungers and stacking them up again was mindless work, but he was happy earning his own money and sometimes he even got overgenerously tipped. Many of the tourists seemed to have little concept of the value of the Cypriot pound, but he was not going to educate them.

Hüseyin's afternoon break gave him time to play an hour of water polo each day, and in the evenings a game of volleyball would take place. When the day was over, the increasingly athletic eighteen year old would buy a cool Keo beer. As the sun went down, he would sit on the sand with his friends and drink it. To him it seemed the perfect life.

The teams were mostly made up of Greek Cypriots, but some of the strongest players were Turkish Cypriot, and he often tried to persuade his younger brother, Ali, to come down to the beach for a game. The fifteen year old, who was taller than Hüseyin, though with a much slighter frame, was reluctant. The simple truth was that he did not want to play in a mixed team.

'I don't trust them,' he said. 'They'll break the rules.'

Ali spent more time at home than Hüseyin and had been more influenced by their father's opinions. Ali knew that Halit Özkan often regretted the fact that they had moved to an area where they were surrounded by Greek Cypriots. He would have preferred to be in the old town, where they would not be in a minority. Ali was aware that his father feared trouble, and when they both read in *Halkın Sesi* of EOKA B's new activities, he fully expected that violence would spread their way.

As the holidaymakers reclined in the sun, sipped cocktails, swam or lost themselves in the latest thriller, Hüseyin noticed that they were always oriented towards the sea. The sunbeds had to be laid in rows, pointing towards the rising sun. These foreigners did not want to look inland. Even Frau Bruchmeyer, who lived on the island now, saw only its beauty and the paradise created by blue sky and sea.

Although during their short conversations she never forgot to ask after Hüseyin's mother, she seemed unaware of the knife edge on which the Cypriots were living.

Markos continued to feel uneasy about Christos' connection with the new movement for *enosis*. It seemed absurd to him that anyone should feel the need to disturb this tourist paradise. He could see from the way the girls sauntered up and down the beach in their bikinis, and how the men casually clocked up ludicrous bar bills, that these tourists, whether from Greece or further afield, did not have a care in the world. In spite of a constant battery of criticism from Christos, Markos maintained his position: why do the one thing that would upset their mother? But above all, why destroy this coastal arcadia?

The Clair de Lune continued to enjoy a full house every night. 'Marilyn' sang three times a week, and on the other nights there was a selection of cabaret acts, all previously auditioned by Markos. One of the most popular was a belly dancer from Turkey. Another comprised three performers from La Cage aux Folles in Paris, who achieved the almost impossible feat of doing a cancan on the tiny stage.

As the holiday season continued, and the reputation of The Sunrise and its nightclub grew, Markos brought in singers from all around Greece, some of them big names in Athens and Thessaloniki, and flew others in especially from Paris or London. Savvas continually studied the accounts, and even with the plane fares, he could see that Markos managed to make a large profit. Membership of the club became highly coveted, and after a few months its cost soared. The drinks were astronomically expensive, but for vintage whiskies, nobody cared what they paid.

For the first time in Cyprus, the high prices became desirable in themselves, making the Clair de Lune a place to be seen. People began to queue for entry to a club where cost and status were synonymous and where spending an evening on one of its purple sofas made them part of an elite, the crème de la crème. To people who could afford luxury, the proximity of modest one-storey homes where families still ground their own wheat, grew vegetables and milked their goats was irrelevant. Inhabitants of these parallel worlds had their own reasons to be content.

'This is what the jet set wants,' said Markos, when even Savvas balked at the new price list that the club manager was proposing. 'They don't want things to be cheap.'

'But spirits only cost two shillings at the bar in town,' fretted Savvas.

'Trust me,' said Markos.

When film stars began to frequent the place, and soon afterwards a famous Hollywood couple spent two consecutive nights there, Markos knew he had proved his worth on every level. From now on, in his boss's eyes, he could do no wrong.

Business in the rest of the hotel had continued to grow. In late September, when the hotel was booked to capacity for the first time, with all five hundred bedrooms fully occupied, Savvas Papacosta announced that dinner would now be held in the ballroom.

With a mosaic floor and slender, elegant pillars at the entrance, the ballroom, like the reception area, had been modelled on the recent discoveries at Salamis. Excavations had revealed tombs filled with treasures from thousands of years before. The architectural and decorative motifs of the once thriving town of Constantia, as Salamis had been known in Roman times, had inspired Aphroditi, and she had taken many of the details and applied them to the grandest space in the hotel.

The ballroom was circular, to reflect the shape of the ancient amphitheatre. Around the edge of the room were a dozen female figures. The limestone originals were no more than thirty centimetres high, but Aphroditi had commissioned hers to be larger than life-size, so that they appeared to be holding up the ceiling, like the caryatids at the Erechtheion in Athens. Each of them held a flower in their right hand. She had resisted the temptation to paint them in the bright colours that would have been used on the originals. She wanted the colour to emanate from the walls, where she had designed a repeated pattern of a woman's face with garlands of foliage, in gold and green. The face had been faithfully produced to mirror the original in the Salamis gymnasium, and yet it looked eerily like Aphroditi herself. Huge eyes gazed from all around the room.

She had even commissioned copies of a chair that had been found in one of the tombs in the ancient city. The excavated fragments were made of ivory, and the cool, smooth texture of the original material had been reproduced in wood. With meticulous attention to detail, an artisan had spent two years on the pair of chairs, reproducing the ornate plaques that embellished them. Everyone marvelled at the carvings of the sphinx and of the lotus flowers. An upholsterer had been given free rein with the padded seats and had chosen gold silk to match the gilding that had been applied to the sphinx's crown. The chairs were sat on by Aphroditi and Savvas at the top table. They seemed like royalty on their thrones.

The two pieces of ornamental furniture were not the only *objets* that had kept the best artisans of Nicosia busy. The gossamer curtains that hung from the very high ceiling had been embroidered with gold thread to match the gilded foliage painted around the walls.

It was a temple to materialism in which some, but not all, of the ancient conventions had been respected. The materials were probably more lavish than those used to construct the originals on which this costly pastiche was based. Aphroditi had combined all the elements that had impressed archaeologists at Salamis and brought them together into one room.

'*Agapi mou*, do you like it?'

'Well I think our guests will love it,' said Savvas tactfully, the first time he saw the finished result, with the drapes in place and the tables arranged in a fan shape round the room.

'Don't you think it's glamorous?'

'Yes, my darling, it's definitely that.'

Crystal glasses, white porcelain plates and brilliantly polished cutlery all caught the light from the chandeliers and sparkled.

In the circular floor space in the middle there was a huge but completed copy of the celebrated Salamis mosaic of Zeus disguised as a swan. This was intended for use as a dance floor – most importantly for the first dance of a bride and groom – or sometimes for theatrical or orchestral events. Aphroditi's ambitions for this space were unlimited. Famagusta had a tradition for theatre and the arts, and she wanted the hotel to be known for something even more spectacular, for a level of performance that no one had seen before.

To mark the end of the summer season and the beginning of their first autumn, Aphroditi realised a dream. She invited dancers from London to perform *Swan Lake*. On this mosaic, in such a setting, it would be unique.

Savvas was nervous.

'Darling, it's a very expensive thing to do . . .'

'We need to have events like this, Savvas. We're the biggest but we have to be the best as well.'

Dancing on mosaic tessellations was far from ideal, but Aphroditi was determined to find a way. The compromise was that the dancers would only perform highlights.

Swans, said the invitation simply, and when the VIP guests came from around the island to Cyprus' most glamorous hotel, they were, once again, speechless at what the couple had achieved.

Few there had seen classical ballet danced in the round, and when the prima ballerina finally came to her graceful, tragic end, they found themselves gazing at a dancer who appeared to be enveloped in the wings of the swan. She and the mosaic had become as one. The audience was on its feet, applauding and calling for an encore. Even men dabbed their eyes.

'It was perfect,' admitted Savvas, 'and everyone loved it, but I do have a few doubts about the cost . . .'

'It's not just about money,' said Aphroditi.

'It *is*, actually, Aphroditi. In the end, that's the only thing it's about.'

Aphroditi had heard the same words from her father over the

years and hoped they were both wrong. It rendered so much of what she did futile. How could the effect of the gold-leaf finish and the unforgettable spectacle of the dying swan ever be measured? On this matter the couple increasingly disagreed.

For Savvas, expenditure of any kind had to be for a purpose and needed justification, whether it was for a certain grade of marble in the bathrooms or a piece of jewellery for his wife. Savvas divided income by number of guests by number of rooms occupied and then calculated profit. For him, it was maths not emotion.

He applied the same principle to staff. His criteria for recruitment were similarly clinical. He wanted the best people working in his hotel and he did not care who they were, as long as they arrived early for their shifts, did their jobs faultlessly, did not steal from guests and did not ask for pay rises.

It was this pragmatic philosophy that had led to The Sunrise having a balance of Greek and Turkish Cypriots among the staff, a ratio that also happened to reflect their relative proportions on the island. For every Turkish Cypriot there were four Greek Cypriots, and all of them (even if Turkish was their first language) spoke both Greek and English. There were a few Armenians and Maronites too. For the foreign guests there was little possibility of differentiating one from another. Every member of staff had to work hard to please the boss, whatever their ethnic origin, whether they went to the mosque or church. What they did and where they went outside working hours was their own business. By the end of the year, the hotel was employing one thousand people.

Though Savvas Papacosta himself was not particularly interested in the cultural richness of Cyprus, he did make one concession in the hotel. Once a week, he agreed that there should be a Cypriot Night, with local cuisine along with traditional dancing.

The Sunrise

On these nights, both Greek and Turkish Cypriot members of staff were asked to demonstrate the steps, wearing specially made local costumes. The men looked dashing in their red waistcoats and sashes, baggy knickerbockers and long leather boots, and the women were pretty in their full-length gathered crimson skirts and white blouses. No one was obliged to take part, but it was noted if they did not. From time to time Emine persuaded Hüseyin to join in. He could earn some extra money that way and he could dance effortlessly.

Although every nationality found the steps challenging (especially the American guests), they were enamoured of the food, getting a flavour for the first time of the 'real' Cyprus. The French-trained maestro chef took the night off, and two cooks from the best tavernas in Nicosia were brought in. They came with trays of ready-made specialities and then spent the day preparing more. Greedily, guests piled their plates high with meatballs, halloumi cheese, stuffed vine leaves and *kleftiko*, and were ecstatic at the range of desserts, *kataifi*, baklava and every type of Turkish sweetmeat. For many, it was their first taste of *zivania*, which was served in generous quantities, and the hotel had even taken delivery of some cheap china so that guests could write on their postcards, 'Having a smashing time!'

Fuelled with alcohol and sweet pastry, guests danced until midnight and then adjourned to the Clair de Lune to dance a little more. When they emerged from the purple and the darkness, they crossed the foyer and stood on the terrace to watch the sun emerging over the horizon. Just as Savvas Papacosta had always intended, The Sunrise provided the best place from which to observe this daily phenomenon. It was a truly awe-inspiring sight.

Chapter Seven

THE BEACH BECAME a little quieter at the beginning of October, but work continued for Hüseyin. He was asked to mend broken loungers and umbrellas, and after that helped repair the hotel boat. This was followed by several other maintenance jobs on the beachfront. Similarly the salon had slightly fewer customers and Emine was able to take a little time off, which she used to visit some of her more elderly clients who liked to have their hair cut or permed at home.

One of these was Irini Georgiou, who lived in the same street. For the first time in several months, Emine went to see her, taking shampoo and a few rollers. While she waited for Irini's hair to set, they had plenty of time to gossip and catch up on each other's news.

'Markos is doing so well,' said Irini proudly.

'The nightclub is obviously a huge success,' Emine replied. 'So many customers tell us about it! One of our regulars is a German lady – easily seventy years old – who goes there every night!'

'Markos has mentioned her,' said Irini. 'And what about your Hüseyin?'

'Well he's certainly earned himself a bit of money in the last few months. I don't know if he wants to be on the beachfront for ever, but at least it gives him time for his sport . . .'

Neither woman brought up the subject of politics. The summer had been a period of intense political instability, of which they had both been aware. Earlier in the year there had been the threat of a military coup against Makarios, and Turkey had put its forces on alert. Turkish Cypriots had even been told to store up food supplies in their homes, and Emine had filled her cupboards. The coup had been averted but Makarios had continued to face opposition, from some of his own bishops now as well as the Greek junta. This ongoing threat and fear made both the women anxious and sleepless, but had had miraculously little effect on tourism.

In his financial forecasting, Savvas Papacosta had expected a steep decline in bookings to begin in the autumn. What he had not anticipated was that people who had come in July would want to return again in November. This meant that occupancy of the hotel was still at fifty per cent. Temperatures were balmy and the sun warm and kind, and the sea promised to hold its heat. The glamorous shops and smart cafés in the city remained open and the Clair de Lune was full to capacity each night.

Once a week, Aphroditi telephoned her parents. Trifonas took a keen interest in everything happening at The Sunrise, and most of the phone call was taken up with answering his flow of questions. Aphroditi was very surprised one day in November when it was her mother who picked up the phone rather than her father. She could hear Trifonas Markides coughing in the background and gathered that he was not even feeling well enough to play golf.

She wondered if she should go and visit them.

'I'd rather you left it a while,' urged Savvas. 'Guests like to see us. Or to see *you* at least . . .'

It was not an idle compliment. Aphroditi's presence thrilled the female guests in the way that the nightclub artistes excited their husbands. What would she have on that night? Would she be wearing a piece of spectacular jewellery? All such questions were on their minds.

'But I'm a bit worried about—'

'Why don't you wait until January? There's bound to be a drop in bookings after Christmas. It would be a much better time.'

A moment passed while his words sank in.

'But . . .'

'You *can't* go now.'

'Savvas! I think my father is—'

'I've *told* you what I think.' He banged his fist on the table. 'We have to put all our energy into this enterprise, Aphroditi.'

It was the first time she had realised that, for Savvas, work came before everything else. And it was the first time he had shouted at her.

She retreated, shaking with anger and shock. For several days she came to the hotel to perform her duties as the boss's wife, but she did not speak a word to her husband.

The popularity of the nightclub never waned. It did not depend on sunshine, and there were more than enough wealthy businessmen in Cyprus wanting whisky and entertainment. Markos found new and better acts all the time and kept the fine brands coming in.

The well-heeled came midweek and the politicians mostly at weekends. They all stayed until dawn. Their host not only knew them by name but also who needed to be given tables and where. He read several newspapers a day and was aware of any rivalry or animosity among the clientele. If his tact had not been exemplary, many of them would have reluctantly gone elsewhere. The Clair de Lune was the place to be.

Markos' confidence swelled as his nightclub became key to his boss's own ambitions. He basked in the praise and respect his clients, colleagues and even competitors gave him. Everyone, in fact, except Aphroditi Papacosta seemed to recognise his talent. To celebrate the first successful quarter since the opening, he treated himself to three new hand-tailored suits, all of them with the wider lapels that were the latest fashion, and gentle flares shaped to conceal his heeled boots. The elegant cut of the suits accentuated his slimness and made him look taller.

When he got to work late each afternoon to ensure that everything was in place in the nightclub, Aphroditi Papacosta was usually arriving at The Sunrise too. One day in December, they came face to face at the entrance. The doorman held open the door and Markos naturally stood aside to let Aphroditi pass. He noticed, as always, how she smiled at the hotel manager with both eyes and mouth.

Something altered when she looked at Markos. Her lips moved, but the subtle creases around her eyes seemed to have disappeared. Her eyes were empty.

'Good evening,' she said politely.

'Good evening, Kyria Papacosta,' he replied. '*Ti kanete?* How are you?'

It was absurd to use such formal language, but even after all this time she had not invited him to call her by her first name, and on this occasion, just as on many others, she did not even bother to reply.

Savvas was crossing the reception area to greet his wife. As happened on the days when he did not collect her from their apartment, she was a little late. Some guests were already gathered in the bar, and she should have been there beforehand.

'Markos! All well?' asked Savvas.

Without waiting for an answer, he turned away, taking Aphroditi's arm and steering her abruptly towards the terrace bar. Markos saw Aphroditi pull away, but he had already left a mark, like a bangle.

Markos went down into the Clair de Lune to make sure that glasses gleamed, bottles were lined up in the right order and bar stools were equidistant from each other. This purple underworld was his to arrange. He brushed his hand across the arm of one of the velvet chairs to move the pile in the right direction, and then pushed a little stack of cocktail napkins more centrally on to the bar. They were printed with the words 'Clair de Lune'.

When he was happy that everything was in order, he went up to the main bar in case he could be of use. He knew Savvas appreciated him being there.

It was busy that night. The hotel was laying on a gala dinner for the feast of Agios Nikolaos. Markos was walking past a crowd of guests on his way towards the bar when an arm reached out like a road barrier to halt him. He recognised the ornate bracelet modelled on an ancient design and the sapphire ring that matched it. It was Aphroditi who had stuck out her hand to give him an empty glass.

It was a peremptory gesture. He had no choice but to take the glass before continuing on his way. It was a silent exchange of contempt and resentful servitude.

Markos greeted the bar staff and then walked to the other side of the terrace to talk to some new guests. The air was still balmy enough for them to be outside. First of all he would say something to make them laugh, then he would enthral them with his description of the cabaret for that evening, before moving on to another group. By the time dinner was served, he knew that all the tables in the Clair de Lune would be full that night.

Aphroditi was always conscious of Markos Georgiou's whereabouts in the room. Wherever there was laughter, he was at the centre of it.

At the end of the year, Savvas reported that the profits of the hotel were double what he had anticipated. The main source of these was the nightclub.

'Of all the staff we have, that man is our greatest asset,' he said to his wife.

Aphroditi listened silently, forcing a smile.

By the time January came, there were just a few residential guests, but the restaurant and bar continued to be popular and the Clair de Lune never shut its doors before four in the morning. Aphroditi essentially felt redundant now. Even though there were a few pieces of upholstered furniture that needed ordering, her role at The Sunrise had run its course.

When she rang her parents one weekend, nobody picked up the phone. She knew immediately that something was very wrong. The Markides never went out on a Sunday evening. Several hours later, the phone rang in the apartment. It was her mother.

'Your father's in hospital,' she said. 'Can you come?'

Aphroditi could scarcely understand what her mother was saying. The words 'tests' and 'weight loss' were almost lost in her muffled sobs.

She got the first available flight to London, but it was Tuesday by the time she arrived.

The tests to which Artemis referred had confirmed that Trifonas

Markides' lung cancer, caused by his forty-a-day habit, was inoperable. His condition deteriorated very rapidly.

When she arrived at the hospital from Heathrow, Aphroditi found her mother holding her father's cold hands. He had died an hour before.

Both mother and daughter were initially paralysed by shock, but they were soon lost in the twin mires of grief and paperwork. Both of them knew how things were done in Cyprus, but here they were adrift. There was so much to organise, so many formalities, and the complexities of a UK funeral to be arranged. Trifonas Markides had plenty of friends in the Greek community close by, and they rallied round, wives bustling and making food, husbands giving sound and practical advice.

Savvas arrived thirty-six hours later.

'Darling, I am so sorry,' he said uselessly.

Sorry for what? she wondered. For keeping her away from her father until it was too late? For that she would never forgive him.

Mother and daughter continued to weep, their mourning full of the deepest anguish. Savvas was excluded from their circle of sorrow.

During the weeks that followed the death and the funeral, Savvas came and went several times, leaving Aphroditi with her mother. Whenever he left Cyprus, he was confident that The Sunrise was in good hands. Markos Georgiou knew exactly how he liked things to be run, even better than the manager himself.

When the forty-day memorial service was over, it was time for the reading of the will. Trifonas Markides had left enough for his wife to live a comfortable lifestyle. There was a small legacy for each of his three surviving sisters, who lived in Cyprus, and his shares in The Sunrise were left to his daughter. There were no additional sums.

'But what about all his other financial interests?'

'Savvas, don't get upset about it,' Aphroditi said, in an attempt to mollify him. 'He invested so much in our business. Maybe he really didn't have much more than that.' She was more preoccupied with the human loss than with any gains they might have made.

'He still had the export business. I am sure he did. There are containers down at the dockside with the name Markides on the side,' Savvas said, losing the struggle to hide his disappointment and disbelief.

With The Sunrise fully booked for the coming summer, he had already had some long phone calls with his father-in-law about totally redeveloping The Paradise Beach. Trifonas Markides had promised that he would be behind it. A hotel that would rival theirs was already under construction, and Savvas knew with a sickness in his stomach that they were going to be left behind. What had happened with the legacy was inexplicable.

Aphroditi could see how her husband felt. A black mood lay over him like a pall.

For now her attention must be on her mother, and she naturally suggested that Artemis should return with them to live in Cyprus. In reality, neither she nor Savvas did much to persuade her, knowing that she would bring her commitment to grief along with her. It was out of the question, given that Trifonas Markides was now buried in Southgate. His wife wanted to stay close to observe the memorial rites, and in any case her feelings for Cyprus had not changed.

When Aphroditi finally arrived back in Cyprus, she could see that while Costas Frangos had managed all the day-to-day issues perfectly competently, it was Markos Georgiou who had really kept everything running, as Savvas was keen to point out to her.

'We are so lucky to have someone like that,' he said. 'He is exceptional. He has such a firm hold on the financial workings of this place. The staff like him, the clients like him—'

'And Frau Bruchmeyer worships him,' interjected Aphroditi. 'Sometimes I think he leads her on . . .'

'Aphroditi! Of course he doesn't! Don't say things like that!'

Aphroditi found it intensely annoying that her husband would never hear a word against the man who had now effectively assumed the role of second-in-command.

Buried beneath her grief was a deep resentment against Savvas for keeping her from her dying father. Her emotions were dominated by an all-pervading sense of anger that she had not been able to say goodbye.

Chapter Eight

Following his father-in-law's death, Savvas decided that if they could not build a new hotel, they should improve on the old. Apart from anything, it would provide a distraction for his grieving wife. He reluctantly met with his architect to see if they could modify the exterior of The Paradise Beach to make it more up-to-date.

Aphroditi began work on refurbishing the interiors, busying herself for some months on the project and glad to have something to occupy her.

One Friday at the end of March she was on her way to meet a fabric wholesaler, whose offices were situated in the middle of Famagusta.

It was a beautiful, clear-sky morning and cafés in the main square were full of people drinking coffee and enjoying the balmy air. The orange trees that lined the streets leading to the square were heavy with white blossom and the atmosphere was filled with sweet scent. One of the city's main annual cultural events, the Orange Festival, was about to take place, and she passed a group of people making preparations. They were constructing a huge ship out of the fruit to be paraded through the streets in celebration of the fact that it brought so much prosperity and good health to the city.

Aphroditi browsed in the shop windows as she passed by. She had her favourites, but there were always new ones opening and fashions seemed to change every day. Next winter she might start to wear the flared trousers, the catsuits even, that many of the mannequins seemed to model, but for now she would stick to dresses. There was so much variety, in shape and colour, and a new fashion for floral.

As she came out of a shop, Aphroditi saw a familiar face. Markos Georgiou. He was sitting at a café table with a young woman and they were smiling and talking animatedly. Aphroditi had never seen her husband's major-domo outside the environment of the hotel and had never thought of him having a personal life. First of all, she took in that he was not wearing a jacket. She had rarely seen him just in shirtsleeves, such was the formality of hotel protocol for their staff, and he was rocking back slightly in his seat, more relaxed than she had ever seen him. The woman was radiant. She had long dark hair, loose around her shoulders, and a wide smile that, like Markos', showed a row of perfect white teeth. Aphroditi thought of her husband's, slightly stained with nicotine.

The pair were noticeably at ease with one another, perhaps more so than many of the other couples at neighbouring tables, between whom the rapport seemed not so intimate. They looked very compatible, and Aphroditi felt a stab of envy at the sight of such companionship.

Markos got up when he saw Aphroditi. He too was conscious that they had never met outside the hotels. After so many years, it was strange. He was impeccably polite as ever and kept to the formal address he normally used with her:

'Good morning, Kyria Papacosta,' he said. 'Can I introduce you . . . ?'

Aphroditi put her hand out and quickly noticed that the other woman was struggling to get to her feet.

'Oh, please don't get up. I didn't realise . . . !'

The young woman was heavily pregnant and her belly bumped into the edge of the table as she tried to rise. She sat down again.

'How many . . . ?'

'Almost eight,' she replied, her expression beaming. She was quite literally in bloom.

'How exciting,' Aphroditi said. 'Just a month away! Well, good luck. Markos will keep us informed, won't you, Markos?'

She turned to her husband's right-hand man and he nodded. It was strange. Perhaps because of the charm he exuded towards female guests in the hotel, she had assumed he was single.

Aphroditi walked away. She had no wish to make further conversation with Markos. It was awkward at the best of times and she could not feign a pleasure she did not feel.

Moments after she had left, the couple were joined by another man.

Aphroditi found herself thinking of the encounter all the way to her meeting and well beyond it into the afternoon. For some reason it was disconcerting to have discovered that Markos had a wife, and even more that he was about to be a father. Exactly why it bothered her she could not explain to herself. In the past year she had begun to hope for a child and month by month had been disappointed. Perhaps this was something to do with her reaction.

The following morning, the phone rang in their apartment. Savvas had left for a meeting at The Sunrise a few hours earlier.

It was a man's voice at the end of the line. British. Aphroditi found herself shaking. Something must have happened to her mother.

'Mrs Papacosta?'

'Yes,' she said, sinking into the nearest chair. Her legs could not support her. 'Speaking.'

'It's George Matthews here. Matthews and Tenby Solicitors.'

There was a silence on the line. Neither of them knew if the connection had broken, as often happened.

'We met a few months ago when your father's will was read.'

Aphroditi needed no reminder.

'Some other papers have come into our hands . . . Are you still there, Mrs Papacosta?'

'Yes,' she replied softly, realising that the call did not seem to be about her mother's health.

'It seems that your father had made changes to the ownership of his companies some time before he died. He transferred everything into your name.'

'But the will . . . ?'

'This was outside of the will.'

It took Aphroditi a few seconds to take it in. Her father was canny with money and would have known how to maximise her inheritance.

'Your mother must have known and approved of this,' the solicitor continued.

There was a long silence from Aphroditi. She realised now that he might even have known he was dying the last time she saw him.

'Mrs Papacosta . . . ?'

'I'm still here . . . Thanks for letting me know.'

'Would you like any more information?'

'Not at this moment, thank you. Not right now.'

Aphroditi wanted to tell Savvas. This news would have an enormous effect on their future. It was exactly what her husband had hoped for.

By the time George Matthews realised that the line really had gone dead, Aphroditi was already in the lift going down to street level.

She accelerated hard along the straight road to the hotel, turned through the iron gates and pulled up next to her husband's car. With a racing heart, she ran towards the entrance.

The angle of the sun on the highly polished glass meant that she saw her own reflection clearly but everything inside was dark. She burst into the foyer and ran straight into Markos, who was on his way out. Her bag went flying, its contents skittering across the floor in a dozen directions.

Markos had never seen his boss's wife moving at any speed greater than a dignified walk. Nor had he ever seen her look less than perfectly coiffed and groomed.

Several members of staff were instantly on their hands and knees, retrieving her possessions from under furniture and in the plants.

She had not fallen, but her irritation was unconcealed. She snatched her car keys from Markos' hand.

'Why the *hell* don't you look where you are going?' she said.

He stood silently to one side. He could do nothing but let the injustice pass. Markos had kept count of the number of times she had dismissed him in this way and added this occasion to the score.

Aphroditi made for the door marked 'Staff Only' in the far corner of the reception area and walked in without knocking.

'Savvas, I have to talk to you.'

Savvas was surprised to see his wife. She looked unusually

flushed, untidy almost, but she was smiling. He got up from his desk and asked Costas Frangos to come back in an hour.

Even before they were alone, Aphroditi began to tell him what had happened.

'We won't need this fabric any more!' she announced triumphantly, pulling a sample from her bag. 'We're not going to refurbish. We're going to rebuild!'

'What do you mean?' Savvas asked.

Soon Aphroditi had explained.

'So our dream is going to come true!' he exclaimed.

Savvas had kept the plans for his next project locked in the bottom drawer of his desk, and now rolled the blueprint out on to his desk. For the first time in ages, he smiled at his wife.

'There's nothing stopping us now,' said Aphroditi.

'Let's call the lawyer again. We need to free up that money as soon as we can. I can get a loan to cover us until then.'

'My father would be happy with that, I think,' responded Aphroditi.

The temperature between them had warmed a little for the first time since the death of Trifonas Markides.

Within three months, Aphroditi had sold her father's businesses and the finances were in place to demolish The Paradise Beach and begin the rebuild.

The new hotel would have twenty-five floors and six hundred bedrooms but it would be built to a lower specification and aimed at a less affluent market than The Sunrise. Its scale meant that profits would be fast and guaranteed. If they threw every cent they owned behind it, and worked to an accelerated schedule, paying out a premium for overtime, they could open in less than eighteen months. They made the decision together. The more they invested, the faster would be their return.

'It might be a little while before you have any new jewellery . . .' Savvas murmured in mock apology.

'I think I have more than enough,' said Aphroditi. 'There aren't enough days in the month as it is.'

This was true. During the first year of The Sunrise, when profit had flowed in almost faster than he could count it, Savvas had regularly commissioned new pieces for his wife. He bought gold by the ounce and sets of stones from different merchants so that he could calculate the initial value of the investment. A jeweller, usually Giannis Papadopoulos, who was the best in the city, was then paid a fee for design and creation, processes in which Aphroditi was closely involved. She favoured the very simple and modern but liked to add details inspired by the jewellery found in the tombs at Salamis. This added value, but the intrinsic value of the raw materials was what mattered to Savvas Papacosta.

Nowadays, Savvas had no time for anyone but the merchants who sold him concrete and glass, and he was already calculating his return in the same way as he had done with his wife's jewels.

Irini Georgiou hardly saw her elder son these days. He was now spending from nine in the morning until four the following day at The Sunrise. He was the best front man a hotel could wish for, charming his way out of any problem or scene created by a guest, whether it was over some glitch with plumbing or an inadvertent error in a bill. Each one of them left completely satisfied and many were even under the impression that Markos was the owner.

Irini hardly saw Christos either. He was evasive or absent and she could not bear to learn the reason. Fortunately, she had something to distract her. Maria had just produced their first grandchild and Irini spent much of the day in her apartment, singing lullabies to little Vasilakis. It was a peaceful antithesis to the violence that was being perpetrated close by. Every time her husband returned from the *kafenion* with news of another EOKA B bomb attack against a police station or a politician, she held the baby closer.

Chapter Nine

Hİgh season came and business boomed at The Sunrise. It had quickly established itself as the number one hotel in Cyprus and they were obliged to turn potential guests away. They simply did not have enough rooms.

Hüseyin sometimes looked at these tourists and realised how unaware they were of the tensions on the island. Vacations were a time for rest and relaxation, a chance for businessmen to enjoy time with their wives and children in a place where the office could not reach them. A few browsed the headlines of the international newspapers available in the hotel's bookshop, but did not remove them from the carousel. The Cyprus papers were not sold in the hotel; only the *International Herald Tribune*, *The Times*, *Le Figaro* and *Die Zeit* stood alongside the glossy magazines and a few paperbacks.

Hüseyin knew that the front pages of local newspapers would have disturbed them. Behind the beautiful tableau of sea, sun and sand, a civil war simmered while tourists remained entirely oblivious. The atmosphere of uncertainty unsettled every Cypriot, whether or not they were directly threatened.

There were always papers lying around in the Özkan home, usually brought in by his father or Ali, and they inevitably provoked discussion and argument. In the past few months there had been dozens of bombings and attacks, mostly against police stations, during which sizeable quantities of arms and ammunition had been seized. In April there had been more than thirty explosions in a single day in Paphos, Limassol and Larnaca.

'Don't fret too much,' said Emine when she saw Hüseyin frowning over the headlines. 'We're not the targets this time.'

'Your mother's right,' said his father, Halit. 'It's not us they're trying to terrorise. And it looks as if Makarios is having some success in any case.'

To counter the activities of EOKA B, Makarios had set up a new auxiliary force, the Tactical Police Reserve. It was used to go on search missions and that month had captured forty Grivas supporters.

'It was different in the 1960s,' Halit Özkan reassured his children. 'We feared for our lives just walking down the street.'

Hüseyin did not need reminding. Even though he had been a boy then, he remembered those times well, especially the summer of 1964 when the island had been close to war. Greeks had attacked the Turkish village of Kokkina in the north, believing it to be a landing place for arms from Turkey. Turkey had retaliated with napalm and rockets. Although an all-out war was averted, the area had been put under an economic blockade and families like his own had experienced severe deprivation.

It was after this that Halit Özkan had moved his family to the enclaved village. They were soon joined by his widowed sister and her son, Mehmet. It was safer, but it was imprisoning too. What Hüseyin recalled most vividly was feeling hungry all the time. They shared everything they had, but it was never enough. Basic foodstuffs were not reaching the community and they were living off whatever his father and cousin could get hold of when they took the risk to leave the area.

He remembered his mother being frantic if they were not back before dusk. She would stand by the door looking up the street for what to the child seemed like hours, and when they finally appeared she would hold her hands out to his father and embrace him as though he had been missing for weeks.

There was a day when his father returned alone. Within moments their street was full of people gathered round him, and lots of people were speaking at once. Hüseyin had been left on the outside of the circle, standing on tiptoe, straining to see one or other of his parents.

The boy was too young to be told what was going on, but there was quiet weeping among the women and an unusual silence between the men. He waited with dread. Something was going to happen.

Not long afterwards he saw his father being driven out of the village. It was July, and a huge cloud of dust rose up behind the truck.

Nobody told him to go to bed that night, and for once he was allowed into a group of older boys to kick a ball around in the street, taking care not to go too close to the barbed wire that sealed off one end of it.

Before it got light, the truck returned and his cousin's body was carried in. His had been the first corpse Hüseyin had ever seen. One moment Mehmet had been playing with Hüseyin in the yard, smiling, teasing, swinging him round, acting as goalkeeper while the younger boy tried to dribble a ball past him. Now he was still and pale. Hüseyin had stood on a chair at the edge of the room to get a better view over the heads of all the people gathered around the dead body. In spite of himself, he wanted to have a good look.

His cousin had been fifteen years older than Hüseyin. He had been training to be a lawyer and the younger boy had hero-worshipped him.

Mehmet had prided himself on looking smart. 'A man should always go to work in a clean shirt,' he used to tell Hüseyin. That day he was dressed differently, the child observed. He was wearing a filthy shirt, one that was as crimson as a Turkish flag.

Although the adults tried to protect the children as much as they could, there was no avoiding the truth. Someone had hacked his cousin to death. They no longer talked of it, but Mehmet remained in their thoughts every day, his memory kept alive in the name the Özkans gave their late, unexpected baby born a few years later.

'It's as if he has been sent to replace your cousin,' said his mother, who at the age of forty-one had imagined that her child-bearing days were over.

During the period that followed the murder, Hüseyin remembered the hunger being more acute. No one in his family was willing to risk going to buy food, so they lived on pulses for many months. Hüseyin was thin then, and had remained slim ever since, even though he was now impressively athletic.

Everything got better when his family had moved to town. They felt safer and his parents smiled again. It seemed that everyone had a tragedy in their family, both Greek and Turkish Cypriots.

'It's something we all share,' said his mother. 'When someone we love dies, it doesn't matter who we are. The pain is just the same, just as terrible.'

Hüseyin noticed that his father stayed silent when his mother was expressing these views. He did not disagree with her openly, but usually found something else with which to occupy himself, suddenly concentrating on an unnecessary repair job, picking up a newspaper to immerse himself in the day's news or going outside to smoke. All of these activities were modes of silent protest.

It was always Ali who challenged their mother, and on many evenings ferocious arguments would ensue.

The endless hours of conversation Emine had in the salon with Savina, when they talked of the past as well as perms, had given her a strong sense of how futile all the violence had been. She was as fond of the younger woman as she was of her sisters. The two women had exchanged scores of similar stories of their families' respective suffering, so she hated it more than anything when her son started his fighting talk.

Emine and Halit knew that Ali was the more politically minded of their two older sons, but neither was aware that he had joined the Turkish Resistance Organisation. The TMT had been formed in the late 1950s to counter the activities of EOKA and the threat to their community. It also campaigned for *taksim,* partition of the island. Ali was sure that his father would be proud to know he was a member, but he could not tell him without his mother finding out too.

Ali had no faith that the Turkish Cypriots were safe. The Turkish government had been prepared to step in when their community had been threatened in the past, but there was no saying that they would do so again. Under the TMT's secret symbol, the grey wolf, Ali was ready to fight.

'We should be able to protect ourselves,' he said to his brother when he was trying to persuade Hüseyin to join. 'Our parents are fooling themselves if they think we are safe. There's no reason to believe the events of the sixties won't happen again.'

Hüseyin did not want to fight. It was not in his nature. When family rows erupted, he wandered out of the house and back towards the seafront, even though he had spent all day there.

Once on the beach, he would hurl himself into the water to cool down before launching into a match, joining whichever team was short of a player. Many times he played in the same team as Christos Georgiou, and sometimes they even walked home together.

As the summer days went by, Hüseyin had noticed that Christos was hardly seen.

While Hüseyin was stacking chairs and daydreaming of sporting victory, Christos had found a new focus, a very different obsession from the one that preoccupied his teammate. He was learning how to construct home-made bombs, and the optimum strategy for surprise attack.

Makarios' enemies were continuing to conspire against him. The police station in Limassol was destroyed in a bombing and the Justice Minister kidnapped. Grivas and his EOKA B were gaining ground. But even as explosions were being perpetrated elsewhere on the island by Christos and others like him, life in the resort continued as normal.

Aphroditi came to The Sunrise several times a week in the afternoon for her hair appointments, and each evening for the cocktail party. Many times she saw Markos, but she avoided speaking to him. Savvas was almost full-time at the Paradise Beach building site, and except for his attendance for cocktails he scarcely appeared. The flagship hotel did not seem to suffer from his absence, but it disturbed Aphroditi that Markos Georgiou was clearly accepted as the man in charge, even though he had no official position. Nothing had been formally said.

At the beginning of August, when temperatures were exceeding forty degrees most days, the foundation stone for The New Paradise Beach was laid. Another reception was held to mark the moment. From then on, Savvas was on site from dawn until dusk, driving straight from the dust of the building works to The

Sunrise and appearing for drinks with his guests still damp from the shower.

One night, following a gala dinner, he and Aphroditi drove home in silence. It was unusual for Savvas not to have a few comments about the guests or complaints about something he felt should have been repaired or redecorated. Once inside the apartment, he walked straight to the bedroom and lay down.

'Savvas?' asked Aphroditi. 'Is there something the matter? Aren't you going to get undressed? Not even your *shoes*?'

'It's hardly worth it,' he muttered. 'I'll be up again before it's light.'

Before Aphroditi had even removed her necklace and put it away in a drawer, her husband had turned out his bedside light.

'Do you *have* to be on site every day?'

He switched on the light and sat up abruptly.

'Of course I do! How can you even ask that question?' A combination of exhaustion and the brandies he had consumed that evening made him irritable. 'I have to be there, but meeting all those people at The Sunrise every night . . . that's something I *don't* need to do.'

'What? But that's important, Savvas. Much more than anything else!'

'Well it isn't for *me*, Aphroditi.'

The process of building had become more interesting to Savvas than the finished result. He enjoyed seeing the figures that showed him how money was being earned to pay for every iron girder and pane of glass, but the day-to-day workings of the hotel and meeting the guests who stayed there had lost its allure.

'So I am supposed to go on my own?'

'Let's talk about it tomorrow, Aphroditi. I'm too exhausted for this discussion.'

'No!' she said. 'Let's talk about it now. Everyone loves coming for cocktails on the terrace – and every party needs a host and hostess. So what do you propose?'

'Markos can stand in for me.'

'Markos Georgiou?' Aphroditi did not bother to conceal her dismay. 'But he's no substitute for you! He's just a *barman*! A nightclub manager!'

'He is a lot more than that, Aphroditi, as you well know. Look, all of this can wait until morning; right now I want to sleep.'

Aphroditi hated her husband dismissing her view in this way. She knew as well as he did what was the source of all the funding. At the beginning, she had felt an equal in the business, but ever since Savvas had begun work on rebuilding The Paradise Beach, he had changed. Nowadays he spoke to her as though she were a child.

Suddenly the words slipped out.

'Don't forget where all the money came from.'

There was a pause. Aphroditi wished she could take them back, but they were out now, like birds freed from a cage.

In silence, Savvas got out of bed and left the room. Aphroditi heard the door of the guest room slam.

She lay awake for hours, angry with herself for losing control but furious at her husband's rebuke and even more so at the suggestion he had made. Under no circumstances would she play the role of hostess next to Markos Georgiou. The idea was totally preposterous. He was, whatever her husband claimed, merely the person who oversaw the alcohol inventory, polished the glasses and booked a few seedy singers.

The following morning, Savvas left without waking his wife. When she got up and wandered into the kitchen, she found a note on the table.

The Sunrise

I meant what I said last night. Today is going to be a long day for me, so I would like Markos to be the host for cocktails tonight. He will meet you at The Sunrise at six thirty. I hope you have had a chance to sleep on this.

No, she thought. I haven't.

The day was the hottest yet that summer, but it was the fury inside that made her boil.

Chapter Ten

Aphroditi got to The Sunrise earlier than usual for her hair appointment. A hotel guest was just having some rollers removed and Savina was backcombing her hair into a fashionable bouffant style.

'Kyria Papacosta, how are you today?' she asked, looking up from her activity.

'A little tired actually, Savina. I didn't sleep too well.'

'It was such a hot night, wasn't it?'

'I didn't get a wink either. And it's going to be even hotter tonight,' added Emine.

Aphroditi forced a smile. How were they to know that her home was constantly cooled by air-conditioning? The sultry weather was not the reason for her lack of sleep.

'So how would we like our hair today?' asked Emine.

Aphroditi shook out her plait and it rippled around her shoulders and down to her waist like melted chocolate. Her eyes met Emine's in the mirror.

'I'd like you to cut it, please.'

'Just the usual?'

Once every six weeks, Emine trimmed Aphroditi's hair by half an inch, just as she had been doing for years.

'No. I'd like you to cut it off, please.'

The hairdresser took a step back. Aphroditi read her look of surprise in the mirror. In all these years, she had kept her hair almost identically long in a style that was infinitely adaptable, for chignons, braids, plaits and other traditional styles that all Cypriot girls wore.

'Cut it *off*?'

The customer had paid and left so Savina now came over and also stood behind her.

'Why? How?' she asked with incredulity.

Aphroditi produced a magazine cutting from her clutch bag and handed it to them. It was a picture of an American actress, her hair just touching her shoulders.

Both the stylists stood there scrutinising the picture. Emine picked up a long shank of Aphroditi's hair and let it fall again.

'It could be done,' she said. 'But do you really want this?'

'You will look so different!'

'What will Savvas say?'

They always asked this of a woman who wanted any kind of radical change. They knew from experience that husbands were rarely pleased.

'This is how I want it,' answered Aphroditi, ignoring the question. 'And hair does grow.'

The two stylists looked at each other in shocked silence. It seemed extraordinary that after all these years Aphroditi should be asking for such a drastic change, and with so little discussion. But they could see that she was absolutely serious.

Emine put a dark gown over Aphroditi's white dress and washed her waist-length dark tresses for the last time. Then, fighting her own reluctance, she picked up her cutting scissors. Skeins of thick, damp hair eighteen inches long fell to the ground. She shaped and layered with expert precision, continually glancing at the picture that lay in Aphroditi's lap to make sure that she was getting it right. When she was done, she put in some rollers and sat Aphroditi under one of the big helmet hairdryers.

Aphroditi watched as Savina swept her pile of dark hair into a mound. It was like seeing the final trace of her childhood being disposed of.

Forty-five minutes later, the timer pinged. Emine deftly loosened each curl and the shape that Aphroditi desired fell into place. With a little backcombing on the crown and some lacquer, the style precisely matched the picture.

Aphroditi smiled at her image in the mirror.

'Let me show you from the back!'

Savina stood behind her with a small mirror. The hair brushed her ear lobes and flicked out slightly at the ends. When she took off the gown, the full effect of the new hairstyle became apparent. It made her eyes seem larger and her neck longer. Any jewellery she had round her neck or in her ears would be more prominent now. Out of her bag she produced a gold and sapphire choker; with her scoop-necked white dress, the effect was spectacular.

The two hairdressers stood back and looked at her with naked admiration.

'My, my, you look beautiful,' Emine said simply.

'It's just how I wanted it,' said Aphroditi, smiling for the first time since she had entered the salon. 'Thank you so much.'

She twirled in front of them, reapplied her lipstick, hugged them both and left. They had not seen her so happy in a long while.

The whole process had taken slightly longer than she had expected, and by the time she got back into the foyer, she could see that a few people were already gathered in the terrace bar. She quickened her step.

Markos was waiting at the entrance, from where he could see the clocks behind the reception desk. It did not surprise him that she was late. He had half suspected that she would want to make a point. Earlier that day, when Savvas had telephoned to request – though perhaps 'order' would have been more accurate – that he act as his stand-in for cocktails, Markos had said it would be his pleasure. For the first time, however, Savvas was asking Markos to do something he resented. And there was no choice.

When evening came, he had arrived early. He was wearing one of his new suits and had stopped to have his shoes shined in the lobby. Catching sight of himself in the mirrored wall, he realised he was overdue for a visit to the barber and ran his fingers backwards through his hair to push a few strands from his face.

Two female guests – Swedish, he assumed, from their deeply bronzed skin and the sheets of yellow hair that hung down their backs – walked across the reception area as he was waiting and he felt the warmth of their approving eyes. One of them looked over her shoulder at him as she passed.

Suddenly he was distracted by the sight of an even more beautiful woman in white striding purposefully across the foyer.

Without the familiar sapphire necklace, Markos would not have recognised Aphroditi. When he realised that it was actually the boss's wife, he stepped forward to greet her, this time breaking into a spontaneous smile, with eyes as well as mouth. The hairstyle was new, but something else was different too.

'Kyria Papacosta . . .'

Aphroditi stopped.

'Your husband asked me to accompany you tonight . . .'

'I know,' replied Aphroditi.

Markos tried to stop himself saying anything complimentary about her appearance, knowing how it might be taken. His boss's wife would want to keep her distance more than ever tonight. He was sure of it.

They walked side by side, with a good metre between them, into the bar. For a while they both joined one group, and then circulated separately for an hour or so, Markos gravitating towards Aphroditi each time he saw that her eyes had glazed over. Some of the guests were short of conversation, or rude enough to make it clear that they would rather be talking to a man.

In spite of herself, Aphroditi was not ungrateful for his presence.

The time passed, and when dinner was served, the pair were placed together at top table. At first they sat stiffly and talked to the person sitting on the other side of them before eventually turning to each other.

There was only one thing that Aphroditi could think of to ask Markos. It had been on her mind.

'Has your baby arrived yet?'

'My *baby*?' he exclaimed.

There was a moment of awkwardness. Had she asked the wrong thing?

'Oh! You mean *Maria's* baby! My *sister's* baby!'

'Oh! Your sister . . . I thought . . .' Aphroditi's eyes had widened. She felt slightly foolish for having made a mistake.

'She had him a fortnight ago. He's to be named Vasilis. After his grandfather. Everything went well.'

There was a moment of awkwardness.

'So you thought I was becoming a father!' A wide smile spread across his face and he laughed, his hand hovering over her bare arm as he spoke. 'I don't think I'm quite ready for that.'

Aphroditi smiled back. She had been right after all. He was not a man ready to settle down.

Markos was much too clever to ask any reciprocal questions, so the matter could be dropped, but in that moment, with his hand almost touching her skin, she felt the ice between them thaw just a little.

In all the time they had known each other, this was the longest conversation they had ever had. She had always shared Markos Georgiou's attention with her husband. That evening, much to her surprise, she found his manners impeccable. He did not behave in any way other than as an employee, and did not even comment on her changed appearance. She rather wished he had.

When the meal ended, Aphroditi drove herself home and Markos went to the Clair de Lune.

Savvas was already asleep when she got into the apartment, but the following morning he was the first to wake.

'What on *earth* have you done?'

Aphroditi sat up in bed, brought out of a deep sleep by his angry voice.

'It was like waking up with a stranger!' he shouted.

He was doing up the buttons of his shirt but continued his rant.

'Why *do* such a thing! You've had that beautiful hair since I've known you.'

'Since I was a child, actually.'

'Well I hope you'll be growing it again.'

'We'll see,' she said sleepily.

He finished dressing in silence. She could hear the small flicking sounds of shoelaces, and even with her eyes shut, she could sense the ill temper with which they were being tied.

'*Tonight*,' said Savvas, getting to his feet, 'Markos can stand in for me again.'

Aphroditi said nothing. It suited her better that Savvas should think this annoyed her.

Over the following month or so, with building work continuing at weekends, Savvas did not attend the drinks reception even once. The noise, heat and dust were an exhausting combination, but he knew that the pace of construction would only be maintained if he were present.

In the few minutes each day that she was with him, Aphroditi saw her husband carrying all the anxieties of the world.

'Why don't you take the day off?' she asked him one morning.

'You know *exactly* why,' he snapped. 'We have a deadline. Unless we open next year, a whole season will be lost. So why do you keep asking about days off?'

Markos, by contrast, seemed carefree. His face broke into a smile with every introduction, every order for a drink, every snatch of conversation. As August turned into September, Aphroditi took it for granted that she would host the nightly reception with him.

Throughout the day she found herself looking forward to the cocktail parties more than she had done in the past, and at five o'clock she was back in the hair salon to ensure that she was perfectly coiffed for the evening.

'She's glowing, isn't she?' Savina commented one afternoon as they were shutting up the salon.

'That hairstyle makes all the difference,' agreed Emine. 'It seemed to have cheered her up. She needed a lift after her poor father . . .'

'I didn't mean that. I wondered if she was . . . you know . . . ?'
'Pregnant?'
'Yes! Wouldn't that be nice for them both?'
'Yes, but with that tiny waist . . . she can't be.'
'Some women don't put on any weight for ages.'
'I think you're imagining it. I am sure she would have told us.'
Something that was not in Savina's imagination was Aphroditi's radiance.

Although formality prevailed between Aphroditi and Markos, with him continuing to address her as Kyria Papacosta, she realised she was beginning to dislike him just a little less.

One evening during dinner he broached a subject that he had long been meaning to mention.

'The Clair de Lune—'
'Is a nice name,' she interrupted, finishing his sentence.
She smiled but he was not certain if she was sincere.

Chapter Eleven

INHALING THE DUST of the building site for fourteen hours a day and poring over paperwork for several more, Savvas Papacosta considered that he worked harder than any other man in Cyprus.

The hours that his right-hand man worked were almost as many. Over the past months, with the nightclub and all his other new responsibilities in the hotel, Markos had spent at least sixteen hours a day at The Sunrise, but he needed little sleep so he did not complain.

In the early hours of each morning when he returned home, he found his brother still awake too. Christos had moved into his own apartment now and was rarely alone. He and his group of friends were in the habit of meeting there, and their cell was becoming increasingly active. In November, events five hundred miles away in Athens fired them up.

For six years, since the coup in 1967, Greece had been ruled by a military dictatorship under George Papadopoulos. Now Dimitrios Ioannidis, well known for torturing political dissidents, ousted Papadopoulos and took his place as leader, bringing in an even more brutal regime.

The unification of Cyprus with Greece had been a goal of the colonels, but the new dictator began to agitate for it more openly. Under Ioannidis, the more moderate Greek officers of the Cyprus National Guard were slowly being replaced by a more fanatical anti-Makarios contingent, and he began to use them as a tool for achieving his aims. EOKA B members knew that this would be a huge boost. The organisation originally formed by Makarios himself had turned squarely against him.

For many people the activities and machinations of politicians and soldiers made little impact on day-to-day life. They carried on as normal, conscious of the undercurrents but facing inwards on their own lives. Irini Georgiou made a fuss of her first grandchild, tended the plants in her little *kipos*, cooked more for her family than they could ever eat and chatted with her canary. Vasilis went daily to check on his ripening oranges, harvested his olives and planted a new crop of potatoes in his dark, fertile soil. These activities took him to the limit of physical endurance, but a rough-skinned orange in his palm, the weight of a net of olives or the sudden sight of a carpet of shoots sprouting from the earth made it all worthwhile. For him such joys transcended all others and helped anaesthetise his pain.

For Christos, the events in faraway Athens meant an acceleration in EOKA B activities. The new leadership was impatient, volatile and extreme in its anti-Makarios position. His unit had been involved with several of the attacks on police stations in the previous year, and had seized arms and ammunition crucial for their movement.

Markos was certain that Christos must be involved, but initially he refused to be drawn in. He found his brother naive and idealistic, like a child trying to achieve something that had been attempted before but had failed.

'Christos, how many times do I have to tell you what people went through in the fifties?'

As a teenager, Markos Georgiou had hung around on the edge of EOKA activities. One of his first assignments had been to paint graffiti. At the time it had felt daring to daub 'Better one hour of freedom than forty years of slavery and imprisonment' on the wall of a police station, but he had never really progressed beyond such activities.

He had plenty of friends who were more involved, however, so he was always a suspect, and at seventeen he had felt a British gun pushed into his back during a search. This was the closest to danger that he had ever found himself.

Many of his classmates believed that the union of Cyprus with Greece was a divine mission and for that reason alone God would protect anyone who fought for it. This had been their understanding of President Makarios' teaching.

Even before one of his school friends was killed by a British bullet, and a second was hanged in 1959, Markos suspected there was no sweetness in martyrdom. Up close, death had a pungent odour. It was ugly and wasteful and the smell of blood was acrid. He knew then that there was no connection between this stench and the sweet smell of incense that was the aroma of religion, even if Makarios himself appeared to condone violence.

By the time the Republic of Cyprus was declared, his residual faith in the teachings of the Church had been wiped out, something he kept from his mother. His belief that *enosis* was a holy cause had vanished.

'The point is, Markos, you all gave up. You didn't reach the finishing line.'

'Without us, Christos, Cyprus would still be under the British,' he said quietly. He was aware of his mother's presence in the apartment below and knew how upsetting she found the sound of raised voices. 'Without us, there would never have been independence!'

'That's not what I mean, and you know it!'

Christos was too young to know how things had changed since then and stubbornly refused to understand why Markos wanted to exploit all the new opportunities that he saw opening up around him. The growth of tourism and the expansion of every kind of trade in Famagusta were part of a bigger economic miracle. Markos remembered the lean years and preferred the present day.

He could see that Christos was inflamed by the cause. Personally he no longer cared about *enosis*, but as the sense of unrest in the country grew, he could imagine the danger his brother might be in.

Although Markos challenged Christos and rather enjoyed provoking him, he did have a little sympathy with him purely because they were brothers. There was no question of him joining the cause himself, but perhaps he could facilitate something that might make Christos a little safer and hence keep danger away from the family home. He was not prepared to make bombs, construct booby-traps or meet at the dead of night to plan sabotage, but there might be a way he could contribute without risk to himself.

'I won't fight for Grivas,' he said to Christos. 'But I'll see what else I can do.'

His plan dovetailed with another idea that had been incubating in his mind.

After years of making himself indispensable to Savvas Papacosta, he had begun to enjoy the status as his right-hand man. But now, when he delivered his weekly accounts, with everything minutely accounted for, there was little gratitude from his boss. The success of the Clair de Lune was taken for granted, along with the huge income it brought in, a sum that was immediately assigned to the new development.

There was no mention of a bonus, or even a yearly pay rise for all the extra hours and effort he put in, and Markos' resentment had begun to fester. If Savvas was not going to recognise his efforts properly, perhaps he would balance things out himself. He felt as if something was owed.

Markos, in fact, had a specific plan. Since he had begun his new project, Savvas' focus had moved entirely away from The Sunrise. He had put aside all that had previously mattered to him and no longer had his eye on the minutiae of his business. This gave Markos freedom.

Most of the clientele at The Sunrise paid in cash, either in dollars, pounds or Deutschmarks, and a day or two might easily elapse before it could be safely banked. In anticipation, a row of safes had been installed in a vault next to the nightclub. They could accommodate not just the hotel's day-to-day money supply, but also valuable papers such as deeds and contracts.

The vault in which the safes were housed had two iron doors and triple locking. The basement contained an extensive network of rooms in addition to the nightclub. It was the invisible part of the hotel, where anything unsightly was hidden, including the laundry rooms and boilers.

Earnings from the Clair de Lune were the single largest element of cash income. Markos had naturally become the keeper of the keys and had the daily task of ensuring that cash was taken to the bank or to Savvas' on-site office on payday. In having total control over the vault, he had discovered the pleasure of power.

'If you want somewhere to keep something secure, just let me know,' he said to Christos. 'I have just the place.'

'Thanks, Markos,' the younger brother responded. 'I'll remember that.'

Shortly after their conversation, Christos took up his brother's offer.

Markos was drinking a coffee in his mother's courtyard before going to work. Even though the end of the year was approaching, the sun still gave enough warmth for them to sit outside. The light was sharp and the sky blue. It was a sweet and pleasant day and Vasilis Georgiou had gone off in the truck to the smallholding to plant carrots.

Markos was admiring some gerania that his mother had asked him to move into the sunshine to catch the warmth.

'*Leventi mou*, they look much happier there. Thank you so much.'

Irini, in shawl and woollen skirt, was sitting at the table having a rest when she saw her younger son appear through the gate.

'Christos, what a nice surprise. You haven't come to see me in days!'

Markos glanced at him, interested to see what excuse he would offer.

'I'm sorry, Mother. It's been busy at the garage . . . Will you make me a coffee?'

'Of course, *yioka mou*.'

She bustled inside, only too pleased.

'Markos,' Christos began, as soon as their mother was out of earshot. 'I need your help.'

Irini Georgiou appeared a minute or two later with a plate of *kourabiedes*. The biscuits were freshly baked and a cloud of icing sugar still hovered above them.

Her sons' conversation was curtailed, but they had exchanged the information they needed to.

'And why aren't you at work?' asked Irini.

'Just taking the day off,' Christos replied quickly.

He nibbled on one of the biscuits and then got up to leave.

'But I haven't even brought out your coffee!'

'Sorry, Mother, I have to go. I've got things to do.'

'Oh,' she said, with obvious disappointment. 'Never mind . . .'

He pecked her on the cheek and left.

Irini disappeared into her kitchen to turn off the stove. The coffee was just coming to the boil.

Markos was still sitting there when she returned.

'That was a hurried visit,' she said. 'Is he all right? There's been a lot of noise upstairs in the last few nights.'

Markos did not answer. Over the past weeks he had been getting home at four or five in the morning, by which time Christos' friends had finally left.

'Is he . . . getting involved?'

'What do you mean, *Mamma*?'

'You *know* what I mean, Markos. Your father might be deaf, but I'm not. I can't hear what they are saying, but I know he and his friends aren't just playing cards.'

Markos drew on his cigarette, filling in time while he tried to think of an answer.

'And I know I don't get out of the house much, but I do hear rumours,' his mother continued.

She swept the crumbs left by the biscuits into the palm of her hand and absent-mindedly dropped them into the pocket of her apron.

'I know Grivas is somewhere in the background and I don't want you two to have anything to do with him. He's an evil man, Markos.'

'*Mamma!*'

'I mean it, my darling. He kills Greeks as well as Turks! There's not an ounce of goodness in that man.'

Irini had tears in her eyes. Her mood had changed from calmness to hand-wringing vexation. She never read a book, but she could read her sons' behaviour with ease. She knew it could not be a coincidence that Christos was so secretive and withdrawn. Even though it operated clandestinely, everyone was aware of EOKA B and was affected by its activities, whether they were specifically targeted or merely leaned on, terrorised even, for support. It took courage to resist.

She had a hunch that Christos was getting drawn in. His behaviour was furtive and she knew he skipped going to work because she sometimes checked up on him. He worked as a car mechanic in a garage at the end of their street, and Irini often strolled by on the pretext of going to the store. If she could not see his mop of dark hair, it meant that he was not there.

His irregular hours gave him away too. Up until now, he had always passed by on his way back from the workshop, his hands still black with oil. These days he rarely did, and when she saw him return, it was often much later in the day, and his hands were clean.

'*Mamma*, you mustn't worry. Christos knows how to look after himself.'

'But it's not just him I'm worried about, Markos. I'm thinking of all of us. I don't want to go back to those terrible years when we were all living in fear. If you didn't support Grivas and his people, there was no saying what could happen to you.'

'You mustn't get so anxious . . .'

'But don't you remember? He even executed that woman in our village! And we nearly lost your father! I still have nightmares about those days.'

'It's not like that now.'

'I don't know what makes you so sure. It's the same man. The same ideas! Grivas hasn't changed his mind about anything.'

'But he doesn't have the same support as he did.'

'Our president isn't behind him, I know that. So *he*'d better watch out too.'

'I think he knows the dangers, *Mamma*,' said Markos.

Both mother and son were silent for a while, as Irini kept busy clearing and sweeping and watering her plants and Markos quietly sipped his coffee.

'Have a word with Christos, will you,' she implored. 'God might not look after this family twice.' She crossed herself and looked at her son, her eyes full of tears.

Markos got up to hug her.

'I'll talk to him,' he said softly, breathing in the sweet, familiar scent of her skin. 'Try not to worry, *Mamma*, try not to worry.'

In the warm embrace of her silken-haired son, all anxieties drifted away. Markos had that effect. She loved him more than anyone else in the world.

Markos drove to work that afternoon knowing that he had not been entirely honest with his mother. He was very conscious of the effect he had on her. He had spent his whole life exercising his charm with Irini Georgiou, and as an adult he had learned how potent it was with other women too. It was like alchemy.

He had understood the effect of a smile even before consciousness and language. As a baby, he was aware that if he moved his mouth into a smile he got a response. It was like a special power.

One reason he had felt such antipathy towards Aphroditi Papacosta was his failure to charm her with his smile when they first met. For him, the bitter cocktail of resentment and rivalry had started there, and grown as they had to compete for Savvas' praise and attention. Since the opening of The Sunrise, eighteen months before, he had been forced to see the boss's wife every day. He acknowledged her physical perfection. The ideals of form and proportion that she embodied made her beauty a fact, not a matter of opinion.

Now, when she turned up each night for the drinks reception, almost burdened by her jewellery and expensive clothes, he still smiled even though he knew not to expect a reaction. Aphroditi was not the sort of woman he liked. To him, she was overtly spoiled, the type who was ruined first by her father and then by her husband.

Obliged to take over Savvas' duties as host at The Sunrise, Markos had continued his almost obsequious courtesy to his boss's wife, and Aphroditi in turn sustained her cool formality. He had begun to detect that she might be simmering with as much anger against her husband as he was, and he started to wonder if she could be useful to him.

Aphroditi's silent fury with Savvas had lasted for months. Until the day when he had announced that he was going to spend almost every waking hour at the building site, she had felt equal in their business and entitled to a half-share in both decision-making and profit. Even though ownership was joint on paper, he began to behave proprietorially. He was too caught up in his work even to notice her annoyance with him. By contrast, Markos' reliable presence and impeccable charm each evening became almost comforting.

One night, she acknowledged to herself that she had become less irritated by Markos Georgiou than before. It was just after New Year, and a Cypriot Night was taking place. Guests stood in a circle to watch the demonstration of basic dance steps.

'Do you know how?' asked Markos as they sat finishing dessert.

Aphroditi looked him straight in the eye, for perhaps only the second time. For the first time, she noticed that they were deep green. Like emeralds, she thought.

'Of course I do!' she said. 'Why wouldn't I?'

'I just imagined . . .'

She knew what was in his mind: that she somehow felt it beneath her to perform the traditional dances.

To prove him wrong, she got up and joined the dancers, showing that she knew the footwork as well as any of them. She took the hands of a couple standing on the edge and patiently repeated the moves for the novices.

Markos watched her, slightly mesmerised. His eyes followed her as she went round in a circle. Yes, he thought, she does know the dances, and as they speeded up, he realised how well.

Frau Bruchmeyer was in the midst of it all, quite accomplished nowadays with many of the steps and able to help the other guests.

Towards the end of the evening, when the movements got faster and the beginners just stood to watch, Markos joined in with the all-male *zeibekiko*. Now it was Aphroditi's turn to be the spectator. The nightclub manager held everyone's attention. His lithe and supple body was perfect for this enthralling, masculine dance. Everyone clapped in time with the music as he rotated, arms outstretched, and performed a series of acrobatic leaps.

When the band stopped, there was rowdy applause from both hotel guests and staff. Nearly two hundred of them had been caught up by the music and the mood. Such a sense of euphoria could not be created to order; it was something almost supernatural.

It was the night she watched Markos dance that she began to see him as someone other than her husband's right-hand man. When he came off the dance floor, strands of shiny black hair sticking to his forehead, his temples glistening, eyes sparkling, clearly exhilarated by the energy of the *zeibekiko*, she could not tear her eyes away. She took a step towards him.

'Oh, don't come too close!' he laughed. 'I'm giving off heat like a lamb on a spit!'

He had taken off his jacket, and sweat had soaked through his shirt.

It was the first time he had told her not to come too near, and it was the first time she had wanted to.

They were close enough to feel each other's warmth.

Many of the guests came up to thank Aphroditi before they dispersed, some of them planning to continue their evening in the nightclub. It was exactly midnight.

Apart from the waiter clearing tables, Aphroditi and Markos were the only ones left in the room.

'You must go,' said Aphroditi.

Without thinking, she touched his elbow. It was a spontaneous gesture and one that was immediately withdrawn.

'My senior barman said he would open up tonight,' said Markos, smiling at her. 'But he'll be expecting me there soon. We have a good act on tonight.'

'Well I must leave too,' she added quickly. 'Thanks for helping with the dance demonstrations.'

She hurried, slightly agitatedly, across the foyer and went outside. It had been very hot in the ballroom and her face shone with perspiration. She stood on the hotel steps inhaling fresh air deep into her lungs.

Markos saw Aphroditi standing outside the glass doors to the hotel, car keys in hand. He had been anticipating her touch, and at the very moment when it happened, an idea finally crystallised.

Chapter Twelve

Through the winter Markos had fulfilled his promise to Christos. Once or twice a week his younger brother gave him a small package neatly tied up with brown paper and string and addressed to one of their many distant cousins who had moved to London. Every Cypriot who had left still craved the fruits of their native island, and friends and family shipped their needs to them on a regular basis. Two thousand miles from home, they continued to re-create home flavours, which depended on aromatic herbs grown in their grandmother's soil, honey from their own mountains and olive oil from the family grove. It was incomprehensible to them all that in England olive oil was regarded as medicinal and only found in small quantities in pharmacies.

He put the packages inside his briefcase or under his arm, sometimes both, and took them to The Sunrise. If he passed his mother on the way out, she would not ask questions. She knew that dozens of relatives looked forward to these essentials, and often took her own to the post office.

The chances of Markos being searched by the police were minimal, and these packages were unlikely to arouse suspicion. Once at the Clair de Lune, he immediately went down to the vault and removed the previous day's takings. He then placed the parcels inside the safe and went to the bank to deposit all the cash.

When Christos wanted the packages – sometimes three or four might accumulate – Markos retrieved them and dropped them off at his garage. Not once did he ask about the contents. That way he kept both his conscience and his hands clean.

Both brothers knew that these terrorist activities demanded as much secrecy as possible. When Irini asked, which occasionally she still did, Markos had no trouble looking his mother in the eye and assuring her that they were all safe and that this time round he would not throw himself behind the cause.

'I'm much too old to be running around with a gun,' he said one morning as he drank coffee in his parents' *kipos*.

'But you're only—'

'Twenty-nine! I'm getting on a bit now, *Mamma!*'

Irini Georgiou laughed.

Markos was by no means old, but the man behind the renewed movement for *enosis* was, and at the end of January General Grivas died suddenly, aged seventy-four.

Grivas' death did not mean the end of the terrorist movement. Instead it marked the beginning of increased involvement from the Greek military junta in Athens, who began to send more officers of its own to Cyprus. It was the excuse they had been looking for and presented the perfect moment for accelerated interference in Cypriot affairs. If they decided to get rid of Makarios and put in their own people, *enosis* could be achieved quite swiftly, as long as the Turks kept out of it. This was their thinking.

As the troop numbers rose, so did Papacosta's new hotel. The New Paradise Beach was a vast concrete shell that cast a great shadow into the sea. Papacosta could only see its beauty, but other hoteliers were shocked by its scale and ugliness. It grew visibly each day, with Savvas demanding long hours from everyone on site. The more income that flowed into The Sunrise, and particularly into the Clair de Lune, the faster the new hotel could progress. Additional labourers were taken on as the building climbed ever higher.

Savvas was rarely seen at The Sunrise now, but Aphroditi had ceased to mind. Nowadays, when she got ready to go to the nightly reception, she realised that she was looking forward to the evening. It no longer seemed a duty. The way Markos greeted her each evening reinforced that feeling, and when they went in to eat dinner her courtesy was now sincere, and she made sure to thank him for pulling out her chair.

Once spring had carpeted the mountains with wild flowers and the fields were verdant with bright shoots, the head chef wanted to celebrate. In mid April, a Gala Dinner was held: 'Farewell to Winter'. It was a theme that provided plenty of inspiration, and the ballroom was lavishly decorated with orchids, poppies and hyacinths. Even for this event, Savvas could not find time.

Winter had been mild, with only the lightest sprinkling of snow on the Troodos Mountains, and Frau Bruchmeyer had continued to swim each day at dawn, her lithe, ageless body cutting a channel through the calm, oily sea. Tonight she sat at the top table on Markos' left, her muscular arms still showing last year's tan.

The menu that night was *fruits de mer*, with sculptures created from lobster, langoustine, scallops and prawns. Oysters had been flown in from France, and there was even caviar and smoked salmon. It was a colourful display, celebratory, glamorous and lavish, and the wine waiters successfully pressed their clientele to accompany their food with champagne.

Markos paid Frau Bruchmeyer plenty of attention. For half an hour or so Aphroditi saw only his back and was obliged to engage in conversation with her neighbour, an elderly Cypriot who had once been a politician and a good friend of her father.

'I miss him,' said the man. 'It must have been such a shock.'

'Yes, it was,' replied Aphroditi, hoping the conversation might not need to last too long. 'My mother still hasn't really got over the loss.'

'Does she live all on her own?' asked the man's wife, leaning across and fixing Aphroditi with a penetrating stare.

'Yes,' replied Aphroditi defensively. 'She didn't want to return to Cyprus. I did try to persuade her.'

'Well, it's understandable after what happened . . .' interjected the man, making an unwelcome reference to her late brother.

The three of them continued eating in silence for a few minutes.

'Perhaps if a little Papacosta comes along, she might change her mind,' said the wife brightly. 'I couldn't be more than a mile from my lovely grandchildren.'

Aphroditi knew that her mother did not like this woman, and she could see why.

'Personally I think she's made a good decision and I don't think she's going to regret it,' said the husband. 'It's just not safe any more. What with all the rumours at the moment, who's to know what's going to happen?'

Aphroditi cut in.

'Rumours?'

'Don't bother Kyria Papacosta with your worries,' interjected the wife. 'I am sure she has heard what's going on.'

There was another pause.

At this moment, Aphroditi felt something on her shoulder. It was Markos, touching her lightly to get her attention.

'Kyria Papacosta,' he said. 'Look!'

He held out his right hand. There, in his palm, was a tiny pearl, the size of a split pea.

'I nearly broke my tooth,' he beamed. 'It was in one of my oysters!'

He dropped it in his glass of champagne to clean it, fished it out with his fork, dried it with his napkin and presented it to Aphroditi.

'Here,' he said. 'A miracle from beneath the waves. Like Aphroditi herself.'

Aphroditi flushed slightly. Savvas had given her dozens of pieces of jewellery over the past years, but none with such a flourish. She picked it off his palm and examined it. It was smooth in texture but rough in shape – and still cool from the champagne.

'Thank you,' she said sincerely. 'I shall treasure it.'

She put it away in her purse, meaning what she said. Her heart was beating hard.

Although everyone was almost drunk on the quantities of rich seafood, there was another course yet to come. The ex-politician and his wife left before dessert to make their way back to Nicosia. It was a long way to drive at that time of night and he had clearly been anxious all evening.

'It's not so safe on the roads at the moment,' was his parting remark to Aphroditi.

Aphroditi rarely left the flourishing town of Famagusta. She visited the shops and The Sunrise and then drove the few hundred yards home, always listening to a music channel rather than the news. She was almost as cloistered as the tourists, whose days were spent in carefree innocence.

As soon as the couple were out of earshot, Aphroditi quizzed Markos.

'What was Kyrios Spyrou talking about just now?'
'When?'
'He mentioned that things weren't very safe.'
'Some people just enjoy unsettling others,' said Markos, nonchalantly. 'I really don't think you should worry.'

The conversation was interrupted by the arrival of waiters with dishes of syllabub. Markos knew perfectly well what the man had been referring to. Army officers were still arriving from the Greek mainland, while EOKA B members were growing ever bolder in their activities and springing attacks on government supporters.

Cyprus was like a leaf on the vine. It seemed opaque and green but held up to the light was lined with veins. The threat of violence coursed invisibly through the island, and while its sunny, sensual image continued to attract visitors, conspiracies were being hatched and whispers clandestinely exchanged behind closed doors.

Markos moved between the two co-existing worlds. The kaleidoscopic tourist playground of blue sky, warm sea, bikinis and cocktails was real enough, but where the sun did not penetrate, there were shadowy places where activities of a different kind took place. Though he never opened the parcels that he ferried on an almost daily basis now, Markos knew that they must contain the toolkits for terrorism, usually stolen from the police: guns, ammunition, detonators and other ingredients for bomb-making. Carefree holidaymakers had no idea what was happening around them, and in the case of The Sunrise, beneath their rooms. The vault was now an arsenal.

By keeping a foot in both worlds and appearing uninterested, non-committal even about current affairs, Markos aimed to ensure he would always be on the winning side. He certainly did not want to be drawn into any political discussions with Aphroditi.

While cutlery was being fussed over and a few glasses removed, Markos used the hiatus as an opportunity to change the subject.

'Kyria Papacosta,' he said, 'what is that perfume you wear?'

Aphroditi flushed slightly. Theoretically, the question was as impersonal as asking who had designed her jewellery, but the knowledge that she had engaged one of his senses other than sight suggested something more.

'It's Chanel. Chanel No. 5.'

'So chic!' he said.

She laughed, easily pleased by the compliment. For months now Savvas had hardly seen her when she went out, let alone noticed what fragrance she was wearing. He never saw her dressed for the evening, and was usually in bed when she returned home, getting a few hours' sleep before rising again at five.

They had left the banqueting room and were standing in the foyer.

'Good night, Kyria Papacosta,' Markos said. 'I should be going downstairs.'

'Markos,' said Aphroditi. 'Can I ask you something?'

He waited, wondering.

'Would you mind calling me Aphroditi? Except in front of staff, of course.'

Markos nodded. 'I'd be delighted.'

'I know it's only a name, but . . .'

'Can I ask you something too? About a name?'

Aphroditi gave him a quizzical look.

'Am I really forgiven?'

'For what?' she asked, disingenuously.

'For the name of the nightclub!'

'Yes, Markos!' she smiled. 'You know you are.'

She noticed him run his fingers through his hair. It was an

unconscious gesture and she had seen him do it before. This time, it made her heart skip a beat.

'Will you come and see one of the acts some time?' he asked, with an expression as vulnerable as a lost child's. 'Then I'll know you mean it.'

'Of course,' she said. 'I'll come tomorrow.'

Aphroditi turned to leave. Most of the other guests had gone now.

'And by the way,' she said, trying to maintain her composure, 'thank you for the pearl.'

In no time, Aphroditi was back in her apartment. She removed her jewellery, slipped off her dress and slid between the sheets. For three hours she listened to Savvas' breathing, only sleeping once she had heard him get up, dress and leave.

When she eventually woke, her mind full of half-remembered images and dreams, light was streaming through a gap between the shutters. It was midday.

She sprang out of bed, slightly disoriented, and tripped over her bag, which she had left on the floor. Suddenly remembering what was inside, she opened it up, took out her purse and looked for the pearl. It was still there, wrapped in a torn-off shred of napkin, knobbly, irregular and smaller than any diamond or gemstone she owned. Its eccentric imperfection was its charm, like a mongrel puppy loved for its lopsided features.

She found a velvet pouch to keep it safe and put it in a drawer with all her other valuables, smiling at the memory of how it had been given to her, and warm with excitement that it had been given to her at all.

In spite of attempts to occupy herself with trivial bits of shopping and unnecessary errands, Aphroditi found that Markos was constantly on her mind. She replayed the moment when she had seen him with his sister and now recognised that she had been jealous. She conjured up the memory of him doing the *zeibekiko* and recalled how animated he had been. Images of him filled her mind, and in all of them he smiled. For a moment she wondered if the presence of his small gift in the drawer had not cast a spell.

She killed time until the late afternoon, when she could change and go to the hotel. She dressed once, then again, and for a third time, uncertain about what to wear. Bright coral? Electric blue? Vivid yellow? A rainbow of outfits lay discarded on her dressing room floor. Eventually she chose lilac. It would complement the decor at the Clair de Lune. Amethysts and diamonds would go perfectly that night.

Markos had had a productive day, taking several hundred pounds to the building site to allow Savvas to settle some large debts with cash, returning a number of packages to his brother and meeting with an importer to place an order for two hundred and fifty crates of fine malt whisky. With the mark-up in the club, he would make thousands of pounds from reselling it. Yes, it had been a good day, but he knew the best of it was to come.

Aphroditi arrived a little earlier than usual. She was already in the terrace bar when Markos appeared for his duties, and they mingled separately until it was time for dinner. Aphroditi did her best to engage her companions in conversation. Markos could sense the effort she was making to keep her back to him. Her interest in the guests on her other side was patently artificial.

Aphroditi was willing time to pass. Eventually it was eleven p.m.

'Are you still going to pay a visit to the Clair de Lune?' Markos asked her. 'You haven't changed your mind?'

'No,' answered Aphroditi. 'Of course not.'

For an hour or so she sat with Frau Bruchmeyer and some Americans, enjoying a French singer whose voice was sexier than Sacha Distel's. She took as long as possible to finish a gin and tonic, and then it seemed the appropriate moment to leave. Other hotel staff would find it strange if she stayed much longer.

Markos read the moment that this thought went through her mind and immediately approached the banquette where she was sitting.

'Can I get you ladies another drink?' he asked.

'Yes please,' chirped Frau Bruchmeyer.

'I think I should go,' said Aphroditi.

'Let me accompany you out,' answered Markos immediately.

Turning first to bid Frau Bruchmeyer and their companions good night, she followed him to the door that would take them to the internal stairs to the foyer. As soon as it closed behind them, she felt Markos take her hand in the darkness. Her fingers automatically folded round his.

Rather than going straight up the stairs, Markos led her through another door that was concealed behind a curtain. A narrow corridor led from here to the vault. Here in the small semi-lit space he turned to Aphroditi and kissed her. The eagerness of her response was just as he had anticipated.

Although it was for different reasons, this was unquestionably what they both desired.

Fifteen minutes later they were in the foyer, and Markos held open the door of the hotel to let Aphroditi through. They used neither surname nor Christian name on this occasion. There was no goodbye.

Trembling so violently that her keys rattled in her hand, Aphroditi got into her car. She wound down the window and sat for a few minutes trying to control her shaking. After a few moments, like a drunken driver, she managed to stab her key into the ignition. She reversed awkwardly out of the space and drove very slowly home.

Markos meanwhile had returned to the Clair de Lune, where the evening was in full swing. Everyone loved the singer. It would be a lucrative night and he could picture Savvas passing his eye over the numbers on the balance sheet and being satisfied. Tonight, though, Markos felt he had taken his share. The real satisfaction was his.

Chapter Thirteen

The following morning, Markos was early at the hotel as usual. He noticed Frau Bruchmeyer in reception, a small case by her side.

'You *can't* be leaving me!' he exclaimed dramatically, striding towards her. 'Where are you going?'

'To Germany,' she said, smiling. 'Just for a week. For a wedding.'

'I'll miss you!' said Markos.

Frau Bruchmeyer blushed slightly.

'Let me help.'

Markos picked up the suitcase and escorted her outside into the sunshine. With a click of his fingers, a taxi was summoned.

Once he had waved her off and the car was out of sight, he went back into reception.

Later that day, he and Aphroditi met in Frau Bruchmeyer's apartment. Throughout that week, while she was in Berlin, they knew they would not be disturbed by chambermaids.

At first it did not occur to Aphroditi that anyone would question her increased presence at The Sunrise and find it strange. She was heedless of the risk and abandoned herself utterly to her passion for Markos. Something had ignited in her and she behaved in new and reckless ways.

Then, as the day approached for Frau Bruchmeyer's return, a sense of anxiety crept in. She had to dream up a scheme that would give her a reason to be at The Sunrise during the day.

It was Markos' idea in the end. She would make an inventory of paintings and other artwork in the bedrooms and then purchase some expensive reproductions of *objets d'art* for the more luxurious rooms. Americans especially would love that, and they could charge more if they advertised them as 'Gallery Suites'.

'It's a stroke of genius, *agapi mou*,' she said as they lay together on Frau Bruchmeyer's bed the day before she returned.

There was often a day or two between the departure of one guest and the arrival of the next, during which time a room would be unoccupied. Each day Aphroditi asked for the keys to those rooms.

Markos was effectively the financial director of the hotel now, so no one questioned the fact that he accompanied Kyria Papacosta to draw up proposals for the acquisition and display of the new purchases. Everything would need to be estimated – the cabinets, the lighting and the items themselves – and Markos wrote up the contract and budget for each element. Calculating the necessary increase in room rates to give a swift return on the outlay would be his job too.

With Savvas preoccupied with his work, his wife lost herself in her obsession for Markos. It no longer bothered her that her husband did not notice her. This now became an advantage. She realised that her feelings for Markos had long since been there, but now he was the focus of her every waking hour.

Each time, as she waited in the room designated for their assignation, she felt her heartbeat must be audible to the world.

By the time she heard the familiar triple tap on the door, her legs were usually so weak she could scarcely stand.

They were careful to leave the room separately. Markos always took the lift and Aphroditi the stairs. She had grown more afraid that someone would notice, but this anxiety allowed her to maintain her coolness towards him whenever they were together in public. Staff at The Sunrise were well accustomed to the apparent dislike between Kyria Papacosta and Markos Georgiou, and their formality provided the ideal camouflage for their affair. Neither Costas Frangos, who was a continual presence in the hotel, nor the head waiter, nor the bar staff detected any change in their behaviour towards each other. On the surface their hostility seemed to have intensified. Waiters would notice that during the reception they never spoke, and when they were together on the Salamis thrones for dinner, they would sit almost back to back.

Emine and Savina would not have recognised the rather stiff figure who dined in the ballroom each day. When she was with them for her daily coiffure, she was radiant and full of laughter.

Savvas' reliance on his right-hand man seemed to be increasing, and Markos' day would often be interrupted by a call from the boss.

'Get here in five minutes, would you?' It was an order rather than a request.

The air inside the site office, a makeshift cabin perched on the edge of the building site, was always dense with dust and cigarette smoke, and Savvas had to shout above the noise of construction work. This made his manner seem additionally rude.

'You need to improve on margins in the terrace bar this week, and I want you to squeeze a bit more from the Clair de Lune before the end of the month.'

Savvas never expected a response. He simply assumed that

Markos would go back to The Sunrise and carry out his instructions.

Markos had no trouble concealing his annoyance with Savvas, but each time he made love to the man's wife, he thought of it. As Savvas' demands on Markos increased, so did Markos' demands on Aphroditi.

Lost in the labyrinth of this new passion, Aphroditi became less and less aware of what was going on outside The Sunrise. She never made time to listen to the news or read the papers. She was oblivious to the events that unfolded daily during June as the police located stolen weapons and arrested members of EOKA B.

When Markos read these reports, he always held his breath in case he should see his brother's name. He also knew that in spite of the talks that were going on, there had been violent clashes between the Greek and Turkish communities, with injuries on both sides.

'Did you see it in the papers, *leventi mou*?' asked his mother. 'About the troubles in Agia Irini? There were lots of people hurt.'

'You mustn't worry too much, *Mamma*. The politicians are having discussions,' Markos said, trying to reassure her.

'But why don't they stop these things happening?' she asked.

'It was some kids daubing something on a wall. They just wanted to provoke a bit of trouble!'

Irini kept her radio almost constantly tuned into CyBC. At this moment, Makarios was reassuring the Turkish Cypriots that there was ample space for them all to live in peace together, and publicly blaming EOKA B as well as those outside Cyprus for aggravating the situation and jeopardising the independence of the island.

'President Makarios is such a wise man,' said Irini. 'I hope everyone will listen to him in the end.'

'With the volume up this high,' said Markos affectionately, 'they won't have a choice.'

'All those people plotting against him,' she said, crossing herself. 'But God is protecting him, I know it.'

He adjusted the radio slightly and gave his mother a quick peck on the cheek before leaving.

Irini Georgiou's faith in Makarios, in God and in the Church never wavered.

One morning in June, even Aphroditi became aware of a new danger in Famagusta. While she and Markos were lying naked in a bedroom on the fourth floor, with the window open to let in a breeze, they heard the sound of an explosion. It was one of ten bombs that went off in the city that day, all of them planted by EOKA B, targeting government buildings and Makarios supporters. Suspects even included some members of the National Guard, and they were quickly rounded up and put into custody. Those accused of feeding and sheltering them were also taken in.

Throughout the month, police were hot on the trail of anyone involved in EOKA B, discovering caches of arms and making further arrests, not only of bombing suspects but also of those responsible for a sizeable arms theft at a National Guard recruitment centre.

Markos continued to be anxious about his brother, but his concern was mostly for himself. If Christos was arrested, the police might want to talk to him too. They were often successful in extracting confessions and repentances.

Every night, Markos knocked with trepidation on his brother's door. Christos opened it smiling. Though the police were trying to close their net, he was proving too wily for them.

One day, a week or so later, as he emerged from the lift at The Sunrise, Markos saw Costas Frangos hastening towards him.

'I've been looking for you!' the hotel manager said. 'Kyrios Papacosta is wanting you. He's telephoned three times already. Can you go and see him at the building site? He asked if you could get there as soon as possible.'

Markos acknowledged the request with a slight nod of the head and immediately left the building. It was eleven o'clock in the morning. He caught a glimpse of himself in the rear-view mirror. There was a tiny spot of pink lipstick on his collar. Savvas would not look at him for long enough to see it, but he himself would know it was there, like the trace of Aphroditi's perfume that he could still smell on his skin.

He drove slowly.

'I'm so sorry to have kept you waiting,' he said to Savvas, with convincing sincerity. 'It's been a busy morning.'

'Just a few points today,' said Savvas brusquely, the last quarter-inch of a cigarette smouldering between his fingers. 'Let me know about the rise in nightclub takings, would you? I need another eight hundred for wages this month and we have to find it somehow. Otherwise we're going to have a problem on our hands.'

That annoyed Markos as much as anything. Why did people say 'we' when they meant 'you'?

Silence, as so often, was his best weapon.

'And do you know anything about these rumours?'

There was a small pause as Savvas sipped some water.

'Rumours?'

'About what all those Greek officers in the National Guard are up to?'

'I only know what I read in the newspapers,' answered Markos. 'And I'm sure it's all exaggerated, as usual.'

His disingenuous answer was what Savvas wanted to hear. In reality, Markos had no doubt that the junta in Athens was planning a coup against Makarios in Cyprus.

'Oh well. Let's hope it doesn't affect business,' said Savvas. 'Tourists are easily scared. Especially Americans. I know we don't have so many these days, but you know what they're like . . .'

He lit another cigarette and swung round in his leather office chair so that he could look out of the window at the huge building site. Fifty or so men in hard hats were visible at various levels of scaffolding. Windows were being put in and a crane was moving panes of glass into position.

'We're getting there,' he said. 'But we need to keep the cash flowing in. I've already got a loan, but it's not quite enough.'

Markos got up. He could see that his appointment with Savvas was over. He had told him what he needed to know.

'Come again in a couple of days,' said Savvas, swinging back to face him. 'And bring some cash next time.'

Markos was already at the door. He was in a hurry to leave for more than one reason. Christos was expecting him at the garage. That morning he had found a note from his brother asking him if he could collect some packages 'to take to the post office'.

There was plenty of activity going on and Christos needed his brother's help more than ever. One of his group had been arrested when stolen weapons were found at his home. Christos did not even know where his friend had been taken. Rumours were flying that imprisoned EOKA B fighters were being tortured, and Christos was terrified that he would be named. It was more important than ever to keep his home clean.

When Markos drew up outside the garage, his brother beckoned him to drive right in. Christos looked exhausted, but there was a gleam of excitement in his eyes.

'I think something's going to happen,' he said. 'We have to be even more careful than before.'

'It's not the first time you've said that,' said Markos sardonically through his open window. After the attempts on President Makarios' life over the past months, plenty seemed already to have happened. With Ioannidis, an uncompromising advocate of uniting Cyprus with Greece, now firmly in control of EOKA B, Makarios was in greater personal danger than ever.

Markos skilfully manoeuvred his car into a space inside the garage but did not get out. Christos opened the boot and in the safety of the shadows carefully loaded in a few packages. Haralambos, who was changing some truck tyres, kept an eye out, watching for the arrival of other customers. Everyone who worked here supported EOKA B, but their customers were of all persuasions; even a few Turkish Cypriots were regulars.

When he had finished, Christos slammed down the lid and came round to the driver's door. He bent down to speak to his brother.

'Thanks, Markos. I'll need these back soon, so you won't have them for long.'

'You'd better be extra careful,' said Markos. 'They're tightening their grip.'

'I know, I know,' answered Christos with impatience. 'There must be informants.'

'And you know what Makarios is saying . . . ?'

'What?' asked Christos, wiping his oily hands on a grubby towel.

'That EOKA B's actions are threatening our independence.'

'It's Makarios who is the biggest threat to this island,' said Christos. 'Not us.'

Markos wound his window up, turned on the radio and drove off.

'*Our love is like a ship on the ocean . . .*'

One of the summer's big hits was playing. Markos knew the words by heart and sang them at full volume. His mother had always told him he had a beautiful voice, and she was right.

The day was idyllic, the sea bright and sparkling, and as he drove towards The Sunrise, he caught a glimpse of a cruise liner coming into port.

'*. . . Rock the boat, don't rock the boat, baby.*'

He hoped nothing *would* rock his boat. At present, he felt things were nicely under control, and Aphroditi's love and devotion were a delicious part of his day.

As soon as the song finished, there was a news bulletin. They were talking about an open letter that President Makarios had written to Phaedon Gizikis, the Greek president, who had been put in place by Ioannidis. It accused the government there of conspiring against him, and made a direct charge that it was following a policy calculated to 'abolish the Cyprus state'.

The broadcaster read out an extract: 'More than once I have sensed, and on one occasion almost felt, the invisible hand stretched out from Athens, seeking to destroy my human existence.'

Makarios demanded that Athens recall the six hundred Greek army officers who were now in the Cyprus National Guard and supplying men and materials to EOKA B.

Against the backdrop of this bright summer's day, Markos asked himself the same question as everyone else who was listening to the radio. What reaction would such a blunt statement provoke? They did not have to wait long to find out.

Chapter Fourteen

A FORTNIGHT LATER, VERY early on 15 July, the presidential palace in Nicosia was attacked. Armoured cars and tanks burst through the gates and shelled the walls. Assailants broke in to find Makarios. Soon the palace was on fire.

News of the coup travelled fast on this small island. In homes all over Cyprus, people gathered round radios. In the Özkan house, in the Georgious' apartment and in the offices at The Sunrise, everyone stood about in stunned silence. On the radio they heard only military music. Then came the announcement:

'Makarios is dead.'

This was followed by a sinister warning:

'The National Guard is in control of the situation. Anybody interfering will be immediately executed.'

News went around that there was a new president: Nikos Sampson, a former EOKA fighter.

Irini Georgiou wept almost inconsolably. She was very sentimental about Makarios. His shifting position on the subject of *enosis* had confused her, but whatever his political aims, she held on to the belief that any man of the cloth must be fundamentally good.

'Another death,' she said to her daughter. 'Another terrible death. Poor man . . . poor man. When will all this end?'

She and Maria, who was pregnant again, listened to broadcasts throughout the day while Vasilakis tirelessly played a game with wooden blocks, lost in his own imaginary world. Makarios was blamed for having caused the situation, and the announcer told them that the National Guard had seized power to avert civil war.

By the time Panikos came home early from the electrical shop to be with his wife and son, Irini Georgiou was beside herself. All her men were missing. Her husband and her two sons had been out most of the day and not returned.

'Where do you think they are?' she kept asking, wringing her hands. 'Do you think they'll be back soon? Do you think they are safe?'

The questions were unanswerable, and neither Maria nor Panikos could do any more than provide futile words of comfort.

Irini paced up and down, walked in and out of the front door, went a little way down the street as if she would find them there, returned to the house, sat down for two minutes and then repeated the process.

'What are we going to do? What are we going to do?' She was on the edge of hysteria and constantly crossing herself.

'I'm sure they'll return soon,' said Panikos, touching his mother-in-law's hand tenderly.

The hours passed slowly, and the first to appear was Vasilis.

'*Agapi mou*, I'm so sorry. There were roadblocks on the way back. Such delays. You must have been so worried.'

They hugged each other and Irini wept copious tears.

'If only we had bothered to get a telephone installed,' said Vasilis, 'then I could have called you.'

Not long afterwards, Markos walked in. He had not realised that his mother would be so anxious.

'I had to stay at the hotel,' he explained. 'We needed to reassure the guests that everything is fine. That it's business as usual.'

Now they were just waiting for Christos.

'He'll come soon, *Mamma*,' Markos reassured her, even though he was not sure he believed it himself.

Irini began cooking a meal. It was the only way she could think of to occupy herself and take her mind off her son's absence. She laid the table, including a place for Christos, and everyone else sat down to eat. The front door was left open so that they would see him as soon as he arrived.

Just as Irini and Maria were clearing the plates, a figure appeared at the door. Irini dropped some cutlery in her haste to reach her son, and Christos enfolded his mother in his embrace. He was thickset and more than a foot taller than her.

Irini inhaled the smells of sweat and car oil that her younger son always carried around with him, and gripped on to him tightly. Finally he pulled away.

'You must be needing some supper,' she said.

'Yes, I'm hungry as a wolf,' he replied.

'You know what's been going on today?' asked Vasilis, wondering if his son had even been aware of the coup.

'Of course I know, Father,' replied Christos, trying hard to conceal his feelings of satisfaction, which had grown with each of the day's developments.

Irini Georgiou realised that her younger son did not share her sadness over Makarios' death, and his general demeanour that evening confirmed to her something she had half known for some time.

Panikos was fiddling with the radio, trying to reduce the interference, and picked up another channel.

Suddenly there was a voice they all recognised. It was Makarios. It was as if he had risen from the dead. Describing how he had escaped from the palace when it was under attack, he told the interviewer that he had stopped a passing car, which had taken him to the Troodos Mountains. From there he had gone to a monastery, and then to Paphos, from where he was making the broadcast on a secret radio station.

'Together we will carry on the sacred resistance and win freedom,' he said. 'Long live freedom. Long live Cyprus.'

For Irini, Makarios' resurrection was even more extraordinary than his death. She was adamant that they were all witnesses to a miracle, and she wept even more that evening than she had done in the morning. All the men she loved had returned.

'God must be on Makarios' side,' she said jubilantly.

Vasilis looked at her. When Irini Georgiou talked about Makarios, she was thinking lovingly of a bearded priest. His God-fearing wife venerated anyone in ecclesiastical vestments. Vasilis, though, believed that there were two very distinct sides to the beady-eyed politician.

Everything at The Sunrise remained calm on that day. Members of staff were given instructions to tell guests that the change in the country's leadership would have no adverse effect on them. The harbours and airports were temporarily shut but everything would be back to normal soon. Nicosia was thirty miles away and any troubles were being contained.

There were still people sunbathing on the beach on the afternoon of the coup. Tourists heard there was a new president, but this did not sound like such momentous news. American and European holidaymakers were more interested in trying to keep up with the developing scandal in Washington. The fate of another president, Richard Nixon, was in the balance, and this would have much greater personal repercussions for most of them.

The following day, for the first time in months, Savvas appeared at The Sunrise. Many of his workers at the building site had not turned up, so progress could not be made as normal. He was in a state of high anxiety.

'Where is Markos?' he demanded of Costas Frangos.

'He is somewhere in the hotel,' responded Frangos. 'I saw him at about ten o'clock.'

Markos and Aphroditi had met that morning as usual, but Markos had been delayed. Aphroditi was always agitated if he kept her waiting. Desire made her impatient. Today there had been an additional cause of tension. She knew that the latest political twist in the island's politics was ominous. More than anything, she did not want it to affect her own daily life. She had never been more fulfilled, never felt more alive, never experienced such intensity of pleasure, and she did not want anything to change. Within the walls of a room with Markos she cared for little but the moment. Clothes, shoes, lingerie – but not always jewellery – were cast to one side. They always let the sunlight stream in wherever they made love, whether it was on the ninth, eleventh, fourteenth or any other floor. Light reflected upwards from the sea, and the sun was usually still on the rise, illuminating every square inch of her skin. With Savvas the lights had always been dim and the curtains drawn.

As his wife and his right-hand man hastily pulled on their clothes, Savvas was calling the staff together in the ballroom to reinforce that all must continue as usual. Most importantly, everything possible had to be done to discourage the guests from leaving. He noted that things seemed to be functioning well and asked that this should continue.

'You all know that we are rebuilding The New Paradise Beach,' he said. 'And the success of The Sunrise and the completion of the new hotel are entirely in your hands.'

Markos appeared at the back of the room and listened. He could hear an unmistakable note of greed clashing with a minor chord of panic in Savvas Papacosta's voice.

The boss is short of information, thought Markos. Typical. He strongly suspected that they would not be able to continue with business as usual. He had called in at the garage that morning to return some parcels. Christos was not there, but one of his colleagues was, working alone.

'Their unit has been ordered to Nicosia,' he said. 'Christos has gone.'

'But isn't it all over?' asked Markos.

'There's still some opposition there . . .' the mechanic answered. 'A few lefties objecting to the new president.'

Whether or not it was a deliberate understatement did not matter. Within a few hours, Famagusta was alive with rumours of what was happening in the capital city, a place that was so close but had always seemed a world away.

Markos had met Nikos Sampson once when he had been active in the original EOKA. Born in Famagusta, Sampson had made a huge impression on the teenager. He was masculine, handsome and charismatic, and men and women alike adored and feared him in equal measure. He had a reputation for being a killer, and wore his ruthlessness like a birthmark. It was part of him, as ineradicable as his steely gaze.

Markos knew that Sampson would not be handing out any amnesties to people who had resisted the coup.

News soon filtered through that the hospitals in Nicosia were overflowing with wounded. Running battles had been fought in the streets. Machine-gun fire and sometimes tank cannon were still occasionally heard throughout that day. In crowded corridors doctors struggled to save the dying, whether they were Makarios supporters, EOKA B, or perpetrators of the previous day's army coup. Wounds were wounds, and once flesh was torn apart by bullets and shrapnel, it did not matter to whom it belonged. The medical staff scarcely had time to register names or look at faces as they cleaned and swabbed and tightened tourniquets. Every doctor and nurse, whether Greek or Turkish Cypriot, had their personal view on what was happening in the streets outside, but performed their tasks without discrimination.

As snippets of news came into the salon, Emine became increasingly anxious. That morning she had noticed that Ali's bed had not been slept in, and she could no longer put aside her suspicion that he was involved in the TMT. As more reports of fighting and the wounded came in, she realised that her hands were shaking violently. She put down her scissors.

'Why don't you go and find Hüseyin?' suggested Savina. 'He might know something.'

Emine found her son raking the stretch of sand in front of the terrace.

'Where was Ali last night?' she asked.

Hüseyin continued with what he was doing without looking up. If he met his mother's eyes, she would see that he knew something.

He shrugged.

'Hüseyin! Look at me.'

Her voice was raised and one or two people glanced up from their sunloungers.

'Mother!' he hissed, embarrassed.

'I want to know!'

Costas Frangos appeared on the terrace and beckoned him over.

'I must go,' Hüseyin said.

He hurried away, leaving his mother standing alone on the sand.

Back in the salon, Savina took one look at Emine and insisted that she go home. She was in no state to work.

Even before she opened the door to her house, her heart soared. She could hear Ali's voice. He had returned.

'Ali! Where were you? Why didn't you come home! We have been so worried.'

She was torn between a desire to slap him hard and hold him tight. She chose the latter, weeping all the while.

Halit was sitting in the corner, quietly clicking his *tespih,* his worry beads.

'Don't get involved!' she urged.

'I have to,' Ali said, his voice cracking. He pulled away from his mother. 'They might kill our people.'

'But you're still a child. You're too young for this!' Emine was beside herself. 'Promise me you'll *never* go again . . .' she pleaded.

'I can't,' he replied.

Irini and Vasilis were still up when Markos arrived home late that night. He had shut the nightclub earlier than normal, as only a handful of hotel guests had turned up. The ones who had come drank plenty to help calm themselves, but did not stay long. Normally, the stage was strewn with flowers by the end of the evening, but tonight only one basket of carnations had been sold.

At first Markos did not see his parents, sitting silently in the darkness of the *kipos,* but then he noticed the glow of his father's cigarette.

'Father?'

'*Leventi mou*,' cried Irini, as Markos appeared at her side. She got up to hug him.

'Irini,' remonstrated her husband. 'He's only been at work.'

He was right, but her anxiety had been building steadily during the course of the day. They had neither telephone nor television, and the radio was not telling her what she wanted to know.

Markos sat down with them and poured from a half-empty carafe of *zivania* in the middle of the table. Irini had persuaded Vasilis not to drive to the smallholding that day.

'I didn't think it would be safe,' she explained to Markos. 'But I had hoped things would have settled down by now.'

'What made you think that?' interjected her husband.

Vasilis Georgiou had been at the *kafenion*, and his speech was slurred. He had spent all day listening to rumour, news and propaganda, and had returned to fill his wife with new anxieties.

'There's a civil war going on out there!' he said, thumping the table. 'They've rounded up lots of Makarios' men. And your mother is none too pleased about that.'

Vasilis Georgiou was one of a large number of people who had turned away from Makarios when the Archbishop no longer put *enosis* at the top of his agenda, but it was only when drink got the better of him that he opened his mouth on the subject. He had no respect for his wife's sentimentality over the man. He knew that Christos, like himself, was for *enosis*, but he was uncertain about his elder son.

'Don't exaggerate!' replied Markos. 'You're just upsetting *Mamma*.'

'Well what do you think is going on, then? You know nothing shut up all day with those foreigners . . . who are you to say what's happening . . .'

Vasilis Georgiou was rambling drunkenly. Markos put his arm round his mother.

'And Christos . . .' she said quietly, appealing to her older son. 'Hasn't he come home?'

Irini shook her head.

'He will, *Mamma*, don't worry. Everything will be fine. He came back yesterday, didn't he?'

'I have an awful feeling,' she said. 'I had a dream last night. A terrible dream.'

She looked away. There were tears streaming down her face.

'I know where he is,' she said at last. 'He's fighting with . . . those men.'

A few uncomfortable minutes passed. Markos was silent. Vasilis lit another cigarette.

Irini went inside to bed. Listening for any footstep, any sound of her son returning, she lay awake until morning staring at the ceiling.

Just before dawn, the cicadas quietened down. Between now and the moment when the dogs began to bark and cocks crowed, there was utter silence. How could a civil war be raging with such total stillness? She persuaded herself it could not be true. Christos would walk in at any moment.

During the morning, tension built up. Hour by hour, scraps of news, real and fabricated, circulated. Sometimes the rumours exaggerated the severity of events, sometimes they underplayed it. Christos had not returned, and when Vasilis went to check at the garage, he discovered that he was not at work for the second day.

Everyone turned up for work at The Sunrise as they had been instructed by Savvas Papacosta, but the atmosphere was tense. Guests bombarded the reception staff with questions.

'How is this going to affect us?'

'Will our flight home be delayed?'

'Will we get a refund if we leave a day or so early?'

'Can we keep the same room if we can't get a flight?'

They were all anxious, self-interested, suddenly feeling a long way from home.

Emine and Savina were alone in the salon that morning. Frau Bruchmeyer, as punctual as ever, appeared at midday for her monthly trim. She kept her silver hair short and gamine, a style that only suited a woman with such cheekbones.

'Good morning,' she said cheerfully.

Emine helped her into a gown.

'Good morning, Frau Bruchmeyer,' she responded. 'How are you today?'

The question was automatic. Emine was totally preoccupied.

'I'm very well, thank you,' came the reply. 'But I think I am alone in this.'

'You might be,' said Savina. 'But most of our customers haven't shown up, so we don't really know . . .'

Frau Bruchmeyer's head was tipped back in the sink for Emine to wash her hair, but she continued to speak.

'I don't like the sound of what is happening,' she said. 'But I think we should all carry on as normal.'

Emine dared not open her mouth to respond.

When her hair was trimmed and dry, Frau Bruchmeyer gave them both a shilling and left. It was lunchtime now and she would take her usual table by the pool, unperturbed by the morning's developments.

Making the excuse to herself that the telephone lines were only working sporadically that day, Aphroditi gave up waiting for a phone call from Markos. She knew from the brief conversation

The Sunrise

she had had with Savvas in the morning that they must continue as though everything was normal, so she dressed carefully, as usual – delicate yellow silk and topaz jewellery – and left for the hotel.

Markos did not seem to be around, so she went down to the hair salon to see Emine and Savina. Perhaps he would turn up a little later. For her, there was nothing in the world that mattered more than a few stolen minutes with this man, and she clung to the hope that he might feel this way too.

Emine and Savina saw a very different Aphroditi from the ebullient woman to whom they had become accustomed in the past few months. She was tense and unusually silent.

'Perhaps she wishes she was in England with her mother.'

'She looks peaky to me . . .'

'Oh Emine! However she looks, you're always imagining she's pregnant! She's just worried, like everyone else!'

Freshly coiffed, Aphroditi went up to reception. There was still no sign of Markos, and she killed time talking to the staff and a few guests who were loitering in the hope of finding out some new information. The dolphins still frolicked in the fountain.

Eventually she approached Costas Frangos.

'Have you seen Mr Georgiou today? My husband was hoping to see him at the building site later.'

'No, Kyria Papacosta,' he replied. 'As far as I'm aware, he hasn't been in since he locked up the nightclub. That must have been at about one this morning.'

'Thank you,' she said, turning away. She was certain that he could read the agitation written on her face.

Aphroditi drove home. As she went up Kennedy Avenue, the main road that ran behind the hotels, she passed a group of National Guard troops. They were in control of Famagusta now. There had been little resistance of the kind that had been put up in Nicosia.

Inside the apartment, she switched on the radio. The newscaster reported that across the island things were generally quiet now. Aphroditi turned it off, put a record on the hi-fi and poured herself a sweet vermouth. With the shutters still down, she stretched out on the sofa, sipped slowly and stared at the phone, willing it to ring.

As Carly Simon sang, the alcohol took effect. Aphroditi closed her eyes.

It was dark when she opened them. The glow that had penetrated the shutters had gone, and night had fallen. She sat up. The needle had got stuck.

'*You're so vain . . . vain . . . vain . . .*'

It must have repeated a hundred times, but she had been oblivious.

Only the sound of the telephone could penetrate her dreams. It was ringing.

She leapt up and snatched the receiver from its cradle, her heart beating. She was about to say Markos' name when she heard her own.

'Aphroditi!' It was her husband's voice.

'Savvas,' she said, breathlessly. 'How was your day?'

'Bloody terrible. Half the workforce didn't show. None of the deliveries arrived . . . Markos Georgiou didn't bring the cash I asked for . . .'

It was as if the true significance of the coup had not even registered with Savvas.

Aphroditi glanced at the wall clock. With a jolt, she saw that it was nine p.m. She must have missed that day's reception. Had Markos been waiting for her?

Savvas was still talking.

'Just tidying up some paperwork here first and I'll call in at The Sunrise on my way home. I'm not letting all this . . .'

While listening to her husband's complaints, she had been watching images flicker on the television screen. There was an old Melina Mercouri film showing.

'Savvas,' she said. 'Have you heard any news?'

'No,' he answered firmly. 'What's the point? That lot won't tell us the truth in any case.'

'It's just that . . .'

Her husband detected the note of anxiety that had crept into Aphroditi's voice.

'Look, I'll be back about midnight,' he said abruptly. 'Don't fret. Things have already settled down again, as far as I know. As long as we can keep going here, everything will be fine.'

Savvas Papacosta seemed oblivious to anything outside the barbed-wire boundary of his building site. Apart from gold and precious stones, everything they possessed had now been liquidated and poured into the project. Even the income from The Sunrise and the sizeable loan he had taken out were not enough to fund the current phase of construction. All he wished for was to hasten the day of the opening. Only then would he begin to recoup this enormous investment.

'See you later, then,' Aphroditi said. She heard a click at the other end.

She was shivering. The air-conditioning had chilled the apartment to freezing point, so she lifted the shutters and went out on to the balcony for some warmer air.

Why hadn't Markos been to the site? she wondered. And why hadn't he called her?

There was no way of finding out.

If she had turned on the radio again, Aphroditi would have discovered that the Turkish government was asking Britain to intervene. The Greek-backed coup in Nicosia, as far as the Turks were concerned, was a final move towards *enosis*, something they would not tolerate. Like her husband, she was too preoccupied with personal concerns to be aware of the danger she and everyone else on the island were in.

The night air was still. All over the town, other sleepless people sat on their balconies gazing out into the darkness and up at the stars. The temperature had not dropped below forty degrees that day. Markos was sitting with his mother, holding her hand and trying to reassure her.

The Özkan family were all awake too, wondering what the next day would bring.

Not far away, across the inky blackness of the sea, Turkish naval units lay in wait.

Chapter Fifteen

When Aphroditi woke the next morning, she saw a dent in the pillow next to hers. Savvas had already left.

The silence in the apartment was oppressive. She had to go and find Markos. Hastily putting on her dress and shoes from the previous day, but leaving her jewellery on the side table, she hurried out.

In the foyer of The Sunrise, suitcases were lined up in organised rows. The guests themselves were less ordered. Several hundred people thronged round the reception desk, eager to settle their bills, the good manners usually observed by northern Europeans all now forgotten. The receptionists tried not to lose their tempers at the demands of the guests, many of whom were insisting on refunds, querying bills, and asking for explanations while dozens of others jostled behind them. There was change to be counted out, exchange rates to be calculated, receipts to be given.

A few small children chased each other round the fountain, squealing and laughing, oblivious to their parents' anxieties. Costas Frangos tried to keep some kind of order, fruitlessly asking people to form a queue, trying to answer queries, organising taxis.

Aphroditi surveyed the scene, looking for one specific face amongst all these near-strangers. Several people approached her, clamouring for information, agitating to get their bills faster and demanding that she should help organise transport for them.

'Mr Frangos will look after you,' she said firmly, directing them to the hotel manager, who remained immaculate amidst the maelstrom of rudeness.

She wandered towards the terrace bar and the pool, and looked out over the beach. A few people stubbornly continued with their holiday routine, applying sun lotion, going for a dip and soaking up the rays. These were their precious annual days of hedonism and sunshine, and they were reluctant to give them up. When the queues in the reception area died down, they would stroll in to check on the situation, but for now they were not going to panic.

In their midst was Frau Bruchmeyer, who had no intention of going anywhere. This was her home. She looked up from her book and waved to Aphroditi from her sunlounger.

Aphroditi did not want to engage in conversation with anybody, so she returned to the foyer and retreated from the entrance. Chaos reigned outside, mostly created by the taxi drivers, who were shouting at each other, their cars clumsily parked and blocking each other's exit.

Over by the door to the Clair de Lune, she saw the man she was looking for. Restraining herself from running, she went across to him.

'Markos!' she called breathlessly.

He spun round, a huge bunch of keys jangling in his hand.

With the noise going on all around them, they could speak without fear of being overheard.

'Where have you been?'

Markos hesitated. 'Look, why don't you come inside? We can talk there.'

He double-locked the door behind them, and they went down the stairs and through a pair of velvet curtains into the nightclub.

'I was worried about you.'

'You mustn't worry about me, Aphroditi,' Markos said, taking her in his arms, stroking her hair.

'It's been two days!'

'An eventful two days,' he replied blandly.

His tone of voice was very matter-of-fact.

'I've missed you,' was all she could think of to say.

'I had to be with my parents,' he said. 'They're very anxious.'

She felt the light touch of his lips on her forehead and the unfamiliar sensation of being dismissed.

'I have a few things to finish off before I leave,' he said. 'But I'll see you soon. I'm sure it won't be long before things are back to normal.'

'Couldn't I stay with you here a while?'

'*Agapi mou*,' he said. 'People will think it strange if they know you are here.'

'I don't think anyone will notice today,' she said.

'Even so, I think it's best not,' he said, stroking her arm in such a way that she was momentarily reassured of his affection.

He led her back to the front door and let her out. She was anguished by a sense of being embraced and pushed away at the same time.

Aphroditi heard the keys turn in the lock behind her, but after that, she was aware of little else. She felt disconnected from the world and drove straight across a crossroads, not registering that she had narrowly missed another car.

In this blind fashion she reached home and went upstairs to

the apartment. She could think of nothing to do, so she rang her mother.

'Aphroditi, I have been trying to call you but I couldn't get through. What's going on? What's happening there?'

'I'm fine, Mother,' said Aphroditi. 'There's a bit of a panic. It probably looks worse on the news.'

'It's terrible. Poor Archbishop Makarios!'

Artemis Markides still regarded Makarios as her spiritual leader, and the fact that he had been deposed was her main concern.

'You should come over to England if things get worse,' she said. 'There's plenty of room here, as you know.'

'I'm sure I won't have to do that,' said Aphroditi firmly. Leaving Cyprus to go and live with her mother was the last thing in the world on her mind. 'We're just coming to the final stage with the new hotel,' she added, 'and Savvas has no intention of stopping!'

'Well, keep in touch, dear. I need to know that you're safe.'

'I will, Mother,' answered Aphroditi.

The following morning, just as the sun was rising, Turkish planes were heard over Cyprus.

In the ground-floor apartment, Markos, Maria and Panikos gathered round the radio with their parents. They were avidly listening to the news on CyBC.

Turkey was demanding the restoration of constitutional order. They feared for the safety of the Turkish Cypriots and the imminent declaration of *enosis* by the perpetrators of the coup. Their ultimatum had not been met, so they had landed thousands of Turkish paratroopers in the north of the island. Kyrenia, just forty miles from Famagusta, was being bombed. It was the family's worst fear.

'*Panagia mou*,' muttered Irini, her head bowed as if in prayer.

Maria sat next to her and took her hand.

'Don't worry, Mother,' she said softly. 'The Greeks will come and save us.'

'Do you think so?' Irini said, momentarily reassured.

'Of course they will.'

Her small son tottered round and round the table, oblivious to the events of the day.

Irini Georgiou looked up at Markos. He knew she was thinking about Christos.

'I'm sure he'll be with us again soon,' he said.

'I can't listen to this,' said Vasilis Georgiou, storming angrily towards the door. 'Why didn't Makarios come to some arrangement with the Turks? Weren't they supposed to want the same thing? They could have got rid of that Sampson together! Now see what's happened!'

He was shouting at the air. Nobody in the room disagreed with him, but the situation was out of their hands and even Markos felt it futile to respond. In the brief silence that followed, a voice on the radio was suddenly audible. All able-bodied men were being called up to defend Cyprus.

Markos exchanged a look with Panikos.

'We'll have to go,' he said. 'I'll drive.'

'*Panagia mou!*' Irini said, crossing herself. 'Not you as well. Please not you as well . . .'

The instruction on the radio was repeated. It was a matter of urgency.

Panikos hugged Maria, who was fighting back the tears. He briefly touched her swelling stomach.

'Don't worry, *Mamma*,' said Markos. 'They'll see that we're not fighters.'

He knew that Savvas Papacosta would find a way to exempt

himself and his right-hand man. As for Panikos, he was in no shape to defend the country.

As they left, Vasilis, knowing he did not qualify, took himself to the *kafenion*, where he continued to argue with his friends for an hour or so. By the time he returned, he would be ready to sleep off an excess of *zivania* and fury.

There was less anger but almost equal fear in the Özkan household. Turkish Cypriots knew that this new development would make each one of them vulnerable. They feared retaliation and knew they could be its victims.

Lots of young men were joining the TMT, preparing to defend their communities, and Emine Özkan begged her son to stay at home.

'What good will it do?' she insisted. 'You don't know one end of a gun from another!'

Ali did not reply. His mother's words were far from the truth. He could take a semi-automatic pistol apart and put it back together in three minutes. There were so many villages that needed armed protection. He could not sit listening to reports on the radio without wanting to feel his finger on the trigger of a gun.

When night fell and everyone was trying to sleep, he whispered to Hüseyin, with whom he shared a room, that he was going.

'Don't try to stop me,' he said, and the elder brother knew there was nothing he could do. Mehmet continued to sleep soundly in a small bed next to them as Ali crept from the room and left the house.

The National Guard were already known to be attacking Turkish Cypriot villages and quarters throughout the island. Turkish troops were heavily outnumbered, so young men like Ali knew they had a role to play.

The Sunrise

That day, the streets of Famagusta were almost empty as people stayed in their homes, glued to their radios. There were developments hour by hour.

Irini and Maria listened nervously to reports of military clashes, praying that Markos and Panikos were safe. Cypriot navy boats, sent out from Kyrenia to engage the approaching Turkish naval flotilla, were sunk by combined Turkish air and naval attack. Greek Cypriot forces failed to dislodge the Turkish landing force, and their tanks and armoured vehicles were destroyed. Fighting then broke out in the mountains behind the town.

Around midday, they heard the slam of a car door. Markos sauntered in, with Panikos behind. The women leapt up and embraced them.

'It was chaos,' said Panikos. 'No weapons, no plan. It was a shambles. They told us we could go.'

'So who's defending us?' asked Vasilis gloomily. 'If the Turkish troops link up between the coast and Nicosia, then it's all over.'

'I'm sure the United Nations will have some influence,' Markos assured him. 'And the best thing is that they are not taking sides . . .'

'It sounds as if they're blaming both sides, though,' said Panikos, holding Maria as if he would never let her go.

Maria did not hide her relief that her husband and brother were back.

The United Nations Security Council was demanding immediate withdrawal of all foreign military personnel unless they were there under the authority of international agreements, and made it clear that they disapproved of the Greek coup that had precipitated the crisis as well as the Turks for taking military action.

'At least if everyone keeps talking, things won't get any worse,' said Panikos optimistically.

There was every possibility that the situation would escalate into an all-out war that would not be confined to Cyprus. Greece had announced mobilisation, and troops were moving towards the border with Turkey.

Meanwhile, the Turks continued to claim that they had invaded purely to protect Turkish citizens, and that they hoped for the recommencement of talks between the communities.

Just down the road, the Özkan family was also anxiously considering events.

'Perhaps it's true,' said Hüseyin. 'They could just be here to protect us.'

Thousands of Turkish Cypriots had been driven from their homes, and many others were now effectively hostages in villages surrounded by the National Guard. Hundreds of others were being held in football stadia.

'If the Turks hadn't invaded, none of this would have happened!' cried Emine in vexation.

'You don't know that,' remonstrated Halit. 'We could have found ourselves living like we did in the sixties. Those Greeks from Athens – they don't want us here! Nothing's changed.'

'So perhaps they *did* come to protect us . . .' repeated Hüseyin.

'But all they've managed to do is put us in danger,' responded his mother.

There was silence for a few moments before she exploded again, this time revealing the true cause of her anxiety.

'And your brother . . .' she cried, now in tears. 'Ali! Where is he? Where has he gone?'

She knew her questions were futile. She left the room, and father and sons listened to the sound of sobbing that penetrated the walls.

The following day, Panikos went out to the electrical shop as usual, but business was dead. No one even came in for a light bulb.

Irini tirelessly tidied and dusted and cooked and then tidied once again. Everyone was on edge.

Vasilis came back home from the *kafenion* bringing plenty of rumour but also plenty of truth. Where one ended and the other began it was impossible to tell.

'They're using napalm!' he exclaimed. 'They could burn the entire island down that way!'

Irini urged him to be calm. 'It might not be true. Sometimes it doesn't help to talk that way,' she said.

Christos' absence cast a huge shadow over their lives, bringing the dread that hung over the fate of Cyprus into their home, into their own souls.

Meanwhile Turkish soldiers were making relentless progress; Cypriots from both communities looked on with fear as they saw well-drilled soldiers marching southwards.

In the chaos and terror following the invasion, waves of people, both Greek and Turkish, began to flee from their homes, taking with them only basic necessities. Many buried money and valuables in their gardens before they left. Thousands sought refuge in the military bases retained by Britain after independence.

Tourists had much more to worry about now. The island's main airport had been bombed, and those still in Famagusta began to hear about the hundreds of people trapped in the Ledra Palace Hotel in Nicosia. Thousands of holidaymakers had already left after the coup against Makarios, but the invasion sent the rest of them into a blind panic.

Chapter Sixteen

When Hüseyin wandered down to the beach very early the following morning, he knew there was no point in unstacking the sunbeds. In spite of the news that the Turks had agreed on a ceasefire, the area in front of The Sunrise was deserted. Or almost.

There was one person in the otherwise empty landscape. It was Frau Bruchmeyer taking her usual early morning swim. The water was particularly still and flat that day, and he could see her effortlessly lapping her way across its glassy surface.

Eventually she stood and waded the last few yards on to the beach, where she picked up her towel. It was like any other morning.

'*Günaydın,*' said Frau Bruchmeyer. 'Good morning.'

Every time she greeted him, Hüseyin was touched by the fact that she had learned a little of his language.

'*Günaydın,*' he replied.

He sat on the sand and gazed out at the view. Close by, he knew that thousands of Turkish Cypriots were effectively trapped within the walled city. He wondered whether Ali was somewhere in that vicinity or if he had gone further afield. Everything seemed so calm, perhaps more peaceful than ever with the lack of traffic and absence of people. He lay on his back to gaze up at the sky and closed his eyes. The gentle lapping of water on the sand lulled him and he began to doze.

His slumber was short-lived. A low roaring sound stirred him, and as he opened his eyes, a huge shadow passed right overhead. The plane was low enough for him almost to see the pilot. Its markings told him that it was a Turkish fighter. Hüseyin stood up. A moment later there was a loud crack. With complete disbelief, he saw the side of a nearby hotel collapse. A sandcastle would not have crumbled so swiftly.

The ceasefire agreement had been violated after only a few hours. The Turks were still carrying out air attacks. Famagusta itself had become their target.

Savvas was in his office at the building site, calculating how much the disruption to the construction work had already cost him, when the bomb tore apart the ten-storey tower close by. It was much nearer to The New Paradise Beach than to The Sunrise, and the mighty *boom* was a thousand times louder than the most powerful lightning strike he had ever heard. When he ran outside and on to the beach, he could see the flames glowing inside the building from the ground floor to the roof. Most of the windows had been blown out in the explosion.

People had emerged from their homes and a few from cafés and shops. Like Savvas, they could not believe their eyes. This simply could not be happening.

The Turkish aircraft had passed over, but nevertheless the danger was still present, and after a few minutes everyone came to their senses. It was quite possible that the planes would return. Having scored a direct hit, they might be encouraged.

Savvas needed to get to The Sunrise. He returned to lock up his office and hastened on foot along the beach. It seemed unlikely that the Turks would drop bombs into the sea, so it felt the safest route.

Usually at this time the foyer was busy. A row of four men would be standing behind the reception desk, uniformed porters would be waiting to ferry luggage and a doorman would be alert to arrivals. Several maids would be dusting the leaves of the enormous pot plants. There would be a steady flow of people coming and going, and outside, to the right of the main entrance, the terrace bar would be full, its elegant striped awning protecting clients from the sun.

Today, there was only one person in the entire space. Costas Frangos was behind the desk, scanning the huge ledger that recorded the names of guests. He looked up to acknowledge Savvas.

'I think we're empty,' he said. 'As far as I can be sure, all the guests are gone.'

'Were all the payments settled?'

'Not all of them.'

'You mean . . . ?'

'The only thing people were interested in was getting out of here.'

'Didn't you give them their bills?'

'Kyrie Papacosta, it was chaos here. I had them all prepared, but everyone just wanted to leave.'

'They were checking out, though, weren't they?'

Savvas folded his arms while he waited for an answer. It was enough to express his dissatisfaction.

'Some of them just threw their keys on to the desk and left. One of the chambermaids told me there are things left in almost every room. I am sure people will be back to collect them and pay what they owe.'

Frangos shut the ledger, hung two room keys on the hooks behind him, lifted the flap of the reception desk and came out into the foyer.

Markos appeared. He looked calm enough. For a few hours he had helped organise the departure of the guests.

'Everyone has gone,' stated Savvas, with utter dismay.

'Not quite,' said Markos. 'Frau Bruchmeyer is still here. I've put her down in the nightclub. It's below ground, so she is safe enough there.'

'She didn't want to leave?'

'No. She has no intention of doing so.'

'Well, this place was built to last,' said Savvas proudly. 'It'll take more than a Turkish bomb to bring it down.'

'I hope you're right . . .'

'My wife,' said Savvas, as an afterthought. 'Have you seen her?'

'No, not today,' Markos replied honestly.

Before leaving, Savvas had another word with Costas Frangos.

'Can you make sure we keep a skeleton staff? I think we should assume that it will only be a matter of time before this is over — and I don't want to find we haven't got the manpower to reopen.'

'But so many have gone to fight . . .'

Before Frangos had finished his sentence, Savvas had turned away and marched out of the hotel.

He retraced his steps along the beach to his office. The phones were not working again, so he quickly drove home so that he could tell his wife what was happening.

Inside the apartment, Aphroditi had listened to the radio and heard news of the ceasefire. The roar of the air-conditioning meant she had been oblivious to the latest developments.

In her hand was the pearl. She played with it in her fingertips and rolled it in her palm, admiring its small beauty. From time to time she glanced out of the window and observed how the buildings down the street seemed to shimmer. The afternoon heat was searing, melting the tarmac, almost bending street signs, and most people would be indoors now trying to escape it.

She looked up into the mirror and gazed at her own reflection. She had idled away almost an entire morning, and though her hair was a little ill-kempt, her eyes had been accentuated with liner.

Inside her apartment and completely buried in her own thoughts, she heard neither the rumble of low-flying aircraft passing over the building nor the sound of the front door opening and shutting. Even a man's voice shouting out her name failed to rouse her.

It was only when she caught sight of a movement in the dressing-table mirror that she turned around. Her hand closed around the pearl.

'Aphroditi!'

'What's happened, Savvas?'

'Didn't you *hear*? Are you *deaf*?' There was unmistakable annoyance in her husband's voice. 'You mean you weren't aware of the *explosion*?'

'No! Where? What's happened?'

'Turkish planes. They're bombing Famagusta!'

Aphroditi stood up to face her husband.

'We need to go to The Sunrise. Even if it gets hit, we'll be safe in the basement.'

Aphroditi furtively opened a drawer to replace the pearl, then grabbed her bag and followed Savvas out.

The streets were empty of traffic, so within a few minutes they were at the hotel. Just before they went inside, they heard a series of deafening bangs. This time the target was a hotel that was being used by the National Guard to attack the old walled city, an area of Famagusta that continued to be held by the Turkish Cypriots.

'Go downstairs,' ordered Savvas.

The last time she had been in the Clair de Lune already seemed an age ago. There was only one thing that mattered. Would Markos be there? She went down the semi-lit staircase and opened the door. The place looked tawdry with all the lighting turned up and the purple velvet seemed sleazy rather than glamorous.

Sitting alone on a banquette by the stage was Frau Bruchmeyer. The elderly woman looked up and smiled.

'Frau Bruchmeyer! What a lovely surprise!' said Aphroditi.

At the same moment Markos appeared through the other door.

'Ladies!' he said. 'My two favourite ladies! All to myself!'

Aphroditi sat down. Her heart was pounding. What she felt lay between pleasure and pain.

'Markos.' Even to say his name made her spine tingle.

'So, what can I get you to drink? They're on the house.'

His light-heartedness was inappropriate given the events happening beyond the walls of this room, and yet both women were delighted by it. What could any of them do? Everything going on outside was entirely out of their control.

The three of them drank whisky, clinking glasses before they took the first sip.

'*Stin yeia sou!*' said Markos, holding Aphroditi's eyes with his own, before turning to Frau Bruchmeyer to do the same.

'*Stin yeia sou!*' he repeated.

'I have something in my handbag,' said Frau Bruchmeyer. 'They might come in handy if we're here for long.'

She produced a pack of cards, and when Markos left, the two

women began to play. Time had no meaning in a room without windows. Perhaps the sun had set and risen again.

Every so often Markos returned, bringing dishes of food from the kitchen. One chef remained there on duty, obliged by the terms of his contract, which did not allow provision for an airstrike, and the fridges were still well stocked with enough fresh ingredients to feed a thousand people.

There was a sound system in the nightclub, and Markos put some records on for them. Over the next few days they worked their way through hours of jazz and blues, plenty of Ella Fitzgerald, Billie Holiday and Ray Charles, all Clair de Lune favourites. For Frau Bruchmeyer, Markos played the complete works of Frank Sinatra.

'If there was ever a man I would marry . . .' she said, her eyes sparkling, 'it would be old *blau ice.*'

Aphroditi giggled at the pronunciation.

'Blue eyes,' she repeated, in her perfect English. The whisky helped their good humour, and as the hours, and then days, went by, they felt less and less connected with the world. They were free to leave their purple prison, but there was nowhere safer to go, and nowhere else they wished to be.

Markos continually came and went from the Clair de Lune, usually taking a package from the safe. Between times, he would go home and spend time with his parents. The outskirts of town were safe enough.

The women always asked him for any news of what was happening outside, and his response remained cheerful.

'It's quiet at the moment, but you're safer down here for the time being.'

When Markos was in the room with them, nothing taking place outside it really mattered to Aphroditi. He flirted with Frau Bruchmeyer in such a way that her eyes sparkled more gaily than her diamonds, but Aphroditi was sure that the smiles he gave her were different. Whenever he could, he touched her hand or arm, casually, fleetingly, but never accidentally.

Together, in this space meant for night-time, she felt the irresponsible pleasure of being removed from the world. There was nothing she could do to affect the actions of soldiers or politicians, and she believed that her moments of intimacy with Markos bound her more tightly to him than anything that had gone before.

Markos had always left before Savvas arrived at the Clair de Lune to sleep.

When he came, he immediately stretched himself out on one of the banquettes and the music had to be turned off. For several hours the women had to keep silent. Savvas' nerves were frayed, his mood dark. During the past few days the Turks had destroyed several more hotels.

In spite of everything, Savvas wanted to believe that this was a hiatus, after which business would continue as usual. Meanwhile, he was feeling angry and frustrated that the days were passing without a solution. The current crisis *had* to be resolved by the politicians. There was too much at stake for everyone. It was July, the peak of the season, and in business terms it was a disaster that The Sunrise was empty and the opening of The New Paradise Beach might be delayed.

Its exterior was nearing completion. All the windows were now in place. They reflected the sky like a mirror, and when the sun rose, it was as if the whole building was on fire. The futuristic design was coming to life, and Savvas was confident it would take Famagusta into a new era.

The huge gleaming tower was an easy target for Turkish planes. Early one morning, they neatly dropped several bombs on to the roof. Moments later they exploded, blasting a huge space through the centre of the building and shattering every window. A fire ripped through the ruins. By the time Savvas reached the site, it looked as if both skin and flesh had been stripped off a body and only the skeleton remained, twisted and charred.

The ghostly figure of Savvas appeared back at the Clair de Lune that afternoon, his face and hair white with dust.

'It's a catastrophe . . .' he whispered to Aphroditi. 'Everything. Everything I've been working for.'

Aphroditi had never seen a man cry. Even when her brother died, her father's tears were wept in private.

This was a different kind of grief. It was fuelled by anger.

She tried to comfort him, but the words sounded hollow.

'We can rebuild it, Savvas . . .'

'You wouldn't say that if you had seen what's happened up there!' he shouted. 'We're finished! *Ruined!*'

Chapter Seventeen

While Savvas' attention was entirely focused on his own patch of the city, Markos brought news that stretched well beyond Famagusta. In Athens, the debacle caused by the Greek-backed military coup in Cyprus had triggered the collapse of the junta itself. After seven years of military dictatorship, democracy was restored. In Greece, this meant the return from exile of former prime minister Constantine Karamanlis. In Cyprus, Sampson had resigned when the Turkish army invaded, and a new president, Glafkos Clerides, was sworn in.

For the new government in Athens, Cyprus remained at the top of the agenda.

'So,' explained Markos to Frau Bruchmeyer, 'the parties responsible for protecting this republic, Britain, Turkey and Greece, are going to sit round a table and talk.'

'An *independent* republic that has the interference of all those outsiders?' exclaimed the German. 'It's ridiculous.'

'As long as it helps get rid of the Turks and brings some kind of peace, does it matter?' interjected Aphroditi.

'And perhaps some *real* independence,' added Frau Bruchmeyer.

'You don't want all these foreigners constantly meddling in your affairs.'

After a few days of sheltering beneath the ground, it finally seemed safe enough to come up again. They climbed the stairs and emerged into dazzling sunshine, feeling grubby and bedraggled.

Everything looked the same. The Sunrise was completely unscathed; the palm trees still stood like sentries at the entrance.

Both women went into the foyer. Savvas had insisted that the dolphins should continue to spout, and the sound of running water cheered the otherwise still and silent space.

Frau Bruchmeyer went over to the lift.

'I shall take a shower,' she said. 'And hope to see you later.'

Aphroditi walked towards the terrace bar, took off her shoes and went on to the beach, from where she could see the line of hotels stretching both south and north of The Sunrise. Many of them had been hit. She could see a gaping hole in the side of one, balconies hanging lopsidedly from another, and some that leaned at dangerous angles. She caught sight of the wreck of The New Paradise Beach. The absence of people on the sand and in the sea was eerie enough. With the damaged buildings as a backdrop, it was an apocalyptic scene.

She stood with her back to the sea and looked up at The Sunrise. Everything was aligned, symmetrical, intact, just as it had been the day the hotel was finished.

At about the same time, Markos was driving his Cortina out of the car park. His boot was loaded up with packages. Christos had still not come home, but Haralambos had rung a few days earlier to ask him to deliver some of the packages to the garage. There was no longer such danger in possessing them, given that EOKA B and the National Guard were both on the winning side of the coup and Makarios' men were now defeated. With the

Turkish army still on the march, Haralambos had wanted their unit to be armed.

When he had dropped everything off, Markos returned home. His mother was sitting at the table in the *kipos*, exactly where he had left her that morning. In the meantime, she had gone briefly to church to light candles and to pray that Agia Irini would bring the peace that her name implied – but more importantly the return of her younger son.

There was a freshly made cake on the table.

Irini was keeping her hands busy making lace. It was something Markos had watched her doing his whole life. She looked up at him. She did not need to ask anything.

'The other boys in the garage haven't heard from him yet. And Haralambos is away too.'

'You mean they're missing?'

'*Mamma*,' Markos said, putting his hand on hers, 'they're just away. Not missing. They're probably on some kind of exercise.'

Even Markos was concerned now, and his mother could sense it.

'*Leventi mou*, what are we going to do?'

'There is nothing we can do. We just have to wait and try to be patient,' he answered, more like a father to his daughter than a son to his mother.

Irini Georgiou crossed herself many times.

'It's your saint's day!' Markos exclaimed suddenly, noticing the cake. '*Hronia Polla!*' He hugged his mother. 'I'm so sorry, I forgot!'

'Don't worry, *leventi mou*. We've all got *so* much on our minds . . .'

There was a moment's pause.

'Emine. She brought it round.'

At that moment Maria appeared with little Vasilakis, who was just over one year old now. The four of them ate large, sticky slices, the thick syrup running down their chins in the sunshine. Vasilakis giggled as he licked his fingers one by one.

'*Ena, thio, tria, tessera,*' his mother counted. 'One, two, three, four.' The small child clumsily tried to repeat the sounds after her, his little brow creased in concentration.

All their attention was focused on his efforts, and together they smiled, though not for a moment were they distracted from the weight of their anxieties.

It was quiet enough in Famagusta that day and the next, but elsewhere villages were still being captured by the Turkish army as it marched across the island. The National Guard continued to put up stiff resistance, but was being overwhelmed.

'There are fifty thousand of them and more coming in by the day,' Vasilis said to Markos.

'That's an exaggeration!' exclaimed Markos. 'You just make the situation worse when you say these things!'

According to the radio, the real figure was half that, but even as politicians and diplomats continued to talk, the numbers were increasing. Intensive talks were now taking place in Geneva between the foreign ministers of Turkey, Greece and Great Britain.

'How can anything be agreed while the Turks have all those troops on the island?' said Vasilis. 'It's not going to work, is it?'

Panikos was dutifully going to the electrical shop each day, and Maria was spending more time downstairs with her parents. Her pregnancy and the heat were exhausting her, and she needed help with Vasilakis.

'*Mamma*, we have to give some clothes for all those refugees,' she said. 'I just heard there was an appeal.'

The Sunrise

Thousands had already fled their homes in Kyrenia to escape from the invasion force. They had left with nothing.

During dinner the next evening, they listened to the latest news bulletin.

'A peace agreement has been reached,' said the announcer.

'You see!' cried Maria. 'Everything is going to be fine.'

'Shhhh, Maria!' said Vasilis. 'We need to listen.'

What they heard reassured them all. The Greek, Turkish and British foreign ministers had all signed. Though the Turkish forces would stay, their numbers would be reduced. Both sides pledged not to violate the terms of the peace agreement.

They sat in silence listening to the good news that the Turkish commander had withdrawn his demand for United Nations forces to leave Turkish-controlled areas. Meetings had been held with Clerides, the new president, as well as the Turkish Cypriot leader, Rauf Denktaş.

'So everything will go back to normal?' said Vasilis. 'Seems unlikely.'

'But it sounds as if a ceasefire has begun already,' said Panikos.

'Thank God for that,' whispered Maria.

For Irini it was all without meaning. If Christos was not there, she could not celebrate any kind of peace. She cleared the plates in silence, but her own food was untouched. As usual, she had laid a place for her younger son.

Close by, the Özkans were eating dinner too. They were relieved to hear news of another ceasefire.

'Perhaps it means that Ali will return,' Hüseyin said reassuringly to his mother.

'I do hope so,' she said, her words almost inaudible.

'And has there been any news on Christos?' her son asked.

'Still nothing, as far as I know,' she said. 'They're as worried sick as we are.'

'Maybe he'll be back now there's been an agreement,' Halit chipped in.

Emine regularly called on Irini, but had done so even more than usual in recent days. The women had been able to share their anxiety about their sons.

'Why do you insist on going so often?' said Halit, who felt that the two families should be keeping their distance.

'Because Irini is my friend!' said Emine firmly.

The days of sheltering in the nightclub had brought Aphroditi and Frau Bruchmeyer close. Although the atmosphere was far from normal in Famagusta, cafés still remained open, and the two of them went out together to pass the time.

'I think I will go back to Germany for a few weeks,' said Frau Bruchmeyer. 'Just until all this blows over.'

Aphroditi's face betrayed her disappointment. Their time together had been a welcome distraction from her constant desire to see Markos.

'Don't worry, dear,' added the elderly German. 'I won't stay away. There's no life like the life I lead here . . .'

The women finished their coffee and left.

The following morning, Aphroditi arrived early to see her friend off. Markos was at the hotel to ensure that transport had been properly organised. The trio stood together.

'Darlings,' said Frau Bruchmeyer, 'I will be counting the days until I am back here.'

They waved her off.

'Markos,' Aphroditi said under her breath, continuing to smile and wave, 'I have missed you so much.'

There were plenty of empty rooms now, but discreetly they

made their separate ways to the penthouse suite and made love as if for the first time.

A few days later, Emine was at the Georgiou home again. The optimism generated by the agreement had almost immediately begun to diminish. There was still much to be resolved, and a second set of talks in Geneva was anticipated.

'My dearest Irini,' Emine said tearfully, 'I feel as if I should apologise.'

'You? What for?'

'For what is happening,' responded Emine. 'How could Turkish soldiers behave in that way? They're shooting women and children now. And men are being taken off to camps.'

'The ceasefire didn't mean very much, did it?'

The women almost clung to each other. They did not always have much to say, but they knew the depth of their anxiety was the same, and this was comforting. They blamed their own sides for creating such chaos, never each other.

Rather than being reduced, Turkish forces and weaponry continued to build up.

Greek Cypriot villages in the mountains close to Kyrenia were attacked and captured, and thousands were still fleeing shells and mortar fire. Larnaca on the south coast became a target too. In spite of the ceasefire agreement, the Turkish troops were making gradual but relentless progress southwards.

As the women talked, there was the dull crump of mortar fire in the distance. Fighting continued on the edge of Famagusta, where thousands of Turkish Cypriots were still under siege, cut off within the old walls. The port remained closed.

Irini was ever hopeful that Makarios would return to save the situation. They had heard that their ousted president was now in Britain.

'He says he wants to see both Greek and Turkish Cypriots living peacefully,' she said.

'But we need to get rid of all those outsiders first,' said Emine. 'While they're still here killing people, that'll never happen.'

Talk of the rape and slaughter of Greek Cypriots behind Turkish lines was now widespread, but at the same time Turkish Cypriots accused Greek Cypriots of murder and looting. Accusations and counter-accusations flew, of violations of human rights and indiscriminate acts of violence. Both sides were holding groups of hostages, and men, women and children from both communities were in flight. Despite the agreement, the island was not at peace.

Older people on both sides began to talk of a similar population exchange that had taken place once before. In 1923, Greeks and Turks in Asia Minor had been forced to pick up their belongings and leave their homes, passing each other on the road as they travelled from east to west and west to east. This time Greek Cypriots and Turkish Cypriots were fleeing and, just as then, communities that had lived in harmony were wrenched apart, the balance of trust on which their lives had been based now destroyed.

Greek Cypriots captured by the army had been taken to Adana in Turkey. Many others had been killed, and families missing their men were desperate for news. The names of those in Adana were to be published, with a promise that they would soon be released. Irini had convinced herself that Christos' name would be among them.

'At least I'll know where he is,' she said. 'Then we'll get him back.'

There were nearly four hundred being held. When Christos' name was not on the list, Irini wept, her hopes dashed. The rest of the family were feeling his absence keenly too.

Meanwhile talks continued in Geneva, with Turkey now demanding separate cantons on the island for the Turkish Cypriots. New demarcation lines in Nicosia were agreed, and both sides were ordered to adhere to the ceasefire.

'Do they really think they can solve this?' slurred Vasilis. 'And come up with an idea about how we can all live together? From thousands of miles away?' He was drunk and belligerent.

'Isn't it better that they keep trying?' asked Maria. 'And keep talking?'

'If they agree on something, who's going to make it work?' he continued, directing his questions at his son. For Vasilis, this was men's talk.

'Markos, what do you think is going to happen?' Irini asked, wringing her hands. 'And *when* do you think we'll get Christos back?'

She relied on her elder son for insight. He was more connected with the outside world. In spite of the hotel and nightclub being closed, he seemed to have plenty of business to attend to and was out a great deal.

'I really don't know, *Mamma*, but I do have faith in the big powers to sort things out for us.'

For the sake of his mother's nerves, he made little of the threat hanging over them all. With general mobilisation in Greece and a large force moving towards the border with Turkey, the possibility of an all-out conflict between the two countries continued to be a real danger.

'Try not to worry too much,' he said. 'I'm sure everything will be fine.'

He gave his mother a peck on the cheek and left.

The casual gesture almost reassured her. She so desperately wanted to believe him.

Chapter Eighteen

Vasilis, ever pessimistic, turned out to be right. Turkey maintained its demand for separate cantons for the Turkish Cypriots and issued an ultimatum. Greece had twenty-four hours to accept the proposal and they would not wait for a decision. Peace talks broke down irretrievably.

Turkish troops were on standby across Cyprus and, before dawn on 14 August, they were issued with new orders to advance. Tanks began to move towards Famagusta. They were slow but sinister, and any remaining sense of security vanished. Their progress was relentless.

'We have the National Guard to protect us, don't we?' said Maria, pale and full of fear.

'I'm not so sure how they'll hold out against the tanks,' answered Vasilis.

'Tanks . . . ?' said Maria quietly, holding the little one tightly to her side.

Vasilis and Irini had been listening to the latest news bulletin when their daughter came in.

It was as if the sudden burst of artillery in the distance had disturbed her unborn child. She felt the baby stir in her belly.

She still had two months to go, but she felt so heavy. It was not like the previous time. This was not a kick, but something stronger.

Irini noticed her react to the pain.

'Come and sit down, *kori mou*,' she said.

For a brief period, fear paralysed the people of Famagusta. It was like a drawing-in of breath, a collective gasp of shock and disbelief that this could be happening to them and to their city.

Less than a month before, in this sophisticated and wealthy resort, people had cruised about in their sports cars, flaunted the latest fashions, studied in the best schools on the island, managed lucrative businesses, put on plays, listened to world-class bands, eaten continental cuisine, enjoyed Sunday outings to Salamis, taken part in pageants and parades, baptised their children, attended grand weddings, flirted and made love until the sun rose.

It already seemed a century ago.

For weeks they had lived with the possibility of invasion, but never imagined it would actually happen. Now they faced a new reality. Everything they knew and had taken for granted was threatened.

Amongst a handful who did not want to acknowledge this fact was Savvas Papacosta. He stubbornly refused to concede that they were in danger. The Sunrise still stood, undamaged and gleaming in the sunshine. It had been built to last, with no corners cut and no expense spared. He believed it would be standing for millennia, long after the others fell, watching over the rising sun like a temple to Apollo.

Now that the building site was a wreck, he was back in his office at The Sunrise every day.

'They'll start talks again,' he maintained to Markos that morning. 'They're still just trying to get their way about the cantons. It's brinkmanship, that's all.'

'I wish I agreed with you,' responded Markos. 'But I'm not sure they're planning to stop. You know about the line?'

'What line?'

'They're making a line – a division – all the way across Cyprus. Apparently it even has a name. Attila.'

Savvas was adamant in his refusal to believe this.

'They won't do it! The Americans and British won't let them!'

Markos did not want to argue with his boss. There was no purpose. Savvas was not always right, but he allowed him to think he was.

'Other people can believe whatever they like. I'm going to give it a bit more time.'

As the Turks continued their slow but inexorable approach, their intentions became ever clearer. Markos' information was correct. They were aiming to close up the line stretching from east to west. In the west, they had their sights set on Morphou. In the east, the seizure of Famagusta was their goal. Orders from the United Nations to stop the advance were ignored. Nicosia was gradually being cut off.

For some, there was an instinct to fight, but it was too late. The suburbs were quickly captured. There was still fighting around the port and bombardment from Turkish warships. Flight was the only option. The people of Famagusta were outmanoeuvred, outnumbered, outgunned. Nobody had come to their rescue. Not even Greece had stepped in to save them.

Once the reality sank in, silence was replaced by terror. And by panic. Where should they go? What should they take?

That night the National Guard realised there was no hope of saving the city, and even nearby United Nations troops seemed impotent. Everywhere, a common cry was heard:

'The Turks are coming! The Turks are coming!'

With this terrifying truth echoing round the streets, forty thousand people looked around their homes and in a moment knew what mattered most. Some picked up icons, some pots, some blankets, some a precious clock, some nothing at all. Some just picked up the irreplaceable: their children. There was no time for vacillation. If they dithered over trivial decisions, all might be lost.

Plumes of black smoke rose from the seafront and the port area as air attacks continued.

Savvas was still at The Sunrise when a powerful bomb landed down the street. The chandelier in the reception area shuddered, the tiny pieces of crystal continuing to jangle for a few minutes afterwards.

'Kyrie Papacosta,' said Costas Frangos, his voice trembling, 'I'm going. Every guest has left now. The staff too.'

He shut the ledger, lifted the flap of the reception desk and came out into the foyer.

'My family will be waiting for me. I want to get them out of here.'

Normally Frangos was a model of subservience, but now he knew he must stand his ground. All he cared about was finding safety for his wife and children. Rumours of the city being overrun were growing by the moment, and even if his boss was behaving as if there was all the time in the world, Frangos had had enough.

Another plane passed low overhead. It was loud enough for them to hear the sound of its engine in spite of the doors being closed. Whether it was Turkish or, as both of them hoped, Greek, anxiety registered on their faces.

'I think you should leave too, Kyrie Papacosta. Nobody thinks it's going to be for long.'

'Yes, you're right. Everyone is expecting intervention; in a few days everything will be back to normal. I'm certain of that.'

Frangos turned his back on Savvas and marched out. He didn't know if he would lose his job, but minute by minute he had begun to realise that his own life and the lives of his wife and children were in danger. His loyalty towards Savvas Papacosta had been pushed too close to the limit.

The glass door shut with a clunk.

Savvas stood there alone. He did not fear for his own life. He merely felt anguish at the emptiness of his hotel. It felt as if there was a void where his heart should be.

Aphroditi was on the balcony when she saw Savvas pull up outside and dash into their apartment building.

In the street below, although it was a quiet residential area and at this time most people would normally have been sleeping, the pavements were full. Looking down to the left, she caught a glimpse of the sea. The sun was dazzling but she could see a continuous stream of traffic on the esplanade. It was all going in one direction: out of the city.

Five floors up, where sometimes there was a slight sea breeze, the air was still. This intensified the fragrance of the jasmine that had been trained along the wall of the terrace, carefully clipped and watered by a gardener who visited three times a week. She buried her face in its froth of white blooms and absent-mindedly picked a sprig.

She had watched people leaving other apartment blocks close by, heard the sound of bombardment and been gripped by fear. Phone lines had ceased to function.

She ran to open the front door for Savvas.

'We have to get out,' he said.

Aphroditi's throat dried.

'I'll pack a few things,' she said quietly, fingering the stone of her pendant.

'There's no time. The only thing we need to think about is your jewellery. We can't leave it here and we shouldn't take it with us.'

'So . . . ?'

'Just get it all and we'll store it in the vault. Markos is waiting there for us.'

Savvas rummaged in his desk for a few moments, retrieving some papers, then went to the door.

'I'll see you downstairs,' he said.

Aphroditi set to work gathering her jewellery.

Each of the drawers of the dressing table — there were five on each side — had a separate key. It was a piece of furniture that had been specially made and was essentially a giant lockable jewellery box, but not one strong enough to withstand someone with real intent to thieve.

She retrieved the ten keys from inside a book whose pages had been cut out to form a box, and unlocked each side. Most pieces were in soft pouches or in their original packaging. As fast as she could, with shaking hands, she cleared each drawer, starting with the lowest and working up. There were a dozen or so small boxes or pouches in each space, and she used both hands, picking up two items at a time and dropping them into a beach bag. If there had ever been any sentimental value attached to the contents, she had forgotten it now. Within three minutes, the dressing table was empty, except for the top left-hand drawer. There was still something inside.

She reached to the back to find the green velvet pouch inside which was her tiny pearl. For Aphroditi it was more precious than anything that now lay in the bulging canvas bag at her feet. She took an embroidered purse from a handbag on the dressing table, put the pouch inside and snapped it shut.

Below the balcony she heard the frantic sound of a car horn. She knew without looking that it was Savvas.

On her way to the front door, she dashed into the bathroom and grabbed a towel to put on top of the jewellery.

In the lift, she caught sight of herself in the smoky mirror, in high-heeled sandals and a new dress. The sense of imminent danger was strong, but nevertheless she used the time it took to descend to the hallway to reapply her lipstick.

As she pushed open the door, once again in the full blast of the day's infernal heat, she could see Savvas, his hand pumping on the steering wheel. He was shouting out of the driver's window.

'Aphroditi! Come on! Come *on*! Come ON!'

Without speaking, she got in, struggling with the heavy bag. She hoisted it on to her lap and put her arms around it to keep it stable. It was too bulky to go on the floor in front of her.

Savvas had left the engine running, and the moment her door closed, he took off at speed.

'What the hell were you doing?'

Aphroditi stubbornly ignored her husband's question.

'I've been sitting here for *five* minutes, for God's sake!'

He continued muttering and complaining as they took the road that led down to the sea.

'Christ! The traffic looks bad already. If you'd been ready a bit faster . . . Markos is expecting us at least.'

As they got closer to the hotel, their exit on to the main road was blocked with traffic. He had seen this from the moment he set off, but nevertheless he slammed on the brakes as if it was a surprise.

'You couldn't sort yourself out any faster?' he said, with ill-disguised sarcasm. 'Not even today?'

Aphroditi had learned to receive blame and equally had learned not to respond. It only provoked argument.

They waited a few moments to turn left out of their street. Nobody was prepared to give way, but within a few minutes, Savvas had forced his car into the flow of traffic.

They crawled along, Savvas thumping the wheel each time he had to brake and cursing continuously under his breath. Aphroditi could feel the sweat breaking out underneath her clothes, trickles running down her arms and legs. Anxiety, stress, the heat of the day, any one of these was enough of a cause, but the real reason was her excitement. Very soon she would be seeing Markos. It seemed as if so much time had passed and she had thought of him a thousand times a day.

Ten minutes later (it would have taken less time to walk), they reached The Sunrise.

Usually there would be two uniformed doormen to greet them. This time, only one man stood waiting. He was not in uniform, but in slacks and a white shirt. He leaned down to speak to Savvas.

'Kyrie Papacosta, I have made some space for you.'

'Thanks, Markos. Be as quick as you can, Aphroditi. I'm just going to do a final check of the hotel.'

As if he imagined that she might miss the sound of his voice for a moment, he felt the need to add another comment.

'Honestly, you could have changed out of those shoes.' He gestured down towards her feet.

Markos had moved round to open the passenger door.

'*Kalispera*, Kyria Papacosta. Let me help you.'

Aphroditi did not look at him, but handed him the bag before getting out of the car and following him sedately through the door of the nightclub. It was true that the height of her heels did not allow her to hurry.

The door shut behind them.

Once in the cool and the half-light of the nightclub foyer, the formality between them disappeared.

'Markos . . . !'

She followed him down the stairs and along the corridor to the metal door of the vault. Markos drew a key from his pocket and turned it in the lock.

Aphroditi shivered. Inside, it was cooler than a refrigerator and the lighting was dim.

He turned, locked the door behind them and touched her lightly under the chin.

'You look beautiful,' he said.

She automatically lifted her head and looked at him; she expected him to kiss her but saw immediately that this was not his wish.

He took her hand and held it loosely. With the other he twisted the dials on one of the safes. The combination was complex but eventually the door swung open. The space inside was empty, and Aphroditi stepped forward and began to unpack the bag that was now sitting on the floor. She tossed in the items, haphazardly jumbling the pouches and boxes in no particular order just to get the job finished.

'Not like that, *agapi mou*,' advised Markos. 'It won't all fit in that way.'

Aphroditi stepped aside as Markos rearranged everything, picking up four or five items at a time and lining them up in neat rows. He was practised at this task.

'We have so little time . . .' she said.

'Pass things to me two at a time, then.'

Aphroditi dutifully acted as Markos' handmaid. In a few minutes the job was done and he stood back to admire it.

'You see? It all fits now,' he said, slamming the door shut, rotating the dials and double-locking the safe with a key.

He turned to face her.

'But what about these?' he said, lifting her pendant and then touching her ears. 'And these?' He raised the hand on which she wore her ring and bracelet and put it to his lips, all the while holding her infatuated gaze with his own.

'Markos . . .'

'Yes?' he answered; this time he embraced her.

Whatever she had planned to say was forgotten. There was nothing in her mind now but the sensation of his lips on hers and his fingers resting gently on her neck.

Meanwhile, having left the engine running, Savvas was inside the hotel, alone in the pantheon of leisure that he had built almost with his bare hands. He glanced up at the rows of numbered hooks behind the reception desk. All five hundred keys were lined up perfectly in place.

In all the months since the opening, there had never been a need to lock up. Today, with a huge bunch of keys in his hand, Savvas went at a run to the various back and side entrances and then to the kitchen, his footsteps echoing around the corridors. Twice he stopped and called out, thinking that the footsteps belonged to someone other than himself, but it was he alone that remained.

His staff, even if they had evacuated earlier than he felt they should have, had at least been diligent. Most doors were already secured. Back in the foyer, he reached over the reception desk and switched off the mechanism for the fountain. The sound of gushing water was silenced for the first time in two years.

Then he turned around and surveyed his magnificent foyer to make sure that all was in place. There was a steady drip-drip-drip from the mouth of one of the gilded dolphins, but apart from that, total silence. The hands of the large electric clocks behind reception continued to turn: Athens, London, New York, Hong Kong, Tokyo. According to the papers, eyes in those distant cities were focused on the events happening on his island, but at this moment those places had never seemed more remote.

On the fob were the master keys for the hotel's main door and the metal grid to protect it. It was the first time they had ever been used. In an establishment that never closed, there had been no need. Having made everything secure, he stepped out into the heat of the afternoon and double-locked the door behind him.

His car engine was still running, but Aphroditi was nowhere to be seen.

During the time he had been inside the hotel, the traffic had built up even further and the pavement was now full of people, all of them carrying bundles or suitcases. Some of the pedestrians stood in front of vehicles to ask for a lift. Something on the edge of panic was beginning to set in.

He strode towards the nightclub, but as he reached it, he saw his wife on the other side of the glass door. Markos was just behind her.

'Aphroditi, can you get in the car, please,' he said sternly. 'And Markos, can we have a word?

'We're going to the apartment in Nicosia,' he told the nightclub manager. 'Is everything locked away?'

'Kyria Papacosta's jewellery is safe,' responded Markos.

'Get away as soon as you can, then. But double-check all the doors before you leave. And can you deal with the locks for the main gates and make sure the fire exits are definitely secure,' he added without pausing for breath. 'And bring Aphroditi's car to Nicosia when you come. I'd rather it was there than here.'

'Okay,' said Markos. 'Mine's empty so I probably will.'

'You know my number in Nicosia; call me when you get there,' said Savvas, touching him on the arm. 'And don't hang around here too long.'

In the car, Aphroditi pulled the rear-view mirror towards her. She could see the two men talking. Savvas was smoking, agitated. Markos looked calm. She saw him run his fingers through his hair and felt a familiar sense of love and desperation. Even in this crisis he looked in command. She noticed how close the two men stood, and she saw Savvas hand Markos his entire collection of keys. He trusted Markos like a brother.

She watched Savvas turn away and walk towards the car. A moment later he was beside her, pulling out of the hotel forecourt and through the gates. Aphroditi took a last glance back. Markos had already vanished.

'I've told him to meet us with the keys as soon as he can,' said Savvas.

His wife looked out of the window to hide her sense of relief that it might not be long until she saw Markos once again.

For a while after that Savvas said nothing more. His mind was elsewhere.

'God in heaven, I hope this traffic eases up once we are away from the city,' he said.

He waved a hand dismissively at a couple standing in the road trying to hitch a lift. They had a small suitcase between them.

'We could fit someone in the back, couldn't we?'

'I think we just want to concentrate on getting to Nicosia,' said Savvas.

His response quietened Aphroditi. There was no point in arguing.

Another plane flew low overhead. It seemed to follow the line of the road that would be taking them out of Famagusta. There was something distinctly menacing about this, as if it was observing them. Fear began to crawl over Aphroditi.

For ten minutes they both sat in silence, united in the need to contain their anxiety. Eventually Aphroditi spoke.

'How long is it going to take to get there?' she asked timidly.

'That's a stupid question, Aphroditi. Your guess is as good as mine.'

She said nothing more. Her anxiety was for herself, but it was for Markos too. She wondered how long it would be before she saw him again.

The heat in the car was building up, even with the cold fan on full blast and the windows firmly shut to keep the even hotter afternoon air outside.

For a few minutes they were stationary outside one of the biggest jewellery shops in the city. They knew the owner well; they were his best customers. The aquamarines, among many other pieces, had been bought from him.

They could see Giannis Papadopoulos carefully removing each tray from the window. His wife was behind him, meticulously stacking them up, but they still had dozens to go.

'They're mad!' exclaimed Aphroditi. 'Why don't they just put their shutters down and leave?'

'That shop contains everything they own!' retorted Savvas. 'You think they're going to risk losing it all?'

'But they're risking their *lives*, aren't they?'

As she was speaking, another plane passed overhead.

Savvas attempted to tune the car radio, but there was too much interference, and the sound of a human voice was almost inaudible through the crackling and hissing.

'Damn! I want to know what is *happening*!' he said, slamming his hand against the dial.

The noise was immediately silenced, but Savvas' anger had been fuelled all the more. He sighed and swore under his breath. Aphroditi noticed that his palms were dripping.

What they were seeing out of the car windows seemed unreal, as if they were watching images on a screen. For more than half an hour, their car moved at a slower pace than the pedestrians. People on foot were all making steady progress with their baggage, babies, even one or two with caged birds. It was like the relentless flow of a wide river. There was just one person whose stillness stood out against the backdrop of movement. A lone boy was poised on the pavement's edge, watching the vehicles, mesmerised.

'Savvas! Look! Look at that child!'

'There are lots of children,' snapped Savvas.

'He looks as if he is on his own!'

Savvas did not take his eyes off the truck in front, keeping nose to tail even though the other vehicle was belching out filthy fumes. His only aim was to carry on moving, inch by inch, and to make sure that nobody else pushed out in front of him from a side road.

As they drew parallel, Aphroditi found herself looking straight out of the window and meeting the boy's gaze. His small stature meant that they were eye to eye. She suddenly felt aware of how she must look to anyone who glanced inside their car. Chic, well made-up, still laden with heavy, expensive jewellery. The truth was that everyone was much too preoccupied with their own journey out of town. Except perhaps for this boy who looked her straight in the eye.

Aphroditi's strong maternal instincts would not allow her to ignore this apparently abandoned child.

'Can't we stop? Ask him if he needs some help?' she pleaded.
'Don't be *ridiculous*. There are plenty of people around.'
'But nobody's taking any notice of him!'

By now the car had moved forward and Aphroditi, craning to look out of the back window, watched the child until he disappeared from view.

Chapter Nineteen

Mehmet was still in the same spot a few moments later. Alone and gazing. He had already forgotten the lady with the light blue stones.

He had wandered out for a few moments when everyone else was distracted at home, to see what was happening, and had been mesmerised by the great tide of people and the flow of cars.

Hüseyin had been sent out to find Mehmet and spotted him as he turned into the main road. As he was sprinting towards him he heard the sound of an explosion.

'Mehmet!' he screamed. 'Come *here*.'

He picked his little brother up and ran to the house.

As soon as they were back, Mehmet received a sharp smack on the leg from his father. It made his eyes smart.

'Don't wander out again like that,' scolded Halit angrily. He and Emine had been frantic.

Emine hugged him, her own eyes wet from crying, and when she mopped his tears with her apron, Mehmet caught the smell of spice. Something very strange was happening, but this at least was familiar.

The Sunrise

A while later, Hüseyin went back down the street to check the situation. Five minutes later, he ran in again to tell his parents what he and Mehmet already knew.

'Everyone's leaving,' he shouted. '*Everyone!* We've got to get out of here.'

'No! We can't go without Ali!' Emine cried. 'He won't know where to find us.'

'Why would we run away from our own people!' said Halit.

'These are not our own people, Father. They're Turks.'

'But haven't they come to keep us safe?' snapped Halit.

'They're hardly going to kill *us,* are they, Hüseyin?' said Emine.

'How do you know that, Mother?' His voice rose with fear and anger. 'It's chaos out there. How will they know who is who? Have you *met* any Turkish soldiers?'

'Hüseyin!' Halit warned.

'You don't know them, Father. You don't know what they are like! You don't know what they'll do when they get here!'

Up until now, many people had defended Turkey's actions. They had believed that it was doing what was within its rights, to try and guarantee the independence of Cyprus. But now it seemed to have transgressed the boundaries. If Emine did not know the reputation of the Turkish soldiers, it was because she did not want to hear. Stories of murder were widespread. Reports of rape were legion.

'I'm more worried about the women in this city than the men,' said Hüseyin.

'Hüseyin! Don't say that kind of thing to your mother!'

'I am trying to save us. We need to get out of here.'

'Maybe he's right,' said Halit. 'Perhaps we shouldn't risk it.'

'But Halit!' pleaded Emine. 'Ali is just a *child*! When he comes back, he'll come back here. We would be abandoning him.'

Halit tried to persuade her, but she refused to even consider it. By now, she was almost hysterical.

'I won't go! I *won't*!'

She stormed out.

'We'll wait a while longer,' said Halit to Hüseyin. 'She'll come round.'

The hours passed, and as night fell, the tension grew.

Hüseyin stirred coffee inside a tiny pan. As the foam rose to the surface, he extinguished the heat beneath it and poured the dark liquid into two tiny cups.

At their small table, Halit smoked one Dunhill after another.

There was silence except for the rattle of the fridge; their *nazar*, the evil eye, seemed to watch over them from the wall. Mehmet sat, unnoticed, on the floor.

Eventually Emine returned, her face streaked with tears.

'If only we'd stopped him going,' she wept, sitting down at the table. 'Then we would all be together and we could leave.'

'It's not too late,' urged Hüseyin. 'Let's go now.'

The debate continued, only suppressed by the need to keep their voices low in case the soldiers were coming closer. Mehmet climbed on to his mother's lap and clapped his hands over his ears. For his entire, though short, life he had listened to quarrels rage within the family.

'*Gavvole!* God damn it!'

His father slammed his fist hard down on the table. One of the small cups bounced off and smashed into a dozen pieces on the stone floor. Everyone in the room froze.

Once more, Emine began to weep into her apron, trying to stifle her sobs.

'I can't believe this is happening again,' she moaned. 'I just can't believe it.'

Silently she picked up the pieces of the broken cup.

'If we carry on like this,' said Hüseyin, regretfully, 'there'll be no hope for any of us.'

Just down the road, most of the Georgiou family were gathered together in Irini and Vasilis' apartment. A low flame flickered before the icon of Agios Neophytos, creating strange distorted shadows on the ceiling. Windows and shutters were tightly closed and the room was airless. It was two in the morning.

On the table were some empty cups and a small glass of *zivania*.

Panikos paced up and down. Vasilis sat slumped in an armchair, running his fingers nervously through his worry beads, but their clacking sound was almost inaudible next to his daughter's panting.

Maria's hands rested on the table next to her father and Irini stroked her back rhythmically, repeating the same words and quietly comforting her: 'Softly now, softly now.' Her hands were clammy, wet from the sweat that had soaked through her daughter's dress from her neck to her waist.

From time to time Maria let out a deep moan as she gripped the edge of the table. Her knuckles whitened and tears of pain dropped on to the lace cloth.

In the corner, on the floor, sat Vasilakis. His head was buried deep in his hands, which were clamped over his ears, and his knees were held to his chest. Certain that it would make him invisible, he kept his eyes tightly closed.

The door opened just for a moment, and a shaft of moonlight fell across the wall, briefly illuminating the glass *mati,* the evil eye, that hung on the wall. Markos slipped into the room.

Irini looked up, her concentration momentarily distracted from her daughter.

'*Leventi mou!* You're still here!'

'Yes, *Mamma*, I'm still here. I wasn't going to abandon you.'

'But you could have left,' said Vasilis. 'Fled like everyone else . . .'

'Well I didn't,' said Markos. 'I'm here.'

He sauntered across to his mother and nonchalantly kissed her on the back of her head as though this was just a casual visit, a normal day.

Unlike everyone else in the room, he was feeling exhilarated. With Savvas gone, he had realised the potential of what he controlled. That morning, he had sold a gun from the safe. There were plenty of people desperate to own the means to protect themselves who were willing to pay anything it cost. And now the vault was filled with something even more valuable than weapons.

From the shadows came Panikos' voice.

'What's going on out there?'

'It seems quiet at the moment. Most people have gone.'

Maria, oblivious to anything but the spasms that gripped her body, let out a low howl, a sound immediately muffled by her mother's hand.

'Shhhh, my darling. Shhhhh.'

'Somehow you have to keep her from making any noise,' whispered Markos. 'Otherwise we're all in danger.'

'I think it's nearly her time,' said the older woman. '*Panagia mou!* Why now?'

Moments later, the heavy, rhythmic beat of boots was heard outside.

Chapter Twenty

THE FIFTEENTH OF August was an important date in the calendar. It was the Feast of the Assumption, the day of celebration for the Virgin Mary, one of the most significant days for the church and for thousands of women who bore her name. Maria would normally be celebrating.

This year it was different. As the final agonising pains of labour tore through her small frame, the Turks broke through the last defences in Famagusta. The remaining members of the Cyprus National Guard had fled. Linking up with Turkish fighters inside the walled area, the soldiers had walked unimpeded into an empty city.

In her parents' bedroom, Maria held her newborn daughter. Two months premature, the tiny baby suckled feebly. Panikos came in and stroked his wife's head.

During the last few hours, Maria had been aware of nothing but the shattering quakes of pain that racked her body. All the windows and shutters had been firmly closed to contain her screams, so the heat had built up.

She was exhausted now, and her eyes were shut. The world outside had ceased to exist.

As long as they remained silent, they might all be safe for a while. Now that the baby had been born, they were talking quietly about what should happen next. When could they leave? Or was it too late?

Markos had gone out again.

When he returned some hours later, Vasilis immediately demanded to know what was happening outside.

'Looting,' he said. 'Ransacking, robbing . . .'

'*Panagia mou* . . .'

His mother sat down. She rocked gently as she sat.

'We have to get out of here, Markos,' said Vasilis.

'Look, there's no question of going out in the streets now. We need to wait, keep as quiet as we can and see what happens.'

'What about food?' asked his mother timidly.

'When we run out, I will go and find some,' he said. 'Everyone has gone. It's just soldiers out there.'

'Turkish . . . ?' asked Irini in a whisper.

'Yes, *Mamma*, Turkish soldiers. They're just going into shops at the moment. But sooner or later they'll begin on the houses.'

'Come on,' said Vasilis decisively. 'Let's get some furniture up against the doors.'

For the first time, Irini wondered if Christos, wherever he might be, was in less danger than they were.

Savvas and Aphroditi had not reached their destination. Several hours into their journey, they had realised that they might have to change their plan. On the congested road out of Famagusta, they began to encounter heavy traffic coming the other way.

A similar exodus was also taking place from Nicosia as residents fled the capital city. People in the capital were familiar with conflict and fear, having lived with the line dividing their city for a decade, but this time many of them were getting out. Rockets had been fired at the Hilton, which was being used as a Red Cross hospital, and even the psychiatric hospital had been a target.

Soldiers at the roadside warned them that Nicosia was as dangerous as Famagusta, and Savvas had to face up to the fact that there was no question of going there.

Along with thousands of others, they were being diverted to the relative safety of the British base at Dhekelia, fifteen miles south-west of Famagusta. Cars were at a standstill now. Families walked between the vehicles; some people even wheeled bicycles laden with their possessions. This teeming mass of thousands was all making for the same destination.

Cars, buses, tractors, fruit lorries and mule-drawn carts passed the checkpoint into the base. Old and young, rich and poor were all in search of the same. Everyone had come to find sanctuary and most had the same dazed and fearful expression on their faces. Tens of thousands of them had abandoned everything they knew for the unknown, leaving their city empty for the taking. Once the National Guard had gone, there had been no other choice.

Aphroditi felt her body temperature plummet, her fear making her cold on a warm day. She was shivering, and her palms felt like ice. If they were not going to Nicosia, what chance did Markos have of finding her amidst all this chaos?

Within two days, nearly forty per cent of the island was under Turkish control. The Attila line that cut off the north from the south was as good as complete.

Inside the base at Dhekelia, conversation was universally bleak. Everyone, male or female, religious or agnostic, was reduced to the same. What they were now and what they had been only a few days before were immeasurably different. For now they were all stripped to nothing.

The Turkish soldiers had brought terror into their hearts. The trauma they had suffered manifested itself in many ways. Some were completely silent; others wept openly. On the first day following arrival in the base, many were numb. After that, there were the practicalities to be dealt with: where to sleep, how to find food, how to get medical attention for the sick. Latrines had to be dug, kitchens erected, and shelter allocated.

Many of them now looked to their religious faith for salvation.

'Only God, the Virgin and the saints can help us now,' a woman repeated over and over again while they were standing in the queue for food.

'What about America?' Savvas muttered audibly. 'Or Britain?'

'Savvas!' scolded Aphroditi, but the old woman was oblivious.

'Blind faith never helped anyone,' he snapped, 'but the Americans could have done.'

'Why not the Greeks?' interrupted another voice.

People were pressed up together in the queue, jostling so as not to lose their places.

'Because the odds are against them winning, that's why.'

'Greece got us into this mess,' said an irate woman close to Savvas, 'so they should get us out of it.'

Her view was a common one, but in their hearts they knew that Greece would already have come to their rescue if it was going to. The prime minister of the newly restored democracy there had inherited more than enough problems from the dictatorship, and taking Greece into a full-scale war with Turkey over Cyprus was something he could ill afford.

Makeshift churches evolved where people gathered to pray. Many were frantic over missing relatives, and their only comfort was to imagine that God would hear their prayers and safely reunite them. They had lost their homes, but this was a small loss compared with the separation from a son, a brother or a husband. The number of those missing was growing by the day.

'*Thee mou!*' was a common cry, uttered with despair. 'My God!'

Priests moved around among the crowds, comforting, praying, listening.

Men were often silent, despising themselves for not having stayed to fight the invader, but knowing it was too late for regrets.

'You *had* to run away!' insisted their wives. 'There was no choice! You had no weapons! Nothing to fight with!'

'And anyway, it's not for ever,' others said. 'We'll be going back.'

Only a few days before, Savvas and Aphroditi had had chambermaids and waiters to do their bidding. Now they had neither bed nor food. They were obliged to join the queues for bread and to sleep on the bare ground.

With a good percentage of Famagusta's population now inside the camp, the couple saw familiar faces. Members of their staff, workers from The New Paradise Beach building site, lawyers and accountants were all there. Nobody looked the same, however, reduced to this level of quiet desperation.

They found themselves almost neighbours with Costas Frangos, his wife and their children. For Savvas this meant someone with whom to exchange ideas and talk about the hotel.

'At least the keys are in safe hands,' he said to his manager. 'And I'm sure Markos will meet up with us in Nicosia.'

Savvas refused to give up his hopes for his Famagusta projects, even though his wife did not seem to care.

While Anna Frangos nursed her youngest through an attack of dysentery, an illness that was becoming more common as the days went by, Aphroditi found herself looking after the older children. It was a welcome distraction.

The Özkans spent the first forty-eight hours of their time in the deserted city inside their dark, shuttered home, still hoping that Ali would return to them.

To begin with, they talked. There was little else to do.

'If they hadn't tried to make us second-class citizens,' said Halit, 'this would never have happened.'

'But you can't blame all Greek Cypriots for that!' said Hüseyin.

'Aphroditi never made me feel that way,' said Emine.

'Well, enough of them did, otherwise we wouldn't be sitting here.'

'Only a few people used to persecute us, Halit,' said his wife. 'But that's how it often is.'

'So everyone is getting punished for the actions of a few?'

'Yes. Greek and Turkish Cypriots – we've all suffered.'

'Why do you always—' Halit Özkan's voice was rising. He found it hard to accept Emine's balanced views.

'Father! Shhhh!' implored Hüseyin.

From time to time they reached the point when they would argue. It was usually over the question of whether they needed to stay. Emine was still absolutely resolute.

'If you leave, it's without me,' she repeated.

A mile or so away, Markos was out in the hauntingly empty city. Alert to the positions of Turkish soldiers, his ears tuned into the slightest sound, he moved stealthily, ducking into doorways if he heard a human voice.

He zigzagged his way across the city, along Euripides Street and down roads named after Sophocles and Aeschylus, all so redolent of the order of the classical past. Everything had been bold and confident in Famagusta, the names of ancient philosophers and poets happily woven into the resolutely modern commercialism of the city. How wrong it was now, he thought, as he turned a corner and found himself looking at the sign for Eleftheria Street. Its name meant 'freedom'.

The wide, deserted streets full of luxurious department stores and glamorous cafés were already ghostly. Even after this short time, it seemed impossible that they had ever been full of people.

There was evidence of looting. Broken shop windows where jewellery had been ripped from displays and clothes hastily ripped from dummies suggested opportunism rather than anything more organised.

It annoyed Markos that he had to edge along the streets of this place over which he felt such a sense of ownership. It seemed that his city had been given away, handed over almost without resistance.

His mission for that day was to find food. Their own supplies were not exhausted, but he wanted to make sure that they had enough for the next few days. Broken glass crunched underfoot as he climbed into a grocery store. The shelves were still fairly full, but beer and spirits had been mostly removed. Markos was more interested in finding tins of condensed milk.

A cushion on the seat next to the till still wore the dent of the shopkeeper's ample backside. He thought about the woman who had worked there. She had a beautiful face, luxurious glossy hair and a plump body. He had always spent a few minutes flirting with her whenever he came in, enjoying her huge smile and the glint of a gold cross that nestled within the crease of her cleavage.

He helped himself to carrier bags still helpfully stacked up next to the till and filled them with several dozen tins. Maria, in particular, needed this sustenance.

Outside the deserted city, the number of refugees on the island's roads continued to grow. It was being said that more than two hundred thousand Greek Cypriots had fled their homes. Thousands of Turkish Cypriots were leaving theirs too, realising that their lives were in danger as the National Guard acted in retaliation for the Turkish invasion. Many of them were seeking refuge in the British base at Episkopi in the south.

For Savvas and Aphroditi, the base at Dhekelia, in spite of the conditions which grew more uncomfortable and overcrowded by the day, was at least some kind of sanctuary. When news came that intense fighting was continuing in Nicosia, they realised that it might be some time before they could leave the camp to go there.

Thousands more streamed in, bringing with them news of what had taken place in the capital over the past few days. Suspicious that the invasion had been a conspiracy between the United States and Turkey, a huge group of protesters had marched on the American embassy and assassinated the ambassador. Many Cypriots were in despair.

'*Infighting!*' said Savvas. 'You'd think that EOKA B and the Makarios faction would realise there's a common enemy now.'

'With the island cut into two, we don't need any more problems,' agreed Frangos.

'And if they can't agree a strategy amongst themselves,' Savvas said, 'how are they ever going to get rid of an organised army?'

'God knows . . .' said Frangos. 'I am sure the British will send some help eventually. They've made some big investments here so it doesn't make sense for them to ignore what's happened. Apart from anything, they're supposed to help protect our constitution!'

There were rumours that a new guerrilla army was being formed to fight back against the Turkish soldiers. Groups of men in the camp were fired up by the prospect of going to war, and those from Famagusta imagined themselves marching to free their city. EOKA B, communists and supporters of Makarios were all active among the vast refugee population.

'They all have a plan of action,' said Savvas, 'but it adds up to nothing! *Tipota!* All we do is sit here waiting for . . . *what?*'

The lack of real activity in the camp was a terrible thing for a man like Savvas. He helped to erect tents and construct latrines, but when those tasks were finished he found himself unoccupied and frustrated.

Aphroditi found it easy to keep silent when Savvas was voicing his point of view. Everyone in the camp was in the habit of giving out opinions. What should happen? What should have happened? What needed to happen? No one knew the answers to any of these questions but they debated them endlessly. The refugees had control over neither their own lives nor anything happening outside the camp. For now their days were spent either queuing for handouts or crowded around a radio hoping to hear news of relatives from whom they were separated.

For Aphroditi, even now, there was only one thing that preoccupied her. Not *if* or *when* they would see the arrival of Greeks, Americans or British soldiers, but *if* or *when* she would see the man she loved. The rest had no meaning.

While rumours proliferated in the camp, in the silent streets of Famagusta there was nothing to inform the Georgious or the Özkans of what was taking place.

After a few days they had lost their electricity, so there was no possibility of listening to the radio. Their city was the focus of the world's attention, but they were unaware of it.

In homes little more than fifty yards apart, the two families were even unaware that the other was there.

The Özkans had not ventured outside even once since the day their city was occupied. Living under siege conditions in the enclaved village a decade before had taught Emine one thing: that her store cupboards should always be full. Lentils, beans, rice and specially dried bread were always neatly stacked there.

'We always need to have them, just in case,' she said.

'Just in case of *what*?' Halit had always enquired teasingly.

Now there was no humour. He was merely grateful that his wife still had a siege mentality.

When they had heard the heavy sound of footsteps several days before, Hüseyin had been sent up to the roof of their two-storey house to ascertain where the soldiers were.

He had raced down again, always swift and impatient in his movements.

'They're at the end of the street,' he panted. 'Half a dozen of them. And it looks as if the city is still full of smoke.'

Since then, there had been nothing but silence and cicadas.

Hüseyin crept back up to the roof.

'Is there still smoke?' his father asked when he returned.

'Not that I could see . . .'

'And sounds?'

'Nothing at all.'

The sound of artillery had ceased; guns were no longer being fired.

In the Georgiou apartments, Maria, Panikos and their two little ones were now staying downstairs with Irini and Vasilis. They felt safer together. Markos continued to sleep upstairs. He came and went, usually after dusk, often not returning until it was daylight.

'Why does he go for so long?' Irini asked Vasilis anxiously.

'He's finding food for us!'

This was true. Markos always returned with plenty for them

to eat. He knew now which stores were still full and that Turkish soldiers mostly used the main streets.

Maria was content to stay inside with the baby, who was named after her grandmother. She would not have gone outside for forty days even under normal circumstances, as was tradition with a newborn.

Irini had brought her canary inside and liked to let it fly around in the darkened room.

'Look how happy it makes him,' she said.

But the bird kept fluttering towards a chink of light between the shutters and she had to put him back in his cage.

'I'd love to let him see the sunshine again,' she said. '*Tse! Tse!* Mimikos! *Tse! Tse!* Please take the table out of the way.'

'But . . .' protested Vasilis.

'I just want to hang his cage outside for a while,' she said firmly. 'I'm not going anywhere else.'

'It's not *safe*!'

'There is no one out there, Vasilis,' she said. 'And if I hear anything at all, I'll come straight back indoors.'

As Vasilis moved the furniture and opened the door just enough to let his wife through with the cage in her arms, the apartment was filled with light. Dazzled by the unfamiliar brightness, Irini went outside and stretched up to replace her bird on his hook. It was seven days since she had been into her *kipos*. Many of her gerania had withered, but there was a huge crop of ripened tomatoes waiting.

'Oh, Vasilis,' she cried. 'Come and see!'

They picked the fruit together, carefully placing them in a bowl. Irini then plucked a handful of basil. She smiled. Her mind had travelled a long distance.

'I wonder how the oranges are . . .' she mused.

Vasilis did not answer. Every day he thought of his precious trees and knew they would be suffering without him. Irini had dreamed that the entire crop had been stripped from the trees and lay trampled on the ground.

Back inside, she carefully sliced some of the tomatoes and covered them generously with olive oil. For the first time, Vasilis opened one of the shutters by an inch to release them from the oppressive darkness.

The five of them sat round the table to eat. It was the first fresh produce they had had for days and the sweetest salad they had ever eaten. Irini had also made a stew with the last of her chickens. In the corner, the baby slept.

They ate in silence. It had become a habit.

At the Özkan home, Emine, Halit, Hüseyin and Mehmet were also sharing a meal. They were eating dried bean stew. Their vegetables had run out.

'How much longer do we have to stay inside?' asked Mehmet.

Emine and Halit exchanged glances. Emine's eyes were swollen from crying. She put down the picture of Ali she had been holding all day and pulled Mehmet on to her lap.

Hüseyin had spent several hours each day on the roof. He reported that soldiers sometimes went on patrol, which told them that the military presence was still there.

'We don't know,' answered Halit. 'We'll only go out again when it's safe.'

At that moment, they heard a sound in the street.

It was a jeep. Then voices: Turkish, but with an accent a little different from their own. They were shouting.

The crunch of heavy boots came closer and then stopped.

Everyone in the room froze.

They saw the door handle being moved from the outside. Many

people had fled the city without pausing to lock their doors, so the soldiers were used to breaking in without effort. A moment later they heard a boot kick against the wood – once, then again, harder the second time.

Emine put her head in her hands and rocked.

'*Bismillah irrah manirrahim*,' she mouthed over and over again, noiselessly. 'May Allah help us.'

The door handle rattled again. Then there was some inaudible muttering and after that something that sounded like scratching.

For some time the Özkans could hear soldiers in the street. It took a while for them to repeat the process with a dozen other doors. When they succeeded, the sounds changed. Soldiers went in and out ferrying anything they could carry, and the noise the Özkans heard was the sound of stolen goods being carelessly thrown into the back of the jeep. Laughter and joking accompanied their task.

Markos was on his way home from finding food when he turned the corner into their street and saw the jeep right next to the Georgiou apartments. The back of it was loaded up, and soldiers were staggering out of the neighbouring block, one with a small fridge, another with a television. A couple of other doors had a mark chalked on them. From watching their movements, Markos knew that if a door did not open easily, the soldiers left the property alone. There were too many places that could be easily ransacked to bother with those that had been made secure. Any locked door was marked with chalk to indicate that the home was untouched. They would come back another time.

He could see that his parents' door was still shut. Perhaps they were the next target. There was nothing he could do but wait and make sure he was not seen. He felt for the gun in his pocket. He would prefer not to use it unless he had to.

Inside, the Georgious waited in silence and terror. Vasilis had moved the women and children into the back bedroom. If baby Irini made a sound, then they would be in trouble.

He took two sizeable knives from the kitchen drawer, handed one to Panikos and gestured that he should stand close to the front door. His son-in-law obeyed the instruction and the pair of them stood trembling as they listened to the sounds only a few inches away.

Vasilis understood enough Turkish to know that the car the soldiers were driving was virtually full.

'Let's go now,' said one of them, to the accompaniment of a scratching sound on the door. 'It's enough for the day.'

They still seemed to be in the *kipos*.

Vasilis could hear a slight creaking, more laughter and then the high-pitched sound of a bird. They had unhooked the canary's cage.

As the sound of the vehicle receded into the distance, Vasilis and Panikos put down their weapons. Vasilis went to open the bedroom door and found his wife, Maria, the baby and Vasilakis sitting huddled on the floor behind the bed.

'They've gone,' he said, his voice trembling. He did not tell Irini about her precious bird.

At that moment, they heard knocking on the door.

'*Panagia mou!*' whispered Irini, clapping her hand over her mouth. '*Panagia mou!*'

'*Mamma!*' It was Markos' voice.

Vasilis and Panikos slid the furniture out of the way to open the door.

'They were here!' said his mother, weeping. 'We thought they were going to break in.'

She was visibly shaking with fear. Everyone else remained calm, but Irini was overwhelmed with thoughts of what might have been.

Markos tried to reassure her.

'But they didn't get in. You're safe, *Mamma*. We're *all* safe. They've gone. Come outside and you'll see.'

Irini went out into the *kipos*. Immediately, she noticed the absence of the cage.

'Mimikos! Mimikos!' she cried out. 'Markos! They've taken my bird!'

She began to weep. The canary, her constant companion in the day, had been her pride and joy, his music immeasurably precious.

'If only I had kept him inside,' she sobbed.

The absence of the bird reminded her of an even greater absence. Christos was still out there somewhere. For several hours, she was beyond consolation.

Although they had no radio, the occasional sound of far-off artillery told them that Cyprus was still at war. In the last hour, that reality had come closer than before.

In Irini's dreams that night, Turkish soldiers overran the whole of the island from Kyrenia in the north to Limassol in the south. She dreamed that every Cypriot had been slain, except for the inhabitants of her own home.

As the days went by, the Özkans began to run out of supplies. All of them were constantly hungry, especially Hüseyin, but Emine was still determined to stay.

'I'm going out,' Hüseyin said.

'Going out where?' his mother asked.

'Look, we need to find some food. And I'm sure there's some still sitting in the shops.'

'Let him go, Emine,' said Halit. 'The boy's a fast runner. He's our best hope.'

'At least wait until it's dark,' pleaded his mother.

That night, Hüseyin rolled up an old flour sack and quietly left the house. Taking a serpentine course through the back streets, he made frequent stops, keeping out of sight in doorways in case soldiers should unexpectedly appear.

Once outside, he was in no hurry to return. After all these days with little food, he was as slim as a wheat stalk and he knew he could hide with ease. He wanted to look round his city. He wanted to see what had taken place outside the prison of his own home.

Were there soldiers everywhere? Were he and his family alone in Famagusta? He walked this way and that, keeping to side roads but occasionally taking a glance down the main streets. He was astonished. The same silence in their own small street extended across the whole city.

Once or twice he saw movement in the distance and hid while soldiers passed. He could hear their laughter and see the glow of cigarettes. They seemed relaxed enough, as though off duty. Clearly they felt their work was done and they were not on the lookout for anyone.

Hüseyin made his way cautiously across the city towards the centre. On the way he peered into several houses and saw tables laid for a meal. In one house there was even food still mouldering in dishes. Apart from the soldiers, he saw no other living creature, not even a stray dog.

Many shopfronts looked the same as normal. In one street, ghostly mannequins in nuptial white stared out blankly. Opposite, in the window of one of the best men's tailors in town, dummies dressed in wedding suits gazed back at their brides. These shops were untouched.

The Sunrise

In other streets it was a different picture. There was a cluster of shops selling electrical goods. He had been passing one shop every day for the past months on his way to the beach and coveted the hi-fi equipment. Every boy of his age wanted a collection of records and the chance to play music when he wanted. He had once plucked up courage to go in, and a young sales assistant had demonstrated a Sony stereo sound system to him. It was like magic, hearing different sounds coming from two speakers. Hüseyin knew his mother walked down the same street because he had heard her mention the idea of a television to his father. She had been firmly turned down.

The price of both was beyond reach but now there was not even the possibility of owning them. Every radio, television and record player had been removed. Even the till was missing. Doors and windows had been smashed and moonlight caught the sparkle of glass sprinkled across the pavement.

Closer to the seafront and the hotels, the shops became more expensive. He knew that one of his mother's friends had worked in Moderna Moda because they sometimes passed it on the way home together and Emine's friend would come out to chat. His mother always commented on the price tags.

'Take a nought off and I'd buy it,' she joked to her friend.

The mannequins were naked now.

Zenon Street, not far from The Sunrise, was where many of the expensive jewellery shops were situated. All of them had been stripped completely bare. The display cases themselves had been ripped out of the walls. In one of them a plastic clock was all that had been left. It told Hüseyin that it was midnight.

He reached the beach and saw his sunloungers neatly stacked exactly as he had left them. Behind was The Sunrise. The dark windows unnerved him. He thought of the day when he had seen his cousin's lifeless body, inside which the heart had stopped and the blood no longer moved in the veins. The hotel itself resembled a corpse.

Hüseyin crept past the gates and peered through the railings. He took in the unlit neon signage and the heavy iron grate across the front doors. He thought he saw some movement inside, but knew he must be mistaken. The nightclub entrance was firmly locked too.

The damage that had been done to the adjacent hotel shocked him. There was a huge hole in its side and many of the balconies were hanging loosely at an angle. If anyone had been inside at the time of the explosion, they would have stood little chance of survival.

There was a moment when he felt he had seen enough. He was saddened by all the destruction. This was a place he loved, and even if he dreamed of playing for a national team, it was the city he would always return to. Hüseyin could see that Famagusta would never be the same again.

It was time for him to find provisions. He had already passed some grocery shops, so he retraced his steps towards home. In the first one he came to, the door pushed open easily. There was a terrible stink. The electricity had been off for days now, so the fridges had shut down and the milk and cheese had gone rancid. The vegetables had rotted. He could not make out exactly what it was, but there were dark shapes in boxes – probably potatoes, tomatoes and, judging by the smell, some bananas. A swarm of flies buzzed close by.

It was hard to see in the darkness, but Hüseyin felt his way along the aisle. He filled the sack with packets of biscuits, various tins picked at random because he could not read the contents in the darkness, and bags of rice. It seemed that no one else had got there before him, as the shelves were still full.

Then he felt his foot touch some bottles and heard the sound of several falling over. They rolled away across the floor and Hüseyin picked up a few, hoping they would be the fizzy drinks his brother so craved.

On his way out of the shop, he took some bars of chocolate. They were soft to the touch, but he ate several as he walked home, their sweetness giving him much-needed energy.

Next door to the grocer there was a butcher. Even with the door shut, there was a stench in the street outside. Hüseyin did not go too close, but he could see that a meat carcass hanging up in the interior was almost swinging, brought to life again by the volume of maggots feasting on it.

Slinging the sack over his shoulder, he started out for home, taking a different, shorter route, ever vigilant for the sound of soldiers. He was soon back in the residential area. This time he noticed a number of suitcases simply abandoned in the street, more evidence of the panic with which people had hastened from the city. Running would have been hard enough in that heat without the weight of such baggage.

Everything was quiet, but at the end of a street not far from home, he noticed something that shocked him more than anything else he had seen.

He put the sack down behind a gate and went up close. Ahead of him, there was a line of barbed wire. He was at the edge of the modern section of the city now, and as he peered in both directions down the moonlit street, he realised that the wire stretched as far as he could see. Famagusta had been fenced off. They were now living in a giant cage.

Chapter Twenty-one

Emine was overjoyed when Hüseyin returned, but she showed it by being angry.

'Where have you been?' she demanded, her voice rising. 'Why were you so long? *What were you doing?*'

He eased the sack off his shoulder and started to unpack it, lining everything up on the table as if it were a small shop. Emine brought a candle over.

'This is what I was doing,' he said, a note of triumph in his voice.

'*Canım oğlum*,' she said. 'My precious boy, thank you.'

Mehmet pointed at the lemonade.

'Can I have some?' he asked.

At the same time, Markos was bringing supplies of food to the Georgiou home. As Hüseyin had also discovered, there were no fresh goods to be had, but Markos reached into people's gardens to pluck a few oranges, and Irini's tomato plants continued to bear fruit.

'You won't let us starve, will you, *leventi mou*?' she said, hugging her son.

Vasilis constantly listened out for the sound of soldiers, always expecting them to return, but as the days passed, it seemed that there were plenty of other places for them to go.

Irini's lacework grew. Now that Vasilis allowed her to have the shutters open for longer in the day, there was enough light to work by. One day, he even said that she could sit in her beloved *kipos*.

She missed the company of her cherished canary, his absence making her yearn all the more for the life they had lost.

'You can stay outside, as long as you listen out,' said Markos. 'At all times.'

With neither his smallholding nor the *kafenion* to go to, Vasilis was restless and difficult company. His supply of *zivania* was running out too, which put him on edge.

Late one afternoon, while they were sitting hidden behind the straggling gerania that Irini had managed to revive, Vasilis saw a movement.

'Irini! Look!'

Down the street, they could make out the receding figure of a man. He was walking fast, glancing behind him.

'That's not a Turkish soldier,' said Vasilis.

'Do you think he's National Guard?'

'No. Doesn't look like military at all . . .'

Mystified, they retreated inside, bolted the doors and moved the furniture back into position.

The following day, at about the same time, they kept a cautious watch and saw the figure again. This time, Markos was at home.

'Look!' whispered Irini. 'I don't think we're alone here!'

Before she could remonstrate, Markos was out of the gate and hastening after the unknown figure, all the time looking around him.

Markos had raided a shoe shop to find crêpe-soled shoes, so his steps were noiseless when he was out on his forays into the deserted streets of Famagusta. For this reason Hüseyin had no idea that there was someone close behind. When he got to the front of his house, he automatically turned round, just as he always did, to double-check that nobody was watching him.

Markos had anticipated this and ducked into another gateway. He had already worked out where Hüseyin was going. He knew every member of The Sunrise staff by sight, even if they had never spoken, and he knew that Hüseyin was the son of his mother's friend Emine, a hairdresser at the hotel. He also remembered that they lived in the same street.

Within minutes Markos was back at home.

'The Özkan family,' he told his astonished mother. 'I think they might still be here.'

'Emine?' she exclaimed.

'Well, I didn't see her,' answered Markos. 'But it was definitely her son.'

'What shall we do?' asked Irini, palpably excited by the thought of her friend being so close.

'We're not going to do *anything*,' answered Vasilis. 'We can't trust anybody. And we're definitely not trusting them *now*.'

Before the invasion, Vasilis had got used to Emine calling at the house, but he had no desire to meet her husband. Moreover, he believed that the presence of another family close by might increase the discovery of his own.

'But Vasilis,' protested Irini, 'we might be able to help each other.'

'Turks? Help *us*?'

'Father! Don't shout! Please!'

Only Markos knew how deep was the silence of the streets. If anyone was even in the next road, the sound of a raised human voice might be audible.

'They're Cypriots, Father,' interjected Maria. 'They're not Turks.'

Irini began to bustle about in the kitchen. It was time for a change of subject.

'Would you like me to try and get another canister?' Markos asked. He'd guessed correctly that their gas was beginning to run low.

For several years it had been the task of either himself or Christos to go and fetch the new cylinders. Vasilis' old leg injury was increasingly slowing him down and he found them hard to lift. Markos' mundane request momentarily diverted his parents' attention from their disagreement.

'Of course, *leventi mou*,' said Irini.

Markos gave his mother a hug. In the warmth of his embrace, he communicated something more than affection. She knew that he would bring her and Emine together.

He had a reason for doing so. He surmised that it would be safer for his own family if the Turkish Cypriots were aware of their presence. At some point, if they were discovered by the Turks, it might make them more lenient in their treatment. It was an insurance policy at least.

Within a short time, Markos had worked out Hüseyin's pattern.

There was more systematic looting going on in the city now, something that Hüseyin had noticed too. He was becoming almost as canny as Markos.

During certain hours of the day, lorries were arriving in the main retail streets and clearing the shops of any valuable goods. These were then driven towards the port to be stored. It was evident that at some point all these goods would be shipped to Turkey.

The scale of this shoplifting operation was enormous, but it meant that some of the food shops were being largely left alone. Neither the Özkans nor the Georgious wanted a fridge or fancy furniture. They merely needed food to survive. The families did not know for how long they might need it, but Irini's dreams told her that it might be weeks rather than days.

For two days running, Markos followed Hüseyin's journey to the general store. On the third day, Hüseyin found a note there waiting for him.

His heart was already beating fast when he arrived at the shop. Even though he had now been there and to other stores dozens of times, he was anxious about discovery on every occasion. His parents always said that though Hüseyin could run with the speed of a panther, it was Ali who had the courage of a lion. When he noticed the letter, propped up on the shelf closest to the door, his heart almost leapt from his chest. His hands were shaking so much he could scarcely unfold it.

Having read the contents, he gathered a few bags of rice and dried peas and made his way back home via a different route from the usual. He did not want to be seen by the Georgious.

'Mother – look!' He was scarcely inside the house before he was showing her the note. 'The Georgious – your friend Irini . . .' he said breathlessly.

'What? What are you talking about?'

'Let me see that piece of paper!' said Halit, snatching it out of his wife's hands.

'We're not alone here!' said Hüseyin.

'Not alone?'

It took Emine and Halit a moment to digest the news.

'I want to go and see her!' said Emine. 'I want to go now!'

She was determined to get her way.

'Go with her, Hüseyin.'

The pair of them silently left the house.

When a timid knock was heard on the door, Irini was expecting it.

The pair on the doorstep could hear sounds from behind the door, and then a crack appeared.

'Irini! It's me!'

Soon the opening was widened enough for them to go inside. The two women embraced, looked at each other and embraced again.

'I just don't believe it!' cried Irini.

'Neither do I,' said Emine. 'When Hüseyin came back with that note, I nearly fainted.'

'It's like a miracle,' exclaimed Irini.

The tearful women continued to embrace for a while, and then Irini offered Emine some coffee and the pair of them sat down to share their reasons for staying. Hüseyin waited outside, keeping watch.

'Maria, how is she?'

'The baby came early . . . the same day as the Turks.'

Emine clasped her hand over her mouth.

'It must have been the anxiety that set off the labour. And Christos being missing,' continued Irini.

'Is he . . . ?'

'Yes,' said Irini. 'Still missing. And Ali?'

'No sign,' responded Emine, trying to hold back tears. 'That's why we've stayed. I can't go until he comes back to us.'

Panikos appeared. He spent most of his time looking after Maria and playing with little Vasilis in the back bedroom. They only came out to the living area when it was time to eat. The irrepressible sounds of baby and child had less chance of carrying into the street this way.

Irini noticed immediately that he was ashen-faced. He did not seem to register that there was another woman in the room.

'Panikos, what is it?'

'The baby . . .'

'What's wrong?'

Before the answer came, Irini had pushed past him and into the bedroom.

Even in the semi-lit room, she could make out the anxious features of her daughter's face. She was cradling the baby, who was unusually silent.

'*Kori mou*, what's happened?'

Maria looked up at her mother and her eyes were full of tears. Irini put her hand on the baby's tiny head.

'*Panagia mou!* She's burning up.'

'And she hasn't fed all day. *Mamma*, I'm really afraid . . .'

Irini had already left the room and a moment later returned with a bowl of cold water. She started to sponge the baby's head.

'We need to cool her down,' she said. 'Otherwise she might have a fit.'

'She already did . . .'

'She needs some penicillin,' said Panikos.

'And how are we going to get that?'

'We'll have to find a way. There'll be some at the hospital.'

The baby was very still and wan. Even little Vasilis sat quietly, sensing his parents' anxiety.

'I'll have to try and find some.'

Irini stroked her daughter's hair and then followed Panikos out of the room. She could see the look of desperation on her son-in-law's face.

Emine was standing outside with Hüseyin waiting to leave. Irini explained the situation.

'I'll go with you,' said Hüseyin to Panikos. 'It will be safer.'

Panikos did not hesitate. They had never met before, but he was grateful for the offer. He did not feel confident about doing it alone. He had been unfit and overweight for a long time, pampered for years first by his own mother and then more so by his mother-in-law.

It was late afternoon when the two of them set off. The hospital was on the other side of the city, so they would have to make their way cautiously. They were bound to see soldiers en route.

They moved silently, Hüseyin going ahead and scouting, beckoning Panikos to follow when he knew it was safe. When they reached the hospital, they encountered their first major obstacle. Peering through the iron railings, they could see that the doors were ajar, but the gates themselves were firmly padlocked.

'Wait!' said Hüseyin. 'I'll have a quick look round the perimeter. There might be another way in.'

Five minutes later, he was back.

'This way!'

He led Panikos to a place where the railings had been prised apart, but he had not considered the man's size. The space was not wide enough and Panikos knew there was no point in trying. Climbing over the top of the railings was even less of a possibility.

'I can go alone,' said Hüseyin. 'But I don't know what I am looking for.'

The minutes were ticking by.

Panikos felt inside his pocket and found a scrap of paper and a blunt pencil. He remembered the name of the penicillin from when little Vasilis had once been sick. He wrote it down and handed it to Hüseyin.

'Can you read that?' he asked. He was not referring to the legibility of his handwriting.

Hüseyin took the paper without answering and scanned it.

Panikos immediately realised that Hüseyin was perfectly able to read Greek and was embarrassed.

In a moment Hüseyin had slipped through the railings. Panikos watched him sprint across the gravelled area and disappear round the corner.

The wide corridors and wards were as eerily deserted as the rest of the city. There was a certain amount of destruction but it was hard to tell if this was wanton or caused by people leaving the hospital in a panic. Trolleys had been overturned and contents spilled from cupboards. Medical files were scattered across the floor.

Hüseyin had no idea where he was going. In his entire life he had never needed a doctor, so even the sour smell of antiseptic was unfamiliar to him. He ran down a corridor until he reached a set of signs. One of them read 'Pharmacy'. He would try that first. Otherwise he would see if he could find the paediatric ward. Perhaps drugs for children would be stored there.

The pharmacy had already been broken into. There were shattered bottles everywhere and cartons emptied of their pills. Abandoned syringes lay on the surfaces. The room was cold. Although electricity had generally gone off in the city, a generator had obviously kicked in at the hospital.

Hüseyin retrieved the piece of paper and began trying to compare what Panikos had written against the labels on the drugs that remained in the cupboards. None of them matched.

He ran back into the corridor and followed signs to the children's ward.

There was less chaos there. Rows of small beds were still neatly made up and Hüseyin noticed a box of toys in the corner. Someone had bothered to put them away before leaving. Doctors' coats hung on a row of pegs and a stethoscope was coiled up on the desk like a snake.

Hüseyin tried the nearest cupboard. Bandages. Blood pressure monitors. More stethoscopes. He realised that he was not going to find what he was looking for here.

Recalling that the drugs in the pharmacy had been stored in a cold room, he began to look for a fridge. He found it soon enough, in a small back room; inside were rows of bottles, dozens of them with a name that matched the one that Panikos had written down. Hüseyin stashed four in his pockets. There was probably nowhere to keep anything cool in the Georgiou house so he left the rest. He could always return if more was needed.

Within moments, he was back at the entrance and round the corner. Panikos was waiting.

They got home as quickly as the corpulent Panikos' pace would allow. He knew that every moment counted with sick babies. If theirs had another febrile fit, it could be fatal. His attempts to keep up with Hüseyin left him breathless, and by the time they were home, he was doubled up with the exertion.

It was Hüseyin who tapped discreetly at the door and entered first. He handed Irini the bottles.

With a teaspoon, Maria fed the baby tiny drops of the liquid. Little Irini's breaths were rapid and shallow. Her grandmother continually dabbed her with a damp cloth.

'We have to try and cool her down,' she insisted.

That night, there was little change.

Maria was as silent as the baby. Panikos paced up and down. Irini wrung out her cloth again and again, praying constantly. Her hands were busy so she did not cross herself, but she looked up at the icon from time to time. At least while the baby was warm, they knew she was alive.

As ever, Vasilis sought comfort in *zivania*.

Late that night, Markos reappeared. He had bags of provisions with him.

'What's wrong, *Mamma*?' he asked. He could see instantly that she was distraught.

'The baby! She's so ill. I think we might lose her . . .'

Markos sat with his father to have a drink.

With such an anxiety hanging over them, he decided to wait until morning before telling them his news. He had learned something that day that was going to have serious consequences for them all.

By morning, the baby's temperature had begun to drop. Life was returning to her. Maria wept, this time for joy.

Irini took her little namesake from her daughter's arms and walked about the room with her. She made little sounds now. This seemed a miracle after the previous day.

They continued to administer drops from the bottles. It was unscientific, but they knew it was curing her.

Maria was exhausted and lay on the bed to sleep. The first thing she saw when she woke up an hour later was her mother's smile.

'She's going to be all right,' said Irini. 'I think she wants feeding now.'

The baby nestled against her mother's breast and suckled. It was the first time in more than thirty-six hours. She was clearly out of danger.

By evening, everything was back to normal and even Maria found herself able to eat again. Markos felt it was a suitable time to give them some news. He was using information like a tincture, knowing that a small amount at the right moment would have a huge effect.

'We're not going to be rescued yet,' he said. 'Or at least it's not going to be for a while.'

There was a look of dismay on his mother's face.

'But . . .'

'How do you know?' demanded Vasilis.

Twenty-four-hour-a-day incarceration with his wife and enforced absence from both the *kafenion* and his citrus grove were making him more irritable than ever. Markos had found some more *zivania* for him and there was a plentiful supply of tobacco, but Irini had told him to put away his *komboloi,* his worry beads. They were a little too noisy.

'I overheard something . . .'

'From who?'

'Turkish soldiers . . . they were standing outside a shop when I was inside. What I heard means that we might have to stay here a while longer.'

'But why? What do you mean?'

Markos sketched out a map of Cyprus on a scrap of paper and drew a line across it.

'As far as I can tell, this is what they've done,' he said.

For the first time, they all understood that they were inside a huge zone occupied by the Turks.

'From the way they were talking, I think we've been completely outnumbered.'

'But there's still fighting?' asked Panikos.

'It seems so,' said Markos.

'Those *poustotourtji*!' It was the strongest word Vasilis could use against the Turks. 'And now we have some living next door!' he spat. His prejudice against Turkish Cypriots had deepened.

'Without Hüseyin,' said Panikos, 'we wouldn't still have the baby with us.'

Vasilis put down his fork.

'What do you mean?'

'She would have died,' he said emphatically. 'He not only found the medicine but I probably wouldn't even have reached the hospital safely in the first place.'

Vasilis carried on eating in silence.

Irini smiled. Her little granddaughter had been saved by Emine's son.

Amongst other provisions, Markos had brought back some semolina that day, so she made *siropiasto,* a sweet cake, and sent him to invite the Özkan family round.

Halit refused to come. Irini and Emine accepted that there might never be a day when their husbands would sit down at the same table. The men made the conflict personal and blamed each other for what had happened. By contrast, the women blamed themselves.

'We're all at fault somehow,' said Emine. 'Aren't we?'

'When something has been going on for so long,' reflected Irini, 'it's impossible to say who started it.'

Now that they were round the table together, Markos asked Hüseyin if he had other sources of supplies in addition to the shop where he had left the note. The younger man was cautious. He did not want to give away the details so he answered vaguely, describing an area in the north-west of the city without mentioning street names.

Irini was passing round plates of cake.

'I think I need to lose a little weight,' said Panikos, his hand on his rotund belly. He pushed away his share.

Hüseyin and Panikos exchanged a smile.

'Can I have it?' asked Mehmet, running up to the table. Up until now he had been on the floor playing a game with Vasilakis.

Mehmet had enjoyed this immensely. Making up the rules and being looked up to by the toddler was a new experience. The last few weeks had passed very slowly.

'With pleasure,' said Panikos, handing his slice of cake to the little boy.

Chapter Twenty-two

IN THE CAMP at Dhekelia, there was no cake. Sometimes there was not even enough bread, and conditions were worsening each day.

Like many there, Aphroditi was sick. Hundreds had been suffering from dysentery, and bacteria rampaged indiscriminately across the generations, from old people to the newborn. There were fresh graves on the perimeter of the camp.

Aphroditi was already slim, but after ten days of violent illness, her grubby dress hung off her. For a few days she was taken care of in a medical tent, lying on a low army bed in the airless space, from time to time doubled up with pain and nausea. Markos was constantly on her mind. She tried to remember his face. When it did not come easily, she questioned whether he was even still alive.

She had not taken off her jewellery since coming into the camp. There was no reason to remove it and nowhere safe to store it. She played constantly with her pendant. It always felt warm, and she held in her mind the last person apart from her who had touched it. She imagined that somewhere deep beneath the layers of her own fingerprints, Markos' remained.

Aphroditi had not looked in a mirror since the last glance she had given herself in the apartment all those weeks ago. It was strange to care so little, a change in her as unexpected as the affection she had developed for the Frangos children.

When her condition gradually improved, she returned to the squalid tent she and Savvas now shared with Costas Frangos and his family.

They had expected to be away for a few days, but it was now five weeks since they had arrived in the camp. Savvas had heard that people were beginning to return to their homes in Nicosia. There was currently no possibility of anyone going back to Famagusta, and many were travelling to relatives or friends who were prepared to give them accommodation.

'Let's leave,' said Savvas. 'The sooner we get out of here, the better.'

'Aren't we going to take the Frangos family?'

'We don't have enough room for them in the car.'

'But we could fit the children.'

Anna Frangos overheard the conversation.

'Don't worry,' she said. 'We wouldn't want to be separated.'

Aphroditi looked at her: four small children, two beneath each arm, like ducklings beneath her wings.

'Of course you wouldn't,' she said.

The five of them made a picture that was both beautiful and full of pathos. At this moment, Aphroditi would happily have swapped places with Kyria Frangos, who had neither home nor possessions and yet at this moment looked like the richest woman in the world. The Frangos family had lived in a small apartment on the outskirts of Famagusta and had left home taking nothing apart from their children. Neither a photo, nor a book, nor any piece of the past was in their hands to remind them of how life had been. They queued daily for food rations or small items such as spare socks for the children. There was little else available. Quite often if a dress or a pair of trousers needed washing, the children had to sit wrapped in a blanket while they dried.

They had no relatives in the south of the island with space to put them up but there was talk that the government was going to build special camps to give the refugees better accommodation.

'If you can get to Nicosia,' added Aphroditi, 'come and stay with us.'

She bent down to give each of the three small girls and their brother a hug. It was the first time she had spent so many hours in the company of children, and they had been happy and rewarding times. Two of them were almost reading now. She had spent days and days working on their letters and making up stories. She was sad to be saying goodbye.

'We'll try and let you know where we end up,' promised Costas as they said their final farewells.

With her handbag over her shoulder, Aphroditi walked away. As usual, her husband was waiting for her and growing impatient.

They drove in silence from the camp and towards Nicosia. The motion of the car brought on a return of the nausea that had so plagued Aphroditi in the past few weeks, and twice they had to stop for her to retch at the side of the road.

Their route was littered with debris and abandoned cars. From time to time they came across a crater in the road and had to drive on to rough ground to get round it. The landscape was dotted with bombed-out buildings. It was unrecognisable. Neither of them spoke. There was nothing to say. Their beautiful island had been ravaged.

Eventually they reached the outskirts of Nicosia. All around, there was evidence of the fierce fighting that had taken place. They passed the damaged Hilton and several apartment blocks that had been completely destroyed.

The apartment that had been owned by Aphroditi's parents was close to the centre of the old town. Many of the older buildings had crumbled easily in the bombardment and it seemed that most of the windows in the city had been shattered.

The car struggled. It was not just the unevenness of the roads and the obstacles of rubble and abandoned sandbags that made the going slow. Savvas pulled in to the side of the street and got out.

'Damn it! Damn it!' he cursed, kicking the car. 'We'll have to walk.'

Two of the tyres were virtually flat.

From where they had to leave the car, it was not far to the apartment. At least they had little to carry. Savvas had his briefcase with various papers and deeds that he had rescued from his study before they left, and Aphroditi merely had her handbag, containing keys to a home that now seemed a world away, some earrings, a purse and a pearl.

When they reached their destination, they were relieved to see that their apartment block was intact. The windows on the ground floor had been boarded up as a precaution but the owners had not returned. They both looked upwards. Their apartment was on the third floor, and from what they could see from the street, it was undamaged.

An elderly woman was pegging out laundry on the balcony above them. Her husband was watering some plants. A caged bird tweeted cheerfully. It was a Saturday morning.

The couple stopped their activities for a moment.

'Good morning, Kyrie and Kyria Papacosta,' called down the man. '*Ti kanete?* How are you?'

The greeting seemed so ordinary, so banal. It was the standard question of everyday life but one that was impossible to answer. The city all around them was in a state of dereliction, everyone was grieving lost relatives and homes, and yet flowers still needed tending and birds feeding.

'I was so sorry to hear about Kyrios Markides,' said his wife.

Aphroditi felt her mouth dry up. It was more than two years since they had been to stay in Nicosia. After the opening of The Sunrise, they had been too busy.

Kyria Loizou knew how to interpret her brave dismissive smile.

'Has anyone been here to find me?' Savvas asked.

Aphroditi held her breath, waiting for the answer.

'Not as far as I know,' the neighbour shouted down.

Aphroditi pushed open the main door and flicked the switch that illuminated the hallway. At least there was still electricity in the building. Markos had not come. They climbed the three flights and Savvas let them in to the apartment with his key. It was exactly as her parents had left it when they last visited.

Aphroditi wandered about opening the windows and shutters. There was a strong, musty smell that almost choked her. She was desperate to let in both light and air.

Savvas went out almost immediately.

'I want to know what the situation is here,' he said. 'And I'll see if I can find any shops open. It looked as if a few areas were returning to normal.'

Aphroditi was more than happy to be left alone.

In spite of the odour, the apartment was tidy and ordered. After the chaos in which they had been living during the past weeks, it seemed a haven. Everything looked so permanent and solid. It was unlike their own apartment in Famagusta, which was almost minimally furnished in 1970s style. Her parents had favoured heavy reproduction antiques. With most of the upholstery in shades of maroon or burgundy, it was a gloomy place.

For Aphroditi, this apartment was burdened by memory and emotion. It was the backdrop to her earliest years and standing in the room brought the past flooding back: visits from her grandparents, early birthdays, saints' days, games with her brother. She even imagined that in the corner cupboard some wooden toys might still be stored.

Her parents' belongings were dusty but undamaged. Most prominent in the room was a dark wood table. Protecting its surface was a white lace tablecloth, on top of which was a collection of photographs. There were wedding photos (Artemis and Trifonas Markides in black and white, Aphroditi and Savvas in colour), pictures of two godchildren and several of Aphroditi as a little girl with waist-length plaits. In another, Trifonas Markides was being presented with an award. The photo had been taken five years earlier. He was holding a plaque on which was etched an image of a ship. The actual plaque now hung on the wall: 'Presented to Trifonas Markides for Achievement in the Development of Export by the Cyprus Chamber of Commerce'. In the photograph, he was shaking hands with a politician.

Larger than all of them, and most prominently displayed, was a graduation photograph of her brother Dimitris. He looked proud and handsome in ermine and mortar board at the ceremony in London. It was in an ornate silver frame, with the image on the left and engraved on the right his name and the dates of his birth and death.

A copy of the photograph sat on a grand tombstone not far away, with the same words: '*Yia panta tha se thimamai. Den tha se ksehaso poté.*'

Forever remembered. Never forgotten.

The tragedy of a short life stolen away in the prime of youth had been repeated many thousands of times. Whatever anyone was saying, this conflict was not a new one. It had been taking lives and destroying happiness on this island for years.

Over in England, Artemis Markides looked at this same poignant image every single day.

Aphroditi felt as if someone had grabbed her heart and wrung it violently. She sat down for a moment. The pain of the past weeks, months and years flooded over her. Everything seemed to have disappeared. Her brother, her father, the man she loved. Nothing that she treasured remained.

Nicosia was where she had expected to see Markos again, but the catastrophe on the island had deepened in a way that none of them had ever imagined. Sooner or later he would bring the keys for The Sunrise. She held on to that thread of hope.

Perched on the edge of a chaise longue, she felt nauseous again and fled to the bathroom. Once she had vomited, she stood up. The small mirror on the front of the cabinet gave her a shock. It was the first time in many weeks that she had seen herself.

She saw a thin face, almost gaunt, with hollow eyes. Her hair was lank and straggly, the skin on her neck sagging and her complexion as white as the shirt that her neighbour had been hanging up. She washed her face and dried it on a towel that had gone crisp with time. It was surprising that Kyria Loizou had even known who she was.

For the first time, she realised how filthy her dress was. She took it off and put it in the bin. After a cold shower, she opened the wardrobe and found something fresh to wear. Her parents had left plenty of clothes in the cupboards and drawers, knowing that they would not be suitable for England. They had always planned to come back on a regular basis.

She chose a blouse and a skirt that she belted around her waist. Both garments almost drowned her. Although her mother was much plumper, the two women had almost the same size feet, so Aphroditi pulled out some flat sandals from the bottom of the wardrobe and buckled them up.

With her wet hair brushed back into a ponytail, she felt a little better. Her stylish bob had long since grown out. Before showering, she had left her showy earrings and pendant on her mother's dressing table; she decided not to put these back on. It seemed inappropriate to wear such things now, and she opened the drawer to put them inside. There was an envelope there with her brother's name on the outside. It was not the moment to cause herself any more pain, so she left it there. In any case, she respected her mother's privacy and did not want to invade it.

Feeling revived, she decided to go out. Like Savvas, she was curious about what had taken place in Nicosia. She shut the door, left the key under the doormat, knowing that her husband would expect to find it there, and crept out of the main door. In due course, she would feel strong enough to make conversation with her kindly neighbours, but not yet, not now.

Aphroditi walked the city's streets like a woman in disguise. When she caught sight of her reflection in the occasional shop window that was neither broken nor boarded up, it was as if she saw someone else.

Taking a route that twisted and turned through the old streets of Nicosia, she occasionally glimpsed the barrier that divided the city in two, old metal drums, makeshift fencing and barbed wire. It had been there for years but in many places was now reinforced. Evidence of the recent violence across the barricades was clear to see. Buildings were pockmarked with bullets, and the interiors of some were exposed to daylight where a hole had been crudely gouged by artillery fire.

A few of the smaller shops were functioning again, mostly grocers or general stores. She had no money with her so she could not buy anything; she hoped that Savvas would return with something for them to eat. Hunger was beginning to nag at her.

When Aphroditi returned to the apartment, Savvas was there.

There was a bag on the table and she could see that he had also spent some money on a new suit.

Even if he had been as tall and slim as his late father-in-law, the row of jackets and trousers hanging in the apartment would have been of no use to him. Savvas would not have worn second-hand clothes. Fortunately, a tailor near the Green Line had recently reopened.

'It was as though he was sitting waiting for me,' said Savvas, smiling for the first time in weeks. 'He had three suits waiting for someone who was exactly my size!'

'And that's one of them?'

Savvas nodded. Aphroditi also noticed that he had been to the barber.

She looked inside the bag on the table. It contained some bread and milk.

'There's not much out there,' he said glumly. 'But the shop-keepers are expecting more supplies any day now.'

Aphroditi cut two slices of bread and ate both of them hungrily.

'The city looks terrible, doesn't it?' she said, between mouthfuls.

'Yes, it's a mess. They say that a huge number of people left not so long ago because they were worried there was going to be more fighting. But the general view is that it's all over.'

'What do you mean, all over?'

'That this is it. That the line is drawn. And there is nothing we can do about it.'

'But what about Famagusta?'

'Oh, don't worry about that,' said Savvas. 'We'll get Famagusta back all right. But not Kyrenia. I don't think we'll be going there for a while.'

'Can we go home?' asked Aphroditi, grasping at the prospect of normal life.

'Not yet,' said Savvas. 'But let's hope it won't be long.'

Aphroditi began to make coffee.

'I'm annoyed with Markos Georgiou for not getting the keys to me,' Savvas added. 'I suppose he'll turn up with them eventually. And all the jewellery's there too . . .'

Aphroditi found some sugar in the cupboard. She usually drank her coffee *sketo*, without sugar, but the sweetness gave her much-needed energy.

'Perhaps we'll be able to start all over again with The New Paradise Beach,' said Savvas. 'I've been checking the insurance policies. We might be covered.'

'And what about The Sunrise? Do you think it's been damaged?'

'Let's hope not,' responded Savvas. 'We'll know as soon as we can go back.'

For the first time in weeks, Aphroditi pictured a return to the old life. Perhaps all the daydreams of lying in Markos' arms, his lips touching hers, would become a reality once again.

Both Aphroditi and Savvas smiled, though their reasons were very different.

Over the following weeks, provisions became more varied and plentiful and a few more people began to drift back to the city hoping to repair their lives.

A new normality began to evolve. One by one the *kafenia* opened up again. On the day when the *zacharoplasteion* where her mother used to take her after school displayed cakes in its window, Aphroditi felt a surge of optimism. The following day, she took one of the tables inside and treated herself. She still needed to regain the weight she had lost and hoped her craving for pastries was going to help.

News of Famagusta had not been positive so far. There had been little progress with talks. The newspapers informed them that there was still much to negotiate before they could return.

'We have to be patient, Aphroditi,' said Savvas.

These words, from the most short-tempered man she had ever known, puzzled her, but when she came in one day and saw him sitting at her father's big desk, she soon realised what had caused him to say them.

Savvas had found some advantage in what had taken place. In front of him were the floor plans of a building.

'Is it The New Paradise Beach?' she asked.

'No,' said Savvas. 'It's another hotel.'

He responded to her quizzical look.

'I was going to wait before telling you,' he said, looking both sheepish and pleased. 'It was too big an opportunity to miss.'

'What was?'

'Nikos Sotiriou decided to sell his hotel. He had been wanting to take early retirement even before this crisis, so he offered it to me for thirty per cent of what it's worth.'

The hotel Savvas had bought was Famagusta's second most luxurious after The Sunrise.

'Even by conservative estimates it was a bargain. Some others might come up. So as soon as we can return to the city, we'll do a few repairs and open again. If I get the other one I have my eye on, it will make me the biggest hotel owner in Famagusta.'

Aphroditi was astonished.

'But—'

'I've taken out a loan. Not a cheap one, but I promise it will pay off. I am absolutely certain of it.'

Aphroditi felt slightly faint. It was almost beyond belief that Savvas had behaved like this in these uncertain times.

'But we have nothing to sell to repay the loan . . .'

'We won't have to,' he said snappily.

A moment passed. Aphroditi said nothing, just stared at her husband. He continued.

'There's always this place . . . your mother has her house in England. And there's the jewellery sitting in the safe. That's a tidy sum. Plenty of security.'

Savvas Papacosta's optimism and the fact that he had acted without consulting her took her breath away.

'I think I'll go out for some fresh air,' she said.

She needed to get away from her husband, and the late autumn weather had even brought a small breeze.

Down in the street, she found herself taking an almost automatic path towards the pastry shop. It was somewhere to go, somewhere comforting. The selection was limited, but a small slice of baklava with a cup of coffee would cheer her, even if it was only for a few minutes. She was totally incredulous that Savvas had risked so much.

As she waited to be served, she surveyed her fellow customers. Most of them were women her age or slightly older, perhaps less *soignée* than they might have been a year earlier, but they had all dressed up to go out. Just as it was for men going to the *kafenion*, meeting friends in the *zacharoplasteion* was a much-needed taste of normality for the ladies of Nicosia. One table in particular caught her eye.

A woman, aged sixty perhaps, with a helmet of backcombed

black hair, was chatting to her friends, a group of three women all with similarly over-tended locks. Aphroditi knew her face. With her politician husband, she had been a frequent visitor to the nightclub. She recalled her from the opening party but knew that recognition would not be mutual.

In the dust and disarray of the city, it was miraculous to see these women chatting as if they had not a care in the world. Wafts of heavy perfume emanated from their table. Perhaps one of them was Aphroditi's own favourite scent, but now the heady mix nauseated her.

The women were noisy and dominating, and their garish clothes and bright lipstick seemed out of place in the dilapidated street. Aphroditi could tell that they had all once been prized for their beauty and were determined not to let their looks fade. With her scrubbed face and her mother's clothes, she no longer felt part of their world.

Suddenly she noticed something. The youngest of them was wearing a ring. It was the flash of its diamonds in the light that caught Aphroditi's eye, but only when the woman's hand stopped waving about (clearly she wanted to draw attention to it) could she get a proper look.

All the sugar she had just consumed seemed to surge through her body.

She saw a yellow diamond, perfectly circular in shape and the size of a small coin, surrounded by smaller ones, also yellow, set in platinum. There could not be two similar rings on the island. There was no mistaking it. It was hers.

Aphroditi was paralysed. There was no question of going up to the woman and accusing her of theft. Sitting in her mother's old-fashioned clothes, trying not to be noticed, it was the last thing she could do.

Trembling like a leaf, she paid her bill and left. How had her ring ended up on this woman's finger? It was not merely that she felt robbed. It was something even more pressing.

How could anyone have retrieved that ring from the safe without Markos' knowledge? Now more than ever, she needed to know what had happened to him.

Aphroditi took the shortest route home, her legs shaking so much they could scarcely carry her.

Chapter Twenty-three

In Famagusta, the habit of visiting the Georgious soon became a daily one for Emine, who was always carefully escorted by Hüseyin and in the company of Mehmet. Little Vasilis was as excited as Mehmet to have a new playmate, even when they ended up playing games of soldiers, an activity that he did not really understand.

Everyone had got used to keeping their voices low. The skies were quiet now, but if they grew complacent about the danger they were in, then all might be lost. There was nothing to indicate to them what was happening outside the city.

'Do we really need to stay now?' Irini asked Markos.

'If the soldiers don't know we're here,' he answered, 'then we're probably better off here than anywhere else. We have food and we're safe.'

'How do we know what's safe out there?' asked Emine. 'If Markos is right about this dividing line, there might be chaos everywhere.'

'If the line is meant to be separating Greeks and Turks, there'll be plenty of people on the wrong side of it, I suppose,' Irini reflected.

'We could go north of the line,' said Hüseyin. 'We still have family and friends in Maratha.'

'If you suddenly appear out there,' interjected Vasilis, 'you'll be putting us in danger too. They'd come looking for others.'

'Well in any case, nothing has changed for me,' said Emine. 'Until Ali comes back, I'm not leaving.'

Once Vasilis became involved, the discussion grew heated. Maria picked up Vasilakis and went into the bedroom, where the baby was sleeping. Mehmet was left once again to listen to the sound of adults arguing.

'Why don't you fetch your father, Hüseyin?' suggested Markos. 'We should see what he thinks too.'

Halit was sitting smoking on his doorstep. He looked very much at ease, just as he would have been in his old life. When he saw Hüseyin, he immediately castigated him.

'Why did you leave them alone there?'

He could never put to one side his anxiety over what might happen to his wife and children in a house full of Greek Cypriots.

'Will you come, Father?'

'What? To that *Greek* house?'

'We're talking about whether to leave. It affects all of us,' he insisted.

'Us? Which *us*?'

'Please. It's important. Just for a few minutes.'

'Well I'll come, but I won't sit down.'

Looking around him, Halit stubbed out his cigarette and crossed the street with his son.

Everyone except Vasilis stood up when Halit entered the room, and Irini greeted him warmly.

'Welcome to our home,' she said. 'Let me make you some coffee.'

Halit remained standing, just as he had said he would. The others resumed their discussion about whether the departure of the Özkans was a good idea. They had scant information on which to base such a decision.

As Halit was about to say what he thought, they all heard the same sound. The slamming of car doors. It was close by but not directly outside. Then came voices.

They all froze. Turkish soldiers had not been on patrol in their street for some days now and they had been feeling safe. There was shouting, the sound of hammering, a door being kicked in, the groan of gears being crunched into reverse and then more yelled instructions. After twenty minutes or so, everything went quiet again. It had seemed a long time.

Irini, Vasilis, Panikos, Emine, Halit and Hüseyin all breathed a sigh of relief. Maria and the children were still in the bedroom and oblivious.

'I think they've gone,' Hüseyin whispered finally. 'Let me go and see.'

He padded towards the door, drew the latch across and stepped outside. In a moment he was outside his family's home. There was debris around it and he realised almost immediately that it was their front door that lay in splinters on the street.

He walked across the threshold. Even though he could see that there were items missing, the overturned tables and chairs and the spilled contents of drawers and cupboards made the house seem more cluttered than it had been before.

His father's precious backgammon board had gone, frames were missing from the walls and the fridge had been removed. The store cupboards had been opened. A chest of drawers where his mother kept some silk cloths had been pulled open and the contents taken. Their small bust of Atatürk had been dropped on the floor, but the valueless *nazar* was intact, so he grabbed that as he left.

He ran back to the Georgious' house to break the bad news.

'You know what this means?' exclaimed Emine.

Nobody spoke for a moment, but the truth had dawned on them all.

'They will know someone was living there.'

When Hüseyin returned to the house with his father and touched the warm pan of pilaf that his mother had cooked for eating that evening, he knew she was right. Even the fragrance of the cinnamon that still hung in the air would have told the soldiers that the house was inhabited.

Back at the Georgious', where Emine was being comforted by Irini, the two families now discussed what they should do.

'They'll be back,' said Vasilis bluntly. 'If they know people were living in that house, they're going to be looking for them.'

'And they might even come hunting for others now,' said Halit.

'So we all need to get out of here?' asked Irini.

Everyone in the room looked at each other with fear and uncertainty. The only sound was the baby crying. She was completely recovered and her cries were lustier than before.

After a few moments, Markos spoke.

'I think we need to leave this street. But . . .'

'But what?' asked his mother. She had already removed their icon from the wall and put it in the pocket of her apron. There was a growing sense of urgency in the room.

'I don't think we should leave Famagusta.'

'What?' Halit Özkan was incensed that this Greek Cypriot was telling him what he should do. 'It's different for us than it is for you! Why shouldn't we leave?'

'Halit, no . . .' said Emine.

'I don't think we have a choice now.' He appealed directly to his wife.

Markos felt a prickle of anxiety. The last thing he wanted was for the Özkans to leave. He felt it was safer for his own family to have them close by; moreover, he needed more time. He was still working out how to profit from his effective ownership of The Sunrise and the enormous riches in its vaults.

'Just a moment,' he said, thinking quickly. 'There's something I need to show you.'

He ran up to his apartment, two steps at a time. In less than a minute he was back with an old newspaper in his hand. It was in Turkish.

'I found this,' he said. 'Some soldiers must have dropped it so I picked it up.'

In spite of his resolution to remain standing in the Georgiou house, Halit sank down into the nearest seat.

'My dearest,' gasped Emine. 'Whatever is it?' She could see from the expression on his face that something terrible had taken place.

He looked up at her but could not speak.

Hüseyin crossed the room, took the newspaper from his father's hands and stared at its front page.

'*Aman Allahım!*' he whispered. 'Oh my God! It's our village . . .'

He looked at his mother and then once again at the front page. It was dominated by a picture of people digging. They were members of the Red Cross, and soldiers in United Nations uniform stood watching them.

The headline was stark: 'MASSACRE IN MARATHA'.

Beneath the photograph there was a detailed account of what had happened. The atrocity had taken place some weeks earlier, on 14 August, but the full scale of it had only been discovered when the bodies were exhumed many days later.

Eighty-eight mutilated corpses, badly decomposed, had been found in a pit. Mothers were still clutching babies, the youngest less than a month old, and there were signs that some of the women had been raped before they were slaughtered. Bodies were decapitated and several were missing one or both of their ears.

Damage to the corpses showed that they had been bulldozed into the pit where they were found.

Emine came round to the other side of the table and pulled the newspaper from her son's hands. As she read it, tears streamed down her face.

A Greek Cypriot eyewitness said that all the males over fifteen years of age had been marched out of the village. Only old men had been allowed to stay. According to the man who had volunteered the information, the perpetrators were both Greek and Greek Cypriots. He thought they might have been EOKA B.

The newspaper claimed that it was the intention of the Greeks to wipe out all Turkish Cypriots on the island, and for that reason the Turkish army had moved south to try and save them. The massacres in Maratha and another village, Santalaris, had only proved that they had been right to take action.

Maratha was Emine's family village, the place where the Özkan family had lived before they had moved to Famagusta. All the names listed there in black and white were familiar to her, but four of them were her own flesh and blood:

Güldane Mustafa 39
Mualla Mustafa 19
Sabri Mustafa 15
Ayşe Mustafa 5

It was her sister and three nieces. Emine began to wail. Her keening drowned out every other sound, the crying baby and the noise of Vasilis gathering together some of their possessions lost beneath her laments.

Several of the families in the village comprised six children, and each and every one had been hacked to pieces, often alongside grandparents. The names of men and older boys were missing as they had been taken prisoner.

Irini drew Markos to the other side of the room and challenged him.

'How long have you had that newspaper?'

'Not that long, *Mamma*,' he answered quietly. 'I had no idea that was where the Özkans came from. I thought it was kinder to protect them from what has been happening to Turkish Cypriots out there.'

Markos knew that there had been other exhumations, not only of Turkish Cypriots but of Greek Cypriots too. Both sides were guilty of atrocities. He had another newspaper under his bed that described the killing of many Greek Cypriots in Kythrea. He would keep that one until it was of use to him.

'But where are we going?' asked Irini, turning to Vasilis.

His impatience was palpable.

'Does it matter?' he snapped. 'But if we don't go soon, those soldiers could be back and we'll still be sitting here.'

Vasilis' primary concern was his own family, but he was still taking in the idea that Greek Cypriots were not the only victims of this conflict. He had not faced this until now.

Halit was trying to comfort his wife. Hüseyin thought of his cousin's engagement and all those broken dreams. Mehmet stood close by, bemused by events.

Emine's fathomless grief would be there forever, but her husband was urging her to stand up. Hüseyin had never seen his father so tender towards her.

'We must leave, *tatlım*, my sweetness,' he said quietly, holding her in his arms. 'We need to save ourselves.'

'I have a suggestion,' said Markos quietly to his father. 'We could all go and stay in The Sunrise.'

'The Sunrise?'

There was something preposterous about the idea of these two families staying in a hotel where under normal circumstances a night would cost them more than they earned in a month.

'I have all the keys,' said Markos. 'The gates and railings are so high that the Turks haven't bothered to try and get in.'

'Perhaps it's not such a mad idea,' said Panikos.

The discussion went around in circles for a while, but time was passing and they could not be sure how long they had. It was clear that there was no better option. It would be impossible for them all to leave the city without being seen. And who knew what capture would lead to?

'We'll have to be careful about getting there,' said Maria. 'There are so many of us. And the baby . . .'

'It's getting dark,' said Hüseyin. 'But we still need to be very cautious.'

He and Markos were the only ones who had experience of moving about in the city with vigilance.

'We should leave now, find somewhere else close by where we can hide. When it's completely dark, Hüseyin and I will lead everyone in.'

'I don't think we should go back home for anything,' Hüseyin said quietly to his father.

He knew that the only things his mother might have wanted were the photographs of lost family members. Hüseyin had seen that they had been stolen for the value of the frames.

Maria had quickly assembled a few things she needed for the

baby, including a bottle of the penicillin, just in case, and some nappies. Vasilakis held a bunch of wooden clothes pegs. They were his soldiers.

All of them filed out of the Georgiou home at the same time and waited for a few minutes in the *kipos*. Vasilis locked up and then picked up a large bag crammed with spare clothes and personal possessions. He could scarcely lift it.

'Why are you bringing that?' asked Maria. 'We may not be there for long.'

She was holding the baby, and Panikos carried Vasilakis. Irini helped her husband with the bag and the two families separated, each taking a different route to a prearranged location.

Hüseyin avoided passing the Özkan home. It took longer, but he did not want his mother to see the mess of their broken belongings on the pavement in front of it. She had suffered enough pain in the past hour.

The Georgious were already waiting in the empty shop when they arrived. It had been stripped completely of its contents. They all sat quietly and immobile for two hours until it was as dark in the street as it was inside the store.

'I think we're safe to go now,' said Markos, taking a look outside.

They stood up. It was time to move into their new home.

Chapter Twenty-four

Markos and Hüseyin led their respective families along different routes, both aware of the safest roads to take.

The rest of them, who had hidden inside their homes for so long, were shocked by what they saw: the silent streets, the ransacked shops, the bomb-shattered buildings, the neglected gardens. The sight of their beautiful Famagusta in a state of shadowy semi-dereliction was painful.

Hüseyin looked at his father and saw him reduced by fear and sadness. Markos saw the same in Vasilis. In their sons' eyes, both men seemed to have shrunk in the past weeks.

Emine, silent and quietly weeping, was apparently unaware of anything.

Markos got everyone to wait in the doorway of the city's grandest department store just across from the hotel entrance. He wanted to unpadlock the gates and open the metal grille across the main doorway before the families got there so that they could all file in quickly. It was a complex process. Savvas Papacosta had been diligent about security. He prized his luxury hotel and had wanted to make it as secure as a diamond in a safe.

Within a few minutes they were inside and Markos locked everything behind them.

The reception area seemed very alien to them. Away from the intimate space of their own home, Irini and Vasilis felt especially ill at ease. In spite of the luxury that Markos had described to them, they already wished they were back at home.

A faint glow of moonlight illuminated the foyer. The families saw the glint of the dolphins and the mysterious silhouettes of the chandeliers. The white marble floor beneath their feet seemed solid yet insubstantial. This was a new world for them in every sense, its size intimidating and strange.

'So this is how foreigners live, is it?' commented Vasilis.

The acoustics amplified their whispers.

'I will find a bedroom for everyone and then tomorrow morning I'll show you all around,' Markos announced. 'It'll be easier in the light.'

He took five keys from the boards behind reception and led everyone up the main flight of stairs to the first floor.

In the half-light, Irini felt her way up, running her hand along the cool marble banister. The deep pile of the carpet and the width of the treads impressed her. The Sunrise was even more like a palace than she had imagined.

Markos opened the doors one by one and the hotel's latest guests went into their rooms. They were all on the same side of the corridor, from 105 to 113.

Before they shut their doors, Markos issued some instructions.

'Don't draw your curtains. It might attract attention from outside. In fact it's best to stay away from the windows. We don't want anyone to spot movement.'

Hüseyin could not help resenting that his family were suddenly being given orders by Markos Georgiou. For the past weeks they had accepted *his* authority, and overnight this seemed to have changed. For now, though, he appreciated that the only thing that mattered was that they were safe.

In the darkness, they all groped their way towards their beds, bumping into other pieces of furniture on the way. The feel of the satin bedspreads and smooth cotton sheets was unfamiliar, but the comfort they offered after their exhausting day was welcome. All of them lay fully clothed on top of the spacious beds and almost immediately fell asleep. The sheets on some of the beds, hastily vacated when the tourists had fled, were tangled.

In Room 105 were Emine and Halit; next door to them came Hüseyin with Mehmet; after that was Irini and Vasilis' room, and then Maria, Panikos and the two little ones.

Only Markos was alone. He remembered that Room 113 was one of the last places he had met with Aphroditi, but the smell of her perfume had long since faded. He lay back on the bed and thought of her for a while, recalling her caresses with satisfaction.

When he had first seduced her, she had seemed like a child, but over time she had become among the most passionate women he had ever slept with. He briefly wondered what had happened to her. The image that stayed with him was of her pale, perfect body naked but for a long chain that snaked down her neck, between her breasts and across her stomach. He enjoyed seeing her wearing nothing but gold.

Glancing at the luminous hands of his watch, Markos got up from his bed. He needed to make sure that all the doors were properly locked, including the inner door to the nightclub. He was fairly certain that everyone would be asleep now. As he crept down the corridor, he could hear the muffled sound of crying.

Except for Emine, they all slept with ease. They had never rested their heads on such soft pillows or felt the comfort of such mattresses beneath them. Just after six thirty the following morning, however, they were woken almost simultaneously by a dazzling light.

Slowly, slowly, slowly, the morning was being born. The clarity of the sky magnified the size and power of the huge orange star that rose steadily in front of them. The floor-to-ceiling windows gave them a perfect view of the bright rays spreading across the sea.

None of them had ever seen day breaking with such a majestic sunrise.

Weary eyes opened and were rubbed. It was magnificent. Every morning of their lives, the same phenomenon took place, but only a few times had any of them felt that the sun was coming up just for them.

Half an hour or so later, when the reds and golds had dissipated and the sun was sitting in the sky, Irini and Vasilis ventured into their bathroom and experimented with the ornate gold taps. They were relieved to find that the water was flowing. At the same time, Halit nervously tried out the shower and sniffed the soap suspiciously. In his bathroom, Hüseyin picked up a thick, soft towel. He had handed similar towels to guests every day but had never expected to use one himself. Mehmet put on a bathrobe and ran around the room tripping and giggling.

Emine was less impressed, as she was well used to the luxurious environment of The Sunrise. In any case, she was very preoccupied. Halit had not been able to make her part with the newspaper. She had even slept with it under her pillow. There was no question of her leaving her room.

'She must grieve today, tomorrow and maybe for a few days

after,' explained Halit to Irini, who expressed concern for her friend.

'Of course,' said Irini. 'But we must take some food to her.' In Irini's mind, a meal would make her friend feel better.

About an hour after sunrise, everyone else had wandered down to the foyer. Wide-eyed, they took in their surroundings. Mehmet and Vasilakis chased each other round and round the fountain, squealing as they went. They felt as if let out of a cage and were intoxicated by the size of the space.

'Shall I show you around?' Markos asked them, in the voice he might use for a guest checking in for a fortnight's vacation. 'The most important place is the kitchen. Let's start there.'

They were astonished by the sheer scale of it. There were rows of silver pans hanging from the ceiling, a multitude of meat cleavers and butchers' blades, sets of glinting whisks arranged like silver flowers, towers of white plates, huge copper urns, banks of gas hobs almost as far as the eye could see. It was a little dusty but otherwise spick and span. The chef was tyrannical, and before they had evacuated, he had insisted that everything was in its place.

'But is there anything to eat?' asked Mehmet.

Markos smiled. 'The food is kept in a special room,' he said. 'Shall we go and see?'

Mehmet made sure that he was close to Markos for the next stage of the tour. They walked into the cold room.

'What are those silver cupboards?' he asked.

'They're the refrigerators,' replied Markos. 'And I'm afraid there won't be much to eat in there.'

'Can we see?' The little boy believed nothing unless it was proved to him.

Without knowing what lay inside, Markos opened one of the

meat fridges. The stench that invaded the room was overpowering, a cloying sweetness that hit the back of the nostrils, descended to the throat and then went quickly to the stomach. The effect was almost instantaneous.

Hüseyin turned away just in time to vomit copiously. Mehmet made a dash from the room, quickly followed by the others. Everyone was coughing and retching.

Only Markos had actually seen the contents of the fridge: whole sides of raw beef that were blue-green and animated by writhing maggots.

He rushed back into the kitchen with the others, and apologised.

'I'm so sorry,' he said, shutting the door to the cold room. 'I had no idea . . .'

He was silently glad that he had not opened the fridge in which fish was kept.

'It won't all be like that,' he promised, seeing that they had lost heart. 'There is plenty we can make use of where the dry goods are kept.'

Fortunately he was right. There was another room off the main kitchen like a small warehouse, where flour, sugar, pulses and rice was kept. It was clear that mice had discovered this, but there were mountains of food still left, along with every other cooking ingredient that a gourmet chef needed to produce meals for hundreds of guests.

Although the chef favoured a sophisticated style of international cuisine, he still had good stocks of dried *koukia* (broad beans), *revithia* (chickpeas), *fakes* (lentils) and *fasolia* (white haricot beans).

Irini especially was wide-eyed. She had not imagined such quantities of food, and the relief was enormous after the weeks of rationing meagre supplies.

There were plenty of tins of tomato purée, cans of vegetables for the times when fresh ones were out of season, and gallons of evaporated and condensed milk.

'Look, Maria! Do you see all that halloumi?' said Irini with excitement.

They might be lacking in meat, but she would still be able to fill hungry stomachs.

Catering for such vast numbers meant that the commis chefs often took short cuts, so there were huge cartons of stock cubes and sesame paste in industrial quantities. On another shelf were enormous jars of pickled mushrooms and capers. There were also the basic ingredients: olive oil, salt, pepper, dried herbs and plenty of spices. Every meal would be flavoursome.

Irini looked up at the higher shelves and realised she would not be short of ingredients for making a dessert or two. There were twenty-pound boxes of whole nuts and packets of ground nuts as well as every dried fruit: sultanas, raisins, dates and figs. In huge jars there were quantities of fruit preserved in syrup: cherries, figs, quince, pumpkin, walnuts and even watermelons. She had never seen such quantities of honey.

To Mehmet's delight, there were also bars of chocolate. They were not a kind he had seen before. They would have looked at home in the giant hands of a colossus. He was allowed one soft square, and even that he could hardly manage to finish.

Irini smiled. She was like a child in a sweetshop herself and could hardly wait to begin cooking.

'We could stay here for ever, Markos,' she said, smiling. 'Can I try to light one of the ovens later?'

In her head were all the recipes from her childhood and the first few years of her marriage, when meat had been a luxury and fish just an occasional part of their diet. She knew a thousand ways to make pulses, rice and spices into tasty dishes, and the sweet things she could create with flour, sugar, nuts and oil were virtually limitless.

Markos saw the animated look on his mother's face.

'Let's do it as soon as we have finished the tour, *Mamma*,' he said. 'And by the way, Father has asked me where the bottles are kept.'

Irini gave her son a disapproving look.

'We don't know how long we'll be here,' he said. 'He can't live without it.'

'I know,' she said. 'But . . .'

'It does seem to help his pain,' said Markos.

From the kitchen, he took them to the ballroom, and his mother and sister were almost lost for words.

'But . . . the . . . oh my goodness . . . look at the . . . I've never . . . !'

They were awestruck by the mosaics, the furniture, the drapes, the murals and a thousand other details that embellished the hotel.

Some hours later, they were all sitting round a table together. Irini had suggested using the big table in the kitchen where the staff usually ate, but Markos had insisted that they should, on this occasion at least, eat in the ballroom.

Without any assistance, Irini had produced three tasty dishes as well as a tray of warm baklava. Markos had gone to the cellar to choose a fine wine to accompany his mother's cooking.

He had laid the top table with silver cutlery, crystal glasses and starched napkins, and candles burned in the sconces around the walls. He put his mother on the Salamis throne where Aphroditi had always sat, and his father next to her. Markos himself sat by his mother, with Maria and Panikos to his right. The Özkan men faced them.

Once they were all seated, Markos made a toast.

'*Stin yeia mas,*' he said. 'To our health.'

They all raised their glasses, except for Halit. Cautiously he tasted the first mouthful of Irini's food. To his surprise, it was delicious and not unfamiliar. Next to him, Hüseyin ate everything appreciatively, as did Mehmet.

'It's even nicer than Mummy's food,' he said loudly.

His father gave him a disapproving look, glad his wife was not there to hear.

Irini Georgiou had never looked so proud as everyone ate hungrily and then asked for more.

Upstairs, Emine gazed out of the window. Images of her slaughtered family members haunted her. Her imagination kept taking her to a vision of her precious sister. Had they killed her first, or had she been obliged to watch the murder of her three daughters? Were they raped? Had they been buried alive? How much did they suffer? Perhaps because she would never know the answer to these questions, her mind would not rest. She was tormented by the unknown.

At times her grief overwhelmed her. She wondered if her brother-in-law and the two boys had survived. Perhaps it would be better if they had not. And what about her other three sisters and their children?

Her mind dwelt constantly on Ali. If innocent women were being slaughtered, what would be happening to soldiers?

Small amounts of each dish were taken up to the first floor, but when the plates were brought down, the food was untouched.

'She just needs time,' Irini kept saying to Halit. 'She just needs time.'

The days passed. Irini was busy. Until Emine was ready to help her, she would be the lone cook for all of them. Maria helped when she could, but she was still nursing the baby most of the time.

With all the sacks of flour in the store, Irini even began to make bread. Each morning as people came down the stairs, the aroma rose to greet them. Three loaves baked for the day lay in the kitchen on a tray, golden, glazed and waiting.

Once they had eaten warm slices, thickly spread with honey or jam, Irini made them coffee. Breakfast was always taken around the staff dining table.

In the first few days, there were plenty of jobs for the men to do. In an extension to the kitchen there was a chilled storehouse where fresh produce was kept. There had been a delivery only hours before the evacuation, and salads, vegetables and fruits of every variety were lined up in neat compartments. During the intervening weeks they had all rotted. The store was full of flies, and judging from the scrabbling going on at the back, rats had also found their way in for a feast.

The odour was foul, but not as repugnant as the meat fridge, and all the men worked at clearing it out.

'Unless we clean it up, those rats will make their way into the kitchen,' Markos said. 'And the smell won't get any better.'

Within a day, the storehouse was scrubbed clean. The debris was piled into sacks, and later that night Markos and Hüseyin took them through the hotel's back gate and dumped them behind the food store. Panikos was rather overweight to be of use with heavy manual labour such as this.

Irini was insistent that their diet should be supplemented with something fresh, so Hüseyin had a daily mission to forage in abandoned gardens for fruit and tomatoes. It was strange that it still gave him a feeling of guilt every time he plucked an orange from a stranger's tree or pulled the last ripened tomato from a vine.

He had usually gathered as much as they needed by midday. After that he felt redundant. There was nothing else to go foraging for, and Markos had given him a strict order not to go out after dark.

'But surely it's safer at night?' Hüseyin suggested timidly.

'No, it's too risky,' Markos responded sharply. 'We can't predict the soldiers' movements then.'

Hüseyin felt put down. He would do what he was told, but nevertheless resented this man bossing him around.

Panikos had witnessed this exchange and could see that Hüseyin would be happy to be sent on a mission.

'We've got most things here,' he said to the young man, 'but all the radios in the rooms are built in. If I give you directions, can you go to my shop? There are some transistors – and there should be plenty of batteries too.'

Hüseyin went willingly. Only one transistor remained in the otherwise ransacked shop, along with a small supply of batteries, but at least it meant that they would be able to keep in touch with the world outside. That night, they took it in turns to listen to CyBC, then Radio Bayrak. It did not matter from which side the news came, it was not good. All around Cyprus there was still chaos, confusion and fear.

Not long after, Panikos came up with another mission for Hüseyin.

'While you're out,' he said, 'would you keep your eye out for a bicycle?'

Hüseyin did not disappoint him. Within days, he brought one back and, wheeling it in, he saw Panikos' face light up.

That afternoon, Panikos began his project to create a generator.

After a week or so, Emine finally emerged from her room. Irini was very happy to see her friend. She had prepared food for her every day, and when she saw that Emine was beginning to eat again, she knew it would not be long before she enjoyed her company. The women immediately began to prepare meals together, but Maria suggested a new task for them all.

Vasilakis had grown a little in the past few months, and Maria wondered if, in the hundreds of empty bedrooms, any small clothes had been left behind. In the final panic of leaving, the occupants of Room 111 had abandoned a full wardrobe. The voluminous sundresses and vast Hawaiian shirts were of no use to any of them, but Maria was certain that somewhere there would be something that fitted her little son and even the baby. There had been plenty of small children staying in the hotel after all.

'Mehmet's trousers are looking too short as well,' said Emine. 'We could start on the top floor and work down.'

Frau Bruchmeyer's wardrobe in the penthouse must have been full of beautiful and elegant clothes, but they did not go into her rooms.

'If anyone is going to come back,' said Emine, 'it's the lady who lived here. So we must leave everything just as it is. In any case, none of us have her figure . . .'

Markos had given them a master key that opened every bedroom on the fifteenth floor, and the baby lay and gurgled on the bed as they went through the possessions that had been left. Many people had tidied their rooms before leaving, straightening their beds, folding towels and hanging them neatly on the rail. Others had just run, grabbing their passports but nothing else. They had not even taken their suitcases.

The task of going through the abandoned clothes entertained and occupied the three women for hours that day.

There was plenty to try on. Most of the guests were wealthy; many of them were elegant and chic. Both Irini and Emine found the new outfits very different from their usual conservative styles, but they were happy to be in clean, fresh clothes. They also took trousers for the men. Panikos had already discovered a huge supply of starched and immaculately ironed shirts waiting unclaimed in the hotel's laundry room.

In two adjacent rooms the women also found everything that was needed for the children.

'Look at these baby clothes!'

There were little dresses and bonnets, tiny trousers, lace-edged vests and small cardigans. Maria read the labels. All of them had been made in France. Little Irini was immediately changed into a new outfit and Maria held her up to be admired. She kicked her legs as if in approval.

Up on the top floor of the hotel, the women felt very free. There was little chance that the sound of their voices would carry to the outside world. Even if there had been Turkish soldiers standing on the beach below, they would not have imagined that there were three women high above them who for a few hours laughed as if they had not a care in the world and almost forgot where they were.

As Maria twirled around in front of the mirror in a full-sleeved floral blouse and matching skirt, Emine exclaimed, 'You look lovely in that!' as though they were out on a shopping trip in one of Famagusta's chic department stores.

'Thank you!' said Maria.

'And look at these earrings!' said Irini. 'Try them on!'

They were made of plastic and the colour was a perfect match with the blouse.

'We're just borrowing all of this, aren't we?' said Maria uncertainly, spraying on some perfume that had been left on the dressing table.

'Well we're not going anywhere with it,' laughed Emine. 'I'll tell you what would make you look even lovelier . . .'

'What's that?'

'If we could do something with your hair . . .'

With clothes slung over their arms, they began their long descent – as yet they had only searched a single floor.

Before they sat down to dinner, Emine washed and trimmed Maria's hair, then put it in rollers. Maria went to the kitchen and sat close to the ovens to dry it, meanwhile chatting to Irini and Emine, who were preparing the meal.

That night all three women wore their new clothes and the men put on fresh shirts. Even Mehmet and Vasilakis had different outfits, though they probably cared the least of anyone.

They ate by candlelight again in the ballroom. The flames picked up the tiny squares of gold in the mosaic floor and passed through the prism of the crystal glasses to make a multicoloured pattern on the ceiling.

Irini had cooked a special dish with anchovies and rice. For the hotel's traditional Cypriot nights, there had been a supply of salted goat's meat, which had survived several months at the back of a fridge. Slices were served on a grand silver platter. They even managed to make a version of *pastitsio* with some preserved sausages – or *fırın makarnası*, as Emine called it.

Emine and Irini both noticed that, for the first time, Halit and Vasilis were engaged in conversation. The wives exchanged a satisfied glance. They had always hoped for this moment. As the days had passed, the two men had started to forget their differences.

After dinner that night, Markos suggested something that had been on his mind: there should be someone on watch. Just because there were strong iron gates and bars, it did not mean that the soldiers might not come looking for spoils, especially if they ever found out that The Sunrise had been the most glamorous hotel in Cyprus. The other hotels might be easier targets but they should be prepared.

He had noticed a pattern with the soldiers' movements. It appeared they patrolled Kennedy Avenue in the late afternoon.

'I think we should take turns and do shifts,' said Markos. 'The rooftop is a good viewing point for all the approaching roads. And they'll never come from the beach side.'

Next day, Halit volunteered to do the first shift.

'There's no reason why I can't do a shift too,' said Vasilis.

'But—' started Markos.

'I'm not too old for it,' he said defensively.

The only problem would be the long climb up fifteen flights of stairs, but Vasilis was adamant.

'We can always go up there together,' said Halit.

The offer made Irini smile. She had never imagined it would happen.

The men agreed that they should go to the rooftop every day before dinner. Markos made them promise that if they smoked, they would stay out of view. As dusk fell, the glow of a cigarette might attract a soldier's attention.

Every day after that, Hüseyin went up to the rooftop to take over from the men. It was only there that he had a sense of purpose. Since being in the hotel, he had yearned to run, not to fight but simply to get away from the stagnation. He wanted to do something other than sit and wait, not even knowing what it was he was waiting for. The lack of activity in the hotel was difficult for him. Earlier in the week he had woken up from a vivid dream in which he was in front of a selection panel for the national volleyball team. Too fat to jump, he had failed. He was now anxious that one day he might even be as corpulent as Panikos.

One night, he could not sleep. Quietly he slid open his balcony door and looked out. It was November now and the air was cool and crisp at night. He looked down at the beach, lit by the moonlight, and imagined he could hear his friends' voices. Every dent and footprint had been removed from the sand by a constant steady breeze. The sunloungers still sat there piled up where he had left them.

He wondered what had happened to the friends with whom he had played beach volleyball and water polo. The best times of his life had been spent on that beach, with boys like Christos. Kyria Georgiou had not mentioned him for a while. It was as if he had become a ghost in their lives.

He knew that Ali was fighting somewhere too. Perhaps the two of them had even encountered each other. Sometimes it made Hüseyin feel like a coward that he had not joined his brother, but he could not picture what he would be fighting for. To kill some Greek Cypriots? To avenge his lost cousins? Both would be pointless.

Night after night, in the flickering candlelight, Panikos tuned the radio. They caught up with the latest attempts to establish a solution for their devastated island and the situation with the homeless and the refugees. They also listened to the lists of people who were trying to find lost relatives, but the names they were hoping to hear were never read out. The batteries were running low, as was their belief that they would ever again see either Ali or Christos.

Chapter Twenty-five

In Nicosia, Savvas and Aphroditi were doing their best to survive. Although their diet was more limited than that being enjoyed by the Georgiou and Özkan families, Aphroditi was feeling much better now. All her symptoms of dysentery seemed to have passed, and a few weeks on, she noticed that, for the first time since she was a teenager, she had actually put on a little weight.

Even if she had packed her own clothes and brought them from Famagusta, she would not have been able to get into them; she was glad of her mother's elasticated waistbands.

Like Irini in Famagusta, the owner of her favourite *zacharoplasteion* could create a mouth-watering variety of results – all of them fattening – out of flour, honey, oil, nuts and various spices. Aphroditi knew that she should stop going there, but her reasons for visiting were no longer just to taste the beautiful pastries.

Day after day she sat at a table close to the window, watching for the woman with her ring. Sometimes she waited in vain, but on other days the person she was waiting for would come in, always with the same group of women.

How they seemed to love themselves, thought Aphroditi, how over-primped and over-preened they seemed against the backdrop of nearby dereliction. They seemed unaffected by everything that had happened. Aphroditi found herself feeling the occasional pang of envy for their camaraderie and their apparent oblivion to everything outside this shop. They appeared not even to notice her, so enthralled were they with each other and their hilarious conversation and unrelenting gossip. If the woman would only come in on her own, just once, Aphroditi could ask how she had acquired this piece of jewellery. As things were, she knew she could not separate her from the crowd. They were like a string of pearls without a clasp.

She tried not to stare. She did not want to be noticed. In spite of the fact that she had put on her aquamarine necklace, she knew she looked dowdy and down at heel.

One day the woman with the ring came in alone and sat down. It was Aphroditi's ideal opportunity and she was about to speak when she noticed something: the woman was wearing the matching earrings. Aphroditi felt the blood drain completely from her face. Even if she had ordered a pastry, not a mouthful could have passed her lips.

Just as she recovered her composure, she heard the ting of the bell. The door opened and the woman's friends danced in. They were even more dressed up than usual.

'*Hronia Polla*, Katerina!' they chorused. 'Many happy returns!'

They all sat down and coffees were immediately brought, along with a huge cream-filled gateau and seven plates.

'*Panagia mou!*' shrieked one of them. 'Your lovely husband has been generous! Look at those earrings!'

In turn, they all inspected the new addition to her jewellery collection. The earrings were indeed very splendid.

'Well, Giorgos says there's nothing worth investing in apart from diamonds at the moment, so I'm not going to dissuade him,' she said coyly.

'My husband says the same,' the one with the helmet hair added, 'but I don't seem to be benefiting like you!'

'Perhaps you should . . .'

The rest was whispered behind a hand, so Aphroditi did not catch what she said, but there were shrieks of mirth before everyone laughed and carried on eating cake.

Aphroditi slipped out, feeling as nauseous as if she had eaten twenty slices of Katerina's gateau. She imagined she could still hear their laughter from a hundred yards down the street.

She had plenty of information; she knew the name of the man who had bought her jewellery and the name of his wife. It would not be difficult to find out who they were. Nicosia was a small place and the number of people with that much money had dwindled. Their connection with the politician whose wife she had recognised would probably lead her to them.

But this was not entirely the issue. Seeing the jewellery that she knew had been in the safe fuelled her burning need to know what had happened to Markos.

It must be something terrible. Surely if he was in Nicosia he would have been to see her. He knew where they were living. But he had not come. Markos was the only person with the keys and combinations to the safes. Perhaps he had been forced to open them and was now a prisoner in Famagusta. The thought made her stomach churn.

She had to get there. It was the only way to find out.

Such a journey would be almost impossible, but there must be a way. She could not think of an excuse for asking Savvas to help without revealing the truth and, in any case, they were hardly speaking. She would have to sell the only things she had. Judging by the woman in the café, there was obviously a market.

Pawnbrokers were already operating in the city. It was the

perfect way to exploit anyone who was desperate for food. Most people had something of value to trade and they would accept a tiny fraction of its worth.

A few days later, Savvas told Aphroditi that he would be going away for a week. Though he was sure that it would not be long before the hotels in Famagusta were up and running again, he was still keen to explore other possibilities and wanted to see some sites on the south coast. Many hotel owners and developers were scared and ready to get out of the island, so prices would soon be hitting rock bottom.

He left Aphroditi a little cash to survive on and took the car. She could not bring herself to worry if he would get back safely.

The next night, after her shower, Aphroditi stood naked in front of the mirror. She had more than made up for her weight loss and was hating her bloated waistline. It seemed ironic to be getting fat when they had so much less to eat than before. Perhaps it was all the bread.

Then she noticed her breasts. They had expanded, and the nipples were enlarged. She looked at herself from the side.

'Oh my God!' she murmured aloud, half with shock, half with pleasure.

She turned to see herself from all sides. It was a long time since she had scrutinised herself in the mirror like this. Her shape had completely changed.

She found a piece of paper, sat down on the bed and, with shaking hands, began to calculate. She must have conceived at the beginning of August. Her lack of periods she had put down to illness and stress. It was now early December. There was no question about who the father was.

In spite of the circumstances, she was thrilled at the discovery. Now, more urgently than ever, she needed to find Markos.

The following morning, she made time to have coffee with the Loizous on the floor below her. For an hour or so they shared their experiences of the war. The Loizous had been in Nicosia for the duration. They had nowhere else to go. All their children had gone to England some years earlier, but they had no desire to leave their beautiful island.

'There were gunshots every day,' said Kyrios Loizou. 'And fires breaking out all over the place.'

'But we stuck it out, didn't we? We still have our home here,' said Kyria Loizou. 'And there's our orchard in the north. I'm sure we'll get it back again one day.'

'That's not to say that we haven't had to pawn a few things,' added her husband.

'Yes, prices have gone up so much!' exclaimed his wife. 'Specially bread!'

Aphroditi's ears pricked up. She thought for a moment.

'That's a shame,' she said. 'What did you have to take?'

'All our silver frames,' Kyria Loizou answered.

Aphroditi noticed a pile of photographs on the side table.

'And an icon,' said the elderly man. 'We got a good price for that . . .'

'But our son has promised to send us some money,' Kyria Loizou said cheerfully, 'so we'll go and retrieve them as soon as it arrives.'

A few minutes later, Aphroditi left the apartment. In her hand she had the address of their pawnbroker.

She felt vulnerable as she walked quickly through the streets. The pawnshop had always been in a seedy part of town, but such areas were even more run-down following the bombardment they had suffered. Slipping through the door, she noticed a row of silver-framed icons and wondered if one of them belonged to the Loizous.

In his white coat, the pawnbroker reminded Aphroditi of a pharmacist. As if scientifically, he examined her necklace, ring and bracelet with his magnifying glass to check on the purity of the stones, and then glanced up at her. He saw that there were earrings to match. She did not look like the sort of woman who would have owned such things, but he was impressed. He could not lie.

'They're good,' he said. 'Real quality.'

'I know,' Aphroditi replied. 'But I need to sell them.'

'I'll give you one hundred for the lot,' he said, laying them carefully on his counter. 'The stones are flawless, but you won't get more than that anywhere else.'

She was feeling bold.

'I need the money for something specific,' she said, 'and I don't know what it will cost. So that's what will help me decide.'

The pawnbroker took off his glasses.

'Well, if you tell me what this something specific is, then perhaps I can help you make a decision.'

It was still early and there was nobody else in the shop.

'Can I sit down?' said Aphroditi, suddenly feeling exhausted.

The pawnbroker pulled a chair round for her.

'Tell me,' he said.

Perhaps for the first time in her life, Aphroditi felt she had nothing to lose.

'I need to go to Famagusta . . .'

The man looked at her. This woman must be insane. Not only was she considering taking one hundred pounds for a set of jewellery worth fifteen hundred, but she wanted to go to one of the most dangerous places in Cyprus. Did she not know that it was fenced off and patrolled by Turkish soldiers?

'But I need someone to take me,' she added.

He realised that she was planning to go alone. She must be desperate.

'Well . . .' he said, with deliberate hesitation, 'I might be able to help you with this.'

His mind had already come up with a plan. This woman certainly had the means to pay whatever it cost, and he would still make a profit out of her. He dealt in desperation, and also in information, and he made money from both.

The pawnbroker had a group of contacts who could be bribed to arrange for safe conduct to the northern part of the island. Many Greek Cypriots had left valuables hidden or even buried in their gardens when they fled from the invasion, fully expecting to return in a short while, but weeks had now turned into months and they were losing faith in the talks and negotiations that might allow them home. All they wanted was to cross the Attila line, make a brief, clandestine visit to retrieve a few valuables, and leave again. It had happened many times and there were networks of people who could help. Anything could be done, as long as payment was forthcoming.

Going right inside the abandoned city of Famagusta was another matter. There were Turkish soldiers willing to accept a bribe, but breaking through the barbed wire was a different proposition.

'Look,' he said, 'come back tomorrow. It won't be cheap but there will be a way. I'll have news for you then.'

Aphroditi gathered up her jewellery, carefully put it back on and left the shop.

That night, she lay awake for hours, thinking.

The discovery of her pregnancy both excited and terrified her. She lay with her hands on her belly. It seemed impossible now that she had not been aware of it before.

Somehow she had to find out whether Markos was still in

Famagusta. The prospect of seeing him gave her such butterflies that she wondered if the baby was already moving inside her.

Eventually she fell into a dream-filled sleep. Markos was waiting for her on the beach outside The Sunrise, and they walked for miles, hands joined, bare feet sinking into deep sand.

When she woke, her pillow was soaked with tears. Was such joy really beyond reach? Later that day she would return to the pawnbroker. This could be her only chance of happiness.

As Aphroditi made her way through the streets of Nicosia, rain was turning the dust to mud. It was cold and yet humid, a combination that brought coughs for the young and aching joints for the old.

She had found an old waterproof coat of her mother's. It was caramel coloured and there was a silk scarf in the pocket that she put on to keep her hair dry, knotting it under the chin just as her mother used to. She caught a glimpse of herself in the mirror and hardly recognised the person she had become. Her bump was well hidden beneath her mother's gathered skirts and shapeless dresses, but she knew that the combination of the outfits and her spreading figure made her look like an old lady. Her reflection, even in broken shop windows, confirmed this.

The pawnbroker seemed happy enough to see her.

'I've found someone to take you,' he said. 'On Monday.'

Savvas was returning on Tuesday evening, so she would have preferred to go sooner.

'It couldn't be any earlier than that, I suppose?'

'No,' the man said roughly, as if reacting to ingratitude. 'There aren't many people prepared to do this, you know.'

In what she now thought of as former days, people had never spoken to her in that way. She had status and beauty back then.

Nowadays, the basic need to survive had changed the way everyone behaved, and manners seemed to matter not at all.

'What time shall I come?' she asked.

'Late afternoon,' he said. 'It's better to do something like that when it's getting dark. And I assume you want to come back the same night?'

Aphroditi had not thought about this at all.

'Yes, yes . . . I'm sure I will.'

'We'll have to settle up now,' he said, not looking her in the eye but staring blatantly at the hand on which she wore the aquamarine ring.

She pulled it off with some difficulty; her fingers had swelled a little in recent weeks. Its absence made her left hand look bare.

She removed the earrings and put them on the counter. Then the bracelet.

The pawnbroker said nothing. He was waiting for the final part of the payment. Aphroditi had not yet undone her coat, but now she did so and looped the pendant over her head.

He leaned over and took it out of her hands. This was the prize.

'Do I get . . .' she began hesitantly.

'A receipt?'

She nodded. There was no reason to trust this man. Only desperation had brought her here.

He got out a small pad, scribbled on the top sheet, tore it off and handed it over.

'In lieu of safe conduct,' it read.

What else had she expected? Folding the paper, she slipped it in her pocket and said an inaudible thank you.

The bell jangled. An elderly couple was entering as she left. Aphroditi knew them by sight, but there was not the slightest flicker of recognition on their distraught and wretched faces.

The next three days passed with agonising slowness. Aphroditi did not know what to do with herself. She slept late and then walked the streets in the afternoons, sometimes losing herself, often coming up against walls of sandbags. The musty smell of emptiness was all-pervading. It did not matter much where these ambles took her. There was always the possibility of finding a shop selling fruit or a tin of milk, and she carried a string bag for this purpose. These days there were very few things that she felt like eating. She had no appetite for sweet things any more and had not been back to the *zacharoplasteion* since Katerina's saint's day, the day she had seen her diamond earrings.

She usually returned from her wanderings late in the afternoon. Having closed the shutters, she slumped, exhausted, in what used to be her father's favourite armchair. In the semi-darkness she was almost too tired to listen to the radio, which reported on little but the state of the refugee camps and the stagnation of talks between Greek and Turkish Cypriot leaders. She had no heart for politics.

One night she rang her mother, who, as usual, urged her to come to England.

'Why don't you come?' she asked. 'I just don't understand you. What is there to stay for?'

'Savvas is still hoping . . .'

'But why can't you go back later on . . . when everything is settled?'

'It's more complicated than that, Mother.'

'It all sounds very simple to me, dear.'

If only you knew, thought Aphroditi. If only you even had the *slightest* idea.

'Well, if you see sense,' continued Artemis, 'you know there's space for you here.'

'I'll call you again next week,' said Aphroditi. 'Bye bye, Mother.'

Their conversations always took a similar path. At the moment when the receiver clicked, both mother and daughter felt dissatisfied.

Finally the day appointed for her journey to Famagusta arrived.

Aphroditi was so full of trepidation that she could not eat. She knew there was a possibility that The Sunrise had been destroyed and the safes broken into. And that something terrible had happened to Markos.

She killed time tidying up the apartment, remembering that Savvas was returning the following day. Then she looked in her mother's wardrobe to see if there was anything that might make her look less frumpy. By late afternoon, five or six dresses lay discarded on the bed. Neither floral prints nor geometric designs flattered her, and most plain colours seemed to drain her. Finally she chose a shirt dress. Green used to suit her so well, but now it seemed as if nothing could improve her looks. The shapeless, button-through style hid her pregnancy.

As she stood in front of the mirror, she realised how much she now looked like her mother. Although she had her father's eyes, her stature and shape were uncannily similar to Artemis Markides'. Her hair at least was still dark brown. It had grown several inches in the last months and was drawn back with a clip. She was not yet ready for the short uniform style of most older Cypriot women.

Aphroditi glanced down at her watch. Apart from her wedding ring, it was the only item of any value she still possessed.

The time had passed. She laced up some flat winter shoes, put on her raincoat and picked up her shoulder bag. Inside it she dropped her key, her purse and the receipt from the pawnbroker. Then she went out of the front door.

She paused on the landing, suddenly remembering something. The small velvet pouch with her pearl was in a bedside drawer for safe keeping. She could not leave without it. Perhaps it would be her lucky charm. She nursed the possibility that she might never come back.

She let herself back into the apartment, retrieved what she wanted and left again.

Aphroditi knew that she was taking a huge risk by going into the occupied part of the island, and there was a brief moment of doubt. Was this fair to her unborn child? The belief that she was on a mission to find the baby's father was the only thing that stopped her from turning back.

Chapter Twenty-six

It was five in the evening and she was due to meet her escort just before nightfall. There was ample time, but she was anxious nevertheless about being late. Something told her that the pawnbroker would not be sympathetic.

Fear and excitement mingled inside her.

The streets were unlit, so she needed to be careful to avoid tripping on broken paving stones or pieces of fallen masonry. As she stumbled along, she realised that the shoes she had chosen felt like boats.

There were very few people around. A cluster of Greek soldiers on one street corner did not appear to notice her as she passed. They were standing in a circle, facing inwards, smoking and laughing, oblivious to anything but the joke that one of them was telling. She saw a mother with two small children. They looked destitute, but she noticed that the little girl was carrying a loaf. She caught its fragrance as they passed.

Aphroditi suddenly felt hungry, but it was too late to do anything about it. Her favourite pastry shop was not far away, but she could not go there now.

Eventually she reached her destination. There were no lights inside the shop, and when she saw that the sign in the window had been turned to read '*Kleisto*' – 'Shut' – she had to fight back tears.

For a few moments she stood pretending to peruse the items in the unlit window. The display was piled high with clocks, watches, ornate silver frames, icons, radios and other things that had once been treasured by their owners. Now they just looked like junk.

She was alone in the street.

She imagined her aquamarines stored somewhere inside the shop, or perhaps they had already been sold. There was no time for sentimentality, but she asked herself if she had been conned. All she had was an unsigned scrap of paper.

A moment later she heard the sound of a jeep, and when she turned, she saw that it had drawn up almost next to her. The window was wound down and a man's voice spoke gruffly.

'Papacosta?'

She nodded.

'Get in.'

Nobody opened the door for her these days. It still seemed strange sometimes.

The driver had left the engine running, and the moment she climbed into the passenger seat, the vehicle moved off again.

Without any preamble, he informed her of the schedule. He sounded Greek rather than Greek Cypriot.

'This is what happens. I take you to a crossroads about ten miles outside Nicosia. Someone picks you up from there and does the next twenty miles. After that, you're taken on foot—'

'On foot?' exclaimed Aphroditi. 'But—'

'It's not far. You won't be on your own,' the driver said impatiently. 'Then with any luck there'll be someone at the wire.'

With any luck. It sounded so casual, but what could she say? What choice did she have now?

She hugged her bag to her. The jeep had already reached the edge of the city and the road was rough and gravelly, worse than in the past. She tried to see if the landscape had changed in any way, but it was impossible in the darkness to make out anything much. They jolted along, sometimes swerving to miss a pothole.

The driver made it plain that he had no interest in talking to her. Most of the time he seemed to be looking out of the side window rather than the windscreen, which terrified Aphroditi.

They passed no other cars on the road, and in what seemed like no time, the vehicle stopped. The driver drew on his cigarette. Aphroditi turned to him for an explanation, noticing for the first time that he looked about eighteen. The youth did not speak, but rudely indicated with a nod of his head that someone was waiting up ahead.

Having opened the door, she swung her legs round and dropped to the ground. The other vehicle had no lights on and its engine was not running. There appeared to be nobody in it.

She walked nervously towards it, her heart beating furiously. The jeep had already driven off. When she got closer, she could see a figure in the driver's seat. He was fast asleep. She tapped on the window and the man woke with a start. Without even looking at Aphroditi, he berated her for being late. Being entirely in these people's hands, she was in no position to argue.

This driver was more ill-tempered than the previous one. He said little, but the stream of curses he uttered under his breath identified him as a Greek Cypriot.

'Have you taken other people to Famagusta?' she asked nervously.

'No,' he said firmly. 'Nobody wants to go back there. Too dangerous.'

This stage of the journey seemed to take an age. The driver's cigarettes made her nauseous, but to her great relief she eventually felt the deceleration of the car.

'This is where you get out,' he said, pulling on the handbrake.

'But there's no one here!' she protested.

'Well it's as far as I go,' he said flatly.

Aphroditi wondered how many people had taken a cut of her payment. Certainly none of them seemed to have been paid to care.

'But I can't just stand here in the middle of nowhere,' she said, determined to hide her alarm.

'I'm not waiting around,' he said. 'That's not what I've been paid to do.'

'But isn't someone meant to be meeting us here?'

'I don't know what you've arranged,' he said rudely. 'I was told to get you to this place, and that's what I've done.'

The thought of being abandoned in this lonely spot filled Aphroditi with terror. She was about to give up her plan and ask if he could just drive her back to where they had come from.

'That's Famagusta,' said the driver, pointing. 'You can walk from here.'

Out of the window she saw the forbidding outline of a city. She had not realised they were so close. There it was. Her home. The place she had loved, now in darkness.

Then she saw a figure coming towards them. It was a man. He seemed to have appeared from nowhere. Slim, medium height. For a fraction of a second she thought it was Markos. He was coming to meet her! She put her hand on the door handle and was about to let herself out and run towards him.

A moment later the man was close enough for her to see that she had been mistaken. He looked nothing like the man she loved. There was not the slightest resemblance.

'I suppose that's your guide,' said the driver.

She got out of the car and without saying anything slammed the door behind her.

Now that he was close up, Aphroditi wondered how she could ever have imagined that this man was Markos. He was around the same age but more thickset, and she noticed that he had several teeth missing. He had a fixed expression, his mouth set in a frozen smile. The dark gaps between his teeth made him look sinister.

She realised immediately that he did not speak Greek, and when she tried some English, that did not work either.

'Famaguthta?' he asked, his missing front teeth giving him a curious lisp.

As if there was anywhere else to go, thought Aphroditi.

She nodded.

They walked side by side. Aphroditi's shoes were giving her blisters, but she plodded along determinedly. Gradually the city loomed larger in front of them and she began to make out the individual buildings, low-rise apartment blocks and houses.

The landscape around them was flat. They passed a few ruined homes and some empty, unlit farmhouses. It was now about midnight and the temperature had dropped. She wished she had worn a thicker coat. Even though they were walking quite briskly, she began to shiver. Fear was taking hold of her.

Only when they were a hundred yards or so away did she notice the fence. She turned towards her guide to see his reaction and saw that he was prepared. He was removing some cutters from his pocket.

The silence was heavy. She recalled her last moments in the city, when everyone was taking flight: the noise of car engines, hooting horns, shouting, the roar of aircraft overhead. Now there was nothing. All she could hear was the thumping of her heart.

Quickly and efficiently he snipped the wires and let her through, not bothering to rejoin the pieces. Presumably they would return the same way.

Then she heard voices. Turkish.

Her guide grabbed her by the wrist. Instinctively she pulled away from him, confused and alarmed. Up until now he had seemed less rough in his ways than the first two men she had encountered, and it took her a moment to realise that this man was not wanting to steal her watch. He was merely pointing at it, making stabbing gestures as if trying to tell her something.

Although he was speaking very quietly, he was miming as well, tapping the watch face and holding up two fingers. Aphroditi understood that she would have to be back in two hours. She also realised that the voices she had heard were coming closer and the toothless Turkish Cypriot was handing her over to someone new.

Two Turkish soldiers sauntered into view. When she looked round, Aphroditi saw that the previous guide had already disappeared. It was all she could do to remain upright. She felt as if her trembling legs might collapse beneath her.

One of the soldiers, his arms folded contemptuously, looked her up and down silently. He was thickset and had a moustache. The other one, slightly taller and fairer, lit a cigarette and drew on it deeply before addressing her in Greek. She felt it was a good sign.

'What do you want here?'

It was the only question that mattered, but she had not expected to be asked. The answer she gave could not be the truth, but she had to say something.

'I want to see our hotel,' she said.

'Our hotel . . .' he repeated.

The other soldier laughed. Aphroditi realised that he understood Greek too, and he also parroted her words. The notion of what was now meant by 'our' clearly amused them.

'So let's go to *our* hotel then, shall we?'

Their disdainful sarcasm was threatening enough, but when one of them put his arm through hers and began to steer her along, fear began to rise within her.

'Shall we go down to the sea?' he asked.

Aphroditi nodded. She was fighting back her tears now. Whatever happened, she must not allow them to see how afraid she was.

The second soldier took her other arm and they strode along like the best of friends, though they were both taller and their steps much longer than hers. She was struggling, her blistered feet now bleeding, though she could not look down to see them.

'*Parakalo*. Please,' she entreated quietly. 'I can't keep up with you.'

The soldiers said something to each other in Turkish but did not slow their pace. In spite of their displays of mocking friendship, they pretended not to hear.

Sandwiched between them, Aphroditi surveyed the dilapidation of the streets. Weeds were growing between the paving stones and the shops were derelict. There was not enough time to take it all in. This was not the city she knew. It was a place she did not recognise. Its soul had gone.

Several times during their march to the seafront, they met other groups of soldiers and stopped for a few minutes. Aphroditi's lack of understanding of the Turkish language fuelled her sense of fear. If only she had been more diligent and bothered to learn more than the basics, it might have helped her now.

Her appearance had already caused her some shame and embarrassment in Nicosia, but now she was grateful for the way in which her shapeless clothes made her look like countless middle-aged women. Most of the soldiers they encountered were momentarily curious about this dowdy Greek Cypriot in a shabby mackintosh and headscarf, but then ignored her completely.

They seemed to have all the time in the world to chat, light each other's cigarettes and pass around a bottle of whisky. None of them were expecting any action. It was clearly just a formality to be patrolling these empty streets, where the only other living creatures were rats and mice. Drunkenness was not going to prevent them from fulfilling their almost non-existent duties.

What bothered Aphroditi most at this stage was that she only had two hours in the city. Time was ticking away, but she knew it would be unwise to point this out.

When the first of the hotels came into view, the taller of the soldiers asked her:

'Where is "our" hotel, then?'

The stockier one spoke to her more aggressively.

'*Pou?*' he repeated. 'Where?'

She had a momentary thought that it might be better not to lead them to The Sunrise, as they might then imagine she had more money. She dismissed the idea, however. Now that she had come all this way, she might as well reach her destination. The smallest possibility that she might see Markos or even be able to work out what had happened to him kept returning to her. It gave her just enough courage to stop her from falling to her knees and pleading with the soldiers to take her back to the wire.

'It's called The Sunrise,' she said. 'It's down towards the end of the beach.'

For a few moments the soldiers jabbered between themselves. She had felt their mood change. As before, she had no idea what they were disagreeing about, which only made the situation more frightening.

Even with their unsympathetic pace, Aphroditi knew that ten minutes' walking still lay ahead. The only thing that had kept her feet moving was hope, but as she took in the state of the city and realised that nobody could possibly be living there, her energy began to drain from her. They walked down Demokratias Avenue and Ermou Street, where the once-gleaming plate glass of her favourite shops was now jagged and broken. Almost everything had been wrecked.

When they got to the strip of hotels, she could see that some of them had smashed windows, but she was not sure if this had been caused by the earlier bombing or if they had been broken into.

In the distance, she could make out The Sunrise. It was still standing, apparently intact, but very eerie in the darkness. She was so close now, only a hundred yards or so away. It was strange how energy could return with hope or excitement.

The soldiers stopped outside a small guest house opposite the hotels.

'We're going for a break now,' said the taller one. 'These friends of ours will get you where you want to go . . .'

It was the fourth time Aphroditi had been handed over to someone new, but the look of dismay on her face did not appear to register with them. Two other soldiers had appeared on the pavement next to her. They were older than the first pair; their crinkly hair had streaks of grey. One of them was wearing a greatcoat over his uniform.

Even from several feet away, Aphroditi could smell alcohol on their breath. One of them reached out and chucked her under the chin. She felt the sharp scratch of his fingernails.

He said something in Turkish and the others laughed.

The first two soldiers must have told them where she wanted to go, and the new ones began walking towards The Sunrise. She followed them meekly. She gathered that they did not speak any Greek.

On the roof of the hotel, Vasilis and Halit were on watch. A few days earlier they had noticed that soldiers were newly billeted in a guest house a short distance away. Markos had insisted that they increase their hours on duty.

Their stomachs were full of good food and Vasilis had enjoyed some wine from the hotel cellar. They kept each other awake by talking; over these past months, there was little they had not told each other of their lives. They were vigilant, though, and took their job very seriously. Although their view was obscured by the hotel next door, they kept a close eye on the soldiers' movements.

'So how often do you prune?' Halit was asking, running his *tespih* through his fingers.

'Well, it depends on rainfall . . .' answered Vasilis. He was sprinkling water on the tomato plants that they were cultivating on the rooftop.

Vasilis' citrus orchard remained his favourite subject, and although Halit had given his up when he had left Maratha to bring his family to Famagusta, he dreamed that he would have trees again one day.

As the men talked, they always faced towards the street, keeping a lookout. Occasionally a vehicle would drive in their direction and turn off opposite the hotel, up a side street that eventually led out of the city. Very occasionally soldiers went past the hotel on foot.

'Vasilis! Look!' Halit whispered, interrupting the other man's flow. 'Down there!'

Three figures were coming from the left and stopped in front of the railings of the hotel.

'It's all locked up, Halit. Nobody can get in.'

'I know, this place is like a fortress, but . . .'

'Don't worry, my friend. Papacosta was prepared.'

Another second passed.

'Pass me the glasses,' said Halit. 'There's something odd.' There was a note of real anxiety in his voice.

Early on in their stay at The Sunrise, when they'd agreed that they needed to keep watch, Hüseyin had come back with a pair of binoculars that had been dropped in the street. They were army issue and powerful enough for them to identify uniforms and faces even in a low light.

'Two soldiers,' said Halit. 'But there's a woman too.'

'A woman? Are you *sure*?'

'Take a look!'

Vasilis saw that there was indeed a woman walking behind the two soldiers. The men sauntered, their gait swaggering. They were apparently indifferent to her.

He drew back from the parapet of the roof, anxious not to be seen. Halit remained poised and still, following their progress as they approached.

Aphroditi saw that they were almost at The Sunrise. It looked so unfamiliar, and the railings that surrounded the hotel so unfriendly.

She had never seen the gates closed before. At more than eight feet in height, both railings and gates were unscalable. Looking through, she could see that the main doors were also still protected by the iron grid and that this had not been forced open.

The soldiers remained on either side of her as she stood in front of the bars, looking in at the intense blackness of the windows. They were talking over her head. She wished she understood even a word.

Halit, hidden in the shadows, tried to focus on the three of them. It was hard to make anything out, with the lines of the bars across their faces.

Perhaps, thought Aphroditi, if she could get them to take her round to the other side of the hotel, facing the sea, there might be a means of getting in. With no common language, all she could do was point. Unless she found a way of getting inside the hotel, her mission would have been futile.

One of the soldiers bent down and said something to her. His face was half an inch from hers and the overpowering combination of bad breath and acrid sweat made her heave. He noticed her recoil and it seemed to infuriate him.

Seizing her arm, he pulled her roughly away from the iron fence. Without warning, his apparent boredom and indifference seemed to have turned into aggression. The other soldier was also shouting at her now. He spat on the ground just in front of her feet.

Still holding her arm, the first soldier hauled her into the passageway to the side of the hotel. This was where Aphroditi had wanted to go, but not like this.

From the rooftop, Halit watched the trio disappear out of sight. He had heard the soldiers' shouts. The sound had carried all the way up to the rooftop.

The Sunrise

'I don't know who she is,' he said, 'but I wish we could help her.'

'We can't,' said Vasilis. 'It'll put all of us in danger.'

'But we need to alert Markos and Hüseyin! They should know there are soldiers right next to us.'

'You go! I'll stay up here. Give me the binoculars.'

Unbeknown to any of them, Markos had gone out that night. As he came southwards down the main road in front of the hotels, the soldiers had already turned into the passageway. Their rough voices alerted him to their presence and he knew his route home was blocked. More than that, he had left the fire door on the latch.

He ducked into the side road opposite The Sunrise and crouched in a doorway. From his hiding place, he could see into the passageway. He realised that there were two soldiers and they were not alone.

In between them was a third person, much smaller. Not a child, but probably a woman. She was caught in the middle of them, held so tightly that there was no question of her getting away. Her feet scraped the ground. She was being dragged.

Then he heard screaming.

Up on the roof, his father heard it too. Aphroditi was screaming as hard as she could for help. In Greek. In English. Just in case someone, anyone, might hear.

Halit had knocked on Markos' and Hüseyin's doors. He did not want to rouse the women, so he had not banged hard. Hüseyin had appeared immediately, but they could not get a response from Markos.

Hüseyin left his father behind as he sprinted upstairs to the roof.

'You won't be able to see them from here,' whispered Vasilis. 'They're out of sight. Almost directly below us.'

They could still hear the sound of the woman's screams, and a short while afterwards loud, incomprehensible sobbing that required no translation.

Her voice. Something stirred inside Markos. He knew that voice. He had heard that whimper before. It couldn't be . . . ? He recalled the last time he had made love with Aphroditi and the noise she had made; how she had sobbed, but with pleasure that time. There was something in its tone that told him it was her, but the person he had glimpsed briefly before she was obscured by the soldiers had looked nothing like the woman he remembered.

The soldiers had not taken Aphroditi far. Pushing her against the rough concrete wall of The Sunrise, they raped her, brutally. Finally she was too weak even to scream. All the fight went out of her.

Hüseyin took the binoculars from Vasilis. He could not see into the side passage, but something else had caught his eye. A slight movement across the road from the hotel. The flash of a white shirt. He adjusted the focus.

There, across the road, he saw a man watching. It was Markos.

Something seized hold of Hüseyin. All rationality left him. He handed the binoculars back to Vasilis, then turned and bolted for the door leading to the staircase. A panting Halit was just reaching the top of the stairs and emerging on to the roof when he met his son running down the other way. Hüseyin did not stay to explain.

Aphroditi lay slumped against the wall of The Sunrise. The two soldiers now had a dilemma on their hands. They could not leave the woman here. She had to be delivered back. If they did not have this obligation they would probably have finished her off there and then. There were plenty of places to leave a body. But if they killed her, there would be too many questions asked.

And they did not want to jeopardise the payment they had been promised.

Without understanding a word, Aphroditi knew that they were arguing about her.

They pulled her to her feet. Her raincoat was still miraculously buttoned up, and even belted.

As Hüseyin emerged through the fire door into the passageway, he saw that the soldiers were dragging what looked like a large rag doll towards the main street. He was too late to help.

At that moment, reason returned to him. If he revealed himself now, coming out of the hotel, he was putting the lives of two families in danger, perhaps to no avail.

His heart was beating furiously, conscience and duty warring inside him. He pressed himself against the wall. He was just in a nightshirt and knew it was poor camouflage.

At some point Markos would have to come down the passage to re-enter via the fire door. What had he been doing out at night? Hüseyin shuddered at the thought of what might have happened if the soldiers had got to the end of the passageway and found this door ajar.

The last thing he wanted was to confront Markos, so he turned round to make his way back inside.

Markos had done his best to remain out of sight, but suspicion that the woman he had seen was indeed Aphroditi urged him to take a step out of the darkness.

The soldiers were now pulling the woman along on her heels. It was less effort than dragging her the other way. They marched in step in the direction of their guest house, entirely oblivious to the presence of a man watching them from behind.

Aphroditi herself was barely conscious, but she forced open the slits of her eyes, swollen by the soldiers' remorseless punching, and wondered if some release was finally being granted her. Was this the vision of heaven that artists tried to paint and poets to describe? The rape had stopped . . . there was moonlight . . . there was Markos . . . He was pushing his fingers through his hair . . . yes, it was definitely Markos. She tried to say his name, but nothing came out of her mouth.

His curiosity satisfied, Markos withdrew into the shadows again.

In his haste to get back inside, Hüseyin's foot caught in something and he almost tripped. Bending down to release himself, he could feel it was the strap of a bag. He picked it up and took it with him into the hotel. He went straight up to the rooftop to speak to his father and Vasilis Georgiou.

'They've gone,' he said.

'I wonder who she was . . . Did you see her?' asked Vasilis.

'Not clearly,' Hüseyin answered. 'I don't even know if she survived.'

'Poor woman,' muttered Halit. 'Those total bastards. A defenceless woman . . .'

'You mustn't tell your mother, or Maria or Irini,' Vasilis said emphatically. 'On any account.'

'Of course not, Kyrie Georgiou.'

'They would all die of fear,' added Halit.

'What's that you're holding?' asked Vasilis.

'I picked it up in the passageway. I suppose it's the woman's bag.'

'Is there anything inside?' enquired Halit. 'It might tell you who she was.'

Hüseyin unzipped it and tipped out the contents. A purse, a key and a little velvet pouch. Inside the purse were a few notes and half a dozen coins. When he tipped the velvet pouch upside down, something fell into his palm. The three men all leaned forward to see what it was.

'Did you ever see such a tiny pearl?' asked Halit.

Hüseyin replaced it carefully. Nothing in the bag identified the owner.

'Look,' he said, 'I'm going to get some sleep.'

He turned away before the two older men had noticed that there were tears in his eyes.

Whoever she was, he thought, I failed to save her.

He was furious with himself, but he was even angrier with Markos Georgiou.

'*Allah belanı versin*,' he muttered. 'God damn you, Markos Georgiou.' He must have seen the whole episode.

Hüseyin sank into a deep sleep filled with nightmares and noise. Aphroditi's bag sat on his bedside table.

The following morning, he went straight down to the kitchen, where the smell of warm loaves greeted him as usual. Mehmet, Vasilakis and Markos were having sword fights with long-handled wooden spoons.

Hüseyin sat opposite Markos and observed him. He could not swallow the bread with jam that was their daily fare, and the rich, dark coffee turned his stomach.

From the minute he got up in the morning, Markos was the centre of attention, the life and soul of the party. It was not just because of his relentlessly happy mood, but also because he always had something to say to everyone. Hüseyin wondered if he put on that charm like other men put on trousers and shirts. He realised that Markos Georgiou was a consummate actor. There was something so calculating in the way he focused on certain people around him.

This morning he had chosen the children to be the object of his attention and exuberance. Even the time he spent playing with Mehmet was a way of finding favour with Emine and probably Halit too. It worked. Hüseyin could see it in their eyes.

This was the same man who only the previous night had watched a woman being raped and done nothing to save her.

Chapter Twenty-seven

THE SOLDIERS HAD dragged Aphroditi back to the guest house, and had half-thrown her into a jeep. The two younger soldiers she had met earlier that night reappeared and drove her back to the fence. Gradually physical pain began to overwhelm her. It was the only thing that told her she was alive. As the shock wore off there was nothing to keep it at bay. Every jolt of the jeep, every bump over every stone, sent waves of excruciating agony through each limb and muscle.

She was indifferent to everything on the return journey. All sense of danger, anxiety and impatience had gone. She no longer cared about where she was going or where she had come from. It did not matter whether she was dead or alive. This sense of emotional neutrality did not even allow her to feel despair. Perhaps this would be the way to survive from now on. To feel absolutely nothing.

Many times during her ordeal she had thought of the baby, but the numbness of her emotions now stopped her from doing so. Perhaps this was all part of the living death that she was experiencing.

Her escorts on the return journey were the same men as before. When it came to the final stage, the brusque Greek was chain-smoking but at least he had noticed that she was unwell. He handed his silent passenger his own water bottle. For Aphroditi, the gesture was one of almost unbearable kindness. She took it and drank.

'Did you find what you were looking for?' he asked.

An overwhelming sense of shame prevented her from replying. She could feel that her eyes and lips were swollen and her raincoat was covered in filth, but perhaps he could not see this as it was still dark. It was only then that she realised she had lost her shoes and her bag.

It would have been impossible to walk all the way from the pawnbroker's shop, so she asked to be dropped closer to home. Since it was on his way into the city, the driver could not object.

At the end of her parents' street, Aphroditi managed to get out and hobble towards the entrance to the block. Without her bag, she had no purse, no key, no pearl.

On the balcony above her, she heard a sweet sound. It was the singing of the canary, blithe, melodious, oblivious. It was six in the morning and the bird was delivering its own private dawn chorus to herald the day. It was also when Kyria Loizou brought its food. Sure enough, she appeared, and as soon as she saw Aphroditi, standing as if frozen to the spot, she hurried down.

'I've lost my key,' said Aphroditi feebly.

'Don't worry, my dear,' answered Kyria Loizou, concealing her shock at the young woman's appearance. 'Your parents always made sure I had a spare one. And they had one of mine too. I'm sure I can find it.'

She took Aphroditi's arm and led her into the hallway. The elderly woman soon found the key inside an old tin, and with her arm round Aphroditi, she unlocked the upstairs apartment and they went in.

'Let's take these dirty things off,' she said. 'And I think we need to bathe that face.'

Aphroditi sat, and very gently Kyria Loizou helped her to undress. Aphroditi could not even unbutton the raincoat. Several of her fingers had been fractured and she had to be undressed like a child.

Beneath the dirty coat, the kindly neighbour could see that the dress was torn and stained with blood.

'My poor child,' she kept saying. 'My poor little lamb.'

Somehow she got Aphroditi down to her underwear, and only then did she realise how broken she was. The bruising on her shoulders and back was beginning to turn from red to purple, and her eyes were almost shut from the swelling. She began to shiver uncontrollably and violently. When Kyria Loizou tried to get her to stand so that she could lead her towards the shower, she saw that the bed where she had been sitting was soaked with blood.

'My poor dear,' she said. 'I think we need to get a doctor for you.'

Aphroditi shook her head. 'No,' she said weakly.

She had felt the warm gush of blood, but she did not want to face anyone's questions. She just wanted to be warm, to sleep and perhaps never to wake up. Yes, to sleep for ever. That would suit her very well.

'Well let's get you into the shower, then,' said Kyria Loizou.

She found fresh towels and took Aphroditi by the hand. She was horrified by the state she was in. It was as if she had been in a car crash or set upon by thugs. Kyria Loizou did not allow herself to imagine what might have happened. All she knew was that Aphroditi must have a warm shower. She wanted to attend to her physical needs before she asked her how she had got to be in this condition.

Gently, with a sponge and soap, she helped Aphroditi clean herself up.

The most worrying thing was that she hardly spoke. It was as if she did not feel. She did not protest or exclaim when Kyria Loizou applied antiseptic to her wounds and taped up her broken fingers. It was as though she was not really there. Her thoughts were somewhere else: as if the lights had been turned out.

Once Aphroditi was dry, Kyria Loizou helped her into a nightdress and got her into bed. She had put on the gas fire in the bedroom and found some pads in a drawer.

For a while, she sat by the bed and watched over Aphroditi. The young woman seemed vacant and was clearly in shock.

'Are you sure about the doctor?'

Aphroditi nodded without lifting her head from the pillow. There was nothing that could be done to save the baby now.

Kyria Loizou had made an infusion with honey and some herbs that she had found in the store cupboard. It sat untouched on the bedside table.

'When is Kyrios Papacosta back?' she asked.

'Today,' Aphroditi whispered.

Once she saw that Aphroditi was asleep, Kyria Loizou went briefly down to her apartment to cook.

It was the smell of soup that eventually roused Aphroditi, along with the sound of voices. One of them was Savvas'. She closed her eyes again, not wishing to face an interrogation from her husband.

She could hear Kyria Loizou telling Savvas that his wife seemed to have had a little accident, but she was sure she would recover.

Aphroditi heard Savvas' heavy footsteps cross the room towards the bed and then retreat again. Then she heard the slam of the front door.

Not long afterwards, her neighbour crept in.

'Are you all right?' she whispered. She lifted the blankets and could see that the sheets needed changing again.

'There are fresh ones in the bathroom cupboard,' said Aphroditi quietly.

Efficiently and without fuss, Kyria Loizou changed the bedlinen without Aphroditi having to get out of bed.

'I was a nurse many years ago,' she offered as an explanation. She tucked the corners in neatly, then gave Aphroditi a thermometer. 'I want to take your temperature,' she said. 'If it's raised, we will have to get a doctor. If it's not, then . . .'

'Thank you for being so kind.'

'It's nothing, my dear. If you want to tell me anything, please do. If you don't, then I understand. Whatever has happened has happened and nothing can change that.'

The elderly woman folded up the sheets that were saturated with blood.

'I'll take these downstairs to wash,' she said before scrutinising the thermometer. 'It's normal,' she declared, pulling the blankets back across.

For a few minutes she continued to bustle about the room.

'I had a miscarriage once,' she said very matter-of-factly. 'So I know it's important to keep eating at times like this. I'm going to bring you something.'

At about the time that Kyria Loizou was tucking the sheets in around Aphroditi, Emine was changing the beds at The Sunrise. It had become her routine to do this once a week. She had calculated that with each of the five hundred beds having seven sets of linen, they would not run out for more than fifteen years. Only then would she have to start washing. It was unimaginably far into the future.

As she was tidying Hüseyin and Mehmet's room, she spotted a bag sitting on a chair. Her first thought was that a former guest must have left it behind, but it was strange that she had not noticed it before. Even stranger, the bag was familiar. It was identical to one that Aphroditi Papacosta often used to bring to the salon.

She unzipped it. Inside was a little purse embroidered with birds, the same one from which Aphroditi had tipped Emine a hundred times. It made her feel a little shaky to see something so familiar not in the hands of the owner.

She left the bag where it was, but later that day she asked Hüseyin where he had found it.

'I picked it up in the street,' he said truthfully.

'But where? Where exactly did you find it?'

Hüseyin blushed. His mother's interrogations made him uncomfortable, as if she thought he had stolen it.

'Close to the hotel,' he said.

'And when exactly? When?'

'Does it matter when?'

'Yes it does. It does matter when.'

'Look, Mother, I didn't want to tell you . . .'

'What, darling? What didn't you want to tell me?'

'It belongs to a woman . . .' he said. 'She was attacked in the alleyway next to the hotel.'

'When? How do you know?'

'It happened last night . . . I ran down to try and stop them, but it was too late. They were dragging her away.'

'Oh my God!' said Emine with horror. 'Oh my God . . .'

'I was ready to kill them. But it's a long way down . . .'

'You mustn't blame yourself, Hüseyin. If you had done that, it would have given us all away.'

Hüseyin saw that his mother was in tears and put his arms around her.

'Poor Aphroditi,' she sobbed. 'Poor, poor woman.'

'You know who she was?' asked Hüseyin.

'Aphroditi Papacosta . . . God knows why she had come back. Perhaps to fetch something,' said Emine. 'I only hope she got out of the city alive.'

Hüseyin was sickened by this revelation. It was bad enough that Markos had witnessed an attack on a woman and stood by, but the fact that it was his boss's wife made it even more shocking.

'Will you look after it?' asked Hüseyin.

Emine took the bag from her son as if it were a piece of precious china.

Knowing the identity of the soldiers' victim made Hüseyin even more determined to find out what Markos had been doing outside the hotel in the early hours. For the next few nights he would be extra vigilant. He was even more appalled by Markos Georgiou's behaviour than he had been before.

He was certain the opportunity would present itself. As he was undressing one night, he thought he saw some movement on the shore. It could have been a trick that the moonlight was playing with the waves.

Against Markos' orders, Hüseyin ventured out on to the balcony, quietly sliding the door shut behind him. He did not want to wake Mehmet.

There was a man below him. In the moonlight, there was no mistaking his identity. The gleaming white shirt made him distinctly recognisable.

Were they not meant to stay in after dark? This had been the instruction Markos himself had given them. Hüseyin's curiosity was aroused when he saw Markos walk along the seafront and disappear out of sight further down the beach. Up on the rooftop, they only kept watch on the street side of the hotel, so he would not be seen from there.

Perhaps he was just getting some air. Hüseyin decided to say nothing, but the next night he stood quietly on the balcony and watched again.

After several hours, he gave up. Nobody appeared. On the third night, the shadowy figure of Markos once again emerged.

Hüseyin knew he had to be fast – and quiet. He ran back into the bedroom, saw that Mehmet was asleep and went into the corridor. Feeling a mixture of annoyance and curiosity, he took the stairs two at a time. He had to get to the beach before Markos disappeared.

His fitness allowed him to reach the hotel's fire door in moments. From there he could get on to the sand.

Footprints gave away the route that Markos had taken, so he followed them, planting his feet precisely in the indentations.

The tracks eventually turned away from the beach and went through a space between two hotels. As he turned into the alleyway, Hüseyin saw Markos silhouetted at the end of it. He knew he must be careful now. The stony ground would not muffle his footsteps.

Soundlessly he followed Markos through the streets of Famagusta. He took a circuitous route, walking purposefully, stopping occasionally at street corners to check if any Turkish soldiers might be in the next road.

Eventually they seemed to be reaching the edge of the city. Hüseyin had not been this close to the limit since the day he had first seen the barbed wire. The younger man hid himself in a garden. From there he could watch Markos as he approached the boundary.

Markos was taking a risk. There was some open space between

him and the fence, and if soldiers came now, he would be seen. Hüseyin watched with trepidation and disbelief.

Markos glanced around him as he approached the makeshift fencing. Within seconds, he had opened a section of the barbed wire, almost like a gate, and gone through to the other side. He then carefully reassembled the wire to cover his tracks. For a short while Hüseyin could see him, but his pace seemed to pick up and he soon disappeared from sight.

Hüseyin had no intention of following him. At least not tonight.

The strange and illogical path that Markos had taken to reach his exit point had brought Hüseyin along streets that he had not visited for a long time. On his forays to find fruit, he wandered mostly into the residential areas, but tonight he found himself once again in what had been the city's lively avenues and squares, where tourists and wealthy Cypriots alike had shopped. Leontios, Volta and Zephyr Streets used to conjure up such images of glamour. Now they were in ruins.

As he returned to The Sunrise, he remained vigilant about his own safety, but he was also distracted by what he saw.

In the main streets, the shops had now been methodically looted. Naked dummies, like cold corpses, lay in obscene tangles in shop windows. Other stores had been more tidily stripped of their contents. The place looked even more desolate than it had done before. A slight breeze was beginning to get up, and a few leaves rustled in the gutter. The darkness of the winter's night and the city's general emptiness chilled him to the bone.

Something black and long-tailed scuttled in front of him. Hüseyin shuddered. He had always hated rats. Without doubt there were more rats than people living in this city now.

He hastened back to The Sunrise, leaving the fire door slightly open just as he had found it, and ran upstairs.

Back in his room, he lay in bed, wide awake.

What on earth was Markos doing? Hüseyin was both shocked and mystified that he was leaving the city without telling them.

He kept vigil for the next few nights, and whenever he saw Markos leaving again, he hastened downstairs and followed him towards the city perimeter. On the first few occasions, Markos went through the wire and was out of sight.

During the daytime, Hüseyin had noticed that Markos sometimes went down to the nightclub. He often re-emerged with a bottle of whisky for Vasilis Georgiou, or a cigar for his father, but Hüseyin now wondered what else he did down there. The doors were always kept firmly locked.

Markos sometimes went out legitimately in daytime to find supplies for the baby, such as disposable nappies. Panikos was still not much use for such errands. He puffed and panted even getting to the first floor.

During one such excursion, Markos found another discarded newspaper; this time it was *Phileleftheros*. It described the discovery of atrocities against Greek Cypriots. In the past few days, both families had been discussing the possibility of departure, but the revelation of the continuing dangers outside their luxury home immediately quashed such ideas. It brought a new wave of anxiety for them all.

Although they did not keep precise track of dates and days, the radio sometimes reminded them. They celebrated festivals and religious holidays simply to break up the monotony of time. Kurban Bayramı had passed in early December, and normally the Özkans would have feasted on a sacrificed lamb.

'We'd have bought new clothes for our children too,' Emine explained to Irini. 'But at least we're not short of those here!'

'The lamb, though . . .' said Hüseyin wistfully. He missed the succulent slices of meat they would have enjoyed.

Not long after that, it was time for Irini to bake traditional Christmas *melomakarona* biscuits, moist with honey and bursting with dates and nuts.

'These are delicious,' said Emine, eating her third one. 'I love your Christmas.'

To sustain a sense of celebration, Markos brought up a record player from the nightclub and installed it in a small lounge next to the ballroom. Panikos found a way to rig this to his generator.

First of all, Markos found recordings of traditional Cypriot music, both Greek and Turkish. Vasilis and Halit joined in when he put these on, and even Mehmet and Vasilakis were encouraged to learn the steps.

Maria preferred top twenty hits, so Markos went down again to find more albums, Abba, the Isley Brothers and Stevie Wonder among them. Irini was persuaded to dance, and with a little encouragement, Emine was soon on her feet too. Halit did not stop her, although she felt his disapproving looks.

'*Leventi mou*,' Irini called out to her son. 'Come and dance with us.'

'Wait!' said Markos. He strolled over to the record player and put on a different song. It was his mother's favourite.

Hüseyin watched them dance

'*Heaven, I'm in heaven,*' crooned Frank Sinatra.

Irini rested her head on Markos' shoulder as he held her close, rocking her to the jaunty rhythm of trumpets and drums and singing along in perfect harmony. Her eyes were closed and she was smiling. In one son's arms, she forgot her worries for the other.

Hüseyin watched his mother watching the dancing couple.

Markos also felt her eyes, and afterwards asked her for a dance. Music was exercising its magic over them all, and so, it seemed, was Markos.

They almost forgot where they were and the circumstances that had brought them there. It was like a party, at the centre of which was Markos Georgiou, smiling, changing records, serving drinks and dancing. He looked as dapper as ever. His shoes shone, his Pierre Cardin suit (borrowed from the abandoned wardrobe of a wealthy guest) was immaculate and his shiny hair neatly trimmed by Emine.

Hüseyin was watching Markos all the time now. He had heard that Frank Sinatra was a gangster, but this was not the reason he would not dance.

Chapter Twenty-eight

WHEN EVERYONE WAS pleasantly tired, the two older men climbed to the roof for their watch and the others retired to bed.

Hüseyin went on to his balcony and waited. Knowing that Markos came and went made him feel more caged than ever. Although they had now established what felt like a way of life, in reality they were quarantined, deprived of access to the outside world and all that it contained. Whatever Markos was doing, he was doing it for himself, Hüseyin was certain of that.

A few days later, he followed him on one of his night excursions and saw that there was someone waiting on the other side of the fence. Markos handed over a package. The recipient took it and unwrapped it. In the moonlight, there was a flash of metal.

In exchange, the man handed Markos an envelope. He opened it and looked inside. Apparently satisfied with the contents, he stuffed it in his jacket pocket and turned away.

Hüseyin realised that Markos would not be going through the fence, and if he was going to get back to the hotel first, he would have to move fast. He turned on his heel and ran, constantly glancing behind him. He pushed open the fire door, making sure to leave it on the latch, and dashed into the foyer.

He paused to catch his breath, realising that he had made it just in time. Within seconds he heard the click of the fire exit being closed from inside. Markos must have run too. It was too late for Hüseyin to make it up the stairs before Markos appeared, so he retreated into the shadows and hid behind one of the huge faux pillars that appeared to support the ceiling.

He saw Markos cross the reception area and reach the door of the nightclub. Within seconds, he had unlocked it and gone down the stairs.

During the day, Markos was always meticulous about locking the door behind him, but this time he had even left the key on the outside. As far as he was concerned, he was unobserved.

Hüseyin, his heart still pounding from the run, but now beating even harder, darted out from the shadows and pushed open the door. He padded down the carpeted stairs into Markos' underworld.

On the left was a door that led to the nightclub itself. Hüseyin opened it an inch, saw a dark space and closed it again. Down the corridor to the right, he could see the beam of a moving torch. He could resist neither the temptation nor the risk. He had left his shoes behind the pillar upstairs and now moved silently towards the dancing light. Both the outer and inner doors that led to the vault were open, and through the crack in the second, Hüseyin could see Markos.

Some of what he saw was just as he expected. The rest totally astonished him.

The table in front of Markos was piled up with guns. This sight was no surprise; Hüseyin had already deduced that Markos was selling them. He guessed that both Greek and Turkish Cypriots would give almost everything they owned for the means to protect their family. Wherever Markos had acquired them, these metal instruments of death must be worth their weight in gold. As Hüseyin watched, Markos picked one up and ran his hand along its barrel. Then he wrapped each one in a cloth and put them back in the safe. Inside the safe Hüseyin could also make out piles of brown envelopes that he imagined must be payments for previous deals.

Markos turned back to his work. Hüseyin could now make out his features. They were dimly illuminated from below by a small kerosene lamp, which cast distorting shadows on his face. The expression of demonic greed was unmistakable, and Hüseyin saw him more clearly in this half light than ever before.

All over the surface there were neat piles of small boxes and a mound of velvet bags. Piece by piece, Markos removed the jewellery and spread it out, concentrating, calculating and making notes on a pad.

Hüseyin could see mounds of glinting gold and dazzling precious stones. It was an astonishing hoard.

He watched as Markos picked up three or four items and dropped them casually into his jacket pocket. The others he carefully packaged up again and replaced in the safe.

Hüseyin backed away and crept up the stairs. The picture was now clear. Finally he understood why Markos regularly left the city. Money, guns and gold. It made perfect sense.

As Markos locked the safes, he looked up suddenly, thinking he had heard a noise. But there was no one there. He gathered his papers and glanced with satisfaction at the numbers written there.

Back in July, Markos had found that the items he was safeguarding for his brother in the vault were suddenly objects of great desire. After the invasion, not only guns but also gold had gone up in value. In addition to Aphroditi's jewellery, in itself worth hundreds of thousands of pounds, he had undertaken to look after necklaces, bracelets and rings for several of the local jewellery stores. He had let it be known that, with its layers of doors and its combination locks, the strongroom at The Sunrise was more secure than anywhere on Cyprus. People felt confident about leaving their valuables there. Some of them had deposited their best pieces with Markos as early as 20 July, when the first of the Turkish troops had landed in the north.

Since then, property, land, stocks and shares had all dropped sharply in value, so Markos was one of the few people on the island with any real wealth. His only problem now was finding enough storage space for the vast amount of cash and jewellery in his possession.

Over the next few weeks, Hüseyin followed Markos every time he could. He realised that Markos had worked out with almost mathematical precision where the troops were positioned and at what time there was a change of duty. Judging by the complex route he took to the wire and how relaxed he seemed at times, he knew where they were garrisoned, where they watched from and the best time to leave The Sunrise. He realised that Markos even took into account the phases of the moon. During the days before and after it was full, he took extra care.

On every journey, he was catlike in his avoidance of Turkish soldiers. In spite of this, Hüseyin knew that Markos' conduct was a risk to everyone at The Sunrise.

He did not know how Markos had come by the guns, but it sickened him that he was clearly smuggling jewellery that was not his own out of the city.

One night, when Hüseyin saw Markos reach the wire, he decided he would follow him out. There were a few buildings and just about enough trees to give a slim man a hiding place. As long as Markos did not look over his shoulder at the wrong moment, Hüseyin would be safe.

He trailed him three or four miles to a crossroads and eventually saw Markos reach a cluster of abandoned vehicles. Hüseyin guessed that they had been there since the mass exodus from the city. He heard the dry, choking sound of an old engine being brought to life and saw a vehicle move off. Amongst all these clapped-out vans and cars, Markos had found one that still functioned.

As he disappeared out of sight, Hüseyin wondered what happened when this snake of a man met Turkish soldiers. He knew instinctively that Markos would find a way. He was fluent in Turkish, as he was always keen to demonstrate in front of the Özkans, so Hüseyin imagined that language would get him through. Clearly he also had plenty of cash and gold with which to bribe them.

Cautiously Hüseyin made his way back to the fence, his curiosity more than satisfied. He began to question everything that had taken place over the past months. He now suspected that Markos was using the Özkans as a buffer to keep his own family safe. There was nothing Hüseyin would put past him. He wondered just how much they had all been manipulated.

He knew, though, that he had to keep everything to himself. Even if Markos was effectively keeping them all there for his own benefit, it would be hard to prove.

The following day, a thick fog came in from the sea. The atmosphere was heavy and the mood at The Sunrise was low.

When Hüseyin saw Markos the next morning, smiling and charming as usual, in spite of the gloom into which everyone else had been plunged, he could not smile back. He could not share the good cheer displayed by the Greek Cypriot.

It was seven months since the beginning of their time alone in the city, and nearly six since they had arrived at The Sunrise. Most of them were still enjoying the ample store cupboards, and for Emine and Irini the luxurious bedrooms with their fine linen and well-appointed bathrooms were a daily pleasure.

Gradually the two older men had lowered their guard with each other. They smoked, sometimes drank and even discussed their political views, clicking their worry beads almost in unison.

Panikos was kept busy doing practical jobs, and Maria helped with the cooking but was mostly preoccupied with the baby, who continued to thrive and grow.

The little boys had become inseparable, playing together all day and every day, chasing up and down the stairs, kicking balls in the corridors and building camps out of cushions and chairs. They knew that their games had to be played with the minimum of shouting and squeals, but they were used to this now. Mehmet and Vasilakis enjoyed more freedom in The Sunrise than they might have done outside it.

It was spring now, and with a change of season came fine rain. The beach, which was out of bounds in any case, now held little allure.

Chapter Twenty-nine

FOR MANY WEEKS, Aphroditi had been lying in her bed. Savvas was grateful to have Kyria Loizou acting as her nurse and happy to have her coming and going to and from their apartment. He had moved into the spare room.

Kyria Loizou was almost constantly at Aphroditi's bedside, dressing wounds, changing sheets and holding her hand. It was clear that Aphroditi did not want to talk about what had happened, and it had not been difficult for the older woman to surmise that she wanted to keep something from her husband too.

Savvas accepted the story that his wife had slipped and fallen down the stairs. It would explain her broken fingers and bruised face. He was solicitous but not over-enquiring. His optimism had returned as the country settled down, and he was far more interested in the business opportunities that this new Cyprus offered.

On his trip to Limassol he had acquired some contacts and was already in discussions over a new hotel.

'I know it's long-term,' he said, 'but we have to think ahead. It might be a while before we can get The Sunrise back.'

He was sitting on a chair at the end of the bed and continued chatting for a few minutes, unaware of Aphroditi's reaction.

'I've no idea what's happened to Markos Georgiou,' he said. 'He never showed up with the keys.'

Aphroditi turned her head away so that he could not see her face.

'Your bruises are going down,' he said brightly. 'I think we should resurface the staircase with something non-slip. There are some very good materials around these days. All the hotels have started using them. I'll get it priced up.'

That afternoon, Kyria Loizou found Aphroditi weeping. It was the first time she had cried.

The mention of Markos Georgiou's name had brought her mind back to the image of him that she had seen that terrible night in Famagusta. Suddenly there was clarity. She knew with blinding certainty that it had not been a hallucination.

The elderly woman took her hand, and when she looked into Aphroditi's eyes she saw a familiar grief. It was as deep as it had been on the morning she had returned with her injuries.

Up until now, Aphroditi had not confided anything, though her demeanour had already told Kyria Loizou a great deal. That day she was ready to speak.

'Have you ever made such a terrible mistake . . . that you can't make it better?' she asked through her tears.

Kyria Loizou squeezed her hand.

'Everyone makes mistakes from time to time,' she answered kindly.

'Not like this,' replied Aphroditi. For a moment she seemed to be speaking to herself, weeping at the same time. 'He was there. He saw. He saw it happening.'

'Whatever happened to you,' the elderly woman reassured her, 'I'm sure it was not your fault.'

For the next few hours she stayed with Aphroditi as the tears continued to flow. Her pillow was soaked. Kyria Loizou could see that whatever the young woman had done, she had paid very dearly for it.

It seemed from that day that her wounds began to heal a little faster. Within a few weeks she could leave her room, making her way carefully down the stairs, holding the banister rail. Kyria Loizou supportively took her other arm and they went out into the sunshine together.

The moment that the scent of the city hit Aphroditi's nostrils, she knew she had to leave. The odour of this island would never change for her now. She smelled dust, rat droppings, decay, blood and bitterness. Everywhere.

'All those things are in your imagination,' said Kyria Loizou. 'Perhaps they'll fade. I can't smell any of them.'

'But for me, they're too strong,' said Aphroditi, with tears in her eyes. 'I don't think it's possible to live with them.'

She told Savvas that night that she wanted to go and stay with her mother.

When she rang Artemis Markides, she got the response she expected.

'I *knew* you would see sense eventually,' said her mother with satisfaction. 'I'll send someone to meet you at Heathrow.'

It would be very simple, since she had almost nothing to take with her.

When she heard the news, her kindly neighbour insisted on taking her shopping for some new clothes, even though they would not be particularly suitable for England.

'You can't arrive wearing a dress of your mother's,' said Kyria Loizou. 'But I expect you'll have to buy something warmer when you get there.'

A few days later, Aphroditi was on a plane from Larnaca.

It was a cloudless day, and as they climbed, she had a clear view of her island from above. With its miles of empty spaces and remote, peaceful beaches where turtles came to lay their eggs, it did not seem possible that such bloodshed and division had taken place. She could make out a few scars on the landscape, but the citrus groves, mountains and villages dotted about on the landscape looked deceptively unscathed. The plane did not need to pass over Famagusta for her to imagine its streets echoing and ghostly and its buildings devoid of life.

Aphroditi pulled down the window blind. She did not want to see the land disappear beneath her. The numbness that she had felt since her last visit to The Sunrise had gone.

As feeling had returned, so too had pain.

Chapter Thirty

WHAT PARTICULARLY ASTONISHED Hüseyin was how casual Markos was becoming in his meanderings around the city. He behaved like a man who would never be caught, acted like someone who thought that everyone had their price, a sum for which they could be bought.

For many weeks now, Hüseyin had been on Markos' trail. It had become an obsession, and yet he still lacked the nerve to confront him.

One night he followed him down a side street on to a main road. About fifteen minutes after he had left the hotel, he realised that a lone Turkish soldier had appeared between himself and Markos. He was thirty or so yards behind the Greek Cypriot, and Hüseyin felt his heart pound.

The young conscript was clearly unaware of Hüseyin, even though there was a similar distance between them. It crossed Hüseyin's mind that he could have spotted Markos on another occasion, and might already know about The Sunrise.

For a few minutes, they followed each other. Suddenly Markos stopped and bent down. He appeared to be doing up a shoelace. It was then that Hüseyin realised the soldier was drawing his gun.

Unless he was very inebriated, the unsuspecting Markos would be an easy target.

Hüseyin was shocked to find that he felt a stirring of pleasure at the thought of Markos being killed by a Turkish bullet. Then it occurred to him that he might not be killed but taken prisoner. Would Markos keep the secret of The Sunrise? He doubted that betrayal was beyond his capabilities.

At the same time as these thoughts were running through Hüseyin's head, he was surveying the immediate vicinity. The only weapons to hand were lengths of metal, shards of glass and other debris from derelict buildings. Then he spotted a jagged lump of concrete. Without pausing, he picked it up and hurled it. Even if it missed, it would distract the soldier and alert his prey.

Although it was a long time since he had played a game of volleyball, Hüseyin had lost neither his skill nor his strength. He could throw with pinpoint accuracy. The solid slab gathered speed as it travelled and met its target.

The soldier knew nothing. The blow to his head felled him instantly.

Markos heard the thud, spun round and saw the soldier lying still on the ground. Hüseyin was a few yards behind him.

The two men looked at each other and simultaneously ran towards the lifeless body.

'We need to hide him,' said Markos.

There was no time for questions or explanations. There was hardly time for Hüseyin to dwell on the thought that he had killed a man.

'Quickly. If they find the corpse, they'll come looking for whoever did it,' said Markos.

'We need to get him as far away as possible from The Sunrise,' agreed Hüseyin. 'There's a big grocery store up that side street. With piles of empty sacks at the back.' It was one of the shops that Hüseyin had methodically emptied in the days before they moved to the hotel.

Silently the two men dragged the corpse through the street. It was heavy, and even between the pair of them it was a huge effort.

Hüseyin wondered if he might have been one of the soldiers who had attacked Aphroditi. The thought did not even enter Markos' mind.

The door to the shop was open and they pulled the body to the dark area at the back, where they covered it with layers of sacking. Only the smell of decomposition would give it away, but by the time anyone came to look, the flesh would be gone and just the bones would remain.

Markos glanced at his watch. This episode had made him late, and he knew that the man he was meeting would be getting impatient. He felt trapped with Hüseyin standing there but knew he needed to get away as soon as he could.

'Why were you following me?' he asked insouciantly as they finished their work.

In those minutes as they were dragging the body, Markos had been calculating how best to win Hüseyin round. There was, of course, a possibility that this was the one and only time he had been followed.

'I wanted to see why you were leaving the hotel when you had told everyone else they must stay,' said Hüseyin boldly.

The effort of moving the body had left them both out of breath. It was hidden now, but the two men were still in the gloomy recess of the shop.

'There was something I wanted to sell,' said Markos, leaning forward and touching Hüseyin on the arm. He wanted to make it seem as if he was confiding in the younger man and perhaps even professing a little guilt. 'I knew it was a risk.'

If he had not watched Markos Georgiou in the strongroom that night and seen for himself the look of lust on his face as he cradled the guns and gems, Hüseyin would have swallowed the man's lie. Over the past few weeks, though, a very different picture of Markos had evolved, and he knew that there was a wide gulf between who he was and who he seemed.

Hüseyin felt he was the only person who had any idea of the reality, but he was inexperienced and did not know what reaction he would provoke. Truth mattered to him.

'I have seen you before,' he said. 'Not just today.'

Markos did not instantly react. Confronted with such simplicity and openness, it was difficult to think of anything to say. Given how carefully he felt he had covered his tracks, and how assiduous he had been in every way, he was astonished to have been found out. In fact he was furious. This had never happened to Markos Georgiou, and the sense of exposure was like having a thousand searchlights beamed into his face.

His body temperature rose. How dare anyone follow him, but more importantly, how dare this Turkish Cypriot boy pass judgement on him? Anger was a rare thing for Markos, but in the back of this huge shop in an isolated part of town, he slid his hand inside his jacket.

Though he could not see Markos' face in the darkness, a memory of the devilish grimace that he had seen in the strongroom came to Hüseyin. The other image that flashed before him was of Markos holding a small gun. He had no doubt that he had it with him now.

When they were concealing the body, Hüseyin had noticed a

knife on the counter close by. It was the tool used for slitting open the sacks.

The younger man's reactions were swift. As Markos was pulling the gun from his pocket, Hüseyin grabbed the knife that lay rusting on the surface. For the second time that day, action had to be faster than thought. He knew that Markos would not think twice. The young Turkish Cypriot was learning that killing was sometimes about self-protection.

The speed of Hüseyin's action came as a total surprise to Markos. He hardly had time to fold his fingers round his gun before the knife was rammed into his chest.

Hüseyin had once helped his father kill a goat. There was the same disconcerting silence as the blade penetrated flesh. The sound it made as it was withdrawn, accompanied by the gushing of blood on to the ground, was more shocking than the stabbing itself.

Until that night, Hüseyin had not realised how sickeningly easy it was to rob a man of his life. He turned away, full of remorse and self-disgust, and leaned against the counter to steady himself. His hands were shaking so violently that he dropped the knife. He feared that the noise of the metal blade scudding across the stone floor would be heard from miles away.

The knife had pierced Markos through the heart. He had dropped backwards to the ground, soaked in blood. For a sudden disorienting moment, Hüseyin's mind flashed back to a decade before, to the bloodstained shirt of his cousin Mehmet.

In a state of disbelief over what he had done, he dragged the body towards the empty sacks. It left a trail of blood that he would have to clean away before he left. Markos seemed weightless, almost insubstantial compared with the Turkish soldier. Hüseyin hid the corpse close to the first one, but not touching, and took the gun.

At the other end of the city, the man who was waiting for Markos had finally lost patience. With increasing fury, he realised that there would be no delivery that day. The Greek Cypriot had let him down, in spite of the fact that he had paid in advance, as always. He had never asked questions, as he had always known that he was getting the better side of the deal, handling magnificent pieces of jewellery for less than half of what they were worth. The item that he had been promised this time was the most valuable and expensive piece he had ever acquired, and now he felt a fool. He would come back each night until Markos turned up. He had been an acquaintance of the manager of the Clair de Lune for a long time, but he was not going to let him get away with this.

Hüseyin hurried back to The Sunrise, stumbling as he went. He arrived just as the light was coming up, hoping to get to his room before anyone saw him.

Unexpectedly, the door to Room 105 opened. Emine saw her son standing there, ashen-faced, his clothes smeared with blood.

'Hüseyin! *Aman Allahım!*' she said. 'My God! What on earth has happened?'

Leaving Hüseyin in the corridor, Emine immediately woke Halit and sent him to make sure that Mehmet was still asleep. 'Bring one of Hüseyin's shirts when you come back, and some of his trousers.'

It was too early in the morning for even Halit to argue, so he carried out the instructions without questioning them. When he returned, bleary-eyed, Hüseyin was in their bathroom.

It was only when he saw his mother's horrified face that Hüseyin realised he was spattered head to foot with Markos' blood. Once he had scrubbed it off his hands and arms, he began to stop shaking. The clothes he had been wearing were rolled into a ball and thrown into a corner.

'Now tell us what happened,' said his mother gently once he was dressed again.

Hüseyin told his parents everything. Neither of them interrupted even for a second. He described how he had been following Markos for some time, had seen him leaving the city and watched him handling guns and jewellery down in the vault.

At first, Emine was full of disbelief. She had been bewitched by Markos' charm. He had made all of them feel loved, from the youngest to the oldest.

'Do you think he was selling Kyria Papacosta's jewellery?' asked Halit.

'It sounds likely,' said Emine.

Then Hüseyin recounted what had happened that day and how he had killed the soldier who was tracking Markos.

'It wasn't Markos I wanted to save,' he said. 'It was the Georgious . . . and us.'

Sitting on his parents' bed, like a child who had wandered in to seek comfort after a nightmare, Hüseyin broke down and sobbed. Emine sat with her arm around him, waiting.

The first killing had felt remote. He had made no physical connection with the soldier. Perhaps it was the same if you shot a man. With Markos it had been different. There had been a true sense of tearing someone's breath from them. Even though he had loathed the victim and was defending his own life, the horror of finding himself Markos' murderer was overwhelming.

'*Canım benmi*,' said Emine. 'My darling, you had to do it. You had no choice.'

Halit was pacing up and down the bedroom.

'You should have done it before!' he shouted. 'He deserved it! *Pezevenk!* Bastard!'

'Halit! Shhhhh! We don't want anyone to hear,' warned Emine.

They sat in silence for a while. Gradually Hüseyin calmed down. He was a young man, but at this moment he looked more like a child.

'Mother, you know the worst thing about him?'

'There were plenty of bad things,' interjected Halit.

'That he was going to kill you?' said Emine.

'No,' replied Hüseyin firmly. 'The worst thing was that he didn't help Kyria Papacosta.'

'What do you mean?' asked Emine.

'That night. He was there. I think he saw it all.'

Hüseyin described what he had seen. For a moment, both his parents were lost for words. Halit could not contain himself for long.

'What man would behave like that?' he roared.

'Halit! Please . . . we don't want to wake everyone.'

'The problem we have now,' said Halit, 'is how to tell the Georgious. They have to know that Markos is dead.'

Emine began to weep. 'Poor Irini,' she said quietly. 'She loves him more than anyone in the world.'

'They have to know what he was doing,' insisted Halit.

'But the truth might kill her,' said Emine. 'And in any case, I don't know if she would believe it. There is no point.'

Together they agreed how they would go about it. Halit's main concern was to protect his son. Emine's was the same, but she wanted to protect the Georgious too, and to be as gentle as possible with them.

By the end of that day, the Georgious were becoming anxious. Especially for Irini, Markos was always at the centre of everything. When he was absent, it was as if the sun was behind a permanent cloud, or the birds had stopped singing on a spring morning.

Hüseyin stayed in his room and Emine made an excuse for him. She told the others he was sick.

In actual fact, Hüseyin felt as though he was. In the eyes of Allah, he had committed a terrible crime.

That evening, just as he had planned with his parents, Hüseyin came down to the kitchen to be told the news that Markos was missing. Irini was in tears. Vasilis sat in silence. Hüseyin knew his mind would forever be haunted by the look on Irini Georgiou's sweet, lined face that night. He saw frantic anxiety, but also gratitude that he, Hüseyin, had volunteered to go out looking.

In the early hours of the morning, moving through the streets carelessly, almost wishing to be caught, he returned to the store. He could see that the lumps beneath the sacks were exactly where they had been left. There had been something of the magician about Markos, and a small part of Hüseyin had almost expected his body to be gone. As he dragged the lighter of the corpses from where it lay, a bunch of keys fell from a pocket.

He rested a moment and then, despising himself for doing it, decided to go through the rest of Markos' clothes. There was nothing else in the jacket. In the trousers he found a velvet pouch, identical to the one that had been in Kyria Papacosta's bag, with the name of a Famagusta jeweller printed on the outside. Hüseyin put it in his left-hand pocket – the keys already filled the right one. He suddenly felt Markos' glassy eyes on him and could not stop himself looking into them. The handsome features were disturbingly unchanged. He took a last glance at his face before covering it with a piece of sacking. With a wave of adrenalin giving him extra strength, he moved the body to another empty shop closer to The Sunrise.

Having 'located' Markos, he returned to The Sunrise. He found his parents waiting.

'I've found him,' he said quietly. 'I'll take Panikos there when he's ready.'

Emine said that she and Halit would tell the Georgious.

The Greek Cypriot couple were sitting at the big kitchen table holding hands. Emine did not have to say anything. Irini read it in the look on her face. Words were superfluous. The elderly woman crumpled forward, her head on the table, and sobbed. Vasilis held her close.

Hüseyin had never forgotten the tidal waves of emotion that he had witnessed with the death of his cousin and more recently his aunt and cousins in Maratha. All of these were premature losses of life, sudden, unexpected and brutal. Such murders elicited an appropriately violent level of grief. Hüseyin vanished to his room and hid beneath the bedclothes. He could not bear to hear the sound of Irini's wailing.

A few hours later, it was agreed that Panikos should accompany Hüseyin to bring back the body. As soon as it was dark, the two men set off. When they got to the shop, Hüseyin realised that Panikos was too unfit to be of much help and found himself taking the brunt of Markos' weight. They seemed the longest fifteen minutes of his life as he lugged the body slowly back to the hotel. Panikos helped him take it down the side passageway and in through the fire door.

They laid Markos on an upholstered couch in the reception area and Emine helped Maria change him into clean clothes. He wore a dark suit and a fresh white shirt, exactly as he always had done in the days managing the nightclub. By the time they had cleaned him up, he looked as immaculate, calm and beautiful in death as he had in life. Finally Maria carefully combed her brother's dark, silky hair in the way he had liked it.

When she saw the body, Irini gave way to even greater grief.

It was unfettered. Emine knew that her anguish would have been the same had she known the truth about her son's character.

'Love is blind,' she said quietly to Hüseyin.

Hüseyin knew from his own mother's love how warm and uncritical maternal devotion could be, but even he had noticed that Irini's feelings for Markos were close to hero-worship.

Maria had prepared a long table in the ballroom with white sheets and gathered armfuls of artificial flowers from the various vases that stood in the darkened corridors of the hotel. The icons that both Irini and her daughter had brought with them when they left home stood close by on a table, gently illuminated by an oil lamp.

This was how Markos lay, while his family prayed close by and watched him. Even in the absence of a priest, they observed what rituals they could.

There was silence except for Irini and Maria's bursts of keening. Vasilis sat, head bowed, next to Panikos. Some respectful distance away, Emine and Halit also remained throughout the night.

A practical issue was the location for burial. There were few places to dig within the grounds of the hotel.

'There are the rose beds,' suggested Emine.

These were at the edge of the terrace outside the bar. There was little choice, and with the early spring rains, the ground was soft enough.

Early the following morning, Markos was buried.

Panikos had found tools and, with great effort, been out to prepare the grave. At five o'clock, they filed outside. Even Mehmet and Vasilakis, bleary-eyed and uncomprehending, had been woken and brought downstairs.

Markos was wrapped in a sheet and lowered into the ground by his father and brother-in-law. Each of them, except for Hüseyin, who hung back, threw a rose into the grave before the earth was shovelled in.

'*Kyrie eleison, Kyrie eleison*,' his family chanted. 'Lord have mercy, Lord have mercy.' They knew the words of the service by heart.

Hüseyin kept his head lowered. He watched his tears drip on to his shoes. In spite of what the dead man might have intended towards him, Markos was the one who had lost his life. There was no sense of justice or of joy. Hüseyin looked at Irini Georgiou's face, creased into a thousand lines of grief, and felt unutterable pity.

Observing the expressions of those who stood around this grave, he realised they were each burying someone different. Each of them had his or her own Markos Georgiou.

Afterwards they ate *koliva*, the traditional food for mourning. Maria had prepared it, substituting rice for wheat. Most of the other ingredients were still plentiful in their store: sesame, almonds, cinnamon, sugar and raisins.

For Irini, no day had ever been blacker. She was beyond tears. That afternoon, she and Vasilis lay silently in their darkened room.

The Özkans went to wash and change their clothes after the burial, as was Turkish Cypriot tradition.

'We don't want to bring bad luck on ourselves,' said Emine.

'It's a bit late to wish that now, isn't it?' observed Halit.

As he stood in the shower and felt the water cascading down over his shoulders, Hüseyin knew that he would never rid himself of the blood he still saw on his hands, or of the guilt he felt. Every time he looked at Markos Georgiou's parents, it only intensified.

A few days later, Irini asked Panikos if there were any churches she could go to.

'There are,' he said. 'But I don't know what state they are in.'

'Irini, you can't leave the hotel,' said Vasilis, quietly but firmly. 'There are Turkish soldiers out there. Turkish soldiers who killed your son.'

'But . . .'

In all the months they had been inside The Sunrise, she had scarcely thought of God. She had kept their icon of Agios Neophytos on display in their bedroom, but it had never seemed that he was watching over them. Each day that Christos had been missing and her prayers had gone unanswered, her faith had waned slightly. With the death of Markos, there was only a little residual conviction. The woman who had once crossed herself many times an hour was almost without belief now.

They had heard on the radio of the efforts Makarios was still making to help bring peace to the island, but she had lost faith even in him.

Perhaps within the walls of a church she might find God's comfort again and He might hear her when she prayed. His absence had left a void in her life and she yearned for her faith to return.

Hüseyin knew what had happened to most of the churches but he hesitated to tell Kyria Georgiou. Icons and treasures had been stripped from them long ago and many of them were subject to wanton vandalism. When they were bringing Markos' body to the hotel, they had noticed several such churches with their doors broken down.

'I don't think the churches are what they were,' said Panikos gently. 'And in any case, it's not safe for you to go out there.'

Hüseyin overheard his mother and Kyria Georgiou talking.

'I can manage not going to church if I must, but these clothes . . . they feel so wrong,' Irini said.

Guests had abandoned many different kinds of clothing in the hotel but none of them had left anything suitable for mourning. Irini could no longer wear her usual colourful floral shirts or button-through dresses, and Emine had nothing to lend her.

'I know where to find something,' Hüseyin interrupted. 'I'll go now.'

Hüseyin had got to know every street and alleyway of the city in the recent months. He knew which shops had been emptied of their contents and which were untouched. There were several small stores that specialised in *yinekeia moda*, ladies' fashions, of the kind that had no value to the Turkish soldiers, even for sending home to their wives. These were the outlets that sold blouses, shirts and dresses for the elderly woman.

At the back of such a shop, Hüseyin found the clothes that every woman needed when she must live out her days like a shadow. There were racks of black garments never wanted or desired, and he brought home for Irini a more than ample supply.

The Georgiou family observed the memorial services over Markos' grave three and nine days after the funeral. Irini did not mention going to a church again.

Irini knew that for every sorrow she had, Emine endured the same. Both their lives had been subsumed in wave upon wave of ever-increasing catastrophe and sorrow. Day to day the two women kept very busy cleaning, tidying and preparing food, and it left them thankfully little time for reflection. Sometimes when their tasks were done they sat together and wept over their losses and their missing sons, who were never far from their thoughts. On other occasions they cheered each other by reading the coffee grounds. Now that her faith had gone, these activities helped to sustain Irini during these dark days.

The atmosphere in the hotel changed after Markos' death. Even the small boys seemed more subdued for a few weeks. They missed the magic tricks Uncle Markos had performed for them, the teasing he subjected them to and the laughter that followed him around. Mealtimes were more perfunctory and there was no longer any music. The record player gathered dust in the corner of the ballroom.

Irini continued to cook. Even the day after she had buried her son, she had immersed herself in the preparation of sweet *loukoumades* and *daktila*. While her fingers were kept busy kneading bread or shaping biscuits, for a few minutes at a time her mind was absorbed by something other than the loss of Markos.

Vasilis' grief was a quiet state of being. He spent most of his days on the rooftop, tending to his pots of herbs and tomatoes, which were thriving in the sunshine, and doing guard duty. Halit kept him company. Vasilis gazed out at the sea for hours at a time, continually smoking but making sure to keep the glow of his cigarette out of sight. He also kept a few bottles on the roof.

Hüseyin continued to be withdrawn for many more days and found himself unable to eat. His mother often brought food up to his room.

'Kyria Georgiou is anxious about you,' she said one day, stroking his cheek.

Hüseyin was lying on his bed and tears began to course down his face.

'My poor boy,' said Emine. 'You did what you had to do.'

Only time would lift the guilt he felt at what he had done to the sweet woman who, even that day, had specially cooked his favourite dish in an attempt to encourage him to eat.

Hüseyin soon realised that the adults needed him in many different ways, not least to lift their morale. With three sons gone, he had to be stronger than ever.

When he had returned after moving the body, he had emptied his bulging pockets and shoved the bunch of keys and the velvet pouch to the back of a drawer. One evening, when there was no one around in reception, he tried out some of the keys. One of them opened the door that led down to the nightclub from the reception area.

He crept down the stairs and made his way towards the strong-room. He unlocked the outer and inner doors. The remaining keys fitted the various safes and there was a satisfying clunk as the mechanisms responded. In spite of this, the doors did not open.

Hüseyin immediately realised that they also required a combination. He suspected that Markos had gone to his grave with these locked firmly inside him.

Back in his room, he replaced the keys in a drawer. The green velvet pouch was tucked in the corner and he took it out to see what it contained. Something glinted inside. As he turned it upside down, a string of dazzling blue stones poured out into his hand. They were a translucent azure, like the sea beyond his window, and even in the half-light they seemed to shimmer. The gems were uniform, except for the clasp, which was bigger than the rest, and each one was set in gold.

He replaced the necklace at the back of the drawer but it pricked his conscience that such a thing should be in his possession. It no more belonged to him than it had done to Markos.

Did it now belong to the Georgiou family? Or should it be returned to the original owner? For now he would keep it in the drawer with the keys. The latter were of no use without the safe codes, but the precious stones must still have a value.

Chapter Thirty-one

It was now July. The days were hot and the nights short.
From their rooftop lookout point, Vasilis and Halit noticed that troop movements had become much more frequent. Hüseyin had seen this too and wondered if it might be connected with the missing soldier. The disappearance of a colleague was bound to have prompted greater vigilance.

It was harder for everyone to remain inside the hotel on these warm days. Even Panikos, whose rotund belly had always made him too ashamed to swim, yearned to go and splash in the waves with his children. For Hüseyin, the gentle lap and swell of the sea was a temptation stronger than a siren's song. One night, he crept out of the fire door and went down on to the sand. He knew he must not make a sound and his body slid into the sea without a splash. In his entire life he had never been alone in the water; it was an infinite space shared by everyone. A dense blackness spread out before him, occasionally illuminated by bright flashes of phosphorescence. He kept his body beneath the water, cutting through it with his limbs and barely stirring the surface.

He swam a long way out to sea and then lay on his back and looked up at the stars. He felt almost delirious with freedom.

His father and Vasilis were keeping watch towards the road, but even if they had been looking the other way they would not have seen the figure in the sea.

After a while, Hüseyin began to swim back to shore. In front of him was the row of giant concrete blocks that lined the coastline. At the far end of the beach he could just make out the huge cranes still keeping watch over Savvas Papacosta's building site. It reminded him of a graveyard and the water suddenly felt cold on his skin. He shuddered.

He looked towards The Sunrise and its dark empty windows. Their hotel looked as sinister and uninhabited as all the others; no one would have guessed that ten people were living inside. Then he saw the lights of a jeep. It was moving northwards along Hippocrates. Almost at the same time, another came from the south. They both stopped out of sight and Hüseyin deduced that they must be somewhere in front of the hotel.

He wondered if his father and Vasilis had seen them. He swam back as swiftly as he could and ran noiselessly up the beach. Still dripping, he slipped through the fire door and retrieved a towel that he had hidden behind reception.

He sprinted up the fifteen flights of stairs to the roof and found the two men frozen to the spot, observing what was going on in the road beyond the car park.

He greeted them with a whisper, but they did not turn around, wanting to keep their eyes on the situation developing in front of them. The strong bars on the gates were enough of a barrier between them and the soldiers, but they could hear shouting. The iron railings did not protect them from that.

'Can you hear what they are saying?' asked Vasilis.

'They're too far away for that,' Halit answered. 'All I know is that they have never taken such an interest in this place before.'

'I'm afraid,' said Vasilis.

'Me too,' admitted Halit. 'It doesn't feel good.'

'Can I have the binoculars?' asked Hüseyin.

He spent a moment adjusting them and then focused on the men at the gates. One of them was not in uniform. He was a small man, much shorter than the Turkish soldiers, with a bald head and a neat beard. Hüseyin remembered seeing him before. He was the man that Markos had been meeting at the wire.

Since the night when Markos had failed to turn up for their rendezvous, the Turkish Cypriot who had been the conduit for guns and jewellery had returned every day to the spot where their meetings had always taken place.

He was angry with himself for being duped but even angrier with Markos Georgiou. He should never have trusted him. He was a Greek Cypriot. After a few weeks, he realised that Georgiou was not going to appear. He had people leaning on him in Nicosia to either get the money back or secure the blue diamonds that had been promised. There was no option but to go inside the city.

He knew that Markos Georgiou had worked at The Sunrise, as he had had business dealings with him even before the war, so that was where he would go and look for him. He unravelled the wire, refastened it and set off.

He had rarely been to Famagusta and was not familiar with its layout, so it took him an hour to find the main street. From here, he reckoned he could find the seafront.

Rats scuttled about in the shadows. It seemed that they had taken over in this city. He saw a troop of three running along together purposefully, unbothered by his presence. From nose to tail they were a yard in length.

He knew to keep close to the buildings. As he was making his way down a street full of shops, he disturbed a snake. He must almost have stepped on it. Since childhood, when a viper had crept across his bed, he had had a phobia. When this one slithered away, leaving a trail in the dust, he let out an involuntary cry of fear.

He no longer felt safe being near the buildings and edged slightly further out on to the pavement. It took him from obscurity to visibility. When an army jeep turned out of a side street, the two soldiers travelling in it saw him immediately. He stood there, blinded by their headlights, not even attempting to run away as the vehicle roared towards him and screeched to a halt. Soldiers leapt out, shouting at him, waving guns and screaming abuse. There was an air of anarchy about them, a madness brought about by months of doing almost nothing except guarding an empty city where nothing stirred except vermin and reptiles. They could smell some action and their excitement was palpable.

The Turkish Cypriot slowly put his hands up. The soldier who had been driving prodded him in the chest with the butt of his gun.

'You!' he roared. 'What are you doing here?'

'*What are you doing here?*' repeated another at a higher pitch.

Both of them suspected him of some involvement with the disappearance of their colleague.

'Answer us!' the first one hollered. 'An-swer-us!' He was almost spitting in the man's face.

'He's Greek!' laughed one. 'He doesn't get it!' He was dancing around, ready to use the excuse that his questions were being ignored as a reason to become violent.

'I do understand,' came the reply in Turkish. His voice quavered so much that he was not certain if they would understand him.

One of the soldiers took a step towards him. Just because this man spoke Turkish, it did not make him a friend.

'Keep hold of him,' he barked to his junior.

The Turkish Cypriot did not struggle. There was no point given the size and strength of the soldiers, and within moments they had a full confession from him. The man had nothing to lose and everything to gain. They might even help him to find Markos Georgiou if he promised them a cut in the deal. He imagined that the diamonds were still at The Sunrise, and if they were lucky, there might be other valuables too. The possibility of personal gain was irresistible to all of them.

When Hüseyin spotted the soldiers and their prisoner, it did not take a moment for him to work out what had happened. Although The Sunrise looked dead from the outside, Markos' middleman had obviously known where the jewellery was coming from.

He realised that they were all in danger now. They would have to leave the hotel.

The only thing that stood between the two families and the Turkish soldiers were the substantial iron railings. There had been too many places that were more easily looted for them to make such an effort, but now they probably knew that it would be worth their while.

The three of them watched the soldiers drive off. The prisoner had gone with them. When the jeeps could no longer be heard, the men turned towards each other.

'We need to leave tonight,' said Hüseyin. 'We can't wait.'

In the past months, Hüseyin had grown wiser than his years. Even Vasilis deferred to this young man, glad to have someone else to assess the situation, just as in the past he had been happy for Markos to take the lead.

Halit, by contrast, argued. He could not be told what to do by his own son.

'But we've been safe for all this time,' he said.

'I think that's over now. And even if they are lenient with us, there is no saying how they will treat the Georgious.'

'Your mother won't want to go,' he snapped, as if this would sway Hüseyin.

'If Kyria Irini goes,' he said firmly, 'then Mother will want to leave too.'

There was a simple truth here. Halit did not contradict it.

The three of them went downstairs to rouse their respective families. It was not yet five o'clock in the morning and everyone was sleeping.

Vasilakis and little Irini were curled up together, innocent, their lashes flickering against their cheeks as though they were having the same shared dream. Maria picked up Irini and Panikos scooped up Vasilakis. Neither child woke up. Their parents needed nothing else. No possessions were worth packing or delaying for.

Mehmet often slept with his mother, as his bad dreams regularly caused him to walk the corridors of the hotel in his sleep. In his mind, bombs were landing on the beach, spraying up storms of sand and combusting everything around him. From the day that peace on their island had been shattered, thousands of Cypriots had been haunted by similar recurring nightmares. Images of bombers flying overhead and the threat of annihilation were hard to shift for adults and children alike.

Emine slept lightly, so it required little to rouse her. She took the *nazar* from the wall. As she left the room, she noticed Aphroditi's handbag still on a chair. She took out the velvet pouch and the purse, leaving the key inside.

For Irini, the precious things were her *mati*, a picture of Christos and her icon.

The only thing that Hüseyin took with him was the necklace.

Within five minutes they were all assembled.

'Where are we going?' asked Irini.

Nobody had really thought.

'Home?' said Halit.

The word sounded strange and empty. Everyone looked at each other. It no longer meant what it used to, but for now it was somewhere to go.

'I always hoped we would leave this place one day . . . but not like this,' said Irini tearfully. 'It's come so suddenly . . .'

Vasilis knew that his wife would be thinking about her son's body. How would she give him the proper memorial? Pray by his grave? Could she walk away from his bones not knowing if she would ever return?

Vasilis said the only thing she wanted to hear.

'I am sure we can come back and find him.'

Irini was the only one who wept as they left. All the others had their minds fixed on the next hour of their lives.

They crept out of the fire door and towards the beach. Hüseyin unlocked the gate and the families went their separate ways, hoping that this would help them avoid detection.

The sun was beginning to come up and the light allowed them to see the decrepitude of the streets that they had not walked all those months. Only Hüseyin and Panikos were familiar with the sight. The others were horrified.

After the spring rains, weeds had sprung up between paving stones and through cracks in the road caused by bombs. Damage to buildings was more extensive than any of them had remembered. The roads were littered with debris and unwanted goods that even the looters had abandoned. Paintwork had peeled, shop signs had fallen, metal balconies had been ripped from buildings and doors kicked in. It was harrowing to see their once beautiful and thriving city in this condition.

The two parties made their way as quickly as they could. They had agreed on their routes before setting off and approached the street from different directions.

Closer to home, there was blossom on the trees and bougainvillea rampaged across many of the houses, their blooms large and blousy. The sight of them was unexpectedly cheerful and softened the overall sense of decay.

The Özkans reached Elpida Street first. Their home was just as they had left it on the day the Turkish soldiers had done their damage.

Halit stepped over the broken fragments of the front door.

Inside, a thick pall of dust lay over everything.

Emine stood with her hand clasped across her mouth. The vision of home that she had cherished during their stay at The Sunrise had not been this. The pan of pilaf that she had left on the stove all those months ago had gone through the stages of putrefaction and decay. Mice had left just a few shreds of paper from bags of rice and flour, and the cupboards were dark with droppings. Rats had burrowed into upholstery and destroyed the curtains for their nesting materials.

Leaving Mehmet and Hüseyin downstairs, Emine and Halit went up to the first floor. It was no better. The smell was pungent and the mattresses and bedclothes were torn to pieces. The open doorway had been an invitation to all the neighbourhood vermin.

'Well, we need to make a start,' said Halit. 'There's work to be done. Let's tidy up first and then see if we can repair the door.'

Hüseyin was looking at his mother. She was shaking her head from side to side.

'We can't stay here, Halit,' she said. 'They have destroyed our home.'

'But this is where we live.'

'Perhaps we will have to go somewhere else now,' said Hüseyin. 'It won't be the first time we have moved.'

Hüseyin was usually reluctant to contradict his father, but the attack on their home was not just an attack on its fabric. It was a violation of their sanctuary, and this sacred status could never be restored.

The Georgiou party was slightly slower than the Özkans. Maria was carrying the baby and Panikos took Vasilakis on his shoulders. Vasilis limped along with his stick, Irini fretting that the constant tap-tap-tap would be heard. Eventually they reached Elpida Street. Their four-storey building looked just the same as it had done when they left it, except that the plants were now either dead or overgrown.

The six of them passed through the low iron gate. Rust seemed to have taken its toll and it needed oiling. Vasilakis was excited to be back in his grandparents' garden. His small tricycle was still sitting in the corner and he ran towards it shrieking with glee.

'Vasilakis!' his mother hissed. 'Come *here*. Shhhhh!'

The whole family stood immobile. None of them had any desire to go inside. It was not what they might find that they dreaded, but what they knew they would not. The absence of Markos and Christos weighed heavily on them.

From the general look of the place, it seemed that Turkish soldiers had not bothered to break in. Doors and shutters appeared intact.

Irini glanced up at the empty hook above her. Mimikos. For her, there could never be another songbird.

The pain of return was even more intense than she had expected. The *kipos* was where she felt her elder son's loss most keenly. It was where they had sat together each morning, where he had sipped the coffee she made for him, where he had embraced her, where he had sung to her more sweetly than any canary.

As Vasilis and Panikos retrieved the hidden spare keys, she sank quietly into a seat. She saw her husband go inside their apartment and Maria and Panikos taking the children upstairs.

A short time later, Maria was back. She was forcing a smile.

'Everything is just as we left it,' she said. 'It's a bit damp and dusty, but nobody has been in there. We'll have it back to normal in no time.'

Vasilis had re-emerged too. He wore his usual unsmiling expression.

'Just as it was,' he said bluntly. 'But a bit dirtier than usual.'

His wife normally kept everything meticulously clean and tidy, so even a small amount of dust would be noticeable.

Irini continued to sit.

'Are you not going in, *Mamma*?' asked Maria. She put her arm around her mother's shoulder.

Irini Georgiou shook her head silently. She could not bring herself to stand up. This place they had all returned to could no longer be called home. The building that they had created for their families and their future felt to her like a broken orange crate, splintered and unusable.

The fate of Christos was still unknown. His apartment had been empty for some time even before they had left. With absolute certainty she knew that the floor above it would never again be occupied. The parental dream of these spaces being filled by daughters-in-law whom they would try to love, and broods of children, was not going to come true. There were lives and futures that would never happen.

Before Irini could speak, Emine appeared, followed by Halit and Mehmet.

'You can't imagine the mess over there,' she said. 'You should see what the mice have been up to! They've done worse things than the soldiers.'

She took a seat next to Irini and put a hand on her friend's arm.

'We can't stay there,' she continued. 'It's been totally destroyed – and it stinks.'

Irini looked at her.

Vasilis reappeared in the *kipos* to find his wife. It was uncharacteristic of Irini not to have followed him inside. He would have expected her to have put on her housecoat by now and to have started dusting and cleaning.

He saw her still sitting, with the Turkish Cypriot couple close by. Mehmet had run upstairs to find Vasilakis.

'Irini?'

'Emine and Halit need somewhere to sleep,' she said. 'So do Hüseyin and Mehmet. Can you find the keys for Christos' and Markos' flats?'

Vasilis silently did what his wife had asked and handed over the keys.

'A thousand thanks, *ahbap*, my friend,' said Halit to Vasilis. 'May Allah bless you.'

Irini stood up and went into her house to start cleaning. She could not sleep in a dirty home.

Their words and actions were almost inaudible, but even if they had spoken in normal tones or slammed a door, there was nobody to hear. There were no soldiers in the vicinity. Most of them had been dispatched to The Sunrise.

When his father and brother had left for the Georgious', Hüseyin had gone to find something to eat.

'The stores can't *all* have been emptied,' said his father. 'And if you can find some tobacco . . .'

Hüseyin made his way through the streets, passing several places that he noted for later. His priority was not food.

There was something he now realised he had left at The Sunrise that he wanted to retrieve: Markos' gun. It was beneath his mattress and it might give them some protection. They had nothing else. While he was there, he would also grab a few food supplies.

Before he could even see the hotel, he knew something unusual was taking place. Apart from the occasional passing of a jeep, the streets had been governed by silence during their time at The Sunrise. Today, this had changed.

The sound of building work had been a common one right up until the war, with new hotels and apartment blocks constantly being erected in Famagusta. Today he heard that sound again, but as he turned the corner, he realised that what he was hearing was *de*struction rather than *con*struction.

In front of The Sunrise there were three bulldozers standing ready, revving their engines. To the side of them were four men, each one operating a pneumatic drill. The sound was ear-splitting, even from a distance.

The drills were being used to undermine the gateposts and the iron railings, and the operators were discovering how solidly Savvas Papacosta had built everything. They had to dig down at least three feet below the ground.

Every so often they stood aside to allow the bulldozers, groaning and roaring as they swivelled from side to side, to scoop up the debris.

At a distance from the din stood a group of at least a dozen soldiers. As the gates came down and a wide enough section of the railings fell, one of the bulldozers crashed its way in. The soldiers cheered and applauded as they followed the monster. Hüseyin watched as it began to tear down the metal grid that protected the front of the hotel and smash its way through the glass behind. There was something anarchic about the soldiers, something savage about their enthusiasm for this brutal destruction. Several of them began to fire their guns into the air.

He imagined that their goal was the vault. No doubt the Turkish Cypriot, who was still with the soldiers, had given them the tip-off, but Hüseyin doubted he was going to get any of the reward.

Hüseyin watched for a few minutes before retreating. What was going to happen next was of no interest to him. He knew the safes were impenetrable even with the keys. He had no way to retrieve the gun now, so his priority was to find food.

He retreated up a side street, feeling that he had witnessed more than enough brutish behaviour. Even though the soldiers' violence was directed against concrete and glass, it was ugly and filled him with fear.

The first general store he came to had been stripped bare. There was nothing except for a few bars of soap and some salt. In the second, he scoured every shelf. Hidden at the very back of the last place he searched were two tins of anchovies. They would have been easy to miss. He put them in his pocket. In the next shop he found a few tins of chickpeas and a small sack to carry them in. He noticed that all the dried goods – rice, beans, flour and sugar – had been consumed already. Quantities of mouse and rat droppings had been left in their place. The Sunrise had been a haven indeed.

He continued his search, going into three or four more shops; in each he found the same piles of animal droppings, shredded paper and cardboard that had once been the wrapping for biscuits and sugar. After two more hours of walking the streets, all he had found were three tins of tomato paste and two of condensed milk. Tired and disillusioned, he returned to Elpida Street.

As he stepped over the threshold, the silence told him that he was alone. He put his hand over his nose. It stank. He remembered walking in after the soldiers had ransacked it, but months later it was much worse.

Putting the small sack of goods over his shoulder, he crossed the street to the Georgious'.

'Your parents are upstairs,' said Vasilis.

As Hüseyin put the supply of food down on the garden table, Irini came out.

'What did you find?' she asked, knowing that everyone would be hungry.

'Just tins,' he said. 'Everything else has gone.'

'I am sure we can make something nice with those,' she said. 'Will you bring them inside?'

One by one, Irini took the tins out of the sack and read the labels. Some of them were looking rusty, but she knew the contents would still be good.

'Did you see what happened to our herbs?'

Hüseyin shook his head politely.

'They've *grown!*' she said, struggling to sound positive. 'Look at this basil! And the marjoram!'

She picked up two huge bunches of greenery that had been sitting in the sink and offered them to him to smell. The combined fragrance was intoxicatingly sweet and fresh.

He buried his face in them to hide his emotions. A few hours earlier, when they had left The Sunrise, he could not even look at Irini Georgiou. The tears had been coursing down her face. Her grief was a great burden to him. He knew he was responsible for it, and even his knowledge that it was self-defence would never assuage his guilt. Now here she was bustling bravely about in the kitchen telling him what she was going to cook from these meagre ingredients.

Making meals for them all was Irini Georgiou's refuge, but when the cooking was completed and the meal had been served and eaten and every knife and fork put away, her sadness would still be waiting for her, like a coat hanging on the back of the door.

He handed her back the bouquet of herbs and hoped she had not noticed how his eyes were glistening.

'With these, these and these,' she said, pointing at three of the tins, 'I can make a bean stew. And there is still some honey, so we will even have something for dessert this evening. Well done, my dear.'

Hüseyin turned away. The affectionate way in which she spoke to him, almost as if he were her own son, was unbearable.

'Will you tell your mother that I'll have something ready in an hour?' Irini called after him.

Hüseyin took the stairs two at a time.

On the first floor, he almost fell into his mother's arms.

'*Canım*, are you all right?'

'Out of breath, Mother,' he said. 'That's all.'

She hugged him. Behind her shoulder, he wiped a tear away on his sleeve.

'I found some food,' he said. 'It's downstairs with Kyria Georgiou. She's cooking.'

'I must go and help her.'

'I'm sure she would like that,' said Hüseyin, for the sake of something to say.

'Oh,' said his mother, almost as an afterthought. 'This is their son Christos' apartment. If you don't want to share a room with Mehmet, then there's always upstairs . . .'

'You mean Markos' apartment?'

Emine realised immediately what she had suggested.

'I'll sleep on the couch,' Hüseyin said.

When they gathered round Irini and Vasilis' table to eat, there was scarcely enough room and extra chairs had to be brought downstairs. Vasilakis sat on his father's lap and the baby on her mother's. Mehmet perched on a small stool.

Hüseyin volunteered to sit in the garden and keep watch. They could not drop their guard now.

Irini brought out a plate for him.

'Can you still smell them?' she asked.

He bent low over the dish. The aroma of the herbs rose up into his face.

'Yes,' he replied. 'Thank you, Kyria Georgiou.'

Within five minutes, his plate was clean.

Inside, Vasilis poured himself and Panikos a glass of *zivania*.

'*Stin yia mas*,' they said, clinking glasses.

Vasilis was happy to be home again. He had missed the strength of home-brewed firewater. The vintage whiskies and French cognacs in the Clair de Lune had been no substitute. They all ate hungrily.

They had got used to the grandeur of The Sunrise, to the porcelain, crystal and silver, but this felt more natural to them: the streaked, shuttered light, the lace cloth, the slightly chipped plates and the touch of elbows round a small table.

The icon was back on the special shelf where it belonged and the *mati* kept watch over them all. The photographs were where they had always been and Irini had even found time to dust them all, deliberately avoiding the gaze of both her sons. They looked out at the lens. Markos: deceased. Christos: missing.

By the end of the following morning, Hüseyin knew the truth of the food situation. He had risen early and walked every street in the neighbourhood, going in and out of every food shop. Most of them did not need to be entered forcibly. Doors were already ajar. He remembered the ones that had been a rich source before they went to The Sunrise, but any dry goods had meanwhile been devoured, and most tins taken, he assumed by soldiers.

When he returned, he found his mother with Irini at her kitchen table.

'Where have you been, darling?' said Emine. 'We've been so worried!'

'We thought something had happened to you,' added Irini with concern.

'I was looking for food,' he answered. 'I thought you would know where I had gone.'

'But you were so long . . .' said Emine.

'I'm sorry you were worried,' he said. 'But . . .' He hesitated. The reality was that he had found almost nothing all morning. In desperation, he had even broken into people's homes to see whether anything edible remained.

Just as he had observed months earlier, there were houses that remained precisely as when their owners had taken flight. In one, plates were stained with the residue of a meal; in another, some dried-out flower petals were scattered in a neat circle around the base of a vase. A baby's bib and an apron were slung carelessly across the back of a chair, discarded before the inhabitants had fled. All around were signs of normal life interrupted by the suddenness of flight. There was a stillness in these homes, as though their owners might walk in at any moment and resume their lives.

The houses that had been looted felt very different. They reminded him of the state of his own home. Chairs were not neatly tucked under tables and plates were not patiently waiting for soup or *kleftiko*. Furniture had been reduced to sticks of wood and china lay in pieces. Cupboard doors were wide open and valuables had been removed. Rumours that people had hidden money and jewellery inside mattresses or under floorboards meant that the Turkish soldiers had sometimes ripped homes apart. Though the vast majority of the houses belonged to Greek Cypriots, the destruction had been equally frenzied in Turkish Cypriot homes.

Over all of them hung an odour of staleness, damp and decay. If buildings were mortal, these were dying or dead.

Whatever the state of the place he walked into, Hüseyin had a single purpose: to see if there was anything edible. The pickings were not rich. In the entire morning, he had found four rusty tins that would scarcely feed them all for a single meal.

The two women watched him expectantly. He felt almost uncomfortable beneath their gaze. Ever since Markos' death, he had been conscious that the adults had been looking to him for guidance.

'This is all there is,' he said, putting the tins on the table in front of them.

Irini and Emine stood silently. They could not conceal their disappointment.

'There is next to nothing out there,' said Hüseyin.

'Go and find your father and Kyrios Georgiou,' said Emine.

The two men were having a cigarette on the rooftop of the building. They had found some stale tobacco in a tin in Christos' apartment.

When Hüseyin arrived, he had a moment to observe them

before they noticed him. Their heads were inclined towards each other as they spoke. So much had changed.

They heard his footsteps and turned towards him.

'Hüseyin!' said Halit, smiling.

'Will you come downstairs?' he asked.

'When we have finished our cigarettes,' responded Halit. 'Is there something your mother wants me to do?'

Hüseyin shrugged. There was a sweet breeze that day and he felt it brush his face as he turned to leave.

A few minutes later, the five of them gathered in the Georgious' apartment.

'Hüseyin has something to tell us.'

'I think we have to leave.'

'But why?' asked Vasilis.

'We don't know what it's like out there . . .' added Halit.

'There's no food here, *Baba*. It's time to go.'

His words were blunt. It was the truth.

They all looked at each other. Even now, growing hunger was telling them that Hüseyin must be right.

'We'd better tell Maria and Panikos,' said Vasilis.

'But how can we just walk out?' asked Irini. 'It can't be safe.'

Hüseyin, who had seen the behaviour of the soldiers, knew that it was not.

'If we leave here,' said Halit, 'we have nothing. We have nothing at all.'

'And Ali won't know where to find us . . . nor Christos,' said Emine.

'We have our smallholding,' said Vasilis. 'And our trees.'

'But nowhere to live,' Irini added, almost inaudibly.

Panikos had appeared at the door. He had left Maria upstairs with the three children and had been listening.

'If Hüseyin says we have to leave, we should listen to him,' he said. 'The children are hungry all the time. And if there is already no food out there . . .'

'But we have to find safe passage,' said Vasilis. 'We can't just walk out of here.'

'And who is going to give us that?' asked Panikos. With two small children and a wife, in a city occupied by Turkish soldiers, he was full of fear.

Once again Hüseyin found that all eyes were on him.

'Give me until tomorrow,' he said. 'But be ready to leave when I come back.'

They all looked at each other. There was little to prepare. The icon, the photos and the *mati* would be repacked. There were no other possessions that seemed of any importance.

Hüseyin raced up to Christos' apartment. Stuffed down the side of the sofa where he had slept was the necklace. He emptied it out of the pouch and held it up to the light. Even he, with his lack of knowledge about such things, admired its beauty.

'Hüseyin!'

When he looked round, he saw that his mother had followed him. Her eyes were blazing.

'Hüseyin – where did you get that necklace?'

'Markos . . . it was in his pocket when I killed him.'

'Let me see it,' she demanded.

Hüseyin had rarely seen his mother so angry. He handed her the necklace; she examined it for a moment and looked at the distinctive clasp.

'There's only one woman in Cyprus who owns anything like this,' she said. She had recognised it immediately as Aphroditi's.

Hüseyin was anxious that she was not going to give it back to him.

'These sapphires are all we have now, Mother,' he pleaded. 'I need to sell them to get us safe passage.'

She looked at him thoughtfully, and then at the necklace that she nursed in her hands. Like Hüseyin, she could see that this provided their only chance. Somehow, one day, they would pay Aphroditi back.

'Something you should know,' she said, 'is that these are not sapphires. They're blue diamonds. It's the necklace that Aphroditi's father gave her for her wedding.'

'So if I can sell them, they'll definitely buy us our safety?'

'I hope so,' said Emine. 'I think they're very rare.'

She did not want to know the details of Hüseyin's plan, but she trusted him to have one.

'Will you cut my hair?' Hüseyin asked. 'I need it really short.'

Emine did not ask any questions.

They found a pair of scissors in Christos' bathroom, and as proficiently as she could with such inadequate tools, she sliced off her son's hair.

Irini was in the *kipos* when he passed by. With everything so overgrown, she felt safe to sit here in the warmth, with the sun filtering through the canopy of early summer leaves. She thought Hüseyin was going out on another excursion to find food and crossed herself several times, saying a little prayer for his safety. Her old habits had begun to return.

Chapter Thirty-two

Hüseyin had a single purpose. First he had to find a soldier's uniform. As a civilian, he would have much less chance of making his way safely to his destination.

There was only one place he knew he would find one. He vividly remembered the location of the store where he had killed Markos. It was impossible to forget. It took him only ten minutes to get there and his heart was racing when he arrived. If he did not do what was needed quickly, if he even paused for thought, he knew he would fail.

As soon as he was inside the store, he pulled off his shirt and tied it tightly round his face, covering nose and mouth. Even from the doorway, he imagined he could detect the smell of decomposing flesh. He walked briskly towards the back and started pulling away the piles of sacks. The soldier's body had not been discovered by vermin and had been left to quietly decay.

Hüseyin quickly unbuttoned the shirt and the trouser fly, trying his best not to look at the face. The boots slipped easily over the feet and then he dragged off the trousers. The shirt was harder to remove. It required rolling the corpse to one side and pulling one arm through at a time. He left the soldier's rotting body in his underwear and covered him up again with sacking.

Taking the clothes towards the front of the shop, Hüseyin shook them vigorously to make sure that no grubs lurked inside. He tried not to gag as he swapped his own trousers for the dead man's, remembering to remove the diamonds from his pocket. Then he put on the shirt and boots and stuffed his own behind the counter.

The clothes were slightly too large, but rolling the top of the trousers over helped them to stay up. The boots fitted as if they were his own. He caught sight of himself in the dirty shop window and knew that he would just about pass. He had no recollection of the soldier wearing a hat. Perhaps it was lost when he fell.

Hüseyin made for the section in the wire that he knew had been Markos' way out of the city, not passing even a single soldier en route. When it was almost dark, he slipped through. It appeared that most of the military now remained at their sentry posts around the edge of Famagusta and did not have a view of his path out of the city.

He made his way across some scrubland, staying close to trees where he could, and walked until he reached a main road. Ten minutes later he heard the sound of a lorry behind him. It was an army vehicle with a group of soldiers in the back. It slowed to pick him up and the grating at the back dropped down for him to climb in.

They squeezed up to make space for him on one of the benches and carried on with their drinking song. When they got to the chorus, they passed around a bottle of firewater and took a large gulp each. Hüseyin mimed both the singing and the swigging. Nobody looked twice at him. Most of the others seemed not to have a hat either.

It was difficult to see very much in the dark, but he noticed dozens of abandoned cars by the side of the road, some of them now pushed into ditches. He wondered if they were vehicles that had run out of fuel on what must have been a terrifying flight from Famagusta all those months before.

They passed a couple of United Nations vehicles on their way and stopped once or twice more to pick up other soldiers who needed lifts, but eventually, in the early hours, they reached Nicosia, where they were dropped at a barracks in the suburbs. Most of the men went inside and a few others wandered off towards the centre of the city. Hüseyin ambled along with them. None of them seemed to know each other that well, so he melted in with their group and managed to conceal the Cypriot accent that might have given him away. From their conversation he gathered that they were off to find a brothel. He kept up with them for a while and then hung back pretending to look in shop windows until they were out of sight.

He was not familiar with the streets of Nicosia. He had been there once or twice as a child, before the Green Line had been run across the city, but he had little recollection of it. Even in the darkness he had been able to see that the island was in chaos. He was anxious enough about his own parents and his brother, but finding safety for the Georgious would be even trickier.

Hüseyin wandered the streets, trying to avoid the groups of soldiers milling about. After a while, exhaustion swept over him and he crept into the dark recess of a doorway and slept. It was only when the shopkeeper pulled up the shutters at five minutes to nine the following morning that he realised he had spent the night outside a watchmaker's. The grey-haired man was only slightly surprised to see him; there were so many soldiers in the city that it was no surprise to find one curled up on his doorstep.

Once the shutters were pulled up, Hüseyin saw that there were hundreds of watches lined up in neat rows. They all looked almost identical. An off-white face with fine golden hands seemed to be the standard. He had never owned a watch and wondered how people chose from this huge selection.

The shopkeeper had been doing good business. Many of the soldiers wanted to buy a watch, as he sold brands that they could not get at home in Turkey, and he imagined that Hüseyin might be such a customer.

'Come in,' he said. 'There are plenty more to choose from inside.'

As Hüseyin entered, a hundred clocks began to chime, each one sounding a different note. For a few moments it was impossible to say anything. It was a percussion orchestra, a morning chorus of repeated single notes. Once they had announced the hour, the sound of ticking took over, insistent, busy and relentless.

'I don't really hear it any longer,' said the watchmaker, knowing what the young man was thinking. 'They say it would drive me mad if I did.'

He was a good salesman and knew to let his customers browse and try on, browse and try on.

'Anything you want to take a closer look at, just tell me,' he said. 'Coffee?'

Hüseyin nodded.

He felt that each moment brought him closer to the question he most wanted to ask.

The watchmaker stepped outside the shop for a second and beckoned to a boy loitering outside the café opposite. A few minutes later, the child appeared with a tray hanging down from a chain and two small cups. The watchmaker knew that coffee helped to focus a customer's mind.

'Where are you from?' he asked, sipping his own drink.

'Not far away,' said Hüseyin elusively. 'On the coast.'

The man would assume he meant somewhere close to Mersin, the port on the Turkish coast where the majority of the soldiers had embarked to reach Cyprus. He had begun to wind his clocks, some of them by hand, some with a key. It was a task that required the utmost patience and dexterity, and the shopkeeper seemed to be blessed with both.

'Sometimes,' he said, 'I feel as if I have all the time in the world!'

Hüseyin knew it was not the first time the man had said this, but he smiled all the same.

'Do you mend watches too?' he asked, to make conversation.

'Of course,' said the shopkeeper. 'I have one to do today. The owner wants to collect it later.'

'I suppose there is always someone with a broken watch.'

'But people like to treat themselves to a new one too,' said the man. 'You soldiers seem keen.'

Hüseyin wandered across to a cabinet full of ladies' watches and peered inside.

'Now those are as much a piece of jewellery as a watch,' said the shopkeeper with a chuckle. The straps were all either gold or platinum, and many of them had jewels around the face. 'Ladies who own those rarely need to look at them,' he added. 'They have a man there to tell them the time . . .'

'They must be very expensive,' Hüseyin commented.

'They are. And I don't think I've sold more than four in ten years. Since the troubles. Lost a lot of business then. So many of my Turkish Cypriot regulars have left Cyprus. And the Greek Cypriots can't come here.'

Hüseyin knew he had to be bold, but so far the man seemed kind enough.

'Look,' he said, dropping his accent, 'I'm not Turkish. I'm a Turkish Cypriot. I can't afford to buy a watch.'

The watchmaker stopped what he was doing and listened. It was a story he had heard before.

'My family has lost everything,' said Hüseyin. 'Except for this.' He pulled the necklace out of his pocket.

The watchmaker's eyes widened with amazement. He only knew about the cost of the tiny gems that were used in watches. Those in the young man's hands were on a different scale. They were bigger than any of the precious stones he had seen in a long while.

'Can I see?'

Hüseyin passed the diamonds across and the man held them up to the light.

'I've never *seen* such beautiful sapphires,' he said, handing them back.

'They're blue diamonds,' said Hüseyin authoritatively.

'Blue diamonds!' The watchmaker took another admiring look at them. 'And I suppose you need to sell them?'

Hüseyin nodded. 'But I need to do it as soon as I can. I need the money.'

'I'm sure you do. Everyone needs money these days.'

'It's to help somebody,' he said.

The watchmaker was beginning to feel confused. There was a vulnerable desperation in the young man's expression. Whoever it was he wanted to help, he clearly cared a great deal for them.

'I'll do what I can,' he said. 'I think we can arrange for that necklace to be sold. And after that, you'll have to tell me how you want to help these people . . .'

'Thank you,' said Hüseyin.

'I'll telephone one of my friends and see what he can do,' he said. 'I shut at lunchtime, so if I can arrange something, we'll go together to see him. But if you're not going to buy anything of mine,' he added, 'I've got work to do. Come back at twelve. On the dot.'

'I won't be late,' promised Hüseyin.

He walked slowly around the city, killing time for the next few hours. He stopped twice for a coffee. It seemed strange to be using money again, handing over coins and waiting for change. He was then lured by the aroma of lamb and hungrily ate some *şiş kebap* from a stall, the first meat he had tasted in months.

When he returned, hundreds of hands on clocks and watches were about to reach their precise vertical position. As he walked in, they began simultaneously to strike the hour.

The watchmaker was ready for him.

'I've found someone,' he said. 'You may not get the price you want, but it's the best we'll do today.'

The fact that Hüseyin planned to use the money to help other people had touched him. Hüseyin reminded him of his son, who was also in uniform but in another part of the island, and it was enough reason to give him a hand.

They walked across the city together and Hüseyin explained what he needed the money for.

'I can't help you with that,' the watchmaker said. 'But we can ask my friend about it. He'll know how.'

He led Hüseyin down a side street and he found himself in a dingy *kafenion*. Across the room, almost invisible through a dense fog of smoke, a pallid, fleshy man was sitting alone. Most others were in groups, playing cards, talking noisily, even shouting. A television blared from the wall, next to a hatch through which coffee was served.

The watchmaker strode towards the solitary man and beckoned Hüseyin to follow. They both sat down at his table. The man was about sixty, with a thick greying moustache, and did not look the watchmaker in the eye when he spoke to him. He remained staring impassively ahead, scarcely responding to anything that was said. Hüseyin even wondered if he was blind, so apparently uninterested was he in anything going on around him. Only when the watchmaker told Hüseyin to show him the diamonds did his expression change.

'Pass them to me, but keep them out of sight.'

Hüseyin handed them to him beneath the table. He could hear the slight jangle of the stones as the man felt them. He was still not convinced that he could see.

'You can have twenty thousand for them,' he said.

'Twenty thousand?' repeated Hüseyin in disbelief. It seemed an enormous sum.

'That's in Turkish lira,' said the watchmaker quietly. 'It's about five hundred pounds.'

Hüseyin repeated the figure. He had no idea if it was enough.

'That's all I'm offering,' said the man, gazing into space.

'There's something else he needs. Tell him, Hüseyin.'

'There are two families, one Greek Cypriot, the other Turkish Cypriot. Nine people and a baby. They need safe passage out of Famagusta.'

'But there is nobody inside Famagusta. Just Turkish soldiers,' stated the man bluntly, in the tone of one who was not used to being contradicted.

Hüseyin said nothing. There was something so cold about this individual and he could see that he was not a man to argue with.

The watchmaker turned to Hüseyin. 'But how . . . ?' he began.

Hüseyin shook his head. He did not want to explain. In this company it seemed safer to keep up his guard.

'I want to get them out safely. Today,' he said under his breath. 'Perhaps to Nicosia.'

'So who exactly are the ten?' asked the watchmaker.

Suddenly the old man was being too curious and asking too many questions. For Hüseyin there was some urgency about their departure, and the longer he sat in this café, the further it seemed to recede.

The dealer leaned forward and spoke directly to Hüseyin for the first time.

'There are rumours of landmines,' he said, showing filthy teeth. 'So the fare isn't cheap. It will cost exactly the price of these stones.'

Hüseyin had hoped there might be some money left. They would need something to live on once they were out of Famagusta, but it seemed he had to take this one step at a time.

The large man held on to the diamonds under the table. They were clearly demanded as advance payment. He said something in the watchmaker's ear that Hüseyin could not hear.

The watchmaker indicated to Hüseyin that it was time to leave. With a slight lift of his head, the dealer summoned a man who had been standing by the door acting as look out. He came over to the table and escorted the pair of them from the *kafenion*.

The transaction had been mysterious. All Hüseyin really understood was that he was glad to get away from this difficult and aggressive man of whom everyone seemed to be afraid.

Once outside on the pavement, the watchmaker explained what was to happen.

'Someone will take you to Famagusta now. They will wait ten minutes and then bring you back to Nicosia.'

Soon Hüseyin was heading back towards Famagusta, surveying more bomb damage on the way. The driver was a Turkish soldier, more than six feet tall, of a senior rank and silent throughout the journey.

They passed several checkpoints on the road, and each time, after heated discussion, they were allowed through. It felt unreal to be driven through the silent streets of Famagusta. Hüseyin asked to be dropped a little way from home. He trusted nobody and was afraid of letting this soldier know exactly where his party was hiding out. Just round the corner from Elpida Street, he climbed out of the jeep.

'You've got ten minutes,' barked the soldier.

He ran into the Georgious' apartment. They were all waiting for him expectantly, and with a mixture of excitement and trepidation he told them what he had arranged.

'Once we are in Nicosia, Kyrios and Kyria Georgiou will be taken across the Green Line with Maria and Panikos and the children. After that, everyone will be free . . .'

His words tailed away. Free. What did that mean now?

Hüseyin felt the eyes of all the adults on him. He had nothing more to tell them, but they clearly looked to him for leadership. He had come up with a plan for the next few hours, but he could not see beyond that.

When the tanks had arrived in Famagusta all those months earlier, they had assumed that everything would return to normal. They all knew now that assumptions could not be made.

'Do you know anyone in Nicosia?' asked Emine.

Irini shook her head.

Emine remembered that the Papacostas had an apartment in Nicosia but stopped herself from mentioning it. It would not have been appropriate given all that had happened.

'I'm sure they'll help us find somewhere to live,' she said brightly.

Even Emine was not certain whom she meant by 'they'.

One of the last newspapers that Markos had brought into The Sunrise had shown a picture of a vast tented refugee camp. For Irini and Emine such a place would be worse than hell: nowhere to cook, no privacy, an inferno in summer and cruelly damp in winter. Perhaps they would have no choice.

They were all ready to leave and filed out of the front door. Vasilis was the last. He locked up and gave the key to Irini, then they followed Hüseyin silently, like an orderly procession of schoolchildren.

When they turned the corner, they saw the army truck. It was hard for Vasilis to climb up into the back, but Hüseyin lent him his strength and gave him a leg-up. They sat on the wooden benches facing each other and bumped along the rutted streets that led them out of the city, the objects of curious stares when they passed any soldiers. When they reached the barrier out of Famagusta, there was a long discussion between the driver and the soldiers on duty. Everyone on the truck stayed silent, even the children. Some papers were handed over and then an envelope. None of the passengers watched too closely, wishing they were invisible.

The roar and grunt of the engine precluded conversation, so even Mehmet and Vasilakis were silent on the journey, simply taking in the landscape as they lurched along the road. The orange groves on the outskirts of the city were laden with fruit, but the rest of the landscape seemed parched and barren. It appeared that no seeds had been planted. They trundled past ruined houses, farm buildings and churches. It was strange not to see farmers working in the fields, and there was a noticeable absence of animals: no goats, no sheep, no donkeys.

The outskirts of Nicosia shocked them, just as they had shocked Aphroditi all those months before. It was not a place any of them were familiar with, but for a capital city, it looked derelict and sad. The lorry roared through the narrow streets of the northern suburbs towards the centre.

Although they all looked down-at-heel, people seemed to be going about their daily business here, old men sitting in cafés, women looking in shop windows and children ambling home from school in scruffy shoes.

Eventually they came to a halt. Up ahead they saw the barricade that divided the city. They had reached the Green Line.

For a moment they sat still in the truck, then there was the scrape of the bolts being drawn back and the grid was lowered. Like cattle, they were being unloaded.

Hüseyin jumped down first and Maria handed him little Irini. It was the first time he had held the baby and he had not realised how sweet she smelled. She reached up and pulled at his nose.

Panikos struggled down next and helped the others – his in-laws, Emine and then Halit. Finally Maria passed Vasilakis to his father and then Mehmet showed off by jumping down on his own. Hüseyin was still holding the baby. He did not want to let her go.

Maria was now standing next him and with some reluctance put out her hands to relieve him of his burden. She could see that the child was happy in Hüseyin's arms.

The soldier was getting impatient. He was not going to stand there all day waiting for these people, and his fee depended on the completion of the job, namely to see these Greek Cypriots safely across the Green Line.

'Go!' he ordered them, pointing to the barrier.

The two families stood looking at each other wordlessly. They were fearful of the soldier's impatience, but even greater was their fear of saying goodbye. This departure had been so hastily arranged that they had scarcely imagined the moment of separation.

There had to be a final moment, a fleeting flash of time, and their instincts told them how to spend it. Both Vasilis and Halit were holding their respective talismans. Vasilis had put the Georgiou *mati* in a napkin to keep it safe. When he held it out to Halit, as if gift-wrapped in its cloth, Halit automatically handed his *nazar* to Vasilis in return. It seemed a natural transaction. They were similar in size and both made of bright blue glass. The only difference was that Emine had used a red cord to hang theirs, and Irini a blue ribbon.

Emine gave Irini the briefest hug.

'We'll never forget how you saved our baby,' Panikos said to Hüseyin.

Hüseyin shook his head, unable to speak.

The small boys were chasing each other around the circle of adults. Maria held little Irini.

The soldier repeated his instruction but more loudly this time.

'Go. Now!'

The Turkish words meant nothing to the Georgiou family, but the gesture was unambiguous. Time had run out. They suddenly realised that this was it. This was the end of their life together. For both parties it felt as if they were being wrenched apart.

It was a year to the day since the coup that had set everything in motion, and there could be neither tears nor any further words.

A few passers-by noticed the elderly lady in black and two younger women, one of whom was wearing a Chanel shift. Their children were expensively dressed too. It seemed unlikely in these times that such smart people should be standing around in the street.

To onlookers they seemed one homogenous party, but only some of them needed to follow the soldier's order. Suddenly they became two groups: Irini, Vasilis, Maria, Panikos and their children moved as one. Emine, Halit, Hüseyin and Mehmet stayed where they were.

The Georgiou family walked towards the barrier, catching sight of some blue-bereted United Nations soldiers on the other side. There was a discussion that they did not hear, but it seemed only a small problem that they had no identification with them. They were soon allowed through.

The Özkans watched their friends until they were out of sight. The Georgious did not turn their heads to look back.

In the years that followed . . .

As the Georgious crossed the Green Line, both they and the Özkans became part of the statistics.

More than two hundred thousand Greek Cypriots lost their homes in the north of Cyprus and forty thousand Turkish Cypriots were displaced from the south. All of them were refugees.

For neither family could Nicosia be regarded as home. Famagusta was the only place that would ever be worthy of that name. The capital city was merely a starting point for their lives in exile.

Eventually both families were allocated places to live that had been left vacant after the conflict, the Özkans in Kyrenia and the Georgious in Limassol. The towns were on the north and south coasts of Cyprus respectively, as far from each other as it was possible to be.

Even if they had known where the others had ended up, they would not have been allowed to cross the border to meet, and communication between the two sides was almost impossible.

To begin with, the Georgious' new apartment was less cluttered than the previous one, simply because so many of the possessions they had accumulated over the years had been left behind. The icon, which had seen them through so much, still watched them. So did an evil eye on a red cord.

It was easy for Irini to replicate some aspects of their home in Famagusta. With Maria and Panikos, they bought a set of similarly mass-produced plastic chairs for the garden, and Irini made a lace tablecloth identical to the one that was still lying undisturbed on their table in Elpida Street. Any possessions that had still been in the house when they first walked in – some photograph albums and a few pieces of china – she stored away for safe keeping in case their Turkish Cypriot owners ever returned.

Gradually too she re-created something that resembled her beloved *kipos* back in Famagusta. With the sunshine and spring rains, things grew quickly, and soon jasmine trailed around the door and gerania rampaged from her pots just as they had done before. She cultivated peppers, tomatoes and herbs, and within two years they would be picking bunches of grapes from their own vine.

It was almost a relief to Vasilis that he no longer had his land. He found it hard to walk far these days and could not bend to dig and weed as he had done before. Many other people from Famagusta were resettled in Limassol as well, so it was not long before Vasilis found some of his old friends. They reconvened daily as before, but in a different *kafenion*, talking of past times and dreaming of future ones.

For the Georgious, the loss of almost every material thing they owned was nothing compared with the loss of their sons. Each day Irini lit three candles in church: for Markos, Christos and Ali. As time passed, her faith had returned even though Christos had not.

Vasilis was determined to be realistic. They might never know Christos' real fate. It had been discovered that some of those who had been killed in the brief civil war around the time of the coup against Makarios had been included among the number of missing, buried by fellow Greek Cypriots in unknown places.

'He might have been one of those,' said Vasilis.

'I just have a feeling,' said Irini. 'And while I am still dreaming of him, I won't give up hope.'

Hope was all she had. *Elpida.*

Routine tasks and daily rituals became Irini's survival mechanism, along with the joys of helping Maria and Panikos look after their children. They provided huge distraction and gave her great joy.

The Georgious lived with the constant anxiety that their house was not their own and that the real owners might come to reclaim it. One day they thought that moment had arrived.

There was an unexpected ring on the bell. Walking slowly, Vasilis went to see who it was. In the old days in Famagusta they had always left the door open, but things were different here.

When he opened it, he wondered if he needed glasses as well as his walking stick. It was a young man. Haggard. Dirty.

Vasilis felt his legs weaken. It was as much as he could manage to say his son's name.

The two men embraced and Christos realised that he was taking most of his father's weight. Vasilis seemed to have aged so much since he had last seen him.

Hearing her husband calling weakly to her, Irini hurried in from the bedroom.

'*Yioka mou, yioka mou, yioka mou . . .*' she repeated over and over again as the tears flowed.

Christos had been released from a Turkish prison camp where he had been for many months, and for a while had been unable to track his parents down. It was disorientating to find that the place he had called home was now behind barbed wire, and it had taken him some time to locate them.

He seemed very fragile in both body and soul, but when they told him the news of his brother's death it seemed to break him completely. He retreated into the darkness of his parents' spare room and for more than a year never went beyond his mother's *kipos*.

As Christos was beginning to return to life, the family suffered another blow. Vasilis had a fatal stroke.

'At least we were with him, *yioka mou*,' said Irini to Christos. 'And he knew we were there.'

With the help of her daughter and son-in-law, Irini managed to remain strong for the sake of her son. She had been wearing black since the day Hüseyin had found her the mourning clothes in Famagusta, and she would always do so.

For some time, Panikos had been mulling over an offer from his cousin, who had lived in the UK since the late 1960s. His chain of electrical shops was expanding and he needed Panikos' expertise to manage three or four of them.

It was hard for Panikos to broach the subject with his brother-in-law. Christos had found work as a car mechanic easily enough, but his mood had remained dark. When Panikos finally plucked up courage to mention the proposition, however, he realised that Christos was ready to make a new start too.

'What can I do here?' said the disillusioned young man. 'Except sit and contemplate how it all went wrong.'

He carried a great guilt with him, too, that his friend Haralambos remained missing while he himself had been freed.

With hindsight, Christos criticised the organisation he had joined for aiding the coup against Makarios.

'We just opened ourselves up for invasion,' he said. 'And look what happened.'

Even Irini proved receptive to the idea of making a break with her beloved island.

'If you and Panikos want to go,' she told Maria, 'and Christos is happy to, then so am I. I can come back from time to time to tend to your father's grave. He won't mind that I'm not there every day . . .'

With help from myriad friends who had gone before them, they moved to north London.

In Kyrenia, the Özkans did their best to make a new life too. But it was almost impossible with Ali still missing. More than ever before, they grieved the theft of their family photographs. Without his portrait, Ali's image was fading from memory. Would they even recognise him now?

Emine got a job in a salon as soon as she could. She could not sit around at home waiting and waiting and waiting. While her hands were busy washing and cutting hair, she was distracted from thoughts of her missing son.

A few tourists started to trickle into the north of the island again after a few years, and Hüseyin got by on part-time work, mostly in restaurant kitchens along with his father. Life did not present him with the same challenges as it had during their time in The Sunrise, however, and he grew bored.

His main focus now was volleyball. He was picked for the Turkish Cypriot team, as had been his ambition from childhood. For a year or so he was thrilled to be fulfilling his dream. But it was not to satisfy him for long. The northern part of Cyprus was not recognised by the international community, and this meant there were many embargoes in place, including for sports teams.

'It's meaningless,' he ranted to his parents. 'If we can't play in any of the big tournaments, then what the hell is the *point*?'

He also found the limitations of being in this restricted area of a small island oppressive. For a young man such as Hüseyin, it was like stretching out both arms and feeling the walls on each side. He wanted to push them until they fell.

When Mehmet came home from school one day with a new question for his mother, Emine began to feel that they should think about leaving.

'You know our friends from the hotel?' he asked. 'Am I supposed to hate them now?'

Emine reassured him that he was not, but she realised that little by little her youngest son's memories of close co-existence with the Greek Cypriots were fading. As more and more victory monuments were erected in the north, place names and street names were changed, and an increasing number of settlers came from Turkey bringing with them their own culture and ways, Emine pressured her family to leave. She had fallen out of love with the country of her birth, and when she discussed it with Halit, she realised that so too had he. The only thing that had been holding them back was that Ali had never returned.

'He's missing whether we are here or somewhere else,' said Halit. 'If he comes back, somehow we will find out.'

They knew many Turkish Cypriots who had left for London. Apparently life was not easy there, but for those prepared to work, opportunities were plentiful. A few months later, with some names and addresses of friends who had done the same, they purchased one-way tickets for themselves and left. There was no sentimentality in saying goodbye to a house that was not really their own, but it was a great wrench to leave their island.

In London, Hüseyin easily found work in the catering trade and soon worked his way up to managing a restaurant.

Water polo was now a memory, but he made time to play

volleyball on Sundays. During the rest of the week he worked for eighteen hours each day. His reward to himself was a second-hand Ford Capri, and Mehmet loved it when his big brother gave him a lift to school.

From the time they had first moved to London, there was something that Hüseyin had been determined to do.

One day, he took a morning off and went to Hatton Garden to search in the shops. Few of them had anything that resembled the diamond necklace as he remembered it, so he tried Bond Street. There was something similar in one of the window displays, but no price. A uniformed doorman guarded the entrance.

Once Hüseyin was inside, a man in a suit politely asked if he could help him.

Trying not to be intimidated – he did after all have a flashy car parked round the corner and was now wishing that he had parked directly outside – Hüseyin said he was interested in the necklace.

'These are premium quality,' said the assistant as he politely and carefully laid the string of blue diamonds on a purple velvet tray, knowing full well that this customer would not be buying it. 'This one is in the region of thirty thousand pounds,' he added, almost as an afterthought.

The diamonds were approximately the same colour and size as the ones Hüseyin remembered. At least he now knew.

Nostalgia for Cyprus was great for them all. Memories of their once delightful lives remained strong. The air, the scent of flowers, the flavour of oranges. None of these things could ever be as sweet again.

In Hackney, close to where both the Georgious and the Özkans lived, there was a community centre where Turkish and Greek Cypriots met together.

Maria heard about it and thought her mother might like to go, so one afternoon she drove her there.

Irini walked into the draughty hall full of tables and chairs. There were a few faces she knew, and she paused, briefly overwhelmed by the exuberant sound of Greek and Turkish mingling.

In a corner of the room, Emine and Halit were drinking coffee. Suddenly something caught Emine's eye.

'Halit,' she said. 'Those women over there . . . the ones who just came in . . .'

'Which women?' Halit's eyesight was fading a little.

Emine had already stood up and was weaving her way through the tables, almost stumbling in her haste to reach the doorway. Tears were streaming down her face.

Beside Irini, Maria gasped and seized her mother's arm.

She gently turned her towards her old friend.

Emine and Irini embraced as if they would never let go. Then they sat down together and shared stories of their lives since they had been separated.

There were moments of immense sadness. Irini had to tell them that Vasilis was dead. Halit immediately lowered his head, trying to conceal his emotion. The continual clack of worry beads ceased. He was a man of few words these days, but was now utterly silent.

'I'm so sorry. You must miss him so much,' said Emine, her eyes glistening.

Irini rested her hand on Halit's arm, and a few seconds went by. There was no need to say anything.

And then she had to ask.

'And Ali . . . ?'

It was hard for Emine to say the words, especially after learning that Christos had returned.

'Still missing,' she said.

They discovered that they were neighbours once more, their houses only half a mile apart. From then on the families met every week and visited each other's homes, sharing dishes such as *gemista* and *dolma* that were identical in all but name.

As the years passed, Hüseyin had taken out a loan for his own restaurant and then a second. Both were doing well and his savings had grown.

When the time came, it was not hard for him to find Aphroditi. Emine remembered that her parents had lived somewhere in Southgate, and he tracked her down.

During the first months of her time in England, Aphroditi had hoped to regain some of her physical strength. The cool climate in itself had given her a little more energy, but she remained frail. She had spent all day at home, as had her mother, but they tried to keep out of each other's way. They rarely left the house and shopping was brought in by the charwoman.

Even after Aphroditi's mother died in the late 1970s, Savvas had stayed in Cyprus. He had less reason to leave than ever, and he barely missed his wife. He was an optimist and still believed in the potential of the island. He had started his business with nothing and was determined to do so again. His fledgling hotel empire in Famagusta still stood: The Sunrise, the twisted skeleton of The New Paradise Beach and, of course, the major acquisition from his former rival.

Like forty thousand others, he was waiting for the revival of his city, sometimes referred to now as Cyprus' Sleeping Beauty. He was sure that one day she would awaken.

Meanwhile, he had new projects under way. At some point the banks might begin pulling in their loans, but until then he continued to borrow money for further acquisitions. Savvas was the kind of man who kept the bankers in business.

On one of his rare visits to the UK, he told Aphroditi that he had begun to build a hotel in Limassol. It would be the jewel of the entire resort, with seven hundred rooms. Aphroditi knew immediately that she would never see it. She had no desire to. Savvas read this in her response. It was clear that their lives could never be lived together again. The divorce was complicated, but Aphroditi's lawyers, Matthews and Tenby, negotiated a settlement to extricate her from the debts that Savvas had built up.

All these years on, she remained like one of the broken caryatids that still lay shattered in the ballroom of The Sunrise.

One day Aphroditi received a letter from Emine. She replied politely, inviting her for a cup of tea. ('How English she must have become!' exclaimed Emine when she opened it.) Mother and son would go together the following week.

Aphroditi did not open the door herself. A carer let them in and they went into the drawing room, where Aphroditi sat alone, a stick leaning against her armchair. She did not get up to greet them and Emine immediately noticed that she was painfully thin. Her hair had gone completely white and was so thin her scalp showed through it. It was fourteen years since Emine had seen Aphroditi, but she had aged by thirty. Her appearance was a shock.

Emine took in every detail of the home Aphroditi had inherited from her mother. It was even larger than she had imagined, and very comfortable, if getting a little faded now. There were bone-china cups and saucers and a teapot on a low polished mahogany table.

They gathered that Aphroditi lived here by herself but Emine did not ask too many questions. It seemed impolite.

Aphroditi wanted to hear about the Özkan family. She recognised Hüseyin from the beach and wanted to know when exactly they had left Cyprus and where they lived now. Was Emine still in touch with Savina Skouros from the salon?

They spoke in English.

Emine loved to talk and went into plenty of detail. Then, a little more tentatively, she started to tell Aphroditi about their time in The Sunrise.

'We were there with Irini and Vasilis Georgiou, our neighbours,' she said. 'Their son suggested it.'

Hüseyin was looking at Aphroditi and saw her visibly pale. He wished his mother would just stop talking. The last person he wanted her to mention was the nightclub manager; besides, talk of The Sunrise might upset Aphroditi. It was more than just a symbol of what she had lost.

In spite of herself, Aphroditi said the name.

'Markos Georgiou.'

'He was killed, sadly,' said Emine.

'Yes, Mr Papacosta was informed,' said Aphroditi rather curtly.

Emine and Hüseyin noticed her change of tone and there was an awkward silence.

'He wasn't all he seemed,' she added.

And then they thought they heard her say:

'I was such a fool.'

The words were under her breath, almost inaudible.

Mother and son glanced at each other, pretending not to have heard.

Emine took a small sip of her tea. How awful it tasted with milk, she thought, putting the cup down again. She looked at

Hüseyin, silently urging him to tell their hostess why they had come.

On cue, he leaned in. It was the first time he had spoken.

'The reason we're really here, Mrs Papacosta,' he said clumsily, 'is to give you this.'

He handed Aphroditi a purple velvet box.

She looked at him with bemusement and then opened it. For a few moments she simply stared at what was inside.

'Where did you find this?' she breathed.

'It's not the original, I'm afraid,' explained Hüseyin. 'We had to sell yours to pay for our passage out of Famagusta.'

There was a strained silence.

'Without your necklace, we wouldn't be sitting here now,' he added.

For years, Hüseyin had been saving, every month putting money into a separate bank account and working overtime to do so. Finally, he was paying the debt for their freedom.

She looked at his earnest face and realised that he could not possibly know the significance of his gesture and how it proved to her beyond doubt that Markos had betrayed her in every way. She did not touch the necklace.

'I'm sorry but I don't want this,' she said firmly, snapping the box shut. 'I really don't want it and I can't accept it. Emine, please make him take it away.'

Aphroditi put the necklace on the table in front of them.

'I am touched by what you have done, Hüseyin, but I want nothing from those days. It will only remind me of awful things and awful times. You must sell it again and spend the money on yourself.'

'But . . .' Hüseyin tried to interject.

'I'm owed nothing.'

Hüseyin leaned forward, awkwardly took the box and tried to stuff it back in his pocket.

The atmosphere had changed. Aphroditi had withdrawn from them and Emine could see how upset she was. Even in her weakened state, she was forcefully resolute.

Emine suddenly thought of something that might relieve the tension.

'I nearly forgot,' she said. 'We found a couple of things that were yours.'

She produced from her handbag the little embroidered purse and the pouch, and held them out.

Aphroditi looked at the miscellaneous items without a flicker of recognition.

At that moment, the carer came in to ask if they needed more tea.

'I don't think so,' answered Aphroditi.

Hüseyin stood up. It was more than clear that it was time to leave.

His mother took her son's cue, placing the two small items on the tea tray as she did so.

Aphroditi remained seated.

Even as they drove away, Hüseyin knew that they had outstayed their welcome. Both of them were shocked by the reaction to the necklace that Hüseyin had worked so hard to buy. And her words about Markos would echo in their ears for weeks to come.

Aphroditi wanted to be alone and told the carer that she could go home early.

She made her way slowly into the kitchen where the tray sat on the draining board. She picked up the velvet pouch, tipped the contents into her creased palm and studied the small, irregular object for the last time. Purposefully, she turned on the tap and slowly rolled it off her hand.

It briefly circled the plughole, then was gone. Within seconds it was washed away from the house in Southgate and flushed through several miles of underground drainage system before arriving at the sewage plant. It travelled on and eventually, after a long voyage, a tiny pearl found itself back in the sea.

News also travelled a long way to reach London from Cyprus. All these years later, Emine's old friend Savina from the salon still wrote regularly. One of the significant things she kept her informed about was the work of the dedicated team of forensic scientists who now endeavoured to identify the bones from unmarked graves. Emine still hoped for news of Ali. Anything would be better than nothing.

One day a newspaper cutting fell out of the envelope. It was not about the missing; it was an article about the rise and fall of a hotel chain. When she began to read it, Emine realised that its owner was none other than Savvas Papacosta. A series of hugely ambitious loans and a change in the financial climate had led to his recent bankruptcy. It took her some time to get through the story (she rarely read in Greek these days, and Savina always wrote to her in English). When she turned the page over, there was a big photograph. It had been taken of Savvas Papacosta and his wife at the opening of The Sunrise. They were standing in front of the hotel's name spelled out in flowers.

She put her hand over her mouth. It was a shock to remember how glamorous and beautiful Aphroditi had been. The long sparkling gown had been a sensation, and Emine remembered doing her hair in preparation for that night as if it were yesterday. She continued to read, quietly but out loud. There was a caption beneath the picture. It said simply: 'Savvas Papacosta and his former wife, Aphroditi, who died last year.'

For a while Emine sat there looking into the pair of dark eyes that stared back from the page.

Since coming to London, the Georgiou family had read of the negotiations and subsequent stalemate, the changes to the texture and make-up of the island, continuous appeals from both sides to find missing relatives, the proclamation of the Turkish Republic of Northern Cyprus and then the opening of the border in 2003.

They were aware too of a failed plan to forge a compromise, and the economic crash in the south. All of these failures and disappointments lodged in their consciousness, but hope never went away.

In 2014, talks began once again. A Good Friday service was held inside a church in Famagusta's walled city, and the US vice president went to visit. He was the most senior American politician to go to the island in more than fifty years.

To the surprise of everyone who had known her in Cyprus, Irini was contented enough in London. Christos, his English wife and their young daughter lived with her, while Maria and Panikos were in the next street; their children were even married now.

The proximity of her children, grandchildren and great-grandchildren sustained Irini and gave her plenty to live for. Most days she still cooked an evening meal for them all, and her only concession to ageing was to take an afternoon nap, just as she would have done on hot days in Cyprus.

During their years in London, barbed wire, plastic netting and guard posts remained in place around Famagusta. The wind whipped through its streets and salty air brought slow destruction. Everything in the town had decayed. Several times a week Irini still woke up imagining herself there.

She was in her late nineties now. Her dreams were more intense these days and sometimes blurred with reality. Other things had faded with age: the dark chestnut brown of her eyes, the pigment of her hair and her physical strength. Her eyesight and hearing were not what they had been either.

One day she opened her eyes to a hazy light. It could have been dawn or dusk; she could not tell, so indeterminate was the glow that filtered through the net curtains. A figure was standing in the shadows of the doorway. It had to be her granddaughter, but her dress was old-fashioned, a white pinafore specked with roses, just as she had worn herself as a child.

'Come and see! Come and see!' Irini heard her call.

The small figure disappeared. Irini rose from her bed and went into the corridor outside. She was drawn to a room at the end where she could see a bluish light.

There on the television she saw Famagusta, its windows vacant, its concrete towers cracked. Supporting herself on the door frame, she gazed at the screen.

There was a huge crowd gathering to enter the city. The barbed wire had been cut away from the perimeter and people began to flow through the old sentry points, younger ones breaking into a run, the elderly walking sedately. Many of them held flowers. Troops stood to one side to let them pass.

In the house there was stillness. The little girl was nowhere to be seen. Perhaps it was a vision, but for Irini it seemed as if the moment she had longed for had finally arrived.

'This is my dream . . . ' she whispered, as her knees began to give way beneath her. 'This is my *dream*!'

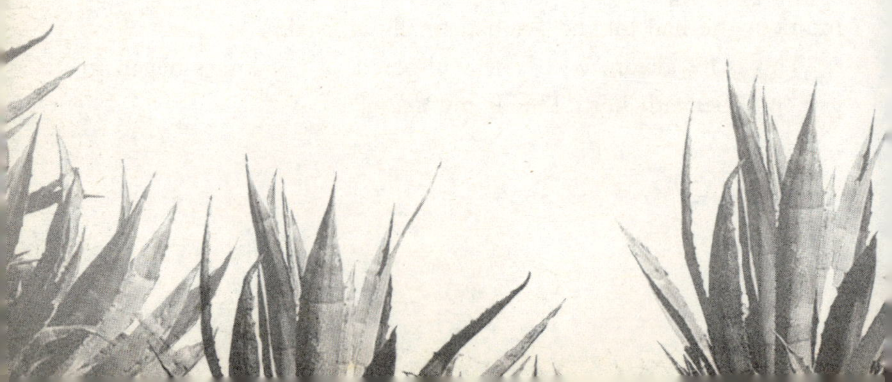

Read on to discover more
about the ghost city of
Famagusta,
by Victoria Hislop

Famagusta, Yesterday and Today

Famagusta, on the east coast of Cyprus, was once one of the most glamorous resorts in Europe: a favourite destination of the 1970s jet-set. It accommodated half of the island's total tourist population, and its miles of pale sand and clear turquoise sea attracted thousands of holidaymakers each year. Along with the tourists, the forty thousand-strong population of the city enjoyed a life rich in culture, with art, music and theatre that was the best on the island.

Famagusta in its early 1970s heyday

As well as tourism, light industry and agriculture thrived. With the deepest port in Cyprus, Famagusta handled more than 80 per cent of the island's cargo, much of which comprised a vast tonnage of citrus fruit, picked from thousands of acres of orchard.

The modern district, where the luxury hotels and apartments were situated, was inhabited mostly by Greek Cypriots, while the adjacent walled city, which contained the historical treasures of Famagusta (including numerous Byzantine churches and a spectacular fourteenth-century cathedral), was lived in largely by Turkish Cypriots. For every four Greek Cypriots in the population there was one Turkish Cypriot.

In August 1974, just over forty years ago, Famagusta's reign as a paradise for both islanders and tourists came to an abrupt and untimely end.

Following the Greek military coup in July 1974 during which the President, Makarios, was deposed, Turkish forces invaded the island, ostensibly to restore constitutional order and to protect the Turkish Cypriot minority. After a brief period of ceasefire and fruitless negotiation, Famagusta was bombarded. Turkish tanks then advanced. On 14 August, the Greek Cypriot population fled in terror, in cars, on buses, by foot, most people taking nothing but the clothes they stood up in. They expected help from a foreign power but none came. Their evacuation, which they had expected to last a few days at most, turned into an absence of weeks, then months, then decades.

My first visit to Cyprus was four summers after the war. I had answered a small ad in a magazine for an overland trip to Cyprus, not realising that I was going to an area under army occupation. I was eighteen years old and very naive. It took the sight of buildings pock-marked with bullets and ubiquitous bomb damage to tell me that this was going to be a strange holiday. There are 40,000 Turkish soldiers in the north of Cyprus today, but back in 1978 there were considerably more.

I found myself on an island where the Turks had effectively drawn a line across Cyprus that divided north from south, cutting off Famagusta and other towns from their Greek Cypriot populations who had now fled southwards. On one of my trips around the north of the island with some soldiers who were on leave, I remember seeing a big modern city in the distance and being told that this was where the best beaches were situated. I asked if we could go. 'No,' they said. 'It's out of bounds.' The city was Famagusta.

A sentry post on the edge of Famagusta

At the time of my first visit the border was entirely sealed, and it remained so for another twenty-five years. Then, in 2003, the Turkish authorities opened it up to allow people to cross from north to south and south to north. Thousands visited their old homes. Many visitors to the north found their homes occupied either by Turkish Cypriots or settlers from Turkey. For most, it was a traumatic experience, particularly if the house had been destroyed or altered beyond recognition. Precious orange orchards and gardens had mostly vanished. For some, however, it was a more positive experience. They knocked on the doors of their old homes and were welcomed in by the new residents, some of whom had kept possessions safe for them in case they ever returned.

For those whose homes had been inside the part of Famagusta that was fenced off, there were no such visits. This section, that still remains entirely sealed off by rusting barbed wire and is fiercely guarded by Turkish troops, is known as Varosha. It represents around 20 per cent of Famagusta and was the prime tourist area with its stretch of golden sand behind which now stand skeletons of bombed and abandoned hotels and apartments. Beyond these are streets of looted shops, restaurants, mansions. All of them are being further destroyed by time and decay.

The 'ghost town', as it is known, is heavily guarded by soldiers, and aggressive signs leave you in no doubt that this is a no-go area. In spite of this, huge holes are left in the plastic netting to afford a provocatively clear view of the dereliction that lies behind. Weeds sprout up through the paving stones and foliage pokes through the broken windowpanes. The atmosphere is eerie and sinister. It seems evident that the point of keeping this area constantly under guard, like a hostage, must have a purpose.

Varosha, seen through the fence

In the area surrounding Varosha, extensive building work has taken place in the last few years that has made the rest of the city unrecognisable to its former inhabitants. There is also a large population of settlers, brought in from the Turkish mainland, whose lifestyle and culture is very different from that of the Turkish Cypriots themselves. It is painful for Greek Cypriots to see their beloved city being reconstructed.

There is plenty of anger among people about this situation, but also sadness. The greatest sadness of course is that tens of thousands of people lost everything they had. Another is that, in the past, many Greek Cypriots and Turkish Cypriots lived and worked happily together.

The Green Line dividing Nicosia

On a recent visit, I entered the fourteenth-century church of Agios Georgios Exorinos, which is located in the old town of Famagusta. Inside, several things caught my attention. Firstly, the defaced frescos. The face and the cross had been crudely scratched out, and stood out white against the walls. There have been numerous cases of cultural vandalism, with icons destroyed and treasures removed from the Greek Orthodox churches in the north. But something else struck me. In the corner was an *epitafios*, a flower-decked bier traditionally carried through the streets on Good Friday. For the first time since 1958, a service had been held in the church in April 2014. Thousands of Greek Cypriots crossed the border to take part in this deeply symbolic moment.

In the summer of 2014, I attended a rally that marked forty years since the people of Famagusta (both those inside and outside of Varosha) lost their homes. To reach the event I travelled along a road that runs parallel to the demarcation line dividing Cyprus. Every few kilometres there was a sentry post on a hill, from which Turkish soldiers looked down, observing us through binoculars. Between us and them was an area of scrubland.

A similar rally has been held each year since the division of the island and takes place in Dherynia, a village in the district of Famagusta close to the 'border'. From this village, the ghost town is clearly visible in daylight, its abandoned multi-storey hotels standing against the skyline with the sea sparkling beyond. At night, it disappears. There are no lights inside those buildings.

The abandoned hotels along the beach

On the night of Famagusta Remembrance Day, I walked alongside the crowd of several hundred people from the Cultural Centre of Occupied Famagusta through the village to present a declaration at the United Nations checkpoint. A letter, addressed to Ban Ki-moon, requested the return of Famagusta to its lawful inhabitants. With their flags waving in the breeze, they sang about their lost city to the UN troops on duty. It was a calm and entirely peaceful demonstration, but beneath it simmered bitterness and grief.

Hugely emotional songs about the city silhouetted by the moonlight were performed and the words of the Mayor of Famagusta rang in our ears. I wondered if the amplifiers carried them as far as the soldiers guarding the city and felt my own conscience, as a European, slightly pricked:

'We left with the certainty that we would soon return, believing that the civilised world would never accept this crime against Cyprus. We were wrong. Days became months, months became years and years became decades,' said Alexis Galanos, who is the mayor in exile (there is also a Turkish Cypriot mayor on the other side of the border).

As they have each year, for the past forty, a huge crowd of 'Famagustians' renewed their commitment and determination to try for reunification and to return to their home town.

Famagusta is known to the Greeks as *Ammohostos*, meaning 'buried in the sand', and many of the previous inhabitants of this city are concerned that the issue of its rightful return will meet this fate.

Setting *The Sunrise* against the backdrop of the invasion and the subsequent years of occupation of this city, I have tried to evoke some of the emotions and experiences that this sudden, dramatic change had on peoples' lives. All the characters in *The Sunrise* are completely fictional. Some are Greek Cypriot and some are Turkish Cypriot. I wanted to tell a story that showed how the events in

Famagusta in 2014

Cyprus were a disaster for both communities – and to suggest that the issue of 'good' and 'evil' is not a matter of ethnicity. I believe that, ultimately, individual choice plays the greatest role.

Victoria Hislop
April 2015

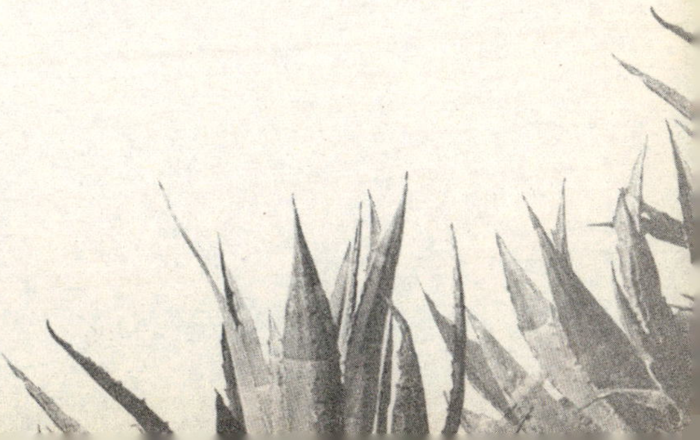

the Island

On the brink of a life-changing decision, Alexis Fielding longs to find out about her mother's past. But Sofia has never spoken of it. All she admits to is growing up in a small Cretan village before moving to London. When Alexis decides to visit Crete, however, Sofia gives her daughter a letter to take to an old friend, and promises that through her she will learn more.

Arriving in Plaka, Alexis is astonished to see that it lies a stone's throw from the tiny, deserted island of Spinalonga – Greece's former leper colony. Then she finds Fotini, and at last hears the story that Sofia has buried all her life: the tale of her great-grandmother Eleni and her daughters, and a family rent by tragedy, war and passion. She discovers how intimately she is connected with the island, and how secrecy holds them all in its powerful grip . . .

'A vivid, moving and absorbing tale, with its sensitive, realistic engagement with all the consequences of, and stigma attached to, leprosy' *Observer*

'War, tragedy and passion unfurl against a Mediterranean backdrop in this engrossing debut novel' *You* magazine

'Hislop carefully evokes the lives of Cretans between the wars and during German occupation, but most commendable is her compassionate portrayal of the outcasts' *Guardian*

the Return

Beneath the majestic towers of the Alhambra, Granada's cobbled streets resonate with music and secrets. Sonia Cameron knows nothing of the city's shocking past; she is here to dance. But in a quiet café, a chance conversation and an intriguing collection of old photographs draw her into the extraordinary tale of Spain's devastating civil war.

Seventy years earlier, the café is home to the close-knit Ramírez family. In 1936, an army coup led by Franco shatters the country's fragile peace, and in the heart of Granada the family witnesses the worst atrocities of conflict. Divided by politics and tragedy, everyone must take a side, fighting a personal battle as Spain rips itself apart.

'What sets Hislop apart is her ability to put a human face on the shocking civil conflict that ripped Spain apart for three bloody years between 1936 and 1939 . . . Stirring stuff' *Time Out*

'[*The Return*] should be required holiday reading for anyone going to Spain' *Daily Mail*

'Brilliantly recreates the passion that flows through the Andalusian dancers and the dark creative force of *duende*' *Scotland on Sunday*

The Thread

Thessaloniki, 1917. As Dimitri Komninos is born, fire devastates the thriving Greek city where Christians, Jews and Muslims live side by side. Five years later, Katerina Sarafoglou's home in Asia Minor is destroyed by the Turkish army. Losing her mother in the chaos, she flees across the sea to an unknown destination in Greece. Soon her life will become entwined with Dimitri's, and with the story of the city itself, as war, fear and persecution begin to divide its people.

Thessaloniki, 2007. A young Anglo-Greek hears his grandparents' life story and realises he has a decision to make. For many decades, they have looked after the memories and treasures of the people who were forced to leave. Should he become their next custodian and make this city his home?

'A sweeping, magnificently detailed and ambitious saga that wrestles with the turbulence of the period Hislop covers'
The Sunday Times

'Storytelling at its best . . . just like a tapestry, when each thread is sewn into place, so emerge the layers and history of relationships past and present'
Sunday Express

'Fresh, unusual and rather intrepid . . . with a tenacious attention to the tangled and controversial history that fuels her plots'
Independent

The Last Dance

AND OTHER STORIES

In ten powerful stories, Victoria Hislop takes us through the streets of Athens and into tree-lined squares of Greek villages. As she brings to life their distinct atmosphere, she creates a host of unforgettable characters, from a lonesome priest to battling brothers, and from an unwanted stranger to a groom troubled by music and memory.

These bittersweet tales of love and loyalty, of separation and reconciliation, captured in Victoria Hislop's unique voice, will stay with you long after you reach the end.

'Beguiling . . . Her characters are utterly convincing and she has perfected her knack for describing everyday Greek life' *Daily Mail*

'Stunning . . . Intricate, beautifully observed and with a painter's eye for imagery, in these stories Hislop evokes Greece, its people, its customs and traditions with a sensitivity that reveals her deep knowledge of not just the place but the human condition' *Express*

'Lyrical, twisty short stories' *Evening Standard*

Be Inspired

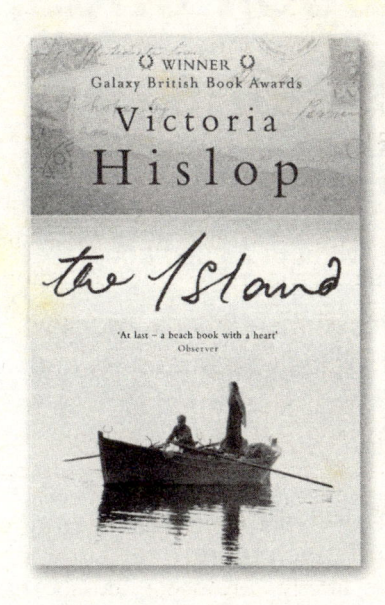

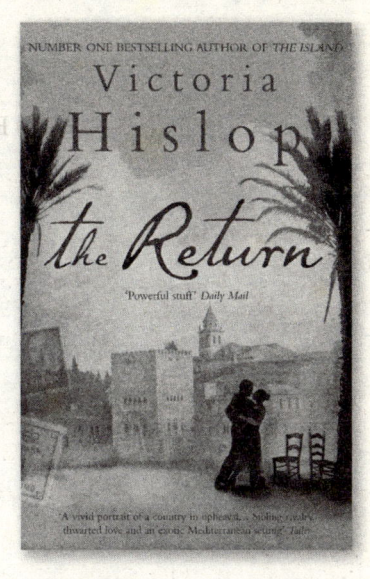

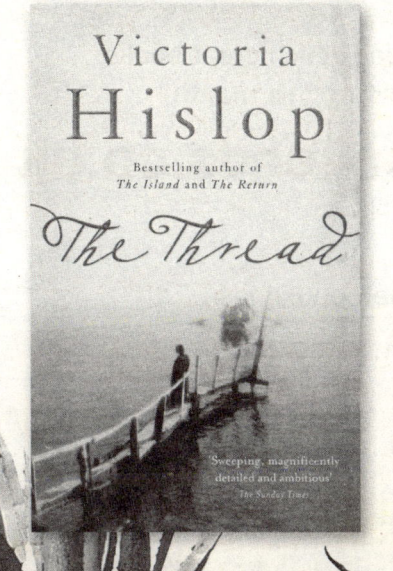

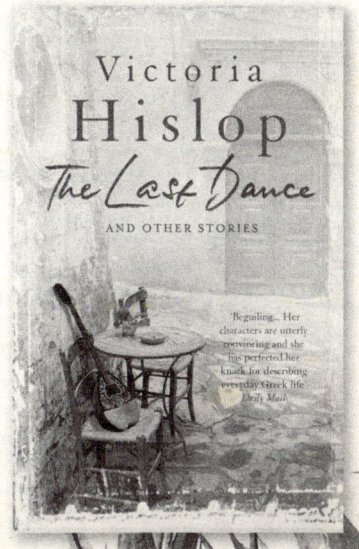

When one book ends, another begins...

Bookends is a vibrant new reading community to help you ensure you're never without a good book.

You'll find monthly reading recommendations, previews of brilliant new books, and exclusive features on and from your favourite authors. We'll also introduce you to exciting debuts and remind you of past classics.

There'll be a regular blog, reading group guides, competitions and much more!

Visit our website to see which great books we're recommending this month.

welcometobookends.co.uk

/welcometobookends
@teambookends

H

FOR
HISTORY

From Ancient Rome to the Tudor court,
revolutionary Paris to the Second World War,
discover the best historical fiction and non-fiction at

H FOR HISTORY

Visit us today for exclusive author features,
first chapter previews, podcasts and audio excerpts,
book trailers, giveaways and much more.

@H_forHistory
/HforHistory
HforHistory.tumblr.com

Sign up now to receive our regular newsletter at
www.HforHistory.co.uk

Victoria Hislop

Discover more

www.victoriahislop.com

🐦 @VicHislop

f facebook.com/OfficialVictoriaHislop